WINGS *of* REFUGE

Books by
Lynn Austin
FROM BETHANY HOUSE PUBLISHERS

Eve's Daughters

Wings of Refuge

LYNN AUSTIN

WINGS *of* REFUGE

BETHANY HOUSE PUBLISHERS
MINNEAPOLIS, MINNESOTA 55438

Published by Bethany House Publishers
A Ministry of Bethany Fellowship International
11400 Hampshire Avenue South
Minneapolis, Minnesota 55438
www.bethanyhouse.com

Printed in the United States of America by
Bethany Press International, Minneapolis, Minnesota 55438

Library of Congress Cataloging-in-Publication Data

Austin, Lynn N.
    Wings of refuge / by Lynn Austin.
    p. cm.
    ISBN 0-7642-2196-5
    1. Women—Travel—Israel—Fiction. 2. Israel—Fiction.
I. Title.
PS3551.U839 W56 2000
813'.54—dc21
                                                    99–051018

To Ken, Joshua,
Benjamin, and Maya
for their unfailing support
and love.

"May you be richly rewarded by the Lord, the God of Israel, under whose wings you have come to take refuge."

RUTH 2:12

"The central paradigm of Jewish religion is redemption. . . . The Jews have given their word to go on living as a people in a special way so that their lives testify . . . to a final, universal redemption."

RABBI IRVING GREENBERG, *THE JEWISH WAY*

CHAPTER 1

TEL AVIV, ISRAEL—1999

Nothing in Abigail MacLeod's life prepared her for the shock of watching Benjamin Rosen die in her arms. She was alone in Israel's Lod Airport, thousands of miles from her home in Indiana, light-years from her routine life as a wife, mother, and teacher. His death from an assassin's bullet was so violent, so unexpected, that she could only cradle his lifeless body in disbelief and hope she would awaken soon from this nightmare. But Mr. Rosen's blood—soaking through her new cotton dress, pasting the material to her skin—felt too warm, too real to be part of a dream.

She never should have crossed the Atlantic. The ocean must have been the dividing line between normal life and chaos. But hadn't her life been in chaos even before she left home yesterday morning? This pilgrimage to Israel was supposed to be a new beginning for her at age forty-two, yet so far she had lost all of her luggage, been forced to board an Israeli Jet Liner in spite of a bomb threat, and had watched the kind, fatherly gentleman who had befriended her on the airplane die sprawled in her lap on the airport floor.

The police interrogation that followed had been like a scene from one of the cop shows her husband liked to watch on TV, except that

Abby couldn't change the channel or escape to her bedroom with a good book. After prying the dead man from her embrace, the police had wrapped a blanket around her trembling shoulders, then led her to a stiff-backed metal chair in the airport security office.

This is where she now sat, clasping her hands in front of her to stop them from shaking. She barely recognized the disheveled, blood-smeared woman in the mirror on the opposite wall. Was it a one-way mirror? Was she being observed from the other side? Why were they questioning her as if she had something to do with Mr. Rosen's death?

"Speak a little louder, please, Mrs. MacLeod," one of the police officers said. The ancient tape recorder on the table in front of her hummed impatiently as the tape slowly fed from reel to reel.

"Umm . . . sorry. He told me his name was Benjamin Rosen," she repeated for what seemed the hundredth time. "I met him on the plane from Amsterdam—he sat beside me. He was making a phone call for me to the Archaeological Institute when somebody shot him. I didn't see who did it." She took a sip of the lukewarm water they had given her, wishing she had never left Indiana. Abby then added feebly, "I didn't have any of those things for the phone. What do you call them? Umm . . . tokens. Mr. Rosen said the phone took special tokens."

There was a knock on the door of the tiny cubicle, and after a brief conversation in Hebrew, the police officers who had been interrogating her filed out. Two men in civilian clothes took their places. The older man was in his sixties, with a milk-commercial mustache and woolly white hair as tightly coiled as a poodle's. His grave, unsmiling features seemed hardened by life, as if violence had left its imprint in concrete. The younger man wasn't much older than Abby's son, Greg, with wavy black hair and a curly beard. Both men wore pistols strapped to their sides and identical expressions on their solemn faces—expressions that clearly said, *You're in big trouble, Abby MacLeod.*

"I'm Agent Dov Shur and this is Agent Kol," the older man told her. He pulled out one of the metal chairs and sat across the table from her. Agent Kol remained standing, as if guarding the door. "We would like you to start at the beginning, Mrs. MacLeod, and tell us everything that happened."

A wave of weary hopelessness washed over Abby. "Again? But I've already told the police everything there is to tell."

Agent Shur pulled an identification badge with his photo on it from his shirt pocket and laid it on the scarred green table in front of her as if the badge might explode if not carefully handled. Abby couldn't read much more of it than his name and *Israel*, but it looked very official.

"You've been talking with airport security and the local police," he said. "We're with the Israeli government. Something like your American CIA." He pulled out a package of cigarettes and offered her one. When she shook her head, he lit up without asking her permission and began to smoke. Then he reached into his pocket again and laid a second badge in front of her. It was identical to his own, except that it had the dead man's name and picture on it.

"Benjamin Rosen worked for us," he said quietly.

Abby choked back a sob. The second-rate cop show had just transformed into a second-rate spy movie—another of her husband's favorites. She wished she had watched spy movies with him more often so she would know how this was all going to end. James Bond was indestructible, but didn't his leading ladies usually die?

The acrid cigarette smoke made her eyes water, and she cleared her throat. "But Mr. Rosen told me that he was an agricultural specialist. He said he was working on . . . What do you call it when you get plants to grow in the desert?"

"Desert hydrology?" the young agent standing near the door offered.

"Yes, that's what he called it." Abby felt relieved, as if the right word could lead them closer to unraveling the mystery.

Shur nodded, exhaling smoke through his nostrils like a dragon. "That is true. Rosen had his plants. Everyone in Israel must play more than one role in order for us to survive. *Ein breira*, we say in Hebrew—no choice." He reached into his other shirt pocket and tossed Abby a small blue booklet. It took her a moment to recognize it as her own passport.

"You are Abigail Ruth MacLeod," he recited. "Maiden name, Dixon. Forty-two years old, married to Mark Edward MacLeod, forty-four, vice president of Data Age, a computer firm. Two children: Gregory William, age twenty, an engineering student at Purdue University; and Emily Anne, age eighteen, who graduated from high school two weeks ago and will attend college in the fall."

A chill of horror shuddered through Abby as he coldly repeated these facts about her family, facts that she knew weren't on her passport. Nor had she told them to the police.

"You live in Carmel, Indiana, a suburb of Indianapolis," he continued, "where you teach history to high school students. You have been separated from your husband for four and a half months and have recently begun divorce proceedings."

Abby started to protest that she had only consulted a lawyer, not actually filed for a divorce yet, then realized how ludicrous it was to say anything at all.

"Now please, Mrs. MacLeod. If you would start at the beginning again and tell us everything you remember up to the time Benjamin Rosen died."

"Can we get anything for you?" the younger man asked suddenly. "You are hungry, maybe? Or thirsty?"

Abby recalled her husband's explanation of the "good cop/bad cop" routine and wanted to cry. She shook her head, her stomach too volatile to risk adding food to the mixture of shock and fear already seething there.

"Then would you kindly repeat your story for us once more, from the beginning?"

Abby drew a shaky breath. "This is the first time I've ever traveled overseas," she began. "You see, I hate to fly. I'm terrified, actually. . . ."

SCHIPOL AIRPORT, AMSTERDAM—1999

Ladies and gentlemen, the captain has begun our final approach to Schipol Airport in Amsterdam, where we will be landing in just a few minutes. Please fasten your safety belts and observe the No Smoking signs." The plane hung suspended in the air for a moment as the droning jet engines changed pitch.

"I hate this," Abby muttered under her breath. "I hate this, I hate this, I hate this!" She clutched the armrests in a death grip and braced herself against the seat. Beyond her window the flat Dutch countryside tilted like a saucer.

She closed her eyes and tried to pray. One of her reasons for making this pilgrimage to Israel was to renew her long-neglected relationship with God, but at the moment all she could recall of her childhood faith was the Lord's Prayer. Asking for her daily bread didn't seem appropriate—it would never stay in her stomach. Nor did asking forgiveness for her trespasses, since she hadn't forgiven Mark for his. She added "learn how to pray" to her mental list of spiritual goals and released her grip on the armrests long enough to dig a roll of antacids from her pocket and pop one into her mouth. She was crunching on her fourth tablet when the landing gear hit the runway and the plane reversed engines with a comforting roar. Only one more takeoff and landing to endure and she would be in Israel.

As the plane rolled to a stop beside the terminal, Abby retrieved her carryon from under the seat and rummaged through it for her passport and map of Amsterdam. Passengers crowded into the aisles, removing tote bags and hand luggage from the overhead racks, but she remained seated, reviewing her plans for a day's walking tour of Amsterdam: the Royal Palace, Anne Frank's house, the Van Gogh Museum.

Local time, the flight attendant announced, was 6:50 A.M. Abby's connecting flight to Tel Aviv didn't leave until 5:20 tonight, freeing her to shop and sight-see for a day—although her internal clock was telling her it was time to sleep, not run around Europe. It was the middle of the night back home, and she hadn't slept on the plane. Who could relax while suspended thousands of feet above the cold Atlantic? Her brother Sam had written her a prescription for sleeping pills, but she hadn't taken one. She wanted to be alert enough to pray if the plane suddenly plunged into the sea.

At last Abby squeezed into the crowded aisle and followed the line of passengers out of the airplane and down the ramp. Signs in foreign languages and international symbols greeted her, while people of every nationality and tongue hurried past in clothing that looked like advertisements for the United Nations. Most disconcerting of all were the camouflage-clad security guards with machine guns standing sentry throughout the terminal, reminding her that she had journeyed into a world of international terrorism.

"Something tells me we're not in Kansas anymore, Toto," she murmured.

Abby had never been out of North America before—had rarely traveled far from her home in Indiana—and found it difficult to comprehend the fact that she was now halfway around the world on her way to Israel. The realization that she was doing it all by herself brought tears to her eyes. She cried easily when she was tired—"sleepy-weepy," her husband had always teased.

The unwelcome reminder of Mark made her angry. It was his betrayal that had catapulted her here to begin with. She slung her tote bag higher onto her shoulder, drawing courage from her anger. Who needed him? She would be fine on her own.

Abby followed the crowd to the customs queue. While she waited, Abby studied her passport picture and saw an attractive middle-aged woman with pleasant "laugh lines"—she refused to call them wrinkles—at the corners of her eyes and mouth. Dark brown hair, cut stylishly short, fell across her forehead above sky-blue eyes. One front tooth bothered her, though—knocked slightly askew after she had fallen from a tree when she was eight. She thought she looked haggard in the picture, but who wouldn't look haggard after grieving the loss of a twenty-two-year marriage?

"You look a lot better in person, Mom," her son, Greg, had assured her. "Passport pictures always come out like mug shots."

"Next? Madame?"

It was Abby's turn to cross the magic line. The customs clerk stamped her visa page and waved her on. She was in Europe, on her own for the first time in her life. She could do this. She didn't need Mark or anyone else to hold her hand.

While the other passengers lined up around the revolving baggage kiosk, Abby made her way to the main terminal, eager to begin her tour of Amsterdam. The travel agent in Indianapolis had assured her that her suitcase would be transferred directly to the flight to Tel Aviv, but he had advised her to check in at the Israeli Airlines desk and get a boarding pass before catching the shuttle bus into Amsterdam.

Abby felt as though she had journeyed out of the Netherlands and halfway through France by the time she reached the Israeli Airlines counter, isolated from all the others at the far end of the terminal. The travel agent had also warned her that the Israelis were fanatics about security, but it still startled her to see all three ticket clerks wearing guns in shoulder harnesses beneath their uniform blazers. Disgruntled passengers crowded around the counter, smoking cigarettes, sitting on suitcases, talking loudly in what Abby guessed was Hebrew. She took her place at the end of the line, frustrated at forfeiting her sight-seeing time.

Ten minutes later she reached the counter and handed the clerk her ticket. "I'd like to confirm my seat, please. I'm booked later tonight on the 5:20 P.M. flight."

The clerk frowned. "Where did you purchase this ticket?"

"At home . . . in Indianapolis. . . ."

"There is no 5:20 P.M. flight," the clerk said abruptly.

"What do you mean? Has it been canceled?"

"No, this flight does not exist. We have no such flight with that number and no flights departing at that time."

Abby told herself not to panic. "Well, is there another flight I could take to Tel Aviv today?"

"Where did you book this ticket?" The clerk fired the question like a weapon.

"I didn't actually book it myself. I'm taking a summer graduate course in archaeology. The school made all the arrangements for me."

"Which school?"

"Western Evangelical Seminary. Dr. Voss's office made—"

"You are part of a group, then?"

"Yes—"

"Where is everyone else?"

"Well . . . they're on another flight. I'm meeting them in Tel Aviv."

"Why aren't you traveling with your group?"

Abby hesitated. The truth was, everyone else was traveling through Athens, which had a bad reputation for terrorist activity. Her fear of being hijacked had overridden her desire to see that ancient city. But should she confess her fear to the gun-toting clerk?

"The seminary is in Colorado," Abby finally said, "but the summer students come from all over the United States. This is an archaeological dig, you see, sponsored by the Israeli Archaeological Institute."

"How well do you know the man who bought this ticket for you?"

"We've never met, but—"

"One moment, please." The clerk hopped off her stool and disappeared through the doorway behind her.

Abby drummed her fingers on the counter. *Great. Just great.* She had saved money from her meager teacher's salary for this trip, and her finances didn't allow for any unforeseen expenses. Maybe she should just take the next flight home.

The ticket clerk returned with an older man whose ID tag indicated he was the manager. His gun was a few sizes larger than everyone else's, too. "Where did you buy this ticket?" he asked.

Abby gestured to the clerk standing silently beside him. "I already explained—"

"Explain again, please."

"Dr. Theodore Voss at Western Evangelical Seminary in Colorado mailed it to me."

"Do you know this Dr. Voss personally?"

"I've never met him. We've only spoken on the phone."

The manager chewed his mustache as he tapped the keys on his computer terminal. Abby's feet were beginning to ache. She shifted her tote bag to the floor, waiting a full five minutes while the manager consulted his computer.

"Did this Dr. Voss ask you to carry anything to Israel for him or give you a package of any kind?"

"Just a package of information about the dig and the graduate course I'll be taking."

"May I see it, please?"

Abby pulled the fat manila envelope from her tote bag and handed it to him. The female clerk disappeared through the door with it. What was going on?

"The flight you are booked on does not exist," the manager said, laying Abby's ticket on the counter in front of her. He made it sound as if she had committed a crime.

"Well, is there another flight to Tel Aviv I could take instead?"

"Flight 1013 departs at eight o'clock this morning."

Abby glanced at the clock above the counter. "But . . . but that's in less than an hour! Isn't there a later flight?" He shook his head. Abby sighed as her plans for a day of sight-seeing in Amsterdam went up in smoke. "Well, I guess I'll have to take it, then." He began tapping keys on his computer again. The clerk returned with Abby's manila envelope several minutes later, and Abby stuffed it back into her tote bag. "What about my suitcase?"

"If it was tagged for Israeli Airlines, it will be sent to our luggage area. You'll be boarding at Gate 96, Concourse C." He handed her the new ticket as soon as the computer spit it out. "Who's next?"

Abby hated changes. There had been far too many in her life these past few months. She slung her tote bag over her shoulder again and followed the signs to Concourse C, passing through airport security. The guards and guns seemed to be multiplying like viruses.

Gate 96 was at the farthest end of the concourse, isolated from the rest of the airport. Abby sighed and sank into a seat. Her nerves felt frayed and the other passengers hadn't started to board the plane yet. They either paced the aisles smoking cigarettes or sat reading Hebrew newspapers in glum silence. The atmosphere seemed unusually tense, like a cheap cloak-and-dagger movie. She should have taken her chances with hijackers in Athens.

At eight o'clock the manager from the ticket counter appeared and picked up the microphone, making an announcement first in Hebrew, then English. "Ladies and gentlemen, Flight 1013 will be delayed until 9:30 A.M. You will be served a complimentary breakfast in the Skyline Coffee Shop."

Abby expected the announcement to be greeted with groans and protests, but the passengers simply rose from their seats and straggled down the long concourse for their free meal. Abby fell in line with them, even though the last thing she wanted right now was food. Her stomach seethed from the long flight and from the tension that seemed to surround the Israeli ticket counter—not to mention all the guns, which never failed to make her nervous.

Halfway to the coffee shop she had a disconcerting thought: *Something must be wrong with the plane!* The free meal was probably a distraction so the passengers wouldn't see the workers frantically repairing the engines. If something was wrong, Abby wanted to know about it. There was no way she would board an ailing aircraft. She hopped off the moving sidewalk at the first break and headed back toward the gate.

The departure lounge was deserted. She looked out the window in time to see the door to the Israeli Airlines jet swing shut and the boarding ramp slowly fold into the terminal. The huge plane backed up, then taxied out of sight. Abby sank into a chair and popped another antacid into her mouth. Great. Something was definitely wrong with the plane.

A lone sanitation worker wheeled his cart into the lounge and began lethargically emptying ashtrays. Abby closed her eyes and tried to doze. When she opened them ten minutes later, the janitor was still emptying ashtrays, in spite of the fact that there was no one in the lounge to fill them. Paid by the hour, no doubt. When he leaned against his cart and lit his own cigarette, she nearly laughed out loud. There's a job she'd like to have—smoking cigarettes and emptying her own ashtray. The janitor took a long drag and, in the same motion, casually turned his head toward her. When their eyes met, he quickly looked away. The man obviously wasn't working—there was no work for him to do in this deserted corridor. And he certainly wouldn't keep his job for very long if he never worked any harder than this.

Abby closed her eyes again and was trying to nap when she heard a faint beeping sound. It came from the janitor's cart. Did he set his watch so he wouldn't miss his coffee break? As he disappeared with his cart behind an unmarked door, something about him struck Abby as wrong. He was too dark-skinned to be Dutch, too young and well-built to be a janitor. Was he a security guard posing as a janitor? If so, who was he watching? A shiver crawled up her spine when she realized that she was the only person in the lounge.

Outside the window, a Dutch National Airlines jet pulled into the gate where the Israeli Jet Liner had been, and workers wheeled a set of stairs to the door. Abby watched in horror as a dozen uniformed guards with machine guns—some leading dogs—hurried up the stairs and disappeared into the plane. She could see them moving around inside it. Beneath the plane, workers opened the luggage hold and several more guards with dogs crawled inside. When they finished their inspection, the guards stationed themselves around the perimeter of the plane, cradling their machine guns. What on earth was going on?

Only one explanation made sense. A bomb threat.

A sickening fear washed over Abby like syrup. *Oh, God, please, no . . .* she prayed. Her heart began to race as if she had just completed a marathon. She couldn't catch her breath. Suddenly she felt so nauseated that she had to sprint into the women's room and kneel in front of the bowl. There was nothing for her stomach to expel, but the toilet flushed automatically. When she realized that she had left her tote bag in the lounge, she tried to stand. Her knees were too wobbly to support her, and she collapsed onto the seat. The toilet flushed again. What was happening to her? She had read about anxiety attacks, but this was the first time she had experienced one.

She rose to stagger from the booth and the toilet flushed a third time. Abby made her way back to where she had left her tote bag, clinging to the sinks, the backs of chairs, and anything she could find to support her rubbery legs. Several of the other passengers had returned. She would have to board the plane soon.

Oh, dear God . . . I can't get on that plane! I can't!

Her nausea was so overwhelming that Abby snatched up her tote bag and ran back into the rest room. Her stomach heaved. As she alternated between sitting on the stool and leaning over the bowl, the automated flush drained repeatedly. Her lungs pumped so hard she felt dizzy.

Pray. She had to pray. She remembered the story of Gideon's fleece from Sunday school and decided to offer a fleece of her own. *Oh, God . . . if something is wrong with this airplane, if I shouldn't get on it . . . let my luggage be the sign. If they can't find my suitcase, then I'll know I'm supposed to wait here.*

She sat in the toilet stall, praying as she hadn't prayed in years, until the loudspeaker announced her flight. She glimpsed herself in the mirror on her way out—her face was as white as the porcelain sink.

The ticket agents had wheeled all of the luggage into the departure lounge on huge carts and were asking the passengers to identify their bags and open them. After the agents inspected each suitcase, it was loaded into the cargo hold and the passenger who owned it was allowed to board.

Abby searched for her suitcase. It wasn't on either cart. It was the sign she had prayed for. She should not get on this airplane. She couldn't breathe.

"Is there a problem, ma'am?" the big-gun manager asked her.

"My suitcase isn't here."

"If you fill out a form stating your address in Israel, it will be forwarded to you. Kindly step aboard the aircraft." Abby glanced around. She was the only remaining passenger in the lounge.

"Umm . . . I'd rather not do that. Everything I need is in that suitcase. I'll wait here until it shows up. I'll take a later flight."

"This is the only flight to Tel Aviv today."

"Well, then I'll stay overnight. It will give me a chance to see a bit of Amsterdam—"

"Why don't you want to board this flight, ma'am?"

What should she say? That God had told her not to? She would sound like a crackpot. They would lock her away somewhere. "I . . . I want to wait here for my luggage."

"But you have a ticket for *this* flight. I must insist that you board it now." He gripped her arm and led her to the door.

"No . . . wait . . ."

"You *must* step aboard, Mrs. MacLeod."

Abby wasn't sure which shocked her more: the fact that he remembered her name or that he was forcing her to get on the airplane against her will. Could he do that? Didn't she have a right to refuse? It didn't really matter what her rights were because she was too weak with fright to do anything but submit. The manager led her down the aisle of the plane to her seat, and she collapsed into it. God had answered her prayer and told her not to board this plane, yet here she sat against her will, buckling her seat belt with shaking hands.

She was surely going to die.

The next several minutes passed in a haze of terror as Abby tried to prepare herself for the explosion she was convinced would come. She had attended church every week as a child, not to mention countless Sunday school classes and Bible camps. She should remember what she was supposed to do, what she should say to God. Yet her mind was a complete blank.

The plane began to move. The flight attendants bustled around, making everything secure, then strapped themselves in for the takeoff. Abby closed her eyes as the jet hurtled down the runway. She battled an enormous surge of nausea as she felt the wheels lift off the ground.

Oh, God, please help me!

"Are you all right, miss?"

Abby opened her eyes and looked into the kind, concerned face of her seatmate. He was about sixty years old, dressed in a dark business suit, crisp white shirt, and striped tie. He wore a Jewish skullcap on his balding head, and his trimmed brown beard was sprinkled with gray, his words sprinkled with the faintest trace of an accent. Yet it was his warm caramel eyes, creased at the corners as if from years of smiling, that won Abby's instant trust. They were the eyes of a gentle grandfather.

"No," she whispered. "I . . . I'm terrified."

He peeled her hand from the armrest and placed it between his own. "May I?" he asked kindly. She nodded gratefully, feeling less alone. "You're perfectly safe, my dear. Israeli Airlines has one of the best flying records in the world. And if you can't bring yourself to trust the pilot, you can always put your trust in God."

She managed a small smile. "That's what I was trying to do. . . . Pray, I mean. I'm a little out of practice, though."

He chuckled, and his laugh was as warm as melted honey. "Then allow me. 'He who dwells in the shelter of the Most High will rest in the shadow of the Almighty. I will say of the Lord, "He is my refuge and my fortress, my God, in whom I trust." ' How am I doing so far?"

Abby was surprised to find her anxiety attack subsiding. "Um, great . . . thank you. Please don't stop."

" 'If you make the Most High your dwelling—even the Lord, who is my refuge—then no harm will befall you, no disaster will come near your tent. For he will command his angels concerning you to guard you in all your ways; they will lift you up in their hands, so that you will not strike your foot against a stone.' "

"That's one of the psalms, isn't it?"

"Yes, that's right. I'm Benjamin Rosen, by the way. And you are . . . ?"

"Abby MacLeod. As you probably guessed, I'm terrified of flying."

He smiled again. "Most people are, Abby, if they're truly honest about it." The plane banked unexpectedly, and she gripped his hand tighter.

"Are you afraid, Mr. Rosen?"

"Well, I suppose I was a bit anxious years ago, but I've flown so many times now that I'm used to it."

"Do you travel on business?"

"Yes. My work takes me to conferences all over the world. I'm a so-called 'agricultural expert,' specializing in desert hydrology. But don't let the title fool you. I'm really a simple farmer at heart, searching for new ways to grow crops in my tiny arid nation. And how about you, Abby MacLeod? What brings you to Israel—despite your aversion to airplanes?"

"I'm a history teacher and an armchair archaeologist. Now that my two children are grown, I decided to fulfill my life-long dream to go on an archaeological dig."

"That's wonderful! Where will you be digging?"

"I'll show you." If Mr. Rosen's plan was to help Abby take her mind off her fears, it was working. Grateful for the distraction, Abby pulled out her packet of materials and pored over the map and details of the expedition with him. Within minutes, she had begun to relax.

"Ah, I see that this is one of Hannah's digs," Mr. Rosen said. "Be sure to say hello to her for me. Hannah Rahov is my cousin."

Abby turned to a blank page in the back of her notebook.

"Would you like to write her a note?" She watched, fascinated, as he quickly scribbled in Hebrew, writing from right to left.

For the next hour they talked as if they were lifelong friends. By the time the flight attendants served their meal, Abby had spilled the entire story of how she had watched the armed guards search the plane and how it had triggered an anxiety attack. She even told Mr. Rosen about her fleece and how the officials had forced her to board the plane against her will. He murmured sympathetically and patted her hand.

"I know the story of Gideon's fleece," he said, and they began to talk about the Bible. Abby showed him the travel-sized one she carried in her purse, a going-away gift from her daughter, Emily.

"I confess I've never looked closely at the Christian Scriptures," he told her as he paged through it. "These first five books are the same as our Torah . . . the Prophets are the same . . . ah yes, and the Psalms are the same."

Benjamin Rosen talked with Abby throughout the flight, leaving her side for only a short time. "If you will excuse me for just a few minutes, my dear, it is time to recite prayers. May I borrow this?" he asked, indicating her Bible.

"Yes, of course."

"Here, you may have a look at mine while I'm gone. Of course, it won't do you much good unless you know Hebrew." He turned the book over in her hands, smiling. "It goes this way—it reads from back to front."

He unbuckled his seat belt and walked to the rear of the plane to join a group of other Israeli men. They stood in a circle in the rear aisle, their heads hidden beneath prayer shawls as they swayed and bobbed in rhythm with the Hebrew verse.

When Mr. Rosen returned, he and Abby talked a while longer about religion and God. "I think it is good for people of different faiths to meet on common ground as we have done, don't you, Abby? It pleases the Holy One." He paged through Abby's Bible for a moment, then began to read:

" 'How good and pleasant it is when brothers live together in unity! It is like precious oil poured on the head, running down on the beard, running down on Aaron's beard, down upon the collar of his robes.' " He sighed heavily. "I'm afraid we have not yet learned to live in unity in my country."

It was nearly time to land. Mr. Rosen fastened his seat belt as the Jet Liner slowly descended over the blue waters of the Mediterranean. Abby could see the flat coastline of Israel ahead.

"I hate landings," she said, feeling sick again. Mr. Rosen took her hand and talked her through each strange noise and dizzying turn the jet made until they landed safely on the ground. As they stood in the aisle, Abby surrendered to the urge to hug him.

"I don't know how I can ever thank you, Mr. Rosen."

"No, no, the pleasure was all mine. It's not every day that I get to spend time with a beautiful young woman. Now, if you will allow me, perhaps I could also help you through customs and see about your lost luggage. I believe there are some forms to fill out."

"You don't have to do that. . . "

"I know, but I would like to."

In the end, Abby was grateful for his help. He seemed to know a lot of people at the airport and was able to cut through the red tape quickly. Before long, they stood in the outer lobby of the terminal by the main exit doors, saying good-bye.

"Is someone from the Archaeological Institute here to pick you up?" Mr. Rosen asked.

"No, they're not expecting me to arrive this early."

"That's right, you said there was a mix-up in your flight times. Would you like me to phone Hannah and arrange to have someone come for you?"

"You've done enough for me already, Mr. Rosen. I know you must want to get home after your long trip."

He smiled kindly. "A simple phone call won't take long. I'll feel better knowing I'm not leaving you at the mercy of our Israeli taxi drivers. Do you have the Institute's phone number

handy?" Abby fumbled in her tote bag for the packet of materials and gave it to Mr. Rosen.

"You sit right here," he said. "I'll be back in a moment
with good news, yes?"

"At least let me pay for the phone call."

He pulled an oddly shaped coin from his pocket. "The
phone requires a special token, like this. Relax. I will be right
back."

He disappeared around the corner where she had seen a
row of telephones. Abby sank into an orange plastic chair, fan-
ning herself with her passport. The heat reminded her of Au-
gust back home, but the little bit of Israel that she glimpsed
through the glass doors certainly didn't look like Indianapolis—palm trees swaying in the breeze, rich golden sunlight,
traffic signs in Hebrew.

Israel! She could scarcely believe that she was in Israel! According to her watch she had been awake for more than
twenty-four hours. Abby couldn't wait to get to her hotel
room to shower and change her clothes. Then she remembered that she had no clothes to change into. Tears pressed
against her eyelids, but she pushed them back. People traveled
and lost their luggage every day. This was not a big deal. She
cheered herself with the thought that she would call her son
and daughter in a little while and let them know she had arrived safely. Would she need telephone tokens to place a call
from the hotel? She had better ask Mr. Rosen where to purchase them, then let the poor man go home. He had done
enough for her.

As she stood and headed toward the phones, she heard a
loud snapping noise, like the electric stapling machine in her
school's office. She rounded the corner and saw Benjamin
Rosen staring at her, his eyes wide, his mouth open in surprise. The telephone dangled from the wall by its cord. The
contents of her packet from the Institute lay strewn all over
the floor. Mr. Rosen held on to the ledge of the phone cubicle
with one hand as if for balance and clutched his chest with
the other.

She thought he must be having a heart attack until she saw the ragged hole in his chest, the dark blood spurting out. A vivid stain spread across his white shirt and seeped between his fingers. Speckles of blood splattered his face, her manila envelope, the glass telephone partition.

"Help him!" she screamed. "Somebody help him!"

He took a step toward her, his eyes pleading, his lips moving as he struggled to tell her something. She opened her arms to him and they sank to the floor together. His voice was urgent, desperate, as he tried to make her understand.

Then, cradled in Abby's arms, Benjamin Rosen died.

———

Agent Shur leaned across the table toward Abby. His breath reeked of tobacco. "Tell me exactly what Ben Rosen said, Mrs. MacLeod. Even if it makes no sense to you. This is very important."

She drew a deep breath. "The only word I understood clearly was *traitor*. He said he was certain there was a traitor. He repeated it two or three times. He also mumbled the word *tore* or *torn.* Something like that. Then . . . then he died. That sweet man . . . died in my arms." The sob she had bravely held back erupted from deep inside her. She covered her face and wept. Neither agent spoke or moved.

"I'm sorry," she said when she was able to control her tears. "That's all I remember. May I please go now?"

"Not until we're convinced you had nothing to do with it."

"*Me?*" The word came out in a squeak.

"We've been observing you ever since you produced the phony airline ticket in Amsterdam. It's a ploy that terrorists sometimes use. They book their luggage on a connecting flight but don't board the plane themselves because of the mix-up with their ticket. Of course, the baggage handlers don't know that. They have thousands of suitcases to deal with, and so the bag carrying the explosive device is loaded onto the plane. You were the only passenger who didn't take advantage of the complimentary breakfast. You were the only passenger paying close attention as the aircraft was inspected. You spent a great deal of time in the ladies' room, flushing something down the toilet. And, you may recall, you were quite insistent about waiting for another flight."

"But I already explained! I was scared! When I saw all the guards and the dogs, I was afraid there was a bomb. That's why I didn't want to get on the plane."

"Indeed. We did receive a tip about the possibility of a bomb shortly before you arrived with your phony ticket. The fact that you never met the man who purchased it made us suspect that you might be a mule."

"A what?"

"Someone who makes a delivery for a second party," the younger agent said.

"For all of these reasons," Shur continued, "Benjamin Rosen was assigned to sit beside you during the flight."

"Assigned?"

"Yes. And now he's dead."

Abby moaned involuntarily. The door opened and a policeman handed Shur a sheet of fax paper. He studied it for a moment, then folded it in half, creasing it several times with his fingernail.

"Your brother lived in Beirut, Lebanon, for a while. Is that correct?"

"Yes, but . . . surely you don't think he's . . . ?" Agent Shur's expression told her that it was exactly what he thought. "No, listen! Sam is a physician. He went to Beirut as a volunteer with a missions organization. That was years ago . . . and he only stayed for a month."

"Your husband's computer firm, Data Age—are you aware that they are one of the subcontractors that does business with the Saudi Arabian government?"

"No, I don't know anything about Mark's work. He and I—"

"What are your views on Palestinian autonomy?"

"I . . . I really have no views. Israel is the Jewish homeland, isn't it?"

"You have close ties to members of the Islamic faith, no? You have a friend . . ." He unfolded the fax and glanced at it for a moment. "Named Fatima Rabadi. She is a Muslim?"

"Yes, she's my friend. We teach at the same school, but we've never even discussed religion."

Abby felt hot and cold at the same time. A nightmare. This was a nightmare. How could she prove to them that she was innocent? Should she ask for a lawyer? Refuse to answer any more questions?

Agent Shur held up the fax. "In light of this new information, Mrs. MacLeod, we would like you to start at the beginning and tell us your story once again."

When he pulled another cigarette from the pack and planted it between his lips, Abby was afraid she was going to be sick. She had read about the many forms of torture used throughout history—from the infamous racks of the Spanish Inquisition to Chinese water torture—but slow suffocation by foul Middle Eastern cigarettes was a new one. If she didn't get out of this tiny room soon, she might confess to anything just for a breath of fresh air.

The Israeli agent was fumbling for his lighter when there was a knock on the door. The younger agent opened it, and a tall bearded man stepped into the blue haze.

"Excuse me," he said. "I'm Dr. Aaron Bazak from the Archaeological Institute. I've come for Mrs. MacLeod." He looked like a dictionary illustration for "archaeologist" with his rumpled khaki shirt and shorts, dusty, flat-soled work boots, and deeply bronzed skin. He extended his hand to Shur, but the agent ignored it. The two men began to argue in rapid-fire Hebrew.

Abby had felt intimidated by Agent Shur's government badge and aura of officialdom, but the archaeologist never flinched. Maybe it helped that he stood well over six feet tall, topping Shur by at least five inches. And that he looked like a gracefully aging Olympic athlete compared to the paunchy, round-shouldered agent. Abby shrank into her chair, exhausted.

Gradually, the argument resolved into the normal volume of speech. She didn't realize that the archaeologist was addressing her in English until he touched her shoulder.

"Mrs. MacLeod?"

She nearly leaped from her seat.

"Forgive me for startling you," he said. "We may leave now."

"Really?" It seemed too good to be true. She stood and the room whirled. He gripped her around the waist to prevent her from toppling over. She felt very small beside him as he helped her through the door. The two agents followed them.

"You will make certain that Mrs. MacLeod is available to us for further questioning, if necessary," Shur said. It wasn't a question but a command.

The man from the Institute nodded. "Do you have any luggage?" he asked Abby.

"Yes, I mean, no . . . I mean, they lost it. But I had a carry-on bag." One of the policemen retrieved it, and the archaeologist slung it over his shoulder. Abby walked out of the terminal at last, a free woman.

2

TEL AVIV, ISRAEL—1999

Abby stepped outside into the sunshine. The ordeal was over. She would go to her hotel, get a good night's sleep, and start fresh in the morning. Hopefully she would stop trembling soon and be able to enjoy the rest of her trip. Israel! She was in Israel, about to participate in an archaeological dig! It was a dream come true.

With the man from the Institute still supporting her, Abby stumbled across the parking lot and climbed into the passenger seat of his battered compact car. She had been warm in the tiny interrogation room, but the inside of his car was like a sauna, the seat like a bed of hot coals beneath her. The archaeologist started the car engine, adjusted the impotent air-conditioner, and they were soon hurtling through the traffic-packed streets of Tel Aviv.

"Mrs. MacLeod, I am very sorry that you had such an . . . eh . . . how should I say . . . *unfortunate* introduction to our country." The archaeologist had a deep, resonant voice and spoke with a thick accent—slightly nasal, with British vowels. "I promise we will do our best to make it up to you in the weeks ahead."

"Thank you. And please call me Abby."

"Of course. I hope we shall become friends . . . Abby." He pronounced it *Ah-bee*.

She took a good look at him for the first

time and saw that he was in his midforties and distinguished-looking, with a dark brown beard and mustache and thick, graying brown hair that fell in curly disarray across his forehead. His eyes, under straight dark brows, were the color of Hershey bars. The muscles in his arms flexed as he wrestled the stick shift into gear, and she could easily imagine him tossing rocks and shifting crumbled pillars to uncover exotic ruins.

"Could you please tell me your name again?" she said. "I'm sorry, but I didn't catch it the first time."

"That is quite understandable after all that you have been through. I'm Ari Bazak, Dr. Rahov's associate. I'll be working on the dig with you."

"Bazak? I don't recall seeing your name on any of the materials Dr. Rahov sent."

He took his eyes off the road to glance at her in surprise. "That's because I joined only a few days ago. The project I was supposed to be involved with fell through for lack of funds. Dr. Rahov allowed me to join her for the summer."

"Listen, Dr. Bazak—"

"Ari. It's short for Aaron."

"I don't know what you said back there to get me out of that awful room, Ari, but I'm grateful. From the way everyone acted, I was sure I was going straight to jail—do not pass 'go.' Do not collect two hundred dollars."

"Two hundred dollars?" he said, frowning. "I don't understand . . ."

"It's just an expression from a dumb Monopoly game. I'm exhausted and I'm not making much sense. But whatever you said to the police, thanks for rescuing me."

"I merely reminded them that Israel is still a democracy and that unless they had evidence of your involvement or charges to file against you, they had no right to detain you any longer."

Abby remembered Agent Shur's accusations and shuddered. "They acted as if I had something to do with . . . with what happened."

"It is their job to be suspicious. Aren't the police in your country the same?"

"I don't know. I've never been in trouble with the police before. Not even a speeding ticket. Umm . . . speaking of speed, do people always drive this . . . fast?" The ride resembled the view from the cockpit of an Indy car, wilder than anything she had encountered back home. Ari and all the other drivers were weaving between lanes, honking, swerving abruptly, barely touching the brakes, while dozens of pedestrians wandered heedlessly among them. She gripped the edges of her seat to keep from being flung about.

"My driving makes you nervous?" he asked.

"Yes, a bit. And I don't think my nerves could survive another rush of adrenaline." He braked and down-shifted, and a chorus of honking horns and angry shouts erupted all around them. Abby sighed. "Never mind. I've caused enough trouble for one day."

"You're not in trouble, Abby," he said as he accelerated again, narrowly missing a tour bus. "There will be no charges filed. They released you, didn't they? In fact, they cautioned me not to talk about the . . . eh . . . incident . . . unless you want to."

"Did they tell you what happened?" She leaned her head against the headrest and looked through the windshield at the cloudless sky, trying to ignore the swerving, racing traffic.

"Only that you witnessed a shooting and that the victim died. I'm supposed to make certain that you enjoy the rest of your visit to Israel. They don't want any negative publicity."

"I'm sure a lot of tourists would be put off if they thought a secret agent might die in their arms." Ari gave her an odd look, a mixture of puzzlement and displeasure. "I'm sorry," she mumbled.

Abby closed her eyes, hoping to avoid conversation and the harrowing traffic. She had been eager to see Israel, but the combination of heat and fear were making her nauseous. She didn't open her eyes again until the car stopped a few minutes later and Ari shut off the engine. "Are we at the hotel?" she asked.

"No. My favorite restaurant."

Abby groaned. "Look, I know you mean well, but the last thing in the world I want is food. I need a shower and a bed and—"

"You don't really think you'll be able to sleep, do you?"

"I'll take a sleeping pill."

"On an empty stomach? Not a good idea." His long bare legs unfolded grasshopper-like as he climbed out of the car and strode around to open her door. "A bowl of soup and a cup of tea, Abby. I promise you won't regret it. Besides, the delay will help us avoid some of this traffic."

"I can't go out in public like this," she said, gesturing to her bloodstained dress.

"Israel is a land of much bloodshed. I doubt anyone will even notice." She guessed by the bitter tone in his voice that he hadn't meant it as a joke. He retrieved a short-sleeved blue dress shirt from the backseat and handed it to her. "Here, wear this."

As he helped her from the car, clothed her in his shirt, and steered her into a restaurant she had no desire to enter, Abby felt angry with herself. She was too passive—too nice—always letting people walk all over her and tell her what to do. She envied assertive women who could get their own way, women like Lindsey Cook, the twenty-eight-year-old systems analyst from Mark's office. She had decided what she wanted—Abby's husband—and then gone after him.

The restaurant was tiny and completely lacking in decor— they would call it a hole-in-the-wall back home. Ari waved away the menus and ordered for both of them in Hebrew. Savior or not, he annoyed her—herding her around like a child, making decisions for her. She decided not to touch the soup, but as soon as the waitress set the fragrant bowl in front of her along with a basket of warm pita bread and a bowl of green olives, Abby's resolve collapsed.

"Mmm. This is delicious," she said, sipping the soup. "What is it?"

"It is made with chicken and some vegetables. I don't know how you call it in English." He broke off a chunk of the bread and dipped it into the soup, chewing slowly. "Tell me about your interest in archaeology. Have you been on a dig before?"

She exhaled. "Look, I know you're just trying to be polite, but I've already answered so many questions today that I really—"

"My apologies. You are quite right."

They ate without speaking until the silence made her feel rude. Dr. Bazak was trying to be friendly, but they weren't connecting at all. Was it the language barrier? Her lack of experience with foreign men? Making small talk with an attractive stranger was too much like dating, and the thought of starting that process all over again now that Mark was gone was too distressing to contemplate.

"Do you have a specialty or something, Dr. Bazak?" she finally asked.

"A what?"

"A special field of archaeology—you know, like Egyptian hieroglyphics or Philistine pottery."

"Ah, yes, yes. I understand. The Roman era. I have a special fondness for Roman mosaics."

"I read about the excavations during last season's dig. Didn't they date some of the ruins to the Roman era?"

He chewed on an olive for a moment, adding the pit to the considerable pile he had amassed before looking up. If it was possible to blush beneath a tan, Ari Bazak was doing it. "I'm afraid I don't know much about this dig. I joined the expedition . . . eh, last minute, and I haven't done my research, as you obviously have."

Another step on the wrong foot with this man. Abby hoped she wasn't assigned to work anywhere near him. "I'm sorry if I've put you on the spot," she said. "Maybe you'd rather talk about your other project."

"My other project?"

"The one that fell through."

"Ah, yes . . . yes, that one." His laugh sounded as though it was rarely used. "That was very disappointing for me. It was a promising site."

"Where was it?"

"Have you heard of Tel Hadar?" She shook her head. "It was Tel Hadar." He returned to his olives and bread as another line of conversation came to a halt. Abby quickly finished her soup and drained her tea.

"That was delicious. Thanks for suggesting it."

"You would like more? A refill, maybe?"

"No, thanks. I'd really like to go to the hotel now."

"We will be staying in Netanya tonight, about thirty kilometers from here. Are you certain there isn't anything you need while we're still in the city?"

"No, just take me to the hotel before I change my mind and fly back to Indianapolis."

They squeezed into the car again, and Abby braced herself for another nail-biting ride. She tried to enjoy the scenery as the car left the city, but the needle on the speedometer hovered around 100. Ari caught her glancing at it.

"Don't worry, it is in kilometers," he said. "One hundred kilometers per hour is about . . . eh . . . sixty miles per hour." It was a small comfort as they hurtled down the busy freeway. Brightly colored advertisements in Hebrew raced past, reminding Abby that she was in a foreign country. Aside from the signs, she might have been on a freeway in any American city.

"Is this your first trip to Israel?" he asked.

"Yes. My first trip to any foreign country, really. Well, we took the kids camping in Ontario once, but Canada hardly counts. We didn't—" She stopped. There was no more "we." Just Abby, alone. How long would it take to break a twenty-two-year habit, to stop thinking of herself as half of a partnership, a marriage? She had meant every word when she'd stood at the altar of her parents' church in Indiana and vowed, "as long as we both shall live." She had never imagined that Mark wouldn't keep his promise.

Abby stole a glimpse of Ari's hands gripping the steering wheel to see if he wore a wedding ring. Like her own, his hands were bare. He glanced at her curiously, as if waiting for her to complete her sentence. She didn't know how to finish it without the "we." "Um . . . have you ever visited the United States, Ari?" she asked instead.

"Not yet. I would like to someday, when there is time."

"Do you work at the Institute year-round?"

"More or less."

Abby wanted to ask how, exactly, did a specialist in Roman mosaics make a living in Israel, but her painful attempts at conversation had already proved too tiring. A tooth extraction would probably be easier than prying information from Ari Bazak. They drove to their destination in silence.

The hotel was a modern high-rise overlooking the Mediterranean Sea. Abby caught a glimpse of the indigo water glimmering in the bright sunlight as they approached the hotel. Normally, she would have kicked off her shoes right away and gone for a long walk down the beach, but she was much too exhausted. Even the elevator ride to her room on the fifth floor made her dizzy. Ari had retrieved their keys from the desk clerk, then accompanied her to her room, unlocking the door for her. He probably meant well, but the way he hovered over her made her feel like a child. She longed to be alone for a while. During the past few months she had finally begun to adjust to living alone.

"If I can be of further help . . ." Ari began.

"Thank you, Dr. Bazak, but I think I can manage from now on."

"My room is right next to yours if you need anything." He pointed to the door beside her own.

"Thank you. Oh, there is one more thing. I want to call home in a little while. How do I make a credit card call to the States from my room?"

"Would you like me to put the call through to the operator

for—? Abby, what is it? What's wrong?"

She leaned against the doorframe and covered her face, her tears unleashed before she could stop them. "That's what Mr. Rosen was doing for me . . . when . . ."

Ari drew her into his arms and clasped her tightly against his chest. "Shh . . . It's all right, Abby. It's all right."

His voice was gentle and soothing, the safety of his embrace exactly what she needed. She wondered how he had known. After a moment, he steered her into the room and sat on the edge of the bed with her, cradling her in his arms, rocking her like a child.

Abby wept, knowing it was finally safe to weep. She cried not only for Benjamin Rosen but for her unrelenting fear on the long flight overseas, for her terror when they had forced her to board the plane in Amsterdam, for the harsh way Agent Shur had questioned her, implying that she was involved in Mr. Rosen's death. And she wept because it should be Mark's arms surrounding her, comforting her. Not this stranger's.

Gradually her tears subsided. Ari continued to hold her tightly, waiting until she was ready to let go. She hoped he understood how grateful she was. She didn't trust herself to speak.

"Will you be all right?" he asked when they finally separated. Abby nodded. He stood and crossed to the door. "I'll be next door if you need anything." He closed the door gently behind him.

Abby lay down on the bed and shut her eyes. Forgetting Mr. Rosen's death wasn't going to be as easy as she had hoped. How much should she tell her children about the experience? All of it? None of it? Abby tried to concentrate on what to say to Emily and Greg, but her thoughts kept drifting back to Ari Bazak and his puzzling behavior. Were all Israeli men like him—cold and uncommunicative one moment, warm and comforting the next? She recalled the sensation of his arms enveloping her—not as a lover but as a friend—and remembered how good it had felt to cling to him, to feel the solid, protecting bulk of the man.

Suddenly Abby remembered something else, and her eyes flew open in surprise. In a shoulder harness beneath his khaki work shirt, Dr. Aaron Bazak had been wearing a gun.

———

Abby tossed on the bed for more than an hour, trying to fall asleep, but she was too overwrought to relax. Against her will, images of Benjamin Rosen played in her mind like a student's poorly edited slide presentation: his warm smile and kind eyes, his dazed horror as the lifeblood pumped from him, his inert gaze as she held the dead weight of his body in her arms. Abby thought she had exhausted all of her tears in Ari's arms, but she found herself weeping again.

She had just finished splashing cold water on her face when someone knocked on her door. She opened it to greet a short redheaded man in his early sixties wearing plaid Bermuda shorts.

"Mrs. MacLeod? I'm Ted Voss from Western Seminary." As soon as he spoke, Abby recognized his high-pitched cartoon voice from their telephone conversations. She had joked about it with her daughter, along with his tendency to emphasize random words.

"Dr. Voss, I'm so glad to finally meet you. Won't you come in?" She swung the door wide in welcome, but he gazed around the hallway absently as if he hadn't heard her. He was perspiring heavily in spite of the hotel's air conditioning. Sweat trickled down his flushed, freckled skin and glistened in his thinning red hair. When he finally extended his hand in greeting, his clammy palm stuck to Abby's.

"My group just got in a little *while* ago," he said, "and they told me at the front desk that you were already *here*, although I was *sure* you'd be arriving later. . . . Well, never mind, I thought I'd stop by and say *hello*. Did you have a good flight?"

Abby stared. "Didn't Dr. Bazak tell you what happened?"

"Who?"

"Dr. Ari Bazak—from the Institute?"

"Sorry, never heard of him."

"He's Dr. Rahov's associate for this season's dig."

Dr. Voss scowled, his flushed cheeks turning a darker shade of red. "I was under the impression that *I* was Dr. Rahov's associate. Hannah didn't mention anything about a *new* man the last time we talked."

"I'm sorry. I'm probably making a hash of things. Dr. Bazak told me that he just joined the expedition a few days ago. He was kind enough to pick me up at the airport. There was a mix-up with my flight and they lost my luggage and . . ." She drew a deep breath, then exhaled. "And the man I sat beside on the plane was shot." She gestured to her bloodstained dress and realized that she was still wearing Ari's shirt.

"*Shot!* On the airplane?"

"No, in the airport lounge. He was helping me make a phone call when . . ." Tears sprang to her eyes again as she remembered. She couldn't finish.

"Good *heavens*! No wonder there was so much extra security at the airport when we landed. But . . . but, oh dear . . . were you injured? Are you all right?" Dr. Voss seemed flustered by her tears.

"I'm fine, just a bit shaken," she said, quickly wiping her eyes.

"What can I *do*?" He pulled out a handkerchief, and Abby thought he was going to offer it to her, but he mopped his freckled forehead with it instead. Abby composed herself.

"I could use a change of clothes," she said. "Do you think one of the women in your group could loan me something to wear until my luggage arrives?"

"I'll send my wife over with something." He looked clearly relieved to shift Abby and her problems into someone else's hands. "Listen, I also came to tell you that dinner is at *seven* in the dining room, followed by a short orientation meeting. But if you'd rather skip the meeting and order *room* service, I'd understand."

"No, no, I think the sooner I get started with the graduate course, the sooner I'll be able to . . . you know, put everything behind me."

"Splendid." He jammed the handkerchief into his shirt pocket, where it drooped like a wilted flower. "We were supposed to have a much *longer* orientation meeting tonight, as you know from the schedule, but Hannah—Dr. Rahov, that is—was called away after a sudden death in the family, and—"

Abby's hands flew to her face. "That's right! He said they were cousins!"

"Who did? Are you *sure* you're all right, my dear?"

"Mr. Rosen—the man who was shot—he told me that Dr. Rahov was his cousin."

"You mean the man *died*?"

"Yes . . . in my arms."

"Oh *my*!" A bead of sweat dripped from Dr. Voss's nose, and he searched his pockets for his handkerchief before finally locating it in his shirt pocket. "Oh my! Then you were a *witness*! It's a wonder they didn't *detain* you!"

"Well, they did . . . for a while. But as I said, Dr. Bazak came to my rescue and—"

"He's the new associate you mentioned?"

"Yes, his name is Aaron Bazak." Abby was growing weary of Dr. Voss and this circular conversation. How many times would she have to relive her ordeal? "Listen, Dr. Bazak's room is right next door to mine if you—"

"Bazak . . . Aaron Bazak," he repeated, as though he were paging through an invisible Rolodex file in his brain. "Wait a minute . . . I know that name! Young hotshot archaeologist, did some brilliant work with Roman sites until he disappeared several years ago. . . . Or did he *die*? Yes, I think I read that he *died* in a terrorist bombing. Shame, really . . ."

"No, he's quite alive," Abby said. She pushed past Dr. Voss to knock on Ari's door. She had already learned from Dr. Voss's rambling telephone conversations that it was sometimes necessary to interrupt him. "He's not so young, either, Dr. Voss. Midforties, I would say." She knocked again, harder. No one answered. So much for Ari's promise to be close by if she needed him.

Abby glanced at her watch and saw that she would have

just enough time for a shower before dinner. "Do you think your wife could bring me that change of clothes now, Dr. Voss?"

He looked at Abby blankly before remembering. "Right! You need some *clothing*. I'll tell my wife."

The shower felt wonderful, even if it didn't last as long as Abby would have liked. A small sign posted in the bathroom discreetly asked hotel patrons to help conserve water in this semiarid nation. It reminded her of Mr. Rosen and his search for new ways to grow crops. Her tears for him fell freely as she showered.

Afterward, Abby changed into the baggy sunflower-strewn shorts and neon-yellow T-shirt that Dr. Voss's wife had loaned her, then studied her reflection in the mirror. Ramona Voss was five inches shorter and at least twenty pounds heavier than Abby. Between the dark circles under Abby's eyes and the ill-fitting clothes, she looked like an appeal for funds for the homeless.

Downstairs, Abby surveyed the crowd around the buffet table before entering the dining room, hoping to avoid Ari Bazak. She was embarrassed to face him again after weeping in his arms. Most of the other twenty-four dig participants seemed to be college students, with perhaps a half-dozen re-tired persons mixed in—no one Abby's age. She filled her plate at the buffet and took the last empty chair at a table filled with students. They all seemed to know one another after touring Athens together, and Abby hoped their conversation wouldn't probe any deeper than who she was and where she came from. She was relieved when it didn't. Ari didn't come to din-ner at all, nor to the orientation meeting afterward.

Dr. Voss explained how the graduate course, entitled "The Life and Times of Jesus the Messiah," would consist of a series of lectures at both the dig site and on weekend bus tours to other ancient sites. His rambling instructions concerning the dig—the four A.M. wake-up call, the need to wear a *hat* in the strong Israeli sunlight, the necessity of drinking several liters of *water* each day—put most of the other participants to sleep. It had the opposite effect on Abby, making her eager to begin discovering Israel that very night. As soon as Dr. Voss dismissed the meeting, Abby headed for the nearest exit to take a long walk on the beach.

The warm night was clear and sparkling with stars, and although it was after nine o'clock, the sandy beach was alive with other strollers like herself, even a few bathers. Abby kicked off her shoes and waded into the Mediterranean, allowing the gentle waves to wash over her ankles. She wished she had a friend to confide in and help lift the weight of the day's events from her heart, but she hadn't sought one among the other dig participants.

She walked through the shallows for twenty minutes before doubling back to the beach below her hotel. The salty water was nearly as warm as bath water. In her mind she rolled down the world map that hung in her history classroom and pointed to the oval-shaped Mediterranean Sea. Of course it's salty, she told her imaginary students; the water flows through the Straits of Gibraltar from the Atlantic Ocean. She smiled to herself. In spite of all the turmoil with Mark this past year, teaching had remained the one constant in her life, her students providing her with a purpose and a small measure of joy. Becoming a teacher had completed her threefold dream, all that she had asked from life—to be a teacher, a mother, Mark's wife.

"Thinking of taking a swim?" someone behind her asked as she stood gazing out at the water.

She recognized Ari Bazak's deep voice and nasal accent even before she turned to see him wading into the water beside her, gripping his boots and socks in one hand. She felt annoyed with him for destroying her solitude.

"I'd love to, Dr. Bazak, but I can't. My bathing suit is with my missing luggage."

He looked her over from head to toe, appraising the flowered shorts and garish T-shirt. "Where did you get those clothes?"

"Dr. Voss's wife was kind enough to let me borrow them."

"They look terrible on you." He spoke with no hint of amusement. His rudeness angered her.

"Well, we have a saying in America—'beggars can't be choosers.' " She waded into deeper water to get away from him, but he stayed stubbornly beside her.

"This beach is one of my favorites," he said a moment later. "Do you know any of its history?"

Abby shook her head, wishing he'd go away.

"Before Israel won its independence, we were under British rule. The Royal Navy used to patrol this coastline to prevent illegal refugees from landing here. Thousands of Jews wanted to come to Israel from war-torn Europe, but the British wouldn't allow them to immigrate." He crouched to dabble his fingers in the water, and a slight smile crossed his face. "Of course, that didn't stop my people from smuggling refugees ashore, right on this beach, by every means they could find."

Abby brushed a strand of hair from her eyes, imagining lights from British patrol ships bobbing on the dark water in the distance, the shivering forms of desperate people swimming to freedom in the night. "What would happen if they were caught?" she asked.

"Many of them were." He stood again. "The British shipped them back to Europe or stuffed them into refugee camps on Cyprus. The Israelis who were caught smuggling them went to prison."

Ari turned to face her. He stood very close, and for a moment she was afraid he was going to embarrass her by mentioning her tears earlier that day.

Instead he said, "If you've finished your stroll, there is someone who would like to talk to you."

Abby's stomach lurched. Agent Shur must have thought of some more questions. Her heart pounded as she walked with Ari across the beach. He led her to a bench near the steps to the hotel where a lone figure sat waiting in the shadows. As

Abby approached, she saw that it wasn't the Israeli agent but a woman about sixty years old with dark gray-threaded hair and a beautiful, serene face. She wore a long, silky caftan that billowed like summer curtains in the breeze. She looked insubstantial, ethereal—like someone you might meet in a dream.

"Hello, Abby," the woman said, smiling. "I'm Hannah Rahov. Thank you so much for allowing me to intrude on your solitude. Won't you sit down?"

Abby sank onto the bench beside the archaeologist with relief, her heart gradually slowing to normal. She was only dimly aware of Ari saying good-night and climbing the stairs to the hotel. "I'm so sorry for your loss, Dr. Rahov," Abby managed to say. "Your cousin seemed like a very kind, gentle man."

"Thank you, dear. He was." She rested her hand on Abby's for a moment. "Don't worry, I'm not going to ask you to relive what happened today. I simply wanted to meet you and to thank you on behalf of our family for . . . for holding Ben until the end. And for caring. Ari told me how you wept, not for yourself but for Ben. Thank you."

Dr. Rahov paused to wipe a tear from her dark, luminous eyes. Then she smiled, and Abby glimpsed the hope in her grief. Once again, Abby was struck by the simple beauty in Hannah Rahov's aging face, the warmth of her smile.

"I hope we shall become friends, Abby. And that you will call me Hannah."

"I'd like that very much." Abby already felt drawn to her, as quickly as she had been drawn to her cousin, Benjamin Rosen. "Please tell me about him," she said. "Was he married? Does he have children?"

Hannah smiled. "Yes, he and his wife have five children, three boys and two girls. I can't even recall how many grandchildren now—dozens of them! They're scattered all over Israel." She spoke of him fondly. "Ben and I grew up together, almost like brother and sister, though he's nearly three years older than me. Our fathers were brothers—as well as business partners—and we all immigrated here together in the 1950s.

Ben has been a foundation stone in my life for so long that I can't quite imagine that he's really gone . . . or how I'll get along without him. I shall surely miss him," she said simply.

"They told me that he was some sort of secret agent for the government."

"A *spy*, yes." She emphasized the word dramatically, but her eyes smiled as she said it. "Though you would never meet a more unlikely candidate for the job—sweet, gentle Ben. I suppose that's what made him so good at what he did. People expect a spy to resemble a suave James Bond, not a jolly grandfather."

"Was that the reason someone killed him? Was it some sort of spy drama? Who would do a thing like that . . . Palestinian terrorists?"

Hannah leaned against the bench and sighed. The sound of it seemed to blend with the sighing of the sea. "Not necessarily. It could just as easily have been our fellow Israelis—one of the many factions that doesn't want to negotiate with the Palestinians. Ben was very involved with the peace process these past few years. He often told me he was willing to risk his life so that future generations could live in peace. He wanted to bring an end to the hatred and the endless cycle of revenge. Blood feuds are a terrible practice that go back for centuries, even millennia . . . you killed my brother for killing your father, so now I'll retaliate by killing your son . . . on and on until no one even remembers who started it in the first place."

"But wouldn't Mr. Rosen's family want to see his murderer caught and punished?"

"Of course, but justice should be accomplished through our court system, not through blood feuds. In ancient times, after Joshua conquered the Promised Land, his first act of government was to establish cities of refuge—safe places where the accused could seek justice and halt the vicious cycle of retaliation. Thousands of years later, we've seen the miraculous rebirth of our nation, yet the cycle of revenge continues."

Abby felt an ember of hatred flicker to life in her own

heart, as if Hannah's words had fanned a smoldering coal. She knew how it felt to wish for revenge.

"In any event," Hannah continued, "though we mourn for Ben, we also know that the Almighty has a plan and a purpose for everything that happens."

"Even for adultery . . . and betrayal?" The words flew from Abby's mouth before she had a chance to stop them. Hannah's dark eyes studied her for a moment. Abby felt as though they were gently searching her heart, probing it as a physician might examine a patient for pain.

"I . . . I'm sorry," Abby stammered. "I didn't mean to say that. . . ."

"It's all right. I think you needed to say it." Hannah reached for her hand again. "What do you hope to gain from this trip, Abby? Why did you come to Israel?"

"Well, the easy answer is that I'm a history teacher. I love ancient history, love reading about archaeology. So when I saw the list of dig opportunities and the call for volunteers, I jumped at the chance to fulfill a dream."

"But there's something more, isn't there?"

Abby paused, staring into her lap. It didn't feel at all strange to unburden herself to a woman she had just met. It felt safe, in fact—as if she had fled to one of the cities of refuge Hannah had mentioned. "Yes. I'm also running away, escaping the pain of my failed marriage . . . the humiliation, the emptiness of what used to be our home."

"You've fled to a good place, then," Hannah said. "Isaiah wrote that this land would be a refuge and a hiding place from the storm."

Abby looked up at her again. "I understand that thirst for revenge you spoke about, Hannah. I've been angry . . . so angry it scares me. I want to hurt my husband as much as he hurt me. Maybe more. I want to get even, strike back at the other woman." She paused, surprised at the vehemence of her feelings as she voiced them aloud for the first time. "I guess I came here to sort through all those emotions. And I also need to decide what to do about my future. Before I left home I applied for a teaching job near Chicago, thinking I might start all over in a new place this fall. I tried to resign, but my superintendent asked me to wait and see how I felt when I got back from Israel. Either way, I'll probably sell our house. My two children will both be in college this fall, and I can't afford it on my salary. Besides, there are too many memories in that house."

Abby closed her eyes, remembering against her will the hours of hard work she and Mark had spent together on that old farmhouse—sanding floors, tearing out plaster and lath walls, their hair white with dust. She couldn't live alone in their house. But what about the handprints Greg and Emily had made in the wet cement on the front porch steps? How could she ever leave those behind?

"Sorry," Abby said after a moment. "I didn't mean to dump all my garbage in your lap."

"I don't mind. You helped me tonight by letting me talk about Ben. When we're carrying a heavy load, it helps to set it down now and then. Or better still, to share it with a friend."

"I sensed that you were safe. I haven't been able to talk to anyone else about my marriage. It wasn't fair to unload on my kids, and most of my friends are also Mark's friends. I'm too ashamed to talk about it at work."

"Why? You're not the one who committed adultery, I assume."

"No, but people think there must be something wrong with a woman who can't keep her husband. And I can't talk to my parents, either. They think it's scandalous for Christians to have marriage problems. They would probably say it's my punishment for straying from the church."

"Is that what you think, too? That God is punishing you?"

"Maybe . . . deep down. I used to be very involved in church activities—like my daughter, Emily, is now. When all this happened with Mark, I realized that something was lacking in my life. So I decided to use this trip to try to . . . rediscover my faith."

"An excellent plan. Jesus said, 'Come to me and I will give you rest.' "

Abby stared. "Excuse me if this sounds rude, but aren't you Jewish?"

"Yes."

"But . . . you just quoted Jesus."

"I'm a Jewish believer in *Yeshua*—Jesus, the Messiah promised in the Jewish Scriptures," Hannah said. "I know that verse firsthand because I also had to suffer pain and loss before I found rest in Christ. I hope there will be an opportunity to share my own spiritual journey with you before this summer is over, but tonight it is late. And I think we are both exhausted from all that has happened today."

Hannah turned and groped beside the bench, retrieving two orthopedic canes fitted with arm braces. She pulled herself to her feet, and as her caftan billowed in the breeze, Abby saw that from the knee down a prosthesis replaced Hannah's right leg.

"Walking on this beach must be difficult for you," Abby said as they began the slow, limping trek through the deep sand to the hotel stairs. "May I help you, Hannah?"

"Yes, thank you, dear."

Abby wrapped her arm around Hannah's waist, supporting her, steadying her.

"This leg of mine is a nuisance, that's for sure," Hannah said. "But I've learned not to be afraid to accept help. It always draws me closer to the one who is offering it. See how we're holding on to each other? I hope you won't be afraid to let me help you with your struggles, Abby."

"You'll have to teach me how to lean on someone. I've had to get used to being independent since Mark left."

"I was pretty independent, too," Hannah said. "But in my line of work I often have to climb around in rough terrain. Archaeological sites can be treacherous, even without these sticks. Quit or accept help, that was my choice. I chose to accept help." They reached the steep wooden stairs to the hotel and started up them.

"I admire your courage," Abby said. "Most of us hate to be dependent on others. Our pride says it's a sign of weakness."

"It isn't, though. It's really a sign of strength," Hannah said, breathless from the climb. "Life has a way of handicapping each of us in one way or another. Those who don't limp have probably quit—or else they haven't come to terms with their loss yet. When I fall—which happens often—I can either lie there feeling sorry for myself or I can accept help, get up, and go on. Perhaps God wants to teach you a similar lesson."

Hannah paused to rest at the top of the stairs and opened her arms wide. Abby hugged her, as she had hugged Benjamin Rosen earlier that day—had it really been that same day? She felt the strength of Hannah's embrace in return. "Thank you," Hannah said. But somehow Abby felt as though she had been the one who had been helped.

When she returned to her room, Abby calculated the time in Indiana and decided that Emily would be home from her summer job by now. Abby sat cross-legged on the bed and dialed the long string of numbers, amazed at how simple it was to call someone halfway around the world. She felt childishly excited, longing for the sound of her daughter's voice. She pictured Emily in shorts, barefooted, sitting outside on the porch swing with the portable phone propped against her shoulder.

"Hello."

A man answered the phone, not Emily.

"Greg? Why aren't you at work?"

"Abby? This isn't Greg, it's me . . . Mark."

Rage boiled up inside her, out of control. "How dare you come into my house the moment I'm gone! Get out, Mark! Get out right *now*!"

Abby thought she had finished trembling for the day, but she began to shake uncontrollably. She heard Mark's muffled voice as he handed Emily the phone, telling her to talk to her mother.

"Mom, I'm sorry . . . please don't be mad." Emily was crying. "I asked Daddy to come over. Somebody broke into our house. They trashed the place, Mom. I came home from work and saw the mess and . . . and I was just so scared! I called the police and then I tried to call Greg but I couldn't reach him, so I called Daddy at work. He just got here a few minutes ago."

Abby leaned against the headboard and closed her eyes, trying to take it all in. What more could happen on this disastrous day? "It's all right, honey. Don't cry. How . . . how much did they steal?"

"It's hard to tell with this mess . . . and we haven't finished looking yet. So far we're missing some cash and that little TV you keep in the kitchen . . . and Greg's portable CD player and maybe your cell phone, unless Greg has them. The police think the thieves were mostly looking for money."

"I'm coming home."

"Mom, no! Don't do that! You worked so hard to save for your trip. I'll be all right. Daddy offered to sleep here for a few nights until I stop shaking."

"Emily—"

"I'm scared, Mom. The police said that sometimes the thieves will wait until you replace everything and then break in again. Besides, I don't have a clue what to do about the insurance and everything."

Abby could barely control her fury. "I don't want your father and that . . . *woman* in my house!"

"She's not here, Mom," Emily said in a lowered voice. "Just Dad. He knows how Greg and I feel."

"Well, your father is *not* moving back in! He can stay tonight, but then I want him gone!"

"All right . . . I'm sorry for dumping all of this on you, Mom. I didn't even ask how you were or how your trip went. Did you survive the flight okay?"

Abby didn't know whether to laugh or cry. For some reason—maybe the fact that Mark was with Emily—Abby suddenly decided not to relate her story. "Well, I'm here," she finally said. "Which is more than I can say for my luggage."

"You're kidding! They lost your luggage?"

"It never showed up in Amsterdam."

"That's awful!"

Not nearly as awful as having an Israeli spy die in your arms, Abby wanted to add. "It happens," she said instead. "Airlines lose luggage every day. In fact, it's a wonder any of it ever shows up in the right place."

"Mom, hang on a minute. Daddy wants to talk to you."

"No! I have nothing more to say to him—"

"Hello, Abby?"

As soon as she heard Mark's voice, Abby slammed down the receiver.

NETANYA, ISRAEL — 1999

A bby awoke the next morning to the soft, distant sigh of waves breaking against the beach. She pulled open the curtains to a breathtaking view of the Mediterranean, the water silvery in the early light.

"Beautiful . . ." she whispered to the empty room.

One of the things she missed the most was having someone beside her to share the sunrise. She and Mark were both early risers, and dawn had been their favorite time of day—especially during the summer months on their family camping trips when they would dress in thick flannel shirts and sip strong coffee together outside the tent, watching the forest nudge itself awake.

She turned from the window. Getting dressed this morning would be simple, her only option Ramona Voss's sunflowered clothes. Abby's reflection in the mirror embarrassed her, especially when she recalled Ari Bazak's blunt analysis.

"I do look terrible," she said aloud. She tried on Ari's blue shirt over the top, tying the shirttails around her waist and rolling up both sets of sleeves. It looked a little better, but since she didn't want to encourage Ari's friendship, it seemed overly presumptuous to continue wearing his shirt. She took it off again.

Breakfast wouldn't be served for another half hour, so Abby settled back on the bed with her Bible and the small book of devotions her daughter had given her for the trip. Abby hadn't realized how far she had drifted from God until her marriage sank and she discovered she was without a lifeboat. Now it seemed like a long journey back to shore, but she opened the devotional, entitled *God of Refuge*, and began to read.

After skimming through the introduction, she reached for her Bible to look up the first Scripture reference. She remembered how reverently Benjamin Rosen had held the small black book as he had paged through it, comparing it to his own. She quickly blinked away her tears and turned to the book of James. *Consider it pure joy, my brothers, whenever you face trials of many kinds, because you know that the testing of your faith develops perseverance. Perseverance must finish its work so that you may be mature and complete, not lacking anything.*

Abby slammed her Bible shut. Consider it joy to suffer the betrayal and loss of her husband? She almost decided against reading the devotional, but then she recalled Hannah's words from the night before: *"I also had to suffer pain and loss before I found rest in Christ."* Drawing courage from her new friend, Abby opened the book and continued reading.

Twenty minutes later, she had just finished praying the printed prayer, asking God to use her trials to draw her closer to Him, when someone knocked on her door. The moment she opened it, Ari Bazak thrust a shopping bag into her arms.

"Here. I thought you could use some decent clothes."

Abby didn't know how to respond. His manner was gruff, as if he was forced to perform this act of charity against his will.

"Um . . . thank you. Where did—?"

"You are closer in size to my wife than to Dr. Voss's wife."

"Please tell her thank you for me."

"Sure."

He returned to his own room before Abby could finish.

What a strange man! She doubted if she would ever understand him, but at least she would feel more comfortable around him now that she knew he was safely married.

Abby took the bag inside and dumped the contents on her bed. There was a sheath dress of pale yellow linen, white slacks with a lightweight navy blazer, several pairs of shorts with knit tops or blouses to match, and even a bathing suit that looked brand-new. Ari's wife was also a size ten—and she had excellent taste in clothes. These were nicer than the clothes Abby had brought from home. Feeling lighthearted, she changed into one of the blouses and a pair of shorts, then took the elevator downstairs to breakfast.

An hour later Abby was seated on the tour bus, listening to the excited chatter of the other dig participants as they rode to the first lecture stop: King Herod's seaport capital of Caesarea Maritima. She noticed that everyone sat in pairs except her: husbands with wives, students with roommates, a few student couples snuggling and holding hands. Abby felt a wave of loneliness, which she tried to push aside by fiddling with her camera. She knew she was still weepy and emotional from yesterday's ordeal. How long would it take her to get over the shock of Mr. Rosen's death? And how long until it no longer hurt to be reminded of Mark?

As the bus parked, she glimpsed the sea again, sparkling in the distance beyond a cluster of ruined buildings. Hannah and Ari were already waiting for the group beside his car, and Abby felt pleased to see Hannah, as if they were old friends, already linked by yesterday's violent tragedy. She quickly climbed off the bus and hurried over to where Hannah stood studying a map Ari had spread out on the hood of his car. Hannah's gestures were so graceful, the way she carried herself in her long caftan so elegant, that once again Abby thought she resembled a celestial being or a figure from a dream. The contrast was especially great as she stood beside Ari, who was as ruggedly solid as a bronze statue.

"Good morning," Abby said.

Hannah looked up, and for the space of a heartbeat, her

face wore an odd expression, as if something about Abby's appearance had startled her. It quickly disappeared, replaced by her warm smile.

"Abby! You look well rested this morning." But before they could speak further, Dr. Voss interrupted them, charging off the bus like an angry bull. He was dripping with perspiration once again.

"We need to talk, Hannah . . . *alone.*"

"Of course, Ted." Hannah finished folding the map and handed it to Ari. "Would you please take everyone through the Crusader ruins for me, Ari, and get the lecture started? I'll meet up with you in the amphitheater."

Ari appeared startled and a little annoyed. "But I . . ."

"Please, Ari?" Hannah begged.

Ari glanced at Dr. Voss, then called to the milling group, "This way, please. Everyone follow me." He set off at a brisk pace, and Abby hurried with the rest of the group to keep up with his long-legged stride.

"I wonder why Dr. Voss is so angry," one of the students said as she walked beside Abby.

"Well, I think his nose is a little out of joint," Abby replied.

Ari whirled around, frowning. "His nose is *what*?"

Abby laughed, guessing at the picture in Ari's mind. "Sorry, it's just a stupid expression. Dr. Voss didn't know you had joined the dig, Ari, until I mentioned your name yesterday. He didn't seem pleased that you were . . . invading his territory." When Ari didn't respond, Abby tried making light of it. "You know, Dr. Voss also thinks you're dead."

"Dead!"

"Yeah, he said he heard a rumor that Ari Bazak, the young hotshot archaeologist, had died a few years ago. It must have been a terrible shock for him to see your ghost." She grinned, but Ari didn't. "I've noticed that Dr. Voss is just a *wee* bit absentminded," she said. "He's the one who booked me on a flight that didn't exist, remember?"

Ari gave Abby a curious look before bringing the group to a halt inside a ruined building. He began addressing the students without further comment. While he may not have been much of a conversationalist, Abby saw right away that he was a gifted teacher. His descriptions brought history to life, and even the travel-weary college students paid rapt attention.

Abby decided that reading about the Crusades in textbooks couldn't compare with standing beneath their vaulted archways or looking out from their battlements. She wandered through the one-thousand-year-old ruins with a sense of awe, reminding herself that this was only the first day of her month-long tour. Then Ari guided them through the remains of Caesarea, explaining how King Herod's engineers had created the seaport city more than two thousand years ago. Two thousand years! Abby couldn't comprehend it. The oldest artifacts she had seen in America were only centuries old, not millennia.

"As a ruler, Herod was a brutal tyrant," Ari explained to the group. "But as a master planner and builder, he was a daring genius. Israel didn't have a natural harbor, so he created one here in Caesarea. But his most famous achievement was the complete rebuilding of the Temple in Jerusalem."

"Is he the same Herod who was king when Jesus was born?" one of the students asked.

Ari nodded. "Herod was called a king, but he was actually under the authority of Rome."

Abby snapped several photographs of the Herodian ruins, then followed everyone inside the restored Roman amphitheater and took a seat on the stone bleachers, warmed by the Mediterranean sun. The theater faced the sea, and Abby felt the gentle breeze on her face as she awaited the lecture. Hannah seemed to have soothed Dr. Voss's temper. They were laughing as the group took seats in front of them. Hannah's laughter had a joyous, musical sound that reminded Abby of children at play.

"Welcome to the Promised Land," Hannah began, "the land God chose for His people. We're sitting beside an ancient travel route—the *Via Maris*, or Way of the Sea, at the crossroads of three continents—Europe, Africa, and Asia. Unfortunately, the route was also a convenient pathway for invading empires. Egypt, Assyria, Babylon, Greece, Rome . . . all of these armies marched across the land of Israel. Now, why do you suppose God would put His chosen people at a crossroads? Why not a place that was more isolated—maybe an island, like Cyprus? Wouldn't it have been easier for the Israelites to keep God's covenant if they lived apart from the other nations? Why expose them to the temptations of pagan religions and cultures?"

She paused, studying the faces in her audience, then smiled when her gaze settled on Abby. "I believe it was because God knew that many trials would help His people grow in their faith. They would learn to depend on Him and discover that He is trustworthy."

Abby recalled her morning devotions. *The testing of your faith develops perseverance . . . so that you may be mature. . . .* She stopped taking notes and listened carefully instead.

"God sent His promised Messiah to a land and a people in crisis. In 63 B.C. the nation lost its freedom to one of those invading empires—Rome. But even before Pompeii's armies swept through the land, the Jewish religious traditions had been contaminated by the pull of pagan Greek culture. The Jews felt their world crashing in on them, and the way of life they had always known was gravely threatened."

Against her will, Abby recalled the night she had discovered Mark's affair, the night twenty-two years of marriage came to an end, shattering her life.

"How would God's people react to this crisis?" Hannah continued. "Would they strike back at their enemies in revenge? Learn to live with them? Or would they pull away, living separate lives from their invaders?"

Abby knew that she had bounced among all three of these reactions during the past few months, becoming bruised and battered in the process.

"These were three of the reactions in Jesus' day," Hannah said. "The Zealots chose to fight against the Romans, the Sadducees to compromise with them, and the Pharisees to withdraw from them. All three groups eagerly awaited the promised Messiah. They hoped He would rescue them from a life that had grown intolerable. All three groups had expectations of what His coming would mean.

"And then, on a star-filled night during King Herod's reign, Jesus the Messiah was born." Hannah smiled as her eyes met Abby's again. "He offered a solution to the crisis in their lives. But in spite of all the words that the prophets had spoken, the answer Jesus offered was not what any of them wanted—or expected."

Abby looked away from Hannah's penetrating gaze, squinting in the glare of sun on water. She wanted her own pain to end, her frightening anger to be extinguished. She wanted the solution to her own crisis to be made clear to her so she could begin all over again—and get on with the rest of her life.

But what if Jesus' solution wasn't the answer she wanted—or expected?

———

"How long have you been a Christian, Hannah?" Abby asked later that afternoon as they drove to their hotel in Galilee. The group had spent a long day visiting several historic sites, including an ancient Roman aqueduct outside of Caesarea. As they were leaving their last stop of the day, Hannah had surprised Abby by offering her a ride in Ari's car. Weighing the pros and cons of sitting alone in the safety of the tour bus or risking Ari's driving again, Abby had decided the risk was well worth the opportunity to talk with Hannah.

"Let's see . . . I've been a Messianic believer for about five years now," Hannah replied. She turned to face Abby in the backseat. "My daughter, Rachel, became a believer first. And I have to tell you that I was quite upset when she told me about her faith. When a Jew hears the word *Christian*, we immediately think of the Crusades and the Spanish Inquisition and all the other horrors committed in the name of Christ. We've quite forgotten the fact that Jesus was Jewish, as were all of

His disciples, the apostle Paul, and most of the earliest Christians."

"I would have guessed it was much longer than five years," Abby said. "I've been a so-called Christian all my life, but your faith seems so much stronger, more real than mine."

Hannah fingered the ancient coin she wore on a chain around her neck. "The central belief of the Jewish faith is that God is working to redeem mankind. Once I saw that Jesus already brought about that promised redemption—*my* redemption—my faith was completed, not altered."

Abby glimpsed Ari's face in the rearview mirror and saw by his frown that Hannah's words made him uncomfortable. Judging by his angry comments in Caesarea about the atrocities committed by the Crusaders, she guessed that he didn't share Hannah's beliefs. He had been silent during their drive, but now he interrupted Hannah to ask her a question in Hebrew. She answered him in the same language. Their discussion grew more and more heated, until Hannah ended it with a shake of her head and a gesture of finality.

"No, Ari. I can't do that." Then she turned to face Abby again. "When we reach the top of this hill, you will have your first glimpse of the Sea of Galilee. . . . There it is! What do you think?"

Abby caught her breath. Below her the sea resembled a deep blue sapphire, mounted in a setting of gentle green hills. The lake was smaller than she had imagined, but much lovelier.

"I never dreamed it would be so beautiful. For some reason, I always thought of Israel as a desert, but it isn't at all. No wonder people have been fighting over this land for centuries."

"Yes, and unfortunately we are still fighting," Hannah said. "You experienced that for yourself yesterday."

Abby gathered her courage to ask the question she had been avoiding. "Hannah, about what happened yesterday . . . do you think I'm still a suspect?"

"I can't imagine that any sensible person would think so! Why?"

"I called home after we talked last night. My house in Indiana was broken into yesterday. Someone robbed it and ransacked the place."

"Is your family all right?"

"No one was home at the time, but my daughter was pretty upset when she discovered the mess. I should call her again tonight and see how she's doing. But I've been wondering . . . Do you think the two events are related somehow?"

Hannah and Ari exchanged glances. Hannah looked very angry. "I'd like to say no, Abby, but I honestly don't know. There are radical groups in my country who would easily stoop to such tactics. Israel is still a nation in crisis, just as it was in Jesus' time. There are people who want to fight and people like Ben who want compromise and peace. . . . You'll probably hear several other points of view, too, while you're here. Once again, Jesus offers us the only real solution. And once again, no one is listening."

Ari mumbled something to Hannah in Hebrew, then they both rode in silence, staring straight ahead.

Abby tried to enjoy the lush scenery as they drove around the lake, passing groves of avocados and bananas, seeing date palm trees for the first time in her life, but she was too upset by Hannah's answer to appreciate any of it. "I'm wondering if I should go home," Abby finally said. "The idea of common thieves invading my home is bad enough—but not nearly as alarming as terrorists. My maternal instincts are urging me to get on the next flight to Indianapolis and protect my children."

"I understand," Hannah said quietly. "How many children do you have, Abby?"

"Two. Gregory is twenty, a college student, and Emily is eighteen. She'll be starting college this fall."

"You don't look nearly old enough to have a grown son!" Hannah said. "You must have been a child bride!"

"Thanks, but at forty-two, I'm certainly old enough. We . . . that is, my hus . . ." Abby drew a breath and started again. "The children were born right after I was married. I wanted it that way. I loved staying home and being a mother. Eleven years ago, after Emily started first grade, I hardly knew what to do with myself. Both of my kids have always been quite independent and self-sufficient. So I applied for a teaching position and I've been mothering entire rooms full of children ever since. I love teaching."

"Is this the first time you've been so far away from your children?" Hannah asked.

"Well, they've been gone from home for summer camp and school trips and things like that—and, of course, Greg has lived on campus for the past two years—but *I've* never left *them* for so long before now. We've always traveled together, as a family."

"Are there other family members living close by who could look in on your children?"

"Both sets of grandparents are within driving distance, and their father is nearby, of course. . . ."

Hannah nodded. "Then if I were you, I would talk to your children again and see how things look today before making any hasty decisions. You did say they were independent and self-sufficient, didn't you?"

"Yes. And in spite of everything, Mark was . . . *is* a good father." She had a sudden memory of Mark sprawled on the farmhouse floor with Emily and Greg, building Lego creations and drinking imaginary cups of tea, reading storybooks and playing checkers. She shook her head. How could she reconcile that image with the man who had walked out of their life?

"Next time you talk to your children," Hannah said, bringing Abby back, "tell them that if they lived in Israel they would have to serve in the military right after high school—your daughter for two years and your son for three."

"Really? That must be tough on them."

"It grows them up in a hurry."

As they pulled into the hotel parking lot, Ari's eyes met Abby's in the rearview mirror. "I have a laptop computer," he said quietly. "You are welcome to use it while you are here if you want to contact your family by email. Telephone calls can be very expensive."

She felt a small measure of relief. "Thank you. That's a wonderful idea. We do have email."

Abby was pleasantly surprised to discover that the Golani Hotel, where they would be staying during the dig, was a plush resort. It perched on a hillside on the eastern shore of the lake, with a view of rolling green farmland and the Sea of Galilee in the distance. The expedition members would be housed in private bungalows that had a pair of rooms in each one. A separate building housed the sprawling hotel, dining room, and gift shop. Signs directed guests to the swimming pool and tennis courts.

"Wow, I had no idea it would be this luxurious," Abby said. "Are we allowed to use all these facilities?"

"Yes, but don't be surprised if you are too worn out after a day of digging to take advantage of them," Hannah said. Her bungalow was the first one in the row, with Ted and Ramona Voss's room next door. Abby's was farther down the path with Ari's room adjoining it.

He glanced at his watch as she unlocked her door. "Give me fifteen minutes and I will have the computer ready to send your email message."

Ari sat outside on the front step while Abby typed a long letter to Emily. After apologizing to her daughter for hanging up last night, Abby described her flight, her impressions of Israel, and as many of today's sights as she could remember. Once again she decided not to mention Benjamin Rosen's death. The idea of terrorists still disturbed her, so she added a postscript: *If you want your father to stay with you for a few more nights, it's all right with me.*

"I'm ready to send this," she called to Ari when she finished. He pushed a few buttons and her message disappeared into cyberspace. "Thank you so much, Ari."

"It's time for dinner," he said. "I will show you the way."

Abby hoped she wouldn't have to eat with him. His abruptness made her uncomfortable. So did trying to converse with him as they walked up the flowered path to the dining room.

"I want to thank you and your wife again for the clothes," she said. "Will I have a chance to meet her? Will she be joining you here this summer?"

"No."

He didn't seem to mind the strained silence that followed, but Abby did. "Listen, I meant to ask . . . is there something I should be doing to help retrieve my lost luggage?"

"I took care of it."

"Thank you. I haven't flown much—and never overseas like this. How long does it usually take for them to find lost baggage?"

"A few days."

"Umm . . . did that horrible man, Agent Shur, say anything more about questioning me?"

Ari shook his head.

The walk back to the bungalow with Hannah after dinner was much more pleasant than the walk with Ari. "I recommend you get a good night's sleep tonight," Hannah said. "Morning will come very early tomorrow."

"I'm so excited about my first day of digging, I may not be able to sleep!"

Hannah laughed. "I hope Dr. Voss warned all of his volunteers that real archaeology isn't like Hollywood. What is that popular movie series called?"

"You mean *Indiana Jones*?"

"Yes, that's the one. Real digs aren't nearly that glamorous. They're mostly a lot of hard work in the hot sun, moving a ton or two of dirt."

"You mean I'm not going to find the lost Ark of the Covenant?" Abby said, laughing.

"Don't we both wish!"

"Oh well, I don't mind. It's thrilling just to be here." Hannah's arm circled Abby's shoulder for a quick hug. "Good night, Hannah."

"Good night, dear."

4

THE GOLANI HOTEL, ISRAEL—1999

Abby's room was dark when the telephone
rang. She bolted out of bed, her heart
pounding. The digital clock read 4:00 A.M. It
was her wake-up call.

"Have mercy!" she said, groaning. It felt
like the middle of the night! She dressed slug-
gishly, then applied a thick layer of sunscreen,
found her hat and her water bottles, and stumbled down the path to the dining hall for a
quick cup of coffee.

She was still yawning and trying to rub the
sleep from her eyes as she walked to the rented
vans that would transport them to the dig site.
Hannah was there already, looking wide awake
as she instructed the drivers and ironed out
last-minute details with Dr. Voss. When she
saw Abby, she limped over to greet her.

"You look like you want to crawl back into
bed," Hannah said, laughing.

"I do. I've never started work this early in
my life."

"You'll understand why we do once you
feel how hot it gets by quitting time. But God
gives you two rewards for rising so early. Look
up, Abby . . . there's your first one."

Abby tilted her head, looking at the sky for
the first time since crawling out of bed. Bil-
lions of stars studded the black velvet expanse,
with the shimmering blaze of the Milky Way

cutting a swath across the middle. The sight took her breath away.

"Wow! I've never seen so many stars! There are too many city lights where I live."

"God told Abraham to look up at the heavens and count the stars—that's how numerous his offspring would be."

The sky was already growing light when they arrived at the excavation site—a jumbled pile of stones and weeds on top of a mound forty feet high. While Dr. Voss issued orders for the equipment to be unloaded—picks, shovels, wheelbarrows, spades, and dozens of black plastic buckets—Hannah drew Abby aside.

"Ready for your second reward?" They walked to the eastern edge of the mound, overlooking a grove of fruit trees. "Have you ever heard the song of praise the birds sing as they greet the dawn? Listen . . ."

The sky above the distant hills resembled an Impressionist watercolor in muted shades of pink and blue. Then, as the hazy sun slowly rose above the horizon, it was greeted by a chorus of birdsong in the trees below. The sound slowly grew in a mighty crescendo of joy.

"You're right," Abby said softly. "It was worth getting up early for this."

"Jesus told us to look at the birds; they don't worry about the future because our heavenly Father feeds them. I think that's why they praise Him, don't you, Abby?"

They enjoyed the ever-changing sky in silence for a few minutes before Hannah sighed and said, "Well, now we must get to work."

She gathered all the volunteers around her to begin the day with a walking tour of the site, deftly maneuvering with her crutches over the rough terrain. "This *tel*, or archaeological mound we're standing on, is like a layer cake of ancient history. Each time the village was destroyed, the survivors would rebuild on the remaining rubble, layer after layer, until the result was this flat-topped tel. The oldest civilizations are on the very bottom, the newest ones close to the surface. This is only our third year at this site, and as you can see"—she gestured toward the eleven-acre plateau that remained largely unexcavated—"we have a long way to go. If you look around among the weeds as we walk, you'll probably find some stray pieces of pottery."

"Can we keep what we find?" one of the college students asked.

Hannah smiled. "That depends. We already have plenty of ordinary potsherds, so you can keep those. But promise me you will show your area supervisor any pieces that have writing or designs on them, okay? All of the artifacts belong to the State of Israel . . . and we still live by the Ten Commandments here—'Thou shalt not steal.' " Everyone laughed.

Hannah stopped at a work site near the village spring. "During our first season, we dug this shaft all the way down to the bedrock and learned that the village was occupied almost continually throughout the Old Testament period, probably because of this freshwater supply. Last year we did more probing, searching for promising sites, and stumbled on a few, including the synagogue that you'll see in a minute. This season we want to concentrate on the top layer of occupation, which dates from the Roman period."

Abby found herself walking beside Ari as they followed Hannah to the next work area. "This should be right up your alley," she said.

"My *what*?"

Seeing his puzzled expression she added, "The Roman period, I mean. Didn't you say it was your area of expertise?"

"Yes," he said after a moment. "Yes, I'm looking forward to it." But there was no enthusiasm in his voice.

"We are still unsure of the name of this tel," Hannah continued. "No one thought to put up a welcome sign on the outskirts of town, announcing the name. But we have tentatively identified it as the village of Degania, which was last occupied in the first century A.D. The name comes from a little blue wild flower, the *deganit*, which grows all over this area in the springtime."

Hannah guided the group across the rocky ground to an impressive pile of building stones and sections of fallen pillars. "Now, what we have over here are the remains of the village synagogue. It would have served Degania as a place of worship and also as the village school. Close to it, over here, we found a public *mikveh*, or ritual bath. Since the Pharisees were very concerned about all the ritual cleansings prescribed by Mosaic Law, we can probably conclude that the Pharisees played a major role in the life of this village. Tell me," she said, addressing the students, "what comes to your mind when you hear the word *Pharisee*?"

"A hypocrite," someone offered.

"The Pharisees hated Jesus."

"They were the ones who crucified Him."

"Does everyone see them as villains?" Hannah asked, smiling. Most of the volunteers nodded their heads. "Well, maybe it will soften your opinion a bit if I tell you that when the movement began, the Pharisees were men of great courage—heroes who were willing to face death rather than deny their faith. The sect originated after the Greeks conquered the nation and began to forcibly impose Greek culture and religion on the Jews. One of the Greek rulers, Antiochus Epiphanes, began a systematic effort to wipe out every trace of the Jewish religion. He even sacrificed a pig on the holy altar in God's Temple. Thousands of Jews were martyred as they defended their faith, and if the Pharisees hadn't remained steadfast in the face of this terrible persecution, the Greeks might have succeeded in eliminating the Jewish faith.

"The name *Pharisee* means 'the separated ones.' That was their response to foreign conquest. They tried to remain strictly separate, having nothing to do with the Greeks or Romans or any other Gentiles—and condemning any Jew who did associate with them. But by Jesus' day, the outward form of their religion had become more important than the state of a man's heart or his relationship with God. They were carefully straining their food to avoid swallowing a gnat—the smallest of the unclean creatures—while at the same time, by neglecting mercy and grace, they were swallowing camels, so to speak—the largest unclean animal."

Gazing at the synagogue's fallen pillars and beautifully carved lintel stones, Abby tried to envision herself coming here to worship under the stern gaze of the Pharisees. It was their modern-day counterparts, with their emphasis on laws and rules, their lack of grace, that had finally driven Abby from the church of her childhood. Her daughter, Emily, insisted that the church she now attended would treat her differently, but Abby had her doubts—especially if she became a divorcée.

"Besides keeping the faith alive during times of persecution," Hannah continued, "the Pharisees made another very important contribution. They helped develop an educational system, teaching the Torah in local synagogues. It was because of the Pharisees' devotion to teaching God's Law that the average person in Jesus' time knew what the Bible prophecies said, even if he was a humble fisherman or a carpenter. And so the Pharisees prepared the people for Christ's coming."

Abby found it hard to imagine that this somber building had once served as a schoolhouse. She smiled to herself as she pictured the village children bursting through its doors into the freedom of the warm Galilee sunlight at the end of the school day. After answering a few questions, Hannah led the group to the next work area, which looked to Abby like a tumbled heap of ordinary fieldstones.

"At the close of last year's season, we found the remains of this typical first-century home," Hannah explained. "We've been eager to finish excavating it ever since. You can see the outline of the house—the main living quarters, an attached storage room, and an enclosed courtyard, where we might even find an outdoor oven." She gestured, using one of her canes as a pointer.

Abby tried to envision the house Hannah was describing among the ruins, but it looked like a pile of rocks to her untrained eye.

"Most of the people who lived in this village were probably very poor," Hannah added, "and lived in houses much like this one. Dr. Ari Bazak will oversee this section, which Dr. Voss and I call the residential area. We think there's a good chance of recovering significant artifacts, since Degania was never burned."

"Then what did happen to the village?" one of the college students asked.

"The people abandoned it around A.D. 67 at the beginning of the Jewish Revolt against the Romans. Jerusalem and the Temple were later destroyed during that same war, in A.D. 70. Since Degania wasn't protected by walls, the inhabitants probably fled to take refuge in one of the fortress cities, like Jotapata or Gamla . . . maybe even Jerusalem. As far as we can tell, the people never returned. Those who survived the war may have been carried into exile. Earthquakes eventually weakened and tumbled many of these structures, until the abandoned village simply crumbled into ruins, buried beneath the dust of the ages."

As Hannah led them across the rubble once more, Abby felt a weight of sorrow settle over her. She could identify with these villagers and the turmoil that had disrupted their lives. She thought of the home she and Mark had worked so hard to restore, with its gabled roof and creaking floorboards, and realized that when her children both left this fall, it, too, would be little more than an empty shell.

Abby returned to the present again as Hannah stopped at the highest point on the flat-topped tel. "And finally, from our preliminary probing, we think we've found the remains of a large, opulent home built in the Roman style. Perhaps the owner was a wealthy Jewish merchant or a prosperous landowner. Dr. Voss will oversee this excavation, which we're hoping will reveal Roman-style mosaics and frescoes."

Abby glanced around, looking for Ari. Why hadn't he been assigned to excavate the villa, since his specialty was the Roman era? But Ari stood with his back to the ruins, watching the flaming sunrise. She couldn't see his face.

When the tour ended and Dr. Voss divided the volunteers

among the various work sites, Abby was disappointed to learn that she had been assigned to Ari's section, not Hannah's. Nevertheless, she made her way across the tel to the residential area, joining the four college students who would also be working with Ari. They all listened as he explained what to do.

"We need to finish excavating this entire area—both the interior and exterior of the house." Ari stood inside a large square crater, which was already two feet deep, gesturing broadly to the jumbled stones all around them. "We'll probably have to dig down another three or four feet before we reach first-century ground level, so you can see that's a lot of dirt to remove. We're going to carefully loosen the hard-packed soil with one of these." Ari showed them a small hand-held pick. "It's called a *petesh.* Then we'll haul the dirt up by the bucketful until our wheelbarrow is full. We can take turns running it to the dump. Proceed carefully! While it's unlikely that we'll find any gold coins in a house this basic, I'd hate to toss one away from carelessness. You also don't want to swing your petesh so hard you smash a two-thousand-year-old oil lamp into bits. And that's what we're much more likely to find—pottery, oil lamps, jugs, household utensils—the simple tools of everyday life."

He assigned each of them a petesh, a shovel-like tool called a *tirea,* a couple of black plastic buckets, and a square patch of ground. Abby's allotment was inside the house itself, following the course of an inner wall. She pulled on a pair of gloves and started to work, carefully swinging her petesh.

The excitement of imminent discovery made her feel like a child digging for buried treasure and conjured up all her favorite treasure-hunting stories. By the time the bell rang for their breakfast break at eight-thirty, she was soaked with sweat and grateful for her straw hat and water supply. As she walked with one of the college students over to the shade of a large canopy for their outdoor breakfast, she glanced at her watch.

"Only eight-thirty!" she exclaimed. "It feels like noon!"

The student agreed. "That's because back home, by the

time we've been awake for four and a half hours, it *is* noon!"

Abby rarely ate breakfast at home, and when she did it never included cucumbers, olives, cheese, and tomatoes. But she was so hungry from her hard labor that she loaded all of those things onto her paper plate, along with bread, hard-boiled eggs, and a container of yogurt. She even went back for seconds.

Shortly after returning to work, Abby's new friend made the first "find"—a long rounded stone, shaped like an over-sized rolling pin. "Anyone want to guess what this is?" Ari asked. He shook his head in reply to all their theories. "Not even close. It's a roller used to pack down the flat clay roof of the house. There would have been a latticework of wood underneath, then a layer of earth, which had to be repaired from time to time with this roller. It probably had a wooden handle attached through these holes on each end."

Abby returned to her labor with renewed fervor after the excitement of the first discovery, and she had dug herself into a good-sized hole by quitting time. But aside from a handful of potsherds, she hadn't unearthed any treasures her first day. The morning had flown quickly. As she climbed into the air-conditioned van, she felt gritty with dust and wilted from the heat.

"I feel like an ancient artifact myself," she joked with Hannah on the ride back to the hotel. "All I want from life right now is a hot shower and a long nap."

"I know how you feel," Hannah said, laughing. "After a long morning on a dig, my daughter, Rachel, used to call me her *mummy*."

By the end of the first week, Abby had indeed moved a lot of dirt, clearing a section of the home's flagstone floor along one wall. She found the work exhilarating—and exhausting. She had gotten to know the four students quite well after working with them all week, but Ari remained a mystery to everyone. He seldom joined in their labor and never joined in their conversation, spending his time drawing detailed sketches of the area, filling out daily field reports, and tagging the bits of pottery and jug handles they found. His large strong hands cradled each artifact reverently, giving the impression of a man who loved his work, even if his manner of relating to the volunteers was more restrained than Hannah's.

Abby began to feel at home in the ancient house once its contours were more readily seen. There was a central living area where she worked, the attached storeroom behind it where the students had already found the remains of several large storage vessels, and the outdoor courtyard, where Hannah said most of a woman's typical tasks would have taken place in good weather. Abby began to wonder about the first-century woman who cooked and slept and ate here with her family, sweeping the dirt from the same flagstone floor that Abby was clearing with her shovel and whisk broom. She didn't believe in ghosts, yet if she tried to imagine this room two thousand years ago, she could almost sense the presence of the people who had lived here in the past—the "great cloud of witnesses," as Hannah called them.

Abby longed to make a spectacular find and was daydreaming about that very thing when her petesh suddenly struck something hard. She slowed down, digging carefully around the obstacle, leaving it in place as Ari had instructed them to do. But it was soon disappointingly obvious that it was only a fist-sized rock. She was about to pry it out when she noticed an indentation in the middle that looked a bit too perfect to be natural. She carefully cleared all the dirt out of the hole and discovered that it went all the way through the stone. When a shadow hovered over her, blocking out the sun, she looked up.

"What did you find there?" Ari asked.

"I don't know . . . a rock with a hole through the middle of it. And when I dug the dirt out of the hole, there were a few strands of this rusty-colored fur or wool mixed in. Do you think it could be something?"

"Let me see." She showed him the tiny fibers she had

saved, and he carefully tucked them into an envelope. "Good job," he said. "You found a weight stone that was probably used on a loom. The weights were attached to the warp threads—the vertical threads—to hold them tight. Keep digging. You might find more of them."

He retrieved his clipboard and began measuring and sketching the location of her find in relation to the house's foundation wall. Within half an hour, Abby had found three more weights. Then her trowel hit something softer than a rock—a piece of wood. She uncovered it carefully, brushing the dirt away with her whisk and saving the almost infinitesimal white fibers she found beside it. The wood was smooth, about ten inches long, and notched on both ends.

"Ari, I've found something else," she said when it was partially uncovered. "Is it a piece of the loom?"

He laid down his notes and crouched to examine it. "It looks like it might be the shuttle. Quite well preserved, too. Uncover it all the way."

"You trust *me* to finish?"

"Most volunteers never would have seen those tiny fibers—much less saved them."

When she had the shuttle exposed, Abby noticed some unusual notches carved into the smooth wood. She used a toothbrush to clean them, operating as painstakingly as a surgeon. The carving looked too neat, too evenly spaced and sized to be natural. Maybe it was her imagination, but it looked to her like Hebrew lettering. She called Ari again.

"Is this writing?" He got down on his hands and knees to look closely, then removed a pair of eyeglasses from his pocket and peered at it again.

"Yes," he said, pulling himself to his feet.

"Is that good?"

Ari didn't answer. Instead, he climbed out of the excavation. "Hannah," he called. "Come here when you have a minute."

Abby thought she detected excitement in his voice. When Hannah arrived, Ari helped her down into the pit. The four college students crowded around them, watching.

"Did you find this?" Hannah asked Abby. "Congratulations! Great beginner's luck!"

Hannah also put on a pair of reading glasses to study it. When she lifted her head again, her excitement was obvious. "This is amazing! We've found other shuttles before, but I've never seen one with writing on it."

Abby felt so elated, the wood might have had rubies embedded in it instead of writing. "What does it say? Can you read what it says?"

"I think it's a name—Leah. Probably the name of the woman who used this loom. You agree, Ari?"

"Yes. The carving is amateur. Looks like crude first-century script."

"Just a name?" Abby said.

Hannah must have heard the disappointment in her voice because she quickly said, "No, it *is* truly amazing! Do any of you know why?" She looked around at the gathered students. None of them knew. "You tell them, Ari," she said.

He grinned from ear to ear. It was the first spontaneous smile Abby had seen on his face.

"Because only boys were allowed to study at the synagogue schools," he said. "Most first-century women—especially poor Jewish women—couldn't read or write."

"Yet in spite of all the odds," Hannah said, "all the prejudice against women, all the hidebound traditions of the Pharisees, a woman named Leah learned how to carve her name into her weaver's shuttle."

Abby gazed at the pile of rocks that had once been Leah's house, the flagstone floor that both she and Leah had swept clean, and wondered what life had been like for her, separated from Abby by so many centuries and traditions. She couldn't imagine how Leah had learned to write her name, but she felt a small shiver of triumph for her ancient friend. "Bravo, Leah!" she whispered.

THE VILLAGE OF DEGANIA—A.D. 46

"Leah . . . Leah!" Her mother's voice finally penetrated Leah's daydream. "Watch out! You're burning the bread!" Leah yanked the loaf of flatbread from the hearthstones before it turned from brown to black.

"It isn't burned," she said as she discreetly scraped off a dark spot. "It's just . . . well done." Leah found it hard not to let her imagination drift when faced with the boring tasks of grinding grain and baking flatbread. The late-winter day had dawned cloudy and cold, forcing Leah and her mother to pre- pare the midmorning meal indoors. With only a hole in the roof for a chimney and no oil to spare for the lamps, the dingy one-room house was smoky and dim.

"It's time you stopped living in a world of dreams," Mama said, shaking her head in reproof. "Any sensible man will choose a hardworking girl for his wife—not a dreamer."

Leah opened her mouth to protest that she was only thir- teen years old and too young to be chosen for a wife, then remembered the terrible event that had happened to her re- cently. She was indeed a woman now—as her budding figure also attested. "I don't want a husband and babies," she mum- bled to herself. But whether she wanted them or not, marriage and motherhood were galloping steadily toward her like a Roman war-horse into battle.

"The Scriptures say that too much dreaming is meaning- less," Mama said. She pushed open the wooden door to the courtyard with her hip and tossed a basin of waste water out- side. The sudden gust of damp air made Leah shiver. "And it is also written that the shiftless man goes hungry," Mama added. "Come, help me make room for the food."

Leah worked quickly, clearing away all the storage vessels and mixing bowls from the low plastered platform that ex- tended along the length of one wall, then she laid out the woven mats for their meal. Her father and three brothers would be home for lunch very soon. She piled the fresh loaves of flatbread she had baked onto one of the mats, then quickly covered them with a cloth, dismayed to see how dry and over-baked the loaves really were.

"May I go and fetch Matthew from his lessons?" she asked after setting out small bowls of seasoned olive oil and wine vinegar to go with the bread. Mama didn't look up from where she bent over the hearth, stirring the lentil porridge. The aromas of cumin and garlic drifted from the pot.

"Your brother knows the way home."

"I know, but I'm all jittery from being cooped up all morning." Leah danced in place, shaking her thin arms and legs as a dog shakes off water. Mama turned in time to see her gyrations and smiled wearily.

"All right . . . go on, then." Leah grabbed her shawl from its peg by the door and wrapped it around her shoulders, hurrying in case Mama changed her mind. "Get all the jitters out of your system," her mother called as Leah fled through the door. "We have things to do this afternoon."

The ground felt cold beneath Leah's bare feet as she ran up the path from her house on the outskirts of Degania and through the narrow village streets to the synagogue. Her long dark hair, frizzy from the humidity, whipped into her eyes as she ran. She hoped she wasn't too late—not to meet her five-year-old brother, but to sit beneath the open window and listen to part of his lessons.

Leah longed to know the God who had created birdsong and the silvery green olive leaves and the peaceful waters of the Sea of Galilee, visible from the hill outside her village. The God whom King David described in his psalms seemed so different from the God the synagogue leaders portrayed. A God who didn't treat us as our sins deserved seemed a far cry from the Pharisees' God of endless rules and consequences. David's God was a shepherd who led him to green pastures and still waters, not a nit-picking master who scrutinized his every move. Whenever Leah hiked up into the pasturelands to take food to her brother Saul and saw the tender care that he bestowed on Abba's small flock of sheep, she longed to know the Shepherd-God whom David knew.

As Leah had hoped, the synagogue school was still in session, and the droning voice of the rabbi drifted from the window in unison with the voices of his young students.

"Once again," he prompted. "All together . . . ' "No longer will a man teach his neighbor, or a man his brother, saying, 'Know the Lord,' because they will all know me, from the least of them to the greatest," declares the Lord. "For I will forgive their wickedness and will remember their sins no more." ' Very good. And again . . ."

By the third repetition, Leah was whispering the beautiful words along with him, wondering what they meant. *They will all know me, from the least . . . to the greatest . . .* Would that include women like her, who were among the very least in society?

"That's all for this morning," the rabbi suddenly said. "You are dismissed."

Disappointed, Leah hurried to the front of the building, watching for Matthew as the boys streamed through the three huge doors and scattered in all directions. He was one of the last ones, and one of the smallest, emerging from the stone building in his slow, shambling way as if walking in his sleep. "Tell me what you learned today," she begged as she fell into step beside him.

He didn't answer right away, concentrating instead on the pebble he was dribbling down the lane between his bare feet. "I don't know . . . words . . . boring stuff."

Leah stopped his pebble with her own foot, then stood in his path."Which words? Come on, please tell me, Matthew."

He squinted in thought. "Names. We're learning to spell our names. I can write mine—want to see?"

"Yes! Show me!" They crouched with their heads together beside the road and Leah helped him smooth a level patch in the dust. She watched, fascinated, as he scratched his name in the dirt with a sharp stone. "Why do those shapes make your name?" she asked when he finished. He sighed in exasperation.

"I don't know. I'm no good at explaining things. And

they're not shapes. They're called letters."

"Letters? Show me again."

Matthew swirled his hand in the dust to erase them, then wrote the symbols again, making one of the sounds in his name each time he drew a letter. "Mm . . . aa . . . thh . . . eww."

"Oh, I get it," Leah said. "Each letter has its own sound." Matthew nodded, relieved that she had caught on without an explanation. "Will you show me my name now?" She tried to brush a lock of his dark curly hair from his forehead, but he pushed her hand away, impatient with her mothering.

"We didn't write your name. You're a girl."

"But you know all the letters and their sounds, don't you? Can't you sort of . . . sound it out?" Matthew planted his hands on his hips in imitation of Abba. Leah worked hard not to laugh at him.

"If I show you, will you let me go home and eat?" he asked.

"Yes. And I'll even share my raisins with you."

"All right," he said, crouching in the dirt again. "I think it's like this. L . . . ee . . . ahh. The letters are *lamed, aleph, heth.*"

"Let me try it." She took the stone from him and copied the shapes he had written, repeating, "Lamed . . . aleph . . . heth. Like that?"

"Yeah."

Leah copied them a second time, then a third. She was so absorbed in the wonder of it, she didn't care that Matthew had started down the lane toward home without her, kicking his pebble. She wrote her name one more time to make sure she would remember it, then brushed the dust off her hands and skipped after him.

Abba and her older brothers, Saul and Gideon, were already seated in their places around the platform. "You are late," Abba said. "You've kept us waiting."

"I'm sorry, Abba." Leah felt his stern gaze following her as she and Matthew quickly washed their hands. She expected another of his almost-daily lectures on the need for her to grow up soon and act more responsibly, but he must have decided that Leah had wasted enough of his time. After Matthew took his place beside his brothers, Abba recited the blessing. Leah helped her mother serve the food, listening in respectful silence to the men's conversation.

"Abba, the new lamb that was born this morning is a male," Saul said. At age eighteen, he worked with Abba every day, laboring in their barley field and caring for their small flock of sheep. His big bearlike frame towered over Abba's, and he even resembled a bear with his shaggy black hair and beard. But Saul was as gentle and docile as one of his lambs.

"Maybe we can take it to Jerusalem for Passover this spring," sixteen-year-old Gideon said. He was as different from Saul as two brothers could be—lean and sinewy, with curly brown hair that bleached to gold in the summer sun. His nature was different, too. Gideon was clever and quick-witted—and quick-tempered.

Saul frowned at his younger brother. "I was hoping to fatten up that lamb to help pay for a bride, not eat for Passover."

Leah felt a sudden chill, as if Mama had opened the door again. If Saul chose a bride this year, it would mean another woman to help her and Mama with their work. But it would also mean that Leah would not be needed as much and could become a bride herself. She waited with her brothers, watching Abba's face for a hint of his decision.

"This lamb will be for Passover," he said at last. "There will be other lambs this spring, God willing, for your bride-price." He scooped a helping of lentils into his mouth with a piece of bread, then added, "We'll bring the lamb down from the pasture about a week before we leave for Jerusalem. It will be Leah's job to care for it." He held up a piece of the burned flatbread and added, "Let's hope she gives it her *full* attention."

Gideon turned to her and grinned. "Remember, Leah, it's the priests' job to offer burnt sacrifices, not yours." All the men laughed, even Abba.

Leah kept her anger and humiliation at bay by savoring her newfound secret: Like all three of her brothers, she knew how to write her own name. Leah was so fascinated with her new skill that for the rest of the afternoon she wrote it everywhere, tracing the letters on the hearthstones with a piece of charcoal, dipping her finger in water to write it on the side of the clay jug, carefully carving it into her weaver's shuttle with a knife. She glowed with triumph at the thought of mastering a skill that few other women possessed. But at the same time, Leah's accomplishment only whet her appetite for more learning. Since writing her name was so easy, why couldn't Matthew or Gideon teach her all of the letters?

She dreamed of learning to read as she methodically wove the shuttle back and forth through the warp threads, barely concentrating on the pattern of russet and gray stripes. The simple loom hung from a crossbeam below the ceiling, and the weight stones, which held the warp threads tight, clicked together rhythmically as she worked.

"Leah," Mama said, interrupting her thoughts, "don't forget, you must go and bathe in the mikveh today."

Leah made a face. She had purposefully forgotten, pushing the unwanted thought from her mind as if shutting it away behind a locked door. "Do I have to go?"

Mama's hands froze in midair, nearly dropping the distaff and breaking the thread she had been spinning. "Of course you must go! The Law commands it! Didn't I already explain to you that after a woman's monthly time—"

"Yes, yes, you explained already," Leah said quickly, wanting to avoid the embarrassing lecture again. "But I still think it's humiliating to have to walk past Reb Eliezer and all his Pharisee friends. Why do they have to hang around outside the mikveh anyway, checking to see who goes inside to bathe? They're so nosy! Besides, the water is probably freezing cold."

"I suppose you expect to take a hot bath, like the Romans do?"

"No, I don't want to bathe at all!"

"It's the Law, Leah," Mama said, stowing her spinning in a

storage basket. "And the sooner we go and get it over with, the better."

Leah dragged her feet as she walked with her mother through the winding lanes to the public mikveh, shivering at the thought of her embarrassing ordeal. By sundown, the entire village would hear that she had paid her first visit to the bath and would know that she was now eligible for marriage. She lifted her shawl from her thin shoulders and wrapped it around her head, trying to hide her face.

"Why can't I just bathe at home?" she mumbled.

"The bath is for purification," Mama explained. "It must be 'living water.' "

"But the water in the mikveh isn't 'living.' It doesn't come from a free-flowing source any more than our water does. They both come from the village well, they are both stored in cisterns . . ."

"They aren't the same," Mama said patiently. "Reb Eliezer sprinkles the mikveh with 'living water' and that makes it—"

"That's cheating! Water is either from a 'living' source or it isn't. Sprinkling doesn't magically change it."

Mama stopped walking. Her shoulders were bent, her face lined with weariness. "Leah, why must you always fight tradition?"

"Because the traditions are stupid! Why doesn't Reb Eliezer sprinkle *our* cistern? Then I could bathe at home. The Pharisees make us follow all their dumb laws, yet they don't have to keep them. It's not fair."

Mama grabbed Leah's shoulders. "You hold your tongue, girl, and keep your thoughts to yourself! Don't you dare bring shame on your father and me by speaking against the village elders! You will do what the Law prescribes without another word!"

Leah would bathe in the mikveh. But she wondered, as she had so many times before, why carefully obeying God's Laws never made her feel any closer to Him.

As Leah had feared, Rabbi Eliezer guarded the door to the ritual bath. Worse, Reb Nahum, the ruler of the synagogue, stood beside him. Leah stared at the ground, her cheeks flaming, as Mama explained why they had come. But instead of quickly allowing them to go inside and have some privacy, Reb Nahum began to lecture Leah.

" 'A wife of noble character who can find? She is worth far more than rubies.' You want to be a good wife of the Torah, don't you, Leah? Fulfilling your duties according to the Law?"

She didn't want to be a wife at all, but she nodded mutely, biting her lip to keep from saying the words aloud. Reb Nahum hooked his thumbs in his wide embroidered belt, rocking on his heels as if lecturing in the synagogue.

"A godly wife will learn to keep a proper kitchen, to separate the clean and the unclean, to sanctify the Sabbath. These statutes were given by God and they are very important, Leah. The Law is our salvation."

Leah bristled. Then why didn't they teach girls to read the Law so they would know exactly what it said?

"A godly wife will make certain the meat is killed and cooked properly, and that meat dishes are never served at the same meal with dairy products. Remember, the Torah says, 'Do not cook a young goat in its mother's milk.' "

Leah had heard enough. Her voice dripped with phony sweetness as she said, "We can't afford to eat meat, Reb Nahum. And any husband who chooses a poor farmer's daughter like me for his wife probably won't be able to afford meat, either."

For a long moment, the two Pharisees simply stared at Leah. Then, as Reb Nahum's expression changed from astonishment to anger, he said, "I can see that you have a great deal to learn, Leah. But for today, one last lesson will do: 'He who guards his mouth and his tongue keeps himself from calamity.' "

He finally allowed Leah to go inside. But as she immersed herself in the mikveh's icy water, she couldn't help wondering if Reb Nahum had dumped snow from Mount Hermon into it just to spite her.

5

THE GOLANI HOTEL, ISRAEL—1999

On a clear, balmy evening near the end of the first week of the dig, Abby trudged down the flowered path to Hannah's bungalow and knocked on her door, fighting the tears that her discovery had unleashed. "I hope I'm not disturbing you. . . ." she began tentatively.

"Not at all! I was just enjoying the view of the Sea of Galilee from my patio. I'd love it if you joined me." Hannah led the way to her balcony, where the silvery lake shimmered in the distant twilight and city lights sparkled in the hills on the opposite shore. "Doesn't this view remind you of the verse, 'A city on a hill cannot be hidden'?" But when Hannah turned for Abby's response, her smile faded. "You didn't come for the view, did you? What's wrong, dear?"

Abby sat in the chair Hannah offered and drew a deep breath, summoning courage. "I've found something that belongs to you, Hannah. I apologize for not giving it to you sooner, but I completely forgot about it." She passed the page she had torn from her notebook to Hannah, trying not to picture the blood-spattered cover. "It's a note to you . . . from Ben."

"From Ben? How . . . ?"

"He wrote it while we were still on the

plane from Amsterdam. Until now, I haven't been able to . . . to go through any of the things—"

"It's all right, Abby. I understand." Hannah laid her canes on the floor and lowered herself into one of the patio chairs to read Ben's note. She smiled slightly at his words even as her eyes filled with tears. "Thank you," she said when she finished. "I'll treasure this." She gently folded the page, then wiped her eyes. "I guess I'm not the only one still grieving. This has been difficult for you, too, hasn't it? I gather your life hasn't been touched so closely by death before—especially a violent one."

"No. Have they . . . um . . . caught the person who . . . ?"

"Not yet, but they will." Hannah sighed. "Ben and I had many discussions—some would say arguments—about the risks he was taking. The Jewish and Palestinian leaders who are willing to work together and negotiate with each other are often considered traitors by their own people who don't want to compromise with their enemies. Ben secretly worked as the middleman between the two sides. I know he was willing to give his life if he thought it would bring lasting peace, but it still doesn't make what you witnessed any easier to forget."

"How are his wife and family doing?"

"They're grieving, but their faith is strong." Hannah pulled a tissue from her pocket and blew her nose. "Ben wasn't always a spy, you know. His first love—his true love— was agriculture. It wasn't until much later in his life that the Agency became his mistress."

"Why did he join?"

Hannah sighed again, looking out at the view that must have appeared blurred through her tears. "Joining the Agency was his reaction to a crisis. Life here in Israel can be very difficult. In fact, it can overwhelm you at times. When it overwhelmed Ben, he felt he needed to do something more than grow plants. For years, making the desert bloom had been his way of fighting back. But that was no longer enough for him. He had to do more. No one in our family was happy with his decision."

There was a knock on Hannah's door, and a moment later Ari let himself in. Abby resented his intrusion, but Hannah didn't seem to mind.

"I followed you over here," he told Abby. "The airline just called to say they will deliver your suitcase tomorrow."

"Finally! I didn't think I'd ever see it again."

"And I have another email message for you." He handed Abby the printout, then he and Hannah talked in Hebrew while Abby read her daughter's letter.

Dear Mom,

I'm so glad you thought of sending each other email. It's been great talking to you every day. Good news! The insurance company sent a check today to pay for the damage and to re-place all the stolen things. Greg already bought a new CD player, but Dad says to wait and let you replace everything else.

Mom, I know that you don't want to talk to Dad or have anything to do with him, and I don't blame you. What he did hurt all of us—you most of all. I didn't want to see him either, but this robbery forced me to, and maybe that was why God allowed it to happen. Daddy and I have had time to really talk. We stayed up until two o'clock in the morning last night. He said that when he walked in the door and saw our house all trashed, and you were gone, and I was scared and alone, it was like seeing a portrayal of what he had done to all of us. He asked Greg and me to forgive him—and he cried, Mom. I don't think I've ever seen Daddy cry before. . . .

Emily had written more, but Abby needed to wait until she was alone to read the rest. The letter made her so angry she wanted to crumple it in her fist. *He hasn't cried nearly as much as I have,* she fumed. She turned her attention back to Hannah and Ari, wanting to push Mark and her problems at home far from her thoughts. Wasn't that one of the reasons she had traveled here—to forget?

Ari leaned against the railing with his back to the lake. His voice had gradually grown louder, his scowling face and brusque gestures betraying his anger. There was a third chair on Hannah's balcony, but Abby was relieved when Ari bid them a curt good-night and left the bungalow. She needed some quiet conversation alone with Hannah to diffuse the anger that Emily's letter had aroused and to soothe the grief that Ben's letter had evoked.

"Is everything all right at home?" Hannah asked, gesturing to the letter.

"Yes, you were right—my kids are coping with the whole incident pretty well. They don't want me to come home." She longed to blurt out her anger and her fear that Mark was taking advantage of her absence and the break-in to worm his way back into their children's lives, but she knew she would sound childish. Instead she asked, "Did I do something to make Ari angry just now?"

"Not at all," Hannah said. "I'm sorry if our discussions get a bit loud. Ari always has been a very . . . intense person."

"To tell you the truth, I can't figure him out," Abby said. "He can be so thoughtful one minute—offering to let me send email, loaning me his wife's clothes—yet he'll barely speak to me the next."

"Please don't take Ari's behavior personally. Like you, he has also had his private struggles. I have known Ari for a long time. He was my first student assistant at the Institute, in fact."

"How long have you been an archaeologist?"

"Let's see . . . more than thirty years, I guess."

"I can tell that you still love it, Hannah. You still get excited with each new find."

"Yes. So does Ari. He just has a different way of showing it."

"What made you decide to study archaeology?"

"That's a very long story," she said, smiling. "Are you sure you're not too tired to hear it after a long week of digging?"

"I'm not tired at all—and we can sleep late tomorrow, right?"

"That's true. We won't leave for our tour of Jerusalem until nine o'clock."

"Nine o'clock!" Abby said. "That's going to feel like noon

after waking up at four all week. Besides, I'm too unsettled to sleep. I keep thinking about Leah, wondering about her life, trying to imagine how she would have learned to write her name."

Hannah smiled. "I do the same thing—give flesh and blood to the people whose lives I unearth. I always have, ever since I found my first artifact."

"Were you born in Israel?"

"No, my family immigrated here in 1951 when I was ten years old. I was born in Iraq, fifty-eight years ago. . . ."

THE NEGEV, ISRAEL—1951

Sunlight radiated off the tin walls of the shack, intensifying the desert's suffocating heat. Perspiration mingled with Hannah's tears as she wept in her father's arms on the front step. "I want to go home! Please, Abba, *please* take me home!"

"We can't go back, Hannah. We can never go back." Sorrow thickened his voice. He patted her head uselessly, offering her no comfort. Every day for the entire two weeks she had lived in Israel, Hannah had pleaded with him to take her back to Iraq. Every day Abba's answer remained the same. "Iraq is no longer our home. We aren't welcome there anymore."

"But I want to go home!"

"We are home. Israel is our home now."

Dirt smudged Abba's handsome face, fatigue etched it with deep furrows. His thick black hair, once glossy and clean, now wore a layer of gray dust. He had always dressed in fine clothes, hand-tailored shirts, and jackets of silk and linen, but now he didn't even smell like Hannah's father. Instead of that wonderful combination of Turkish coffee, expensive tobacco, and lemony cologne, he reeked of sweat, like a common servant.

"I hate it here! I hate Israel!" Hannah clenched her swollen eyes shut, remembering their clean, spacious villa in Baghdad, the servants who took such luxurious good care of them, the juicy lamb and luscious fruit that seemed to overflow from their table. Hannah had lived a pampered life in Iraq, stuffed as plump as a melon with pastries and sweets. After her mother died, she and Abba shared the villa with Uncle Mordecai, Aunt Shoshanna, and their three sons. Now she couldn't understand why they had left it all behind to live in squalor in a crude shack in the melting heat of the desert. And she was much too numb with her own grief to notice by the slump of Abba's shoulders, the quiet despair in his voice, that he longed to return to their old way of life in Iraq as much as Hannah did.

"Why can't we go home?" she sobbed.

"Enough. I give up," Abba said suddenly. "It is useless to try to console you. You don't hear a word I say. I have work to do." He didn't sound angry—Abba never spoke angrily to Hannah—simply weary of plowing the same old ground. Hannah slid from his lap as he stood. He pulled his shirt off over his head and tossed it through the open door of the shack. "Benjamin," he called to his nephew, "see if you can do something with your cousin, please." Ben emerged from the neighboring hut and shuffled over to take Abba's place, while Abba took over Ben's job of helping Uncle Mordecai mix cement for a new floor.

"Whew! It's hot, isn't it?" Ben said, wiping his face with his shirttail. Hannah wept in reply. "Want to play a game or something, Hannah?"

She thought of the games she and Ben used to play in the shady courtyard of their villa and wailed, "I want to go home!"

"Let's go for a walk," Ben said, yanking her to her feet. He dragged her by the arm like a stubborn puppy on a chain, down the road in front of the long row of shacks and across an empty field. As soon as they were out of earshot of their fathers, Ben grabbed Hannah by the shoulders and shook her until her teeth rattled. "Stop bawling! We're all sick of it! You're not a baby!"

No one had ever treated Hannah like that before. Stunned,

she wiggled out of his grasp and fled to the shade of a spindly broom tree, one of the few that managed to grow in their desolate immigrant camp. Ben followed right behind her, his face red from his anger and the heat. Afraid he would shake her again, Hannah finally took control of her tears.

"Go away and leave me alone!" she yelled. Instead, Ben flopped down beside her.

"I'm not supposed to leave you alone, Hannah. I'm supposed to teach you stuff so you can start school as soon as it's built."

A belated sob shuddered through her. "What . . . kind of . . . stuff?"

"The Hebrew alphabet, for one thing. I already learned it when I studied for my bar mitzvah in Iraq."

"I don't want to go to school." Hannah crossed her plump arms, content to remain illiterate.

"Well, you don't have a choice," he said. "It's the law here in Israel. . . . And don't start bawling again about how much you hate it here. Everyone for miles around already knows." They sat in silence for a moment, watching their fathers mix another bucket of cement and haul it inside. They looked as small as ants from this distance, performing a wavering dance in the heat. "They sure could use some help," Ben muttered.

Hannah knew without asking that he was thinking of his two older brothers who had been inducted into the army shortly after arriving. "Do you miss them?" she asked.

He lifted his shoulders slightly in resignation. "No use thinking about it."

Hannah stared at the shacks, the vertical lines in the corrugated tin shimmering in the heat until the houses appeared to be melting before her eyes. She wished that they would melt. It would be unbearable inside tonight as she and Abba tried to sleep.

"Why can't we have a nice house?" she asked. "I saw nice ones when we first arrived in Israel. Why did they send us here where it's so hot that even grass can't grow?"

"Because we're *Sephardic*." He spat out the word as if it

made a bitter taste in his mouth.

"What does that mean?"

"There are two kinds of Jews—*Ashkenazi* and Sephardic. Ashkenazis are lighter skinned and come from European countries. They hold all the power in Israel and make all the important decisions. Sephardis like us are darker skinned and have no power at all. We're descendants of the Jews who fled the Spanish Inquisition."

"What's that?"

"The Inquisition? One of the many bad ideas the Gentiles have come up with to kill our people."

"Kill us? Why?"

Ben took a breath, about to speak, then shook his head. "Don't ask. Anyway, our ancestors left Spain and settled in Iraq. But we really belong here, in Israel. *This* is the land God promised to Abraham and his descendants."

Hannah had heard the name Abraham mentioned at the synagogue and knew he was an important man. "Is Abraham Ash-*whatever* or like us?" Her question amused Ben. His eyes filled with warmth and laughter. They reminded Hannah of the dark, sweet candies that had been her favorites in Iraq.

"Neither one. Abraham was just plain Jewish."

"How do you know so much?" she asked, grateful that Ben had taken her mind off home for a few minutes. He grinned and tousled her hair.

"Because I go to school. And now that you'll be going to school, too, you'll be as smart as me someday."

"I don't want to go to school," she repeated. Ben sighed. "Don't be such a baby."

In the distance, Aunt Shoshanna straightened from the tub of laundry she was bending over and rubbed her aching back. When she finished washing their clothes, she would hang them out to dry on the rope that stretched between their two huts. It looked to Hannah like an endless job. With a house full of servants in Baghdad, Ben's mother had never scrubbed laundry or cooked a meal in her life. Now that she was forced to do servants' work, she appeared exhausted by dinnertime as she laid their daily fare of fish and steamed vegetables on the table. Hannah had seen her aunt crying several times since they'd left Iraq, but unlike Hannah, Aunt Shoshanna shed her tears in silence.

"We were all spoiled in Iraq," Ben said, as if reading Hannah's thoughts. "But the truth is, it has always been hard for our people. One of the Torah passages I had to learn for my bar mitzvah said that our ancestors were slaves in Egypt, but when they cried out to the Lord, He brought them to this land flowing with milk and honey—"

"Milk and honey! *This* place?" Hannah gestured to the dry, barren landscape all around them, the row upon row of ugly tin shacks. "Our home in Baghdad was paradise! Israel is Sheol!"

Ben shook his head. "That's just what our ancestors said after God delivered them from slavery. 'That was Paradise,'" he said, mimicking her whiny voice. "'Why did you bring us here to die?' But Iraq wasn't our home, Hannah. We were hated there. And ever since the Iraqis lost the war three years ago, they've hated our people even more. Why do you think we're so poor now? They let us leave the country, but only if we left all our valuables behind."

Tears welled in Hannah's eyes as she remembered the confusion and fear she'd felt the night the Israeli government airlifted her family out of Iraq. Along with 120,000 other Iraqi Jews, they had left with only one suitcase apiece and the clothes on their backs, city clothes that proved to be ridiculously inappropriate for the rugged desert life they now faced in Israel.

"So quit blubbering about Baghdad," Ben finished. "Israel is our true home. We belong here. And now that we have our own country, no one can ever persecute us again."

"Well, if you ask me, they're persecuting us here in Israel," she said, unconvinced by Ben's speech. "Why were we sent to the desert? They have cities in Israel. I saw them."

"It's not a desert. It's called the *Negev*. And I already told you why. Besides, this is where most of Israel's unsettled land is."

Hannah scooped up a handful of hot dry dirt and flung it into the wind. "How is Abba supposed to grow food out here? We'll all starve!"

"Oh, we'll grow food here all right," Ben said, gazing into the distance. "You wait and see. The prophets said that one day the desert would blossom like a rose. It *has* to happen, Hannah. And I'm going to *make* it happen!"

———

The first week after school opened, Hannah ran away from it at least twice a day. It was easy to do; her classroom had no walls, only a roof made of discarded packing boxes to shade students from the sun. She sat on a bench made from a board and two rocks, sharing all her textbooks with a seatmate named Dara. Hannah hated her. Dara hogged all the nice books with the colored pictures, holding them on her lap instead of in the middle, and she poked Hannah in the ribs with her bony elbows every time she flipped a page. Whenever the teacher turned his back, Hannah bolted.

Her favorite place to hide was in the "lost city," a pile of tumbled stones on a hill behind the immigrant settlement. Abba said it had once been a town. It was nothing but a jumble of rocks and broken pillars now, but Hannah had discovered enough intricately carved fragments among the ruins to see that it had once been beautiful—like her home in Iraq had been. Now both places were lost forever. After fleeing from school again this day, she sat down on a short flight of stairs shaded by a section of wall that hadn't fallen and dreamed of home.

"You can't keep running away from school!" Ben yelled when he found her. He was breathless from the search and angry that he'd been sent to fetch her again. "What's your excuse this time?"

"That stupid Dara who sits beside me won't stop wiggling. I got tired of trying to keep my balance on that dumb board."

"Oh, that's just great!" Ben said, rolling his eyes. "I'm missing class again because you were uncomfortable!"

"I hate school, and I hate—"

"Save your breath. I've heard it all before." He flopped down on the step below Hannah's and leaned his back against the wall.

"Well, I'm not going back to school—ever!" she said.

"Fine. You don't have to go back."

"I don't?"

"Nope. Not if you don't want to."

Although this sounded like good news to Hannah, there was a look in Ben's eye that put her on guard. He was plotting something, she could tell. She wiggled closer to the wall to get away from him, waiting.

"Come back to the house with me," he finally said. "I want to show you something."

"Is this a trick?" Hannah folded her arms against her body so he couldn't grab her and haul her to her feet. When he turned to her she saw that he was very angry. But when he spoke, his voice was as deathly quiet as the stones all around her.

"Listen, Hannah, your days of being a spoiled brat are over. All of us have to work harder than we've ever worked before to make a new life for ourselves here. Ein breira, the Israelis say. *No choice.* My brothers were drafted—no choice. Our fathers have to struggle out there in the heat to grow sunflowers—no choice. But you do have a choice, Hannah. You can go back to school and *stay* there this time, or you can go back to the house and help my mother scrub clothes and cook fish."

Hannah's heart began to pound like a trapped rabbit's. "But I don't want to—"

"No? Well, guess what? My mother doesn't want to do all the washing and cooking either, but—no choice." He stood again, brushing dust off the seat of his shorts. "I'll go down and tell her that she doesn't have to fix dinner for you and your father tonight, since you won't be going back to school."

"I hate you, Ben! I hate you!" Hannah curled into a ball and buried her face in her lap. A few moments later, Ben crouched beside her again.

"What's really going on, Hannah? Why do you keep running away?" After a moment, her secret sprang to the surface like an enormous ball that she was tired of holding underwater.

"I feel so stupid," she wept. "Everyone knows their numbers and letters but me, and if the teacher ever finds out, he'll put me in the baby class."

"Then why won't you let me help you?" Ben asked.

She shrugged uselessly, not understanding the reason herself.

"Well, one of these days your stubbornness is going to trap you into a corner with no way out. You mark my words."

Hannah pictured herself chained to a laundry tub like Aunt Shoshanna, and a small crack splintered her wall of pride. "Will you teach me, Ben?" The words stuck in her throat like dry bread.

"On one condition. You can't run away from school anymore. Promise?"

"I promise."

Hannah kept her word for almost six months. Ben and her father tutored her every night until the electric generators were switched off and everyone had to go to bed. She caught on quickly, motivated by the sight of Aunt Shoshanna gutting fish or plucking chickens. Hannah even learned to arm-wrestle with Dara until the textbooks were square in the middle where they belonged.

Then one day Hannah's teacher showed the class pictures of the Holocaust. Cattle cars stuffed with people. Gas chambers and crematoriums. Piles of shoes and discarded clothing. Bodies stacked like cordwood in mass graves. Liberated survivors with protruding ribs and hollow eyes.

"These were families, like yours and mine." Tears washed

down the teacher's face as he spoke. "They were forced from their homes, tortured, and killed for only one reason—they were Jews. Like us."

Hannah didn't wait until the teacher's back was turned to run. Nor did she stop when she heard him calling her name. Ben found her among the ruins of her lost city an hour later.

"You broke your promise!" he shouted. "You said you wouldn't run away again!"

She lifted her head. "I'm sorry," she whispered.

All of Ben's anger released with a rush of air when he saw her face. "What's wrong, Hannah? You're white as a ghost . . . and your hands are shaking! What happened?"

"Why does everyone hate us? You said our ancestors went to Iraq because people wanted to kill them. And you said the Iraqis hated us, too. But what if they had lied to us, like they lied to the Jews in Europe? What if they had tricked us and put us on trains and taken us to gas chambers and burned us in ovens . . ."

"Shh . . . Hannah . . ." He laid his hand on her head. "That's why we got out of Iraq—before something like that did happen." He exhaled wearily as he sat down on the rock beside her. "I'm sorry you had to find out about the Nazis. But now do you understand why we can't go back home?"

"What if it happens here?" she whispered. "What if all those people who hate Jews come here?"

"The Israeli military will beat them back again," Ben said angrily, "just like they did the last time!"

For a terrible moment, Hannah was afraid she might be sick as images of the Holocaust replayed in her mind. "You mean . . . you mean they already *came* here?"

Ben groaned. "Don't tell me you never heard about the War of Independence, either?"

"Tell me."

He plucked a weed from between two rocks and slowly tore it into little pieces, taking his time answering. "As soon as Israel declared its independence in 1948, the Arab nations went to war against us. They refused to recognize the nation of Israel and vowed to push every last Jew into the sea. There weren't even a million of us against thirty million of them—from six different nations. But we won, Hannah. And we'll win again if we have to. This is *our* land, *our* home, and they're never going to push us off it again!"

Something shifted inside Hannah's heart, the way her body would suddenly shift in the backseat of the car when their driver in Baghdad turned a corner too fast. By learning about the Holocaust, she had also turned a corner—faster than she would have liked, certainly—but now, for the first time, she hadn't bristled when Ben called Israel their home. Her teacher had explained that Jews were scattered among the nations—other people's nations. That's why countries like Germany could pass laws to kill them. But Israel was a Jewish nation. Their homeland.

"These rocks you're sitting on prove that this is our land," Ben said. "There are ruined cities like this one all over the country, and whenever archaeologists dig them up, they find stuff that once belonged to our ancestors. Like when they found the Dead Sea Scrolls down by Qumran a few years ago. Those were Jewish scrolls, buried for two thousand years. They prove that Israel belongs to us."

Hannah looked around at the stones of her beloved lost city. They had always seemed more like home to her than the ugly shack she shared with Abba. "Do you think there might be some scrolls buried here, too?" she asked.

"Maybe. Nobody has dug up these ruins yet. They're not very important compared to all the others."

"Then *I'll* dig them up." She would prove that these ruins were once a Jewish city, this bit of land, Jewish land. As much as Hannah hated this broiling patch of desert in the middle of nowhere, it was still Abba's land, Abba's corrugated tin shanty, and no one had the right to take it away from him as they'd taken away his villa in Baghdad.

"You can't just start flinging dirt around," Ben said. "You have to know how to do it properly."

"Then I'll learn how," she said. And Hannah meant every word.

6

Hannah stood in the doorway of her tent at the archaeological site as the first jeep pulled into the desert compound. "Hey, Rivka," she called to her roommate in the tent behind her. "I think the eggheads have finally arrived."

"Any good-looking ones?"

"Too soon to tell, but don't count on it. After all, they're *engineers* and *botanists*." She wrinkled her nose, as if describing two species of vipers. Rivka sauntered up behind her.

"Come on, Hannah. Let's go welcome them. Remember what Professor Evanari said?"

"You mean his little speech about how this is an important interdisciplinary project that will have positive long-range effects on Israel's food supply?"

"No, I was thinking of the one where he said, 'Be nice to them.'"

Hannah watched as two more jeeps pulled in behind the first. "What do you want to bet those sissies don't even last the summer?" she said. "After all, they're not accustomed to rugged desert conditions like archaeologists are." At age twenty, Hannah felt smug, the veteran of one summer season as a dig volunteer, plus one week already spent on this site located thirty miles south of Beersheba.

"Well, I'm going over to say hello," Rivka said, patting her hair into place. "Come on."

In spite of her feigned indifference, Hannah was excited about the project. The Desert Runoff Farms Unit was an experimental team of archaeologists, biologists, and engineers who would attempt to rebuild a first-century Nabatean farm in the Judean desert. Based on the archaeologists' discovery of an ancient system of catchment basins, terraces, and water conduits, the engineers would reconstruct the irrigation system designed by the Nabateans, preparing the way for the botanists to grow grain, fruit, and other crops. It seemed like a miracle to Hannah that the Nabateans could have once harnessed the scant rainfall of the desert—a mere four or five inches a year—and grown enough food to sustain tens of thousands of settlers. The fact that she had been selected from scores of volunteers to be part of the team seemed like another miracle.

"Hey, they're not bad-looking," Rivka said as she and Hannah drew closer to where the scientists were emerging from the vehicles. "And so far, they're all guys. I like those odds."

"They look like a bunch of pale-faced intellectuals to me, without enough common sense to wear a hat. Engineers and botanists! They won't last a day in this—" Hannah stopped midsentence when the last man climbed from the vehicle. "Oh, my goodness! It's Ben!" Her cousin looked up when he heard his name, but Hannah was already running toward him, arms outstretched. "Ben! Why on earth didn't you tell me you were coming?" He pulled her into his arms, lifting her off the ground.

"I thought I'd surprise you. I haven't seen you in ages!" They had both served in different branches of the military, then attended different colleges, with Hannah away for the summer at dig sites.

"It's been too long—since your father's funeral . . ." she said. "But I saw the list of botanists and your name was _not_ on it." He lifted his duffel bag and showed her the identification tag. "Benjamin _Rosen_?" she said. "That's not you!"

"It is now. I changed my name after Abba died."

"Why did you do a stupid thing like that?"

"I wanted an Ashkenazi name. I was tired of being shoved aside because I'm Sephardic."

Hannah remembered the day Ben had explained the difference to her and recalled the bitterness she'd heard in his voice. That was before she'd graduated from school with honors at the age of sixteen; before she'd spent the required two years in the military; before she was accepted into the Institute to study archaeology.

"Hey, there's someone I want you to meet," Ben said suddenly. "Jake! Get over here!" The man who separated himself from the group and strode over to them was no pale-faced intellectual. He stood at least a foot taller than Hannah, with long tanned legs, wide shoulders, and a chest like a brick wall. His biceps seemed about to split the seams of his short-sleeved shirt. He had a face to match his impressive build—the kind they put in magazine advertisements, with dark dreamy eyes and thick arched brows. No doubt he knew the effect he had on women, too. Rivka was staring shamelessly at him, her mouth agape. Hannah would never stoop so low as to be enticed by a man's flashy good looks.

"This is my best friend, Jacob," Ben said. "Jake, meet my cousin Hannah."

Jake simply smiled as he shook her hand, then Rivka's hand after Hannah made the introductions. But then, men like Jake didn't need to talk. They were much too good-looking to waste the energy, thank you very much. Hannah had met his type in the army. They invariably relied on their physical charms—not words—to pursue their hobby of seducing women. She linked her arm tightly through Ben's and started walking away, leaving Jacob to her speechless roommate.

"Come on, Mr. *Rosen*, I'll show you to your tent. If we hurry, you can grab the best cot."

"So what do you think of Jake?" Ben asked as they strolled across the compound.

"He's okay." Hannah would submit to torture before

admitting she was attracted to him. "I hope you didn't plan on playing matchmaker."

"Me? Match my shy, gentlemanly best friend with my stubborn, unrestrained cousin? No way! That would be like throwing a lamb to the wolves!"

"I think I know a wolf when I see one," she said, laughing. "And you seemed pretty eager for me to meet him."

"That's because he's a great guy. We were in the same tank squadron in the army, then we ended up rooming together—although he's studying engineering and I'm in agriculture. When we heard about this joint project, we decided to sign up together."

"And you had no plans for introducing the two of us, of course."

"He has a steady girlfriend, Hannah."

"I'll bet he does."

"Speaking of girlfriends," he said, looking wistfully over his shoulder. "Why did you pry me away from your roommate so fast? She seems nice!"

"You'll have all summer to get to know her, sweetie."

But for the first week, the three groups were involved in separate aspects of the project, leaving little opportunity for socializing. Everyone rose early to avoid the heat, then retired early, as well—usually in a state of exhaustion. Hannah ate dinner with Ben every evening, both of them talking nonstop as they tried to catch up on each other's lives. His conceited friend rarely spoke, quietly watching Hannah like a predator, biding his time, waiting to pounce.

Halfway through the second week, Professor Evanari proposed the first cooperative venture. "I need a volunteer," he told the archaeology students, "to hike up the mountain with one of the engineers and explore the catchment area. They want to follow the ruins of the water channels and see how much rebuilding will need to be done."

"I'll go!" Hannah said, eager for the chance to roam free.

"Not so fast. The desert can be very dangerous—"

"I know, Professor. I grew up in the Negev."

He looked around at the other students, but no one else volunteered. "All right, Hannah. Come meet your new colleague."

The engineer was Jacob, of course. Ben had probably told him she would be the first to volunteer. Jake's knowing smile infuriated her.

"Get some food and water from the mess tent, and a couple of backpacks," Professor Evanari said. "Don't wander too far, Hannah, and make sure you two stay together. We want you back before dinnertime."

The snickering laughter she heard from the other men made her furious. Oh, she would stay aloof to Jacob's charms, no matter how tempting his full lips might be.

Hannah set a brisk pace as she led the way up the valley where the orchards and farm plots were being restored. She didn't know one tree from another, but the tags on the saplings that Ben and his team were planting waved like banners in the breeze: almonds, peaches, figs, apricots, plums.

"Your engineering team had better produce some water pretty soon," she said to Jake over her shoulder, "or those poor trees are going to burn to a crisp out here." She found the remains of a narrow conduit channel and began following it up the steep hill above the plain.

"Just who are these mysterious Nabateans, anyway?" Jake asked after they had hiked for a while. "And if they were so brilliant, how come you archaeologists are the only ones who have ever heard of them?"

"Plenty of people have heard of them. They were an Arab tribe that took over this territory from the Edomites around the fourth century B.C. Ever hear of King Herod the Great? His father was an Edomite and his mother was Nabatean."

"Who would want to live out in this wasteland?"

"Besides the Nabateans? *I* would. I think the desert has a rare beauty all its own."

"I guess beauty is in the eye of the beholder," he said, laughing. "So what else did they do out here besides enjoy the desert's rare beauty and grow fruit?"

His cynical attitude irritated Hannah, but she battled to remain coldly aloof. "They monopolized the main trade route from southern Arabia to the Mediterranean, among other things. Their caravans passed through all these settlements on their way to the port of Gaza. They were incense traders."

"Incense! Seems like a lot of bother for nothing." Jake was breathless from the climb.

Hannah was out of breath, too, but she refused to be the first one to stop and rest. What had appeared to be a smooth brown hill from camp was proving to be a rugged, rock-strewn obstacle course.

"Oh, it was well worth the trouble," she said. "The Romans used enormous amounts of incense in their religion. It was sent all over the world, wherever the Romans settled. The Nabateans became quite wealthy from it."

"Maybe that's what they meant when they said the Nabateans turned the desert green. Hold up a minute," Jake said. "I need to rest."

Satisfied that he had grown tired first, Hannah sat down on a rock and took a swig of water. "You sound as though you have your doubts about this project," she said.

"Not at all—I hope it works. More than a third of the world's land is as dry as this. If we can get your cousin's trees to grow out here, it will be good news for millions of people."

They continued hiking for well over an hour, following what Hannah hoped were Nabatean water conduits. Jake stayed close behind her, never once pausing to examine the channels or even to take notes. If he was carefully studying the catchment area, he certainly showed no signs of it. Hannah would never admit it, but she was no longer certain that the runoff channels were man-made. Nor was she certain that she knew the way back to camp, which had disappeared from sight an hour ago. Now that the sun stood directly overhead, she would have to wait until it began to sink to see which direction was west. She would rather die than ask Jake if he'd remembered a compass.

"How about lunch?" she said, stalling for time. "There's a

WINGS of REFUGE 111

patch of shade down in this gully." She led the way down a steep embankment and pulled her lunch from her backpack—pita bread stuffed with heat-wilted lettuce, warm tomatoes, and melting cheese. The apricots were smashed to a pulp but she ate them anyway. The water in her canteen was blood-warm. Hannah took her time eating, waiting for the sun to move. Neither of them spoke until they were finished.

"So . . . you've lived in the Negev all your life?" Jake asked as he tucked waxed paper and apricot pits into his backpack again. Something about the way he said it sounded like a challenge.

"Since I was ten. Why?"

He shrugged nonchalantly. "I'm just a little surprised that you've lived this long if you're in the habit of sitting in dry riverbeds."

Hannah realized her mistake as soon as he said it. Of course. Dozens of people drowned every year when *wadis* like this one suddenly became rushing torrents that swept them away. Jacob was already climbing up the embankment, so she couldn't see his gloating face. Nor, thank heaven, could he see her embarrassment.

"If you were so worried about it, why didn't you speak up sooner?" she said as she scrambled up behind him.

"I figured I could use a little excitement in my life." He gallantly stepped aside, gesturing for Hannah to lead the way. "After you . . ."

"Where to? Are you finished exploring up here?"

"I saw what I came to see."

Whatever *that* meant. His face offered no clue to his thoughts. Hannah glanced up at the sun, which seemed glued to the top of the sky, then started blindly down the hill, following the path of the wadi below them. She had the disturbing feeling that he was laughing behind her back. She decided to lead the conversation as well as the hike.

"So are you convinced yet that archaeology can make as valid of a contribution to mankind as the other sciences?"

"Are you?"

"Absolutely! Look what archaeologists have already done! Nelson Glueck found valuable copper deposits after excavating ancient mining camps. And Yigael Yadin led a surprise attack against the Egyptians during the war using a Roman road he had discovered."

Hannah expected an argument or at least a sarcastic comment about archaeology not being a true science. Instead, Jake suddenly cried out behind her. She turned to find him lying on the ground, clutching his ankle.

"What's wrong?" she said impatiently.

"Hold up a minute . . . I stepped in a hole and twisted my ankle. Oh, *man*! I think I sprained it!"

He was quite a good actor, rolling on the ground, cradling his foot, wincing in pain. He might have convinced Hannah if she hadn't seen this little act performed too many times before in the army. She planted her hands on her hips and stared down at him in disdain.

"That's the oldest line in the book—you sprained your ankle. I'm not falling for it."

"Ow! . . . *Ow!* What are you talking about?"

"I'm supposed to sit down beside you and feel all this gushing sympathy for you, right? And the next thing I know you'll have me in a clinch, trying to make out with me. Sorry, I'm not falling for it. You played your little game with the wrong woman this time. I trained as a medic in the army, and I've seen guys like you pretending to be sick countless times."

"Guys like *me*? You barely know me!"

"But I know your type—too handsome for your own good, convinced that every girl you meet is panting to be alone with you. Well, I know a *real* sprained ankle when I see one. You may have a swelled head, but I'm willing to bet you don't have a swollen ankle."

Jake stared at her for a long time, holding his ankle, not saying a word. The look in his eyes reminded Hannah of a time-delay fuse she had seen in a demolition demonstration—the kind that did a long, slow burn before finally exploding. Of course he was angry—she had exposed his little scheme. He would have to stand up now and start walking again. Oh, he might fake a limp for a while, but they both knew he was a fraud.

Instead, Jake sat up and began to untie his boot, very slowly, pulling out the laces, opening the tongue wide. He grimaced rather convincingly as he struggled to pull it off, then he carefully rolled down his sock and slid it off his foot. From where Hannah stood, ten feet away, she could see that the contour of his ankle bone had already disappeared beneath a mound of puffy flesh. Deep indentations revealed where the seams of his boot had been. His skin had already started to discolor, and she knew it would soon be a deep purplish blue. Jake wadded up his sock and stuffed it into his empty boot before looking up at Hannah again.

"So . . . what's your diagnosis, Miss Medic? No, wait! Don't get too close! This might be a trick. I might be making my ankle swell just so I can kiss you."

Hannah felt her cheeks flaming. "I'm sorry," she mumbled.

"What did you say?" he shouted. "I can't hear too well. My swelled head interferes with my hearing sometimes."

"I said I'm sorry."

"Sorry for what? Sorry it wasn't a trick? Sorry we didn't make out? Sorry you were wrong? You're certainly not sorry that you misjudged me! Or that I really am in pain!"

"I'm sorry that I didn't believe you." She started to crouch down to examine it, then paused to ask, "May I see . . . ?"

"Shouldn't you tie me up first, so I don't lunge at you?"

Hannah ignored him, carefully examining his foot for signs of a fracture. When she didn't see any bones poking through the skin she asked, "Does it hurt much?"

"Yes, as a matter of fact it does. It hurts like the devil. You don't happen to have a first-aid kit handy, do you?"

She didn't like the accusing tone in his voice. "No, do you?" she shot back.

"I don't . . . but then, why should I? I trained to be a leering woman chaser in the army, not a medic. Since you assumed that I brought along my little bag of tricks, I just assumed you might have brought along yours."

"Look, I'm sorry I said all those things—"

"Right. You sound more embarrassed than sorry."

"What do you want me to say?"

"Well, you can start by saying my name. It's Jake. You haven't used it once all day. Then you can get rid of that chip on your shoulder and tell me how to fix this stupid ankle so we can make it back to camp."

"There's really nothing I can do . . . Jake. It might be broken. If it hurts just sitting there, you'll never be able to put any weight on it."

"I'll hop. Would you mind helping me up?"

"You can't hop down a mountain! Are you crazy? It's treacherous enough walking on two good feet with all these loose stones. That's how you fell in the first place."

"Well, at the risk of being accused of making a pass . . . maybe I could lean on you?"

Hannah shook her head. "Then we'll both end up falling off the cliff. Nothing doing."

"Then what do you suggest? There doesn't seem to be any wood around here to make a pair of crutches or a splint."

"I'll try to fashion some sort of shade for you, then I'll hike down and get help."

"Absolutely not! The first rule of desert survival is to stay together."

"No, the first rule of desert survival is to survive! I'm going for help."

"I'm not letting you wander off alone, Hannah. It's much too dangerous. Suppose you got lost or hurt? Professor Evanari said to stay together. They'll come looking for us sooner or later."

"We're wasting time," she said, tightening the straps of her backpack. "I'm leaving." But before she could take two steps, Jake reached out and grabbed her by the ankle, pulling her leg out from under her. Hannah landed in a heap in a cloud of dust.

"You idiot!" she said, spitting sand. "I might have broken my neck!"

"Sorry, but I outrank you. I can't let you go. And if you try it again, I'll tackle you."

Hannah sat with her legs drawn up, her arms hugging her knees, fuming. The sun was hot and still directly overhead. It would be hours before they were even missed. "Okay, now what?"

"You said you could rig us up some sort of shade?" He removed his hat and used it to fan himself. "That sounds good for starters."

Hannah scanned the barren landscape. Nothing but rocks and scrub grass as far as she could see. "I made that up. I'm studying archaeology, not desert survival. Unless you want to sit down in the riverbed again, I don't know how we'll find shade."

"I could probably crawl down there, but I'd never be able to climb out in time."

"There isn't a cloud in the sky!" she said, gesturing.

"There never is. The water comes out of nowhere. Have you seen the size of the retaining pond your little Nabatean friends built? They were expecting a *lot* of water. I'd rather not be in the path of it."

"Have you ever seen a wadi fill up?" she challenged.

"Clear to the top. Washed a bus away. And the sky was just as blue as it is now."

His eyes were deep green, not brown. Hannah looked into them for the first time, then quickly looked away.

"I can't fix your ankle, I can't go for help, I can't make shade. . . . What else do you want from me?" She lifted her palms, then let them fall to her lap in frustration.

"Talk to me. Take my mind off the pain."

"Fine!"

Hannah talked for more than an hour—a long, rambling monologue about her childhood in Iraq, her training as a medic, her fascination with archaeology. That led to a lengthy, one-sided discourse about the importance of the Dead Sea

Scrolls and how they belonged in an Israeli museum, not a Jordanian one. She talked about everything but her shoe size before finally pausing to glance at her watch. "It's two-thirty. We should have been arriving back in camp right about now." She sighed, then added absently, "How are you doing?"

"I was wondering when you would remember to ask."

Hannah had a sarcastic reply on the tip of her tongue, but she swallowed it when she looked up and saw how pale he was. Rivulets of sweat ran down his face and neck, soaking the front of his shirt. She could tell he was in a lot of pain.

"You have to be the most self-involved person I've ever met," he said. "You've made a lot of assumptions about me, but you haven't bothered to get to know me at all. Instead, you seem intent on proving yourself, for some reason. Proving you don't need anyone or anything—least of all a lecherous womanizer like me."

His words stung, but she tried not to let him see how much. "You're the one who asked me to talk," she said. "If you wanted a turn, why didn't you say so?"

He gave a short laugh, shaking his head in disbelief. Hannah waited until he finished taking a drink from his canteen before saying, in the sweetest voice she could muster, "Please tell me about yourself, Jake." He seemed to consider his words for a moment before answering.

"I'm not a woman chaser. I grew up on a kibbutz in Galilee, tossing bales of hay and milking cows. I have a steady girlfriend. I'm religious—observant, in fact. I believe that what the Torah says is true. And I don't think it conflicts with scientific truth, either. I believe science can accomplish a great deal, but I also believe that man has limitations. The Holy One knows that, and once we reach those limits we usually remember to call on Him. That's why He lets us come to the end of ourselves. You didn't tell me what you thought about God, Hannah. Do you ever think about Him?"

She didn't answer, embarrassed into silence. He paused to take another swig of water from the canteen before continuing.

"You seem fascinated with the Dead Sea Scrolls, and you obviously know a lot about their significance as artifacts. But do you know what the Isaiah scroll actually says? Do you know what the Holy One's message to us is? Besides promising to gather us from the ends of the earth a second time and give birth to our nation in a single day, He also promised to redeem us and make us His own. Think of that! The Holy One breathes His very breath into us and gives us the most precious gift He could give—*life*! And he places us in a world that is filled with wonderful things to see and do . . . wonderful people to know and to love. And He says, 'There! Enjoy! *L'Chaim!*' And all He asks in return is that we don't squander this gift on ourselves, but that we give it away. That we show others that He is a God of redemption and love."

Hannah didn't try to force back the tears that filled her eyes. "I feel like such a fool, Jake. I'm really sorry I misjudged you. Want to have a go at me? Put me in my place? Tell me what you really think?"

He smiled. "Ben told me so much about you, I felt like I knew you before we even met. He's very proud of you, you know."

"I can just imagine what he said, but you may as well tell me anyway."

"You're the youngest in the family, the only girl. Quite spoiled, but very smart. Also very opinionated, stubborn, headstrong, and obstinate. Tough as nails one minute, you wear your heart on your sleeve the next. He described you to a 'T' except for one thing." Hannah looked up, waiting. "He forgot to mention that you're beautiful."

His words stunned her. How could he see any beauty in her after the way she'd treated him? "Can you ever forgive me?" she whispered.

"I already have."

All of Hannah's defenses crumbled into ruins. They talked for hours—about God and life, about everything and nothing. The more Hannah learned about Jake, the more she felt drawn to him—for reasons other than his good looks. By the time the sun began to set, she had fallen under the spell of his quiet manner, his gentle humor. She envied the woman who had won his heart.

"Tell me about your girlfriend," she said quietly. His brows lifted in surprise.

"Devorah? Well, we've been going together since we were both fifteen. We grew up on the same kibbutz, started out in the same nursery, slept in adjoining cribs. She's in charge of the nursery now. She loves kids. And horses. She rides every chance she gets."

"Are you going to marry her?"

"We've always assumed we would be married some day . . . after we got out of the army, after I finish college. And I didn't chase any women when I was in the army, by the way. Ask Ben. He chased enough for both of us."

"Was that because of Devorah?"

"It was because I didn't really know how."

"You must love her a lot."

"Yes, I must." His face was deadpan, his voice without inflection.

"Why did you say it like that? I can't tell if you're being sarcastic or serious."

"Me neither. I've been going with Dev for so long . . . there are so many family attachments, so many assumptions made about the two of us. I can't tell what I really feel anymore and what's . . . habit. I've never even kissed another woman besides Devorah."

"Have you been tempted to?"

He paused, lightly touching his ankle. "Truthfully? Yes." He was blushing. "You know, it's strange, but I was never attracted to another woman—until recently."

"And. . . ?" Hannah prompted.

"Then I met someone, and . . . it got very confusing. If I'm in love with Devorah, if I'm going to marry her—"

"Are you?"

"—If I'm going to marry Devorah I shouldn't feel so . . . captivated by someone else, should I? I shouldn't lie awake at night wondering what it would be like to bury my fingers in her hair or hold her in my arms . . . or feel her lips on mine."

Against her will, Hannah's gaze wandered to Jake's mouth. She imagined his full, soft lips on hers and swallowed. "Is that all it is with this other woman? Physical attraction?"

"I don't know . . . maybe . . . except that I keep comparing her to Devorah in other ways, and Dev comes up short every time. I know that sounds terrible, but Dev is very traditional. 'Whatever you say, Jake . . . You know best, Jake.' I can't help but wonder if she even has an opinion."

"Most men love that type of woman. I thought they hated women like me who actually have a mind of their own."

"Devorah and I have never had a conversation like the one we've been having. We know everything there is to know about each other. There are no surprises for either of us."

"And this other woman you're attracted to?"

When Jake looked away, blushing again, Hannah's heart began to race.

"I think I could spend a lifetime with her and still be surprised," he said softly.

Hannah wished she had a cigarette to fiddle with, even though she rarely smoked. Something, anything to break the exquisite tension that was slowly building between them. Or was she the only one who felt it? She scooped up a handful of pebbles and began tossing them, one by one, down the slope.

"So what are you going to do, Jake?" He looked startled, as if he had spoken a forbidden thought out loud.

"What do you mean?"

"What are you going to do about Devorah? And this other woman you're attracted to?"

"I'm going to do exactly what everyone assumes I'll do— forget the other woman, marry Devorah, move back to the kibbutz, and raise a family."

"How very honorable."

"Well, what else can I do?" he said wearily. "What would you do?"

"You mean, if I'd been stringing along some guy I didn't love for ten years?"

"I never said I didn't love her—"

"Ah, but you never said that you did love her, either."

Jake let out a sigh and went back to massaging his ankle, which was swollen to nearly twice its normal size. "What *would* you do?" he finally said.

"You're asking the wrong person, Jake. I'm a spoiled brat, like Ben says. I've never done the honorable thing in my life. In fact, I usually do the most selfish thing I can. But if I were in your shoes, I'd want to live a little . . . play the field . . . kiss a few other girls just to see what it felt like. Then, if no one could compare to Devorah and she was still patiently waiting . . ."

"I can't do that. It would hurt her too much."

"Listen, Jake, if you're bored with her now, it's not going to improve once you marry her. Can you honestly imagine sitting across the dinner table from each other for the next forty years with nothing to say? And you'll hurt her a lot more if you start kissing other women *after* you're married."

When Jake didn't say anything for a long time, Hannah was astounded to discover that she was jealous—jealous of Devorah, of his loyalty to her, his sensitivity to her feelings. And she was jealous, too, of the unnamed woman who was so attractive she had made Jake question his feelings for Devorah. She wished she were that woman.

"So what does Devorah look like? Do you carry her picture in your wallet?"

"Stop it, Hannah. I don't want to talk about her anymore."

Hannah didn't know why, but she was suddenly close to tears. "May I have a sip of your water, please," she said. "Mine's all gone." He picked up the canteen and shook it.

"Better go easy—mine is nearly empty, too."

"Great! Then what are we going to do, Mr. Water Engineer? Pray for the wadi to fill up? We've been sitting here all day. The stars are coming out already. If you had let me go for help six hours ago, I would have been back by now."

"No, you'd still be wandering around lost out there, getting eaten by jackals."

"I wouldn't have gotten lost," she said haughtily.

Jake laughed out loud. He laughed long and hard, rolling on his back in the sand.

"Who are you kidding?" he said, wiping his eyes as he sat up again. "We're lost right now! We're way off track, and we have been for most of the day!"

"If you thought we were lost, why didn't you say something sooner?"

"Because I—" He stopped and looked away from her, biting his lip. Hannah grabbed his chin and yanked his head back, forcing him to look at her.

"Tell me why, Jake, or admit you're lying!" He took her wrist and gently pried her hand away, as if wary of her touch.

"If I tell you, you'll get mad."

"I'm already mad! Tell me why you didn't speak up if we were lost!"

Jake stared at his ankle for a moment, then met her gaze. "Because if we were lost, I'd be able to spend more time with you."

Hannah fought the urge to smile. "And did you step in that hole so you could spend more time with me, too?"

"No, that was pure clumsiness."

He grinned and she lost the battle to keep a straight face. They both laughed until the tears came. Then, without even thinking, Hannah threw her arms around his neck and kissed him. At first he seemed stunned. He didn't kiss her back. Hannah feared she had made a fool of herself again. Then she felt his hands rest lightly on her back, and he began kissing her in return.

"I'm sorry," she said when they finally pulled apart. "I hope you're not going to be consumed with guilt now because of me."

"Should I be?"

"I don't know . . . have you given Devorah an engagement ring?"

"No . . ."

"Set a date for the wedding?"

"No . . ."

"Picked out any children's names?"

"Well, as a matter of fact, if it's a daughter we thought we'd name her Hannah, after you." This time it was Jake who moved first, taking Hannah's face in his hands, kissing her forehead, her eyelids, and finally, her lips. His kisses were even better than she had imagined they would be.

"Those army guys were right," he whispered when they paused for air. "That old sprained ankle trick works like a charm."

They were in the middle of another laughing fit when Jake suddenly froze. "Listen! Did you hear that?"

"Hear what?"

"Voices. Someone shouting." He scrambled to his knees and cupped his hands around his mouth. "Hey! Over here!"

Hannah waited, holding her breath, until they both heard an answering cry. She saw the flicker of flashlights in the distance.

"Over here!" Jake yelled again. Hannah's shoulders sagged.

"What rotten luck," she mumbled. "They found us."

———

Jake returned from the hospital in Beersheba with a cast on his broken ankle. There would be no more private desert hikes with Hannah. And since he could barely maneuver around their camp on his crutches, she could invent few opportunities to be alone with him. But Hannah got to know Jake very well that summer as they worked together during the day, then gathered with the other team members each night for lively discussions beneath the stars. She had dated a lot of men—her usual criteria being good looks or a good time. But with Jake she saw beyond outward appearances for the first time and discovered character, intelligence, and a heart that was tender toward God.

While most of the other scientists were secular Jews, Jake

was one of the few who took his faith seriously. Once his natural shyness wore off, he engaged the others in passionate debate.

"If the universe is governed by a set of physical laws, why wouldn't there be moral laws, too?" he asked the other scientists. "If you hold proof in your hands of the factual truth of Scripture," he argued with Hannah's colleagues, "how can you still dismiss all of its spiritual claims?" Each new argument, each new insight into Jake's heart, made Hannah hungry for more.

The work they did for Professor Evanari's Desert Runoff Project was some of the hardest Hannah had ever done. Then the rain fell on the reconstructed Nabatean farm, gathering in the catchment area, flowing down the channels and conduits, nourishing the fields and orchards in the arid valley below, and joy overwhelmed all of them. On the last night of the project, they hugged and danced and celebrated until the early morning hours. But as Hannah watched Jake trying to dance the *hora* on crutches, her joy was bittersweet. She had kissed him twice. She had never held his hand. There were always dozens of people hovering around them. How could she have fallen so deeply in love with him?

When the song ended, Jake maneuvered to a folding campstool to rest. Hannah followed him, sitting on the ground cross-legged in front of his outstretched leg. She swallowed the knot of pain in her throat. "Will I ever see you again after tomorrow?" she asked.

"Israel isn't a very big country. And I am your cousin's best friend." He had tossed out the comment lightly, but his smile seemed strained.

"Does that mean I'll be invited to your wedding when you marry Devorah?" she asked.

Jake closed his eyes and looked away, unable to mask his sorrow.

"That wouldn't be wise . . . for you or for me." After a moment, he leaned forward and took her hand in his, twining their fingers together. "I've never met anyone like you, Hannah. You've probably guessed that you're the woman who . . . never mind. It doesn't matter. Because regardless of what I feel for you, I made a promise—"

"Stop. You don't need to say any more. Just my rotten luck to fall for a guy with integrity."

"Hannah—"

"Look, I'll make this easy for both of us. Good-bye, Jake." She lifted his hand and kissed the back of it. Then she quickly released it and walked away without looking back. He didn't follow her. She stayed in her tent the next day until his jeep was gone.

Back at college that fall, Hannah tried dating other men. Then she tried *not* dating other men, studying for her classes as if getting straight A's was a matter of life or death. But she couldn't forget Jake. She was love-sick, plain and simple. Whenever she saw a tall man with broad shoulders striding down the street, she would run up behind him, shouting, "Jake! Wait!" It was never him. He was probably back on his kibbutz in Galilee by now, with Devorah.

Finally, on a cold, rainy day in January, Hannah called Ben and invited him to lunch. They both seemed subdued by the gloomy weather as they sat across the table from each other, drinking sweet Arabic tea and eating *schwarma*. After exhausting every other conceivable subject, she finally asked the question she was dying to ask.

"So how's your friend Jake doing these days?" She tried to sound casual, but her shaking voice betrayed her. Ben took a sip of tea before mumbling a reply into his cup.

"I haven't seen him around."

"But I thought you two were roommates?"

"He moved out."

Surely Ben knew what Hannah was really asking. Why was he was making this so difficult? "Did he . . . um . . . marry that steady girlfriend of his?"

"Not yet." Ben concentrated on his plate, a strange look crossing his features as he nibbled on the loose fillings from his sandwich.

"What aren't you telling me, Ben? He was your best friend—why so mysterious all of a sudden? You two have a fight?"

She had meant it as a joke, but Ben nodded. "Jake isn't speaking to me."

"Why not?"

He didn't answer.

"Out with it, Ben . . . or do I have to track down Jake and pry the truth from him?"

Ben gripped the table edge as if steeling himself, then finally looked up.

"I'm in love with Devorah."

"*What?*"

"You heard me. I'm in love with my best friend's fiancée."

Hannah wanted to laugh out loud at the absurdity of it, but Ben's face was such a mask of tragedy, she reached across the table for his hand instead. "Oh, Ben! How on earth did *that* happen?"

"It's your fault. Jake was fool enough to confess to Devorah that he had been attracted to you last summer and that he had kissed you—"

"And she got mad at him?"

"Furious! Hell hath no fury like a woman scorned. Jake was devastated to think that he had hurt Devorah . . . and when Devorah wouldn't speak to him, he begged me to help patch things up between the two of them."

"And you fell in love with her."

"Hannah, you can't imagine what a wonderful woman Devorah is. I've never met anyone like her. She's so sweet and loving . . . I could talk with her for hours."

Hannah remembered Jake saying that he and Devorah had nothing to talk about anymore, and she wanted to scream at the injustice of it.

"How does Devorah feel about you?"

"I don't know. At first I was just a shoulder to cry on. Then we both felt something happening between us. So one night I kissed her and now . . . now she says she's confused." Hannah began to laugh. "It really isn't funny, Hannah."

"Oh, poor Ben. I know it isn't, but—" She lost control, laughing in spite of herself, then her laughter suddenly turned to tears. "I know how you feel, Ben. I'm in love with Jake!"

"*Oy*, what a mess," he mumbled, squeezing her hand. "I love Devorah . . . you love Jake . . . Devorah and Jake can't decide who they love . . ."

"What are we going to do?" she asked, wiping her eyes with a napkin.

"I don't know. Too bad we can't just have a big shoot-out, like they do in those American westerns. The winners get to gallop off into the sunset together." Hannah pictured it in her mind—all four of them in western dress, guns blazing in the streets of some dusty cowboy town. She leaned toward Ben.

"You know, that's not a bad idea."

"No, Jake is a much better shot than I am."

"Not with guns, sweetie. Let's plan a peaceful confrontation—all four of us in one room. No one leaves until Devorah and Jake decide who they're in love with."

Ben looked thoughtful. "You know, that just might work."

"And if it doesn't, you and I can shoot each other and put ourselves out of our misery."

They arranged to meet at a sidewalk fish restaurant in Tiberias the following Sunday at two o'clock. It was Ben's job to think of a way to lure Jake and Devorah there and Hannah's job to think of something to say once he did.

Hannah arrived first, nervously gulping down two Cokes while she waited. After three different women approached the restaurant and then passed by on the sidewalk, she realized that not only was she nervous about her competitor, she didn't even know what Devorah looked like.

Fifteen minutes later, Ben arrived with her—a petite brunette with a perky nose and impressive curves. She could've played the part of a wholesome all-American cheerleader in an Elvis Presley flick. Jake approached from the other direction a moment later, and Hannah's heart began to hammer. There was no doubt at all in her mind: She was in love with him, every inch of him—from his gorgeous dark head to his no-longer-limping feet.

Jake looked at all three of them in confusion, then said, "What is this, Ben? What's going on?"

"Why don't we all take a seat," Hannah said, "and I'll explain." Chairs scraped as everyone sat. The atmosphere was so tense as the waiter took their orders that Hannah expected him to throw down his pad and run for cover. When everyone finally had their soft drinks, she cleared her throat.

"In case you haven't figured it out, Devorah, I'm Ben's cousin Hannah. The *other woman* Jake met last summer. I want to set the record straight—I'm the one who kissed Jake first, not the other way around. He made it very clear that he was committed to you." Everyone studied their beverages as if carbonation had just been invented. Hannah cleared her throat again.

"I'm sorry you found him first, Devorah. He's an unforgettable guy. I know, because I've been trying to forget him for months now, and I haven't been able to. He's not only the handsomest guy I've ever met, but he's also a man of integrity and—*Ouch!*" Hannah rubbed the spot on her shin where Ben had kicked her.

"And also for the record, my cousin Ben is in love with you. He's a wonderful guy, too, Devorah—thoughtful, sensitive, funny, loving. I could fall in love with him myself if he wasn't my cousin. The woman who marries him will be very lucky indeed. So I can see how you might have a tough time choosing between the two of them. But that's the point, Devorah. You aren't leaving here until you make up your mind which one you want. And that goes for you, too, Jake. It's time you both made up your minds. Are you in love with each other or not? I think Ben and I have a right to know."

For a long time, no one moved. Hannah was aware of cars rushing past, people hurrying down the sidewalk . . . but for her, time seemed suspended. She wanted to scream. Then Devorah finally looked up from her drink. Her eyes traveled from one man to the other for what seemed another eternity. When

Devorah rested her hand on Jake's arm, Hannah's heart stood still.

"Oh, Jake, honey . . . I understand how you might have been attracted to . . . her. Can you ever forgive me? I'm so sorry. I . . . I never meant to fall in love with Ben." She slipped her arm through Ben's and leaned against his shoulder. He closed his eyes in joy.

Hannah's gaze never left Jake's face, waiting . . . for what? Tears? A burst of anger? Maybe a fistfight? But after another eternity of waiting, his face slowly split into a grin. He began to laugh as he had the day they were lost on the mountain. No one joined him. Ben looked very pale.

"This is absolutely unbelievable!" Jake said at last. "I've been eating my heart out for the last five months—worried about the way I hurt Devorah, upset about losing my best friend, heartsick with love for you, Hannah . . . and it was all for nothing!"

Heartsick with love.

Hannah didn't need to hear more. Her chair toppled as she scrambled to her feet.

"Watch, Devorah. I'll show you exactly what I did." She threw her arms around Jake's neck and kissed him on the lips, right in the middle of the fish restaurant on the main street of Tiberias, in broad daylight.

Four months later she became Mrs. Jacob Rahov.

WEST JERUSALEM, ISRAEL—MAY 16, 1967

Turn off the radio, Hannah," Jake said quietly. "We've heard enough bad news for one night."

He sat cross-legged on the floor of their apartment with two-year-old Rachel on his lap, their dark, perfect heads bent over a picture book. They looked so beautiful together, so content, that a shudder rocked through Hannah as she thought of the radio announcer's words.

"I'll turn it off in a minute. I want to hear what the United Nations plans to do."

"We'll know soon enough. Please, Hannah." She switched it off. The sound of Jake's calm voice replaced the crackling static and urgent bulletins as he pointed to objects in the book and asked, "What's that, Rachel?"

"Kitty," she replied.

"Very good. And what are those?"

"Birdies!" The birds were her favorites. She and Jake walked to the park every day to feed them. But Hannah knew that if the United Nations gave in to Egypt's threats, if they withdrew their peace-keeping forces from the Sinai three days from now, there would be no more walks to the park. There would be war.

"Jake . . . I'm scared."

"Come here, love." He reached for her hand and pulled her down to the floor beside him.

"I know what you're going to tell me," she said, laying her head on his shoulder. "I need to trust in God's unfailing love." Jake had reminded her of those words often since Rachel's birth two years ago. Hannah had wanted to clutch her beautiful newborn tightly, protect her from every threat, never let her out of her sight.

"Her life is a gift from God," Jake told her. "Whatever happens, we can trust Him with it because His love reaches to the heavens, His faithfulness to the skies. And that's a very long way."

Hannah had learned the morning prayers from Jake. They recited them together before they began each day: " 'How priceless is your unfailing love! Both high and low among men find refuge in the shadow of your wings.' " But it hadn't been easy for Hannah to lay aside her stubborn self-sufficiency and surrender control to God. It had taken six years of marriage for her to get over her fear of losing Jake each time he left for work or when he went away for his yearly military exercises with the reserves. This current crisis reminded her of the fragility of everything she cherished.

"It's a lot easier to trust God in peacetime," she told him. "But if there is going to be a war . . . Jake, we're surrounded by enemies who are committed to our destruction. I don't think Nasser is just mouthing vague threats this time. He intends to destroy Israel. I've never had to take refuge beneath God's wings when there were bombs falling all around me."

"We still have today," Jake told her. His eyes were very green. "We have Rachel and we have each other. Let's not spoil today by worrying about what might happen tomorrow."

He turned the page of the book and calmly continued reading to Rachel. As Hannah watched them, she saw her daughter's dependence and trust in her father as she rested securely in his arms. She must do the same, resting in her heavenly Father as He turned over each new page in her life.

But three days later, Hannah huddled on the sofa beside

Jake, listening in stunned disbelief to the news. The UN peace-keeping forces had yielded to Egypt's demands, evacuating the positions they had held in the Sinai since 1956. Prime Minister Levi Eshkol called it an act of war. Jake seemed as worried as she was.

"It's only a matter of time now," he said, "before Egypt blocks all shipping to Eilat and we lose our only southern port."

Hannah gazed around their tiny spartan apartment, wondering what shortages the blockade would bring, what new ways she would have to find to adapt. On a bookshelf across the room, shards of ancient pottery and jar handles were piled around wedding photographs and Rachel's baby pictures, as if offering evidence of Israel's endless cycle of destruction and rebirth.

"Why are people so bent on destroying us?" she asked. "In every generation there has been someone who tries to start a crusade or an inquisition or a pogrom to wipe out the Jewish people. Why us?"

"Because we bear witness to the Holy One's plan to redeem mankind. In fact, His redemption will come from our race, from Abraham's seed. If Satan can destroy us, he thinks he can destroy all memory of God and keep mankind under the curse. But Satan's plans won't succeed."

"Do you think there will be a war?" she asked quietly. "Tell me the truth, Jake. Don't say I'm borrowing tomorrow's worry." He reached over her shoulder to turn off the radio before taking her in his arms.

"Yes. I do. But I also believe that what our enemies intend for evil, God is going to turn to our good."

"Our *good*? How?"

"The Holocaust wiped out six million of us, but God used their sacrifice to reestablish us in this land. Our enemies declared war the day we declared independence, but God used it to increase Israel's territory. Who knows what good will come from this?"

"If we live through it," Hannah mumbled.

The following day, Jake's reserve unit was mobilized. He was ordered to report to the area of the Golan Heights to defend Israel's border against Syria. No one needed to remind Hannah that Syria's troops were backed by the powerful Soviet Union. As she lay on their bed watching Jake put on his uniform and lace up his boots, she broke down and wept.

"Hannah . . . don't. Please don't." He lay down beside her again and held her close. "The woman I fell in love with was strong and fearless. She strode up mountains without a map or a compass and ate her lunch in dry riverbeds without a care in the world. What happened to her?"

"She fell in love with you. We became one like Scripture says, and now that we're being torn apart, it's the worst pain I've ever known."

"I know, love. I know. Just pretend that I'm leaving for reserve exercises and that I'll be home in a couple of weeks."

"I can't, Jake. I know exactly where you're going."

"Listen, every time one of us walks out that door, we have no guarantee that we'll ever see each other again. Life isn't forever, Hannah. But our love is, and so is God's love." He kissed her and wiped away her tears. " 'He who watches over Israel will neither slumber nor sleep,' " he recited. "I don't know what God is doing, but I know we can trust Him." He kissed her again, then stood. "Come to the window. I'll wave to you."

He crossed to the crib where Rachel was napping and bent to kiss her forehead. Hannah stood and took her husband in her arms one last time. She felt the strength of his embrace and clung to him with all her might. Love and fear choked off everything she wanted to say.

"I'll see you," Jake whispered. Then he pried her loose and quickly picked up his kit bag, walking away so she wouldn't see his tears.

She had felt them, though, gently falling into her hair. As soon as the front door closed, she ran to the living room window and pulled back the curtain. Jake emerged from the apartment building a few minutes later. He looked up at the window and waved. Then he rounded the corner and disappeared from sight. Hannah wondered if she would ever see him again.

Hannah knocked on the door of Ben and Devorah's apartment and waited. Ben's five-year-old son opened it. "It's Auntie Hannah!" he shouted.

"Hi, Itzak. Where's your mama?" Hannah asked.

"In the kitchen. Can Rachel play?"

"Of course." Hannah set Rachel on the floor where Itzak and three-year-old Samuel were playing with a ball and a set of toy bowling pins. She followed the sound of a scratchy radio broadcast into the kitchen. Ben and Jake had been gone for ten days. Hannah had promised to look after Devorah, who was eight months pregnant. She found her sitting at the kitchen table in tears. Hannah switched off the radio.

"No, Hannah, wait—"

"That's what Jake always does when the news starts to upset me. He drove me crazy at first, but I'm beginning to think he's right."

"But I want to hear the news."

"Sweetie, it's not just news. Those commentators can't shut up, and all their 'what ifs' and 'maybes' might never even happen."

She crossed to the sink and poured Devorah a glass of water. In spite of Devorah's condition, her kitchen shone—no dirty dishes piled on the counters, no sticky spots of spilled juice on the floor, no mysterious smells drifting from her tiny refrigerator each time she opened the door. Unlike Hannah's apartment, which resembled an archaeological ruin most of the time, Devorah's was always neat and clean. Hannah often wondered if Jake regretted his choice of a wife.

"Here," she said, handing the glass to Devorah, "you need this to replenish all the water that's leaking from your eyes."

Devorah didn't return her smile.

"Did you hear the latest?" Devorah asked. "Egypt has signed a defense pact with Jordan. They were enemies a couple of months ago, and now they're suddenly friends, pledging to help each other destroy us."

Hannah hadn't heard, and the news shook her. The border between Israel and Jordan ran right through the middle of Jerusalem, just a few miles to the east of them. But she waved the news away as if swatting a fly, feigning indifference as she pulled out a chair and sat down.

"Oh, so what! Egypt signed one with Syria, too. It doesn't mean a thing. Those fools break their word easier than you can break an egg."

Devorah managed a weak smile. "Maybe you're right about the radio, Hannah. They keep saying that Iraq is going to send troops to help Egypt, too. And they keep bringing up that speech Nasser gave a few days ago."

"You mean the one where he said, 'Our basic objective will be to destroy Israel'? That's not news. That's been his objective for years. The man is a broken record." But when Hannah had first heard the speech four days ago and learned that Egyptian armored units had crossed the Suez with 100,000 troops and taken positions in the Sinai, she had covered her face and wept. Images of the Holocaust circled her mind and settled on her heart like birds of prey waiting to snatch her peace. The only way to keep them at bay was to keep moving, keep working, keep praying.

"Have you heard from Ben?" she asked.

"Yes. He told me to brace myself for war." Devorah rose and set the empty glass in the sink, then stood near the living room doorway watching the children play, gently massaging her ponderous belly as she spoke. "Ben says once the war starts, Israel has no alternative but to win. He says if we lose, they'll kill every last one of us."

Hannah knew Ben was right, but she said, "He's wrong. The British and the Americans will never let it come to that."

"Well, so far the Americans haven't done a thing to help.

Their promise of a multinational navy to break the Egyptian blockade was an empty one. Israel will be forced to fight alone."

"Devorah, listen. I came to ask a favor." Hannah needed to steer Devorah's mind away from her fear before they both crashed into despair. "Would you be willing to watch Rachel for a few hours every day so I can go to work? I know it's difficult in your condition with two kids of your own to watch, but nearly every man in Israel is mobilized for war, and if the women don't take over their jobs, everything is going to come to a screeching halt around here."

Devorah's shoulders straightened, and she seemed to grow stronger before Hannah's eyes as she was offered a useful alternative to sitting and waiting. "Of course, Hannah. I'd be glad to. Where are you going to work?"

"They're converting some of the hotels into emergency first-aid stations. Since I trained as a medic, I thought I would volunteer. I tried taking Rachel with me when a bunch of us cleaned out the basement of our apartment building to make an air raid shelter, and she was constantly underfoot. A couple of days ago I took her with me to help fill sandbags, and I'm still cleaning sand out of her hair." She laughed, but Devorah didn't.

"They made a shelter in this building, too," she said. "It's supposed to be a good, sturdy one. Rachel will be safe here, Hannah. And I'm all packed and ready to go down whenever we need to." She pointed to a small overnight bag by the back door. Hannah had a similar one ready beside hers.

Hannah feared the bombing raids the most. The Egyptians had a huge airforce that could be airborne and dropping bombs on Israel almost before the warning sirens had a chance to go off. Because her nation was so small, civilians were certain to be in the way of enemy targets and would likely be spending a great deal of time in air raid shelters. Hannah tried not to think about what would happen if Devorah couldn't make it downstairs in time with three small children in tow.

Rachel toddled into the kitchen with a smile on her face and a plastic bowling pin in her fist. "Wha's dat?" she asked. Hannah pictured Jake, paging through books for hours on end, asking *"What's that, Rachel?"* Would their daughter even remember her father if anything happened to him?

"It's a bowling pin, sweetie." Hannah caressed Rachel's dark curls before she tottered away again.

"I admire your courage," Devorah said. "I know how hard it will be for you to leave her."

"I'm really not courageous at all. It's like Ben always says—'no choice.' Jake would tell me to trust Rachel to God's unfailing love." She stood and drew Devorah into her arms for an ungainly hug. "But you're right—it will be hard. I think I know how Jake and Ben must have felt when they had to leave us."

Two days later, the director of the Israel Museum telephoned Hannah. "Can you possibly help us? We need to move all the antiquities into the basement for safekeeping in case the bombs start to fall."

Hannah left Rachel with Devorah and rode whatever transportation she could find to the museum, walking a good portion of the way. Armed soldiers, troop transports, and even tanks roamed the streets, while Israeli fighter jets roared overhead, patrolling the skies. They were accompanied by the nerve-wracking stutter of helicopters. The tension that loomed over West Jerusalem was palpable, like a huge billowing thundercloud that would surely pour rain and split the earth with lightning at any moment.

Walking the museum hallways, Hannah felt as though she were returning home. She hadn't worked since Rachel was born and hadn't realized how much she missed the dusty texture of clay pots, the warm luster of ancient bronze. The task of packing thousands of precious artifacts and hauling them down to the safety of the basement was nearly as exhausting as excavating them had been in the first place, but she was protecting her daughter's heritage, the proof that Israel belonged to Rachel's ancestors as well as to her descendants.

With the Arab nations poised to wipe the land clean of all Jews, it seemed as important a task as shouldering a machine gun.

At midmorning, she took a lunch break with her friend Rivka, who worked part time at the museum. They sat outside in a patch of shade, enjoying the warmth of the early summer day, if not the ominous rumbling of jets and vehicles or the stench of diesel fuel.

"This endless waiting is driving me absolutely crazy," Rivka said. "I feel like there's a gigantic time bomb ticking in the background and you know it's about to explode, but you don't know exactly when."

"I know what you mean. And if it's this tense for civilians, imagine how the soldiers must feel. Jake is sitting in a tank beneath the Golan Heights, waiting to be bombarded by Syrian guns. The Syrians have had twenty years to fortify the Heights, and their hateful Soviet friends to help them do it."

"My husband is sitting under a camouflage net in the sands of the Negev, waiting to face the Egyptians. He says that all they do all day is wait and train and wait some more. They can't stand it much longer." Rivka paused as an Israeli Defense Forces fighter jet screamed overhead. She and Hannah covered their ears. "Now that Jordan is going to bed with Nasser, we'll have to fight a war on three fronts. They said on the radio last night that huge mobs have been demonstrating in Cairo and Damascus and Baghdad, calling for Israel's destruction."

"I try not to listen to the radio too much," Hannah said.

"We're so small and vulnerable—and so incredibly outnumbered!" Rivka said in a trembling voice. "Do you think there is any way in the world that Israel can survive this war? Our nation isn't even twenty years old—can this really be the end of us already?" Rivka's fear was contagious. Hannah felt panic rising from its resting place, overshadowing her heart like a flock of vultures darkening the sky. She knew of only one way to put it to rest again.

"Do you ever pray, Rivka?" she asked, reaching for her friend's hand.

She gave a nervous laugh. "You know me, Hannah. I wouldn't know what to do inside a synagogue even if they did let me through the door."

"I wasn't raised in a religious home, either, but I've been attending Sabbath services with Jake ever since we were married. . . ."

"Rabbi Jake!" Rivka said, laughing. "That's what everyone called him that summer we worked on the Desert Runoff Project, remember? But they meant it in a nice way. Everybody respected him, even if they didn't always agree with him."

"Well, you won't be surprised to learn that his faith has started to rub off on me after six years of marriage. I didn't know how to pray either, so I started by praying the psalms. Try it. With this crisis, it really helps keep my fear down to manageable proportions."

"Thanks," Rivka said. She squeezed Hannah's hand before releasing it. "I will."

"You know," Hannah said, "there were so many times in the past when Israel was outnumbered by her enemies—just like we are now—but every time they called on God they won the battle."

"Do you think we could win this war, too?"

"I'm trying to believe it. Jake was reading the prophecies of Ezekiel to me the week before he left. You probably know that famous part about all the dry bones coming to life, right?"

"I've heard people say that's supposed to be Israel, coming to life on the ashes of the Holocaust."

"Well, the chapter right after that one talks about a huge army coming against Israel after the Jewish people are gathered here from many nations," Hannah said. "It sounds just like this crisis, with enemy troops advancing like a storm, covering the land like a cloud, plotting to invade peaceful, unwalled villages. And it says that God will allow them to come so that He can show His greatness and His holiness before the eyes of the whole world."

"Wow! I sure would like to believe that!"

"Yeah, me too." They gathered up their lunch wrappers and returned to work inside. The air was hushed and cool in the museum, a welcome relief from the clamor and warmth outside.

"You know," Rivka said as they began packing a display of Iron Age pottery, "it would be very ironic if these artifacts survived three thousand years of careless warfare and mayhem only to be destroyed in a bombing raid after we've been so careful to protect them."

"But they did survive for three thousand years, Rivka. And so will Israel. Even if we lose this war, the evidence will be here, safely buried for a future generation of Jews to unearth, proving once again that this land belongs to us."

Two days later, Hannah attended Sabbath services with Devorah. It comforted her to imagine Jake and Ben and a *minyan* of ten men reading the same Torah passages and reciting prayers as they huddled beside their tanks. When she and Devorah took the children to the park that afternoon, they were surprised to find it crowded with picnickers, as hundreds of officers enjoyed a short home-leave from the front. Rachel pointed to the men in uniform, saying, "Abba . . . Abba."

"You'd never know that we're teetering on the brink of war, would you?" Devorah said. "It almost looks like a normal Sabbath afternoon. Maybe there won't be a war after all."

They learned a few days later that it was precisely what the Israeli government wanted the Egyptians to think. Sending so many officers home on leave had lulled them into believing that Israel wasn't ready to attack. But at 7:45 A.M. on June fifth, Israeli fighter jets launched a surprise air strike on eleven Egyptian air bases, destroying or disabling ninety percent of their aircraft. In a huge gamble, Israel had left behind only twelve planes to patrol Israeli airspace and committed the remainder to demolishing Egypt's huge airforce. Syria and Jordan soon lost their airforces as well when they scrambled to Egypt's aid.

"Thank heaven we don't have to live in fear of air raids anymore," Hannah said as she and Devorah listened to the news in astonishment.

"Yes, but we're really at war now, Hannah. Do you know what that means? If we lose we die. That's what Itzak Rabin said in his speech—it's either victory or annihilation."

"Then may God help us win."

In the days that followed, Hannah worked to near exhaustion as an emergency medic. The ground-fighting was heavy in Jerusalem, and the rumble of artillery fire echoed off the surrounding hills like thunder. The air smelled as she imagined hell would smell—of smoke and burning and destruction. Even though there had been no fighting in the Golan Heights yet, where Jake and Ben were stationed, she was afraid to look at the faces of the wounded men, afraid she would see someone she knew. She returned to Devorah's apartment each night after work and listened in amazement to reports of Israeli victories in the Sinai, the West Bank, and in the Old City of Jerusalem. With air superiority, Israel was able to capture huge tracts of land. After only four days of fighting, the Israeli Defense Forces had miraculously defeated their enemies.

When Devorah told her that the UN was already trying to negotiate a cease-fire, Hannah's faith soared. "Maybe Ben and Jake won't have to fight at all!" she said. The war was nearly over. God had answered her prayers. He had kept Jake safe.

On the fifth day of the war, Hannah was changing the dressing on a wounded soldier's leg when one of the other medics came to her. "You must be pretty upset by the news, Hannah. Your husband is in the Golan, isn't he?"

The roll of bandages nearly slipped from Hannah's hand. "What news?"

"You didn't hear? Moshe Dayan ordered the IDF to attack the Golan Heights."

Hannah sank onto the bed as her knees gave way. All her reserves of faith in God bled from her heart as if the news had severed an artery. She was barely aware of the discussion between the medic and the wounded soldier, nor did they seem aware of how upset she was.

"I think it was a stupid thing to do," the medic said. "The war was over, so why are they prolonging it?"

"Dayan had to do it," the soldier insisted. "As long as the Syrians sit up on those fortified heights, aiming their guns down on us, life in the Galilee isn't going to be worth living for any Israeli within shelling range. We've been tyrannized by them long enough. If we don't win the Golan in this war, it will haunt us in the next."

"But the Syrians outnumber us. And the Heights are thousands of feet above sea level in places. How are we going to launch a successful assault uphill? Even if we somehow manage to do it, our losses are going to be staggering."

At the medic's words, a terrible premonition gripped Hannah's heart: Jake was going to die. She saw it as clearly, as vividly as if watching a motion picture. He was trapped inside his disabled tank on the Golan Heights under heavy Syrian artillery fire. In a horrifying burst of flame, the tank exploded. Jake and everyone else on board were burned to death. She would never see him, never hold him again. Hannah slid from the bed to the floor as she fainted.

The doctors sent her home when she revived. She knew by Devorah's bloodless face that she had also heard the news. Hannah didn't mention the premonition to her. Ben and Jake often manned the same tank. She and Devorah clung to each other throughout that day and into the night, listening to the news. There was no question of turning the radio off now, even when it reported severe fighting in the Golan, sometimes hand-to-hand, and heavy losses for both sides. Against her will, Hannah's mind replayed the image again and again: a flaming tank, her beloved Jake trapped inside.

The next day the news finally came. Against all odds, the Israelis had captured the Golan Heights from Syria. They would now sign the cease-fire agreement. Six days after it had begun, the war was over. According to the jubilant newscaster, the IDF could have easily overrun Cairo, Amman, and Damascus. Exhausted, Hannah turned off the radio, kissed Devorah good-bye, and took Rachel home to wait for news of Jake.

The apartment smelled stale after being closed up for two days. Hannah decided to clean it, filling buckets with hot water and soap, scrubbing walls and floors and sinks until her hands were raw. In the bedroom, she took her prayer book off the bedside table and stuffed it into a drawer. It was useless to pray.

When the telephone suddenly rang, Hannah stared at it, her heart pounding wildly. She couldn't answer it. She was certain that it was Jake's commanding officer, calling to break the news of his death to her. She let it ring and ring. When it finally stopped, she yanked it off the hook. As long as she delayed hearing the terrible words that he was dead, Jake would remain alive a while longer.

Throughout the day, Hannah fed Rachel but could eat nothing herself. Instead of sleeping, she spent the long night reliving each moment of her six years with Jake. She was feeding Rachel her breakfast the next morning when the doorbell buzzed. Hannah froze with the spoon in midair, her daughter's mouth open like a baby bird's. Of course. The IDF didn't telephone widows. They came in person with the bad news. She snatched Rachel from her chair and ran into the bedroom, clapping her hands over her ears to drown out the insistent buzzing. Thinking it was a game, Rachel did the same. At last the buzzing stopped.

The following afternoon, Hannah was lying on the bed trying to nap with Rachel when someone pounded on her door. "Open up, Hannah!" she heard Devorah shouting. "Or I'll get the key from the superintendent!" When Hannah finally opened the door, Devorah pushed her way inside with her two kids in tow and sprawled onto the living room sofa, her lungs heaving with exertion.

"It would serve you right . . . if I went into labor . . . right here and now!"

"Dev, I'm sorry." Hannah's voice was barely audible.

"We've been trying to reach you for two days! Do you

know your telephone isn't working?" She gestured to it, then frowned when she saw that the receiver was off the hook. "Hannah! What is wrong with you? What's going on?"

"Jake—" It was all she managed to say before tears choked off her words.

"Jake is worried sick because he hasn't been able to reach you!"

Hannah stared. "He . . . he called you?"

"No, Ben called and asked if you were at my place. He said Jake has been going out of his mind because he couldn't get through to you."

"Jake is . . . all right . . . ?" Her voice sounded very tiny. Devorah suddenly seemed to comprehend.

"Oh, Hannah, yes! Yes, they're both fine! They're exhausted and nearly stone-deaf from all the shelling, but they're fine. They'll be home before you know it."

Jake was all right. He wasn't dead. He was coming home. Hannah collapsed onto the nearest chair and wept.

Devorah began to laugh and cry at the same time as she struggled upright and reached for the telephone. "For goodness' sake, Hannah, put this miserable receiver back on the hook and talk to the poor man!"

"I pray that I never have to go to war again," Jake said as he and Hannah finally lay in each other's arms. "I thought the weeks of waiting were bad, but the battle was worse—much worse than I can ever describe."

"The world marvels that we won in *only* six days, but they weren't here, Jake. They don't know that those six days seemed like an eternity. Each day wasn't twenty-four *hours* long, but twenty-four *years*! I wondered, sometimes, if we were facing another holocaust."

"I know." Jake's arms went slack and he rolled onto his back, staring up at the darkened ceiling. "They were talking about passing out medals for bravery, but I told my C.O. I didn't want one. I didn't feel brave, Hannah. I felt terrified most of the time. Before the fighting we joked around and acted tough, but we were all shaking inside. When they gave the order and the assault began, I did what I was trained to do, but I knew this wasn't another exercise or a drill. The shells were real, the machine-gun fire was real . . . and there was an enemy out there who wanted to kill me."

Hannah moved closer, gripping him tightly, letting the warmth of him assure her that he was indeed alive. "When I was working at the hospital and all the wounded were coming in, I remembered the words you read to me in Isaiah where God promised to swallow up death forever. I kept thinking, 'Now would be a good time, Lord.' "

"Yeah. It would have been. Men I knew died, Hannah. A lot of them." He waited until he could go on. "I always wondered if it would be hard to kill the enemy. They tell you in training that the reason we drill so much is so that we'll fire automatically, without thinking. But it was still hard. Ben and I talked about it while we were waiting to start the assault. He told me to think about you and Rachel, to imagine the Syrians overpowering our defenses, imagine them running up the stairs to our apartment and battering down our door like the Gestapo . . ." Jake's voice broke. He paused again. "When the time came, I made myself fight so that you and Rachel wouldn't have to be afraid. But I pray to God I never have to fight again."

"No choice, Jake. They gave us no choice."

"You know, the world is busy spinning myths about the amazing Israeli military and how we won against overwhelming odds, but they don't understand that we were fighting to survive."

"I hate the Arabs for putting us through that."

Jake rolled onto his side and took her in his arms again. His dark brows creased into a frown. "Don't hate them, Hannah. They win if you hate. The Holy One is a God of redemption, and it's our job to show His redemption to the whole world. We can't do that if we hate."

What Jake was asking her to do was impossible. Hannah

wondered if he would feel the same way if Israel had been defeated, if they were the ones who were prisoners of war in an occupied land instead of the Palestinians. "Our victory was miraculous, wasn't it?" she said instead. "All of the ancient historical land of Israel is ours now—the Sinai, the Gaza Strip, the West Bank, the Golan Heights! And Jerusalem! Think of it! The Old City, the Wailing Wall—we can pray at the wall for the first time in our lives, Jake! The Rockefeller Museum and the Dead Sea Scrolls are ours, too. And all those ancient sites are just waiting to be excavated."

"You need to be part of it, Hannah. You need to go back to work. We won the city, but the battle for Jerusalem is far from over. You need to help excavate it and prove that it's ours. Jerusalem is our ancestors' most important legacy."

"But what about Rachel?"

"Give her a shovel and let her dig alongside you. What kid wouldn't love a giant sandbox?" Hannah hugged him harder still as tears of joy filled her eyes. "They intended to harm us," Jake whispered, "but God intended it for good."

As Hannah kissed him, she knew that her cup overflowed. She not only had Jake back in her arms, but all of Jerusalem at her feet.

CHAPTER 8

W hat an incredible city!" Abby said as the bus rolled through the streets of Jerusalem. "I can hardly believe I'm here!"

"You aren't disappointed, then?" Hannah asked. "People sometimes are. They say it's so much smaller than they imagined, or they complain because it's too modern."

Ari leaned across the aisle and added, "And some people can't help noticing how dirty certain sections are, and how much tension there is."

"I think it's beautiful," Abby said. "I can understand why people still fight over it."

Their bus had traveled down the Jordan Valley for a day of touring and lectures, stopping at the oasis of Jericho before climbing up the desolate Judean hills to Jerusalem. Hannah had explained how the mountain ridge divided the region, with green, productive land on the western slopes and parched, barren land on the eastern slopes, down to the Dead Sea. "You can see where King David got his inspiration for some of the psalms," she said. "We thirst for God in a dry and weary land, then find Him enthroned on His holy hill."

"I suppose if you live in a wasteland long enough you don't realize what you're missing," Abby said. "I know it took this crisis with Mark to make me realize how thirsty I was."

She thought about how empty her life would be when she returned home with her husband gone, her children grown. She wondered if a closer relationship with God would really make a difference. Life in Israel had been immensely difficult for Hannah, yet her faith gave her a vitality and strength that Abby knew she lacked. As the bus climbed up into the cool green hills, the difference in landscapes was as stark as the contrast between Abby's faith and her friend's.

"The Dead Sea is the lowest place on earth," Hannah said. "I think it was part of God's design to require the Israelites to climb *up* from there to worship Him—from death to life. When the pilgrims finally reached His dwelling place in Jerusalem, they found it had been well worth the long, rugged journey. I know it's a lesson I had to learn: Faith in God often comes by way of a hard upward road."

Abby hadn't expected Jerusalem to be surrounded by such lovely rolling hills. The city perched on the mountaintop like a proud, golden ship riding a wavy green sea. From a distance, it had appeared gilded, all of its buildings hewn from the same creamy limestone that had been quarried and used for construction since King David's day. Hannah pointed out the golden dome of a Muslim mosque, standing where Solomon's Temple had once stood. "According to tradition, the Temple also had a golden roof. The pilgrims would have seen it from afar as they climbed to the city."

Portions of Jerusalem looked like any other modern city, with high-rise buildings, shopping plazas, and the bustle of traffic and buses. Other sections, like the Arab bazaar near the Damascus Gate, could have been a scene from Bible times, with bleating sheep and haggling merchants, sacks of aromatic spices and mounds of fruit. Abby could scarcely take it all in. A montage of pedestrians hurried across the intersection as the bus paused at a traffic light—Eastern Orthodox priests in black cassocks and glinting crosses, bearded Jewish men in dark suits and fur hats, Muslim women with ankle-length skirts and veiled heads. Arabic prayers blared from the top of a minaret, competing with the clamor of ringing church bells.

"This has to be the most religious city I've ever seen!" Abby said.

Ari frowned as he leaned toward them again. "It's probably the most religious city in the world. The Jewish poet Yehuda Amichai says the air over Jerusalem is so saturated with prayers and dreams it is hard to breathe."

At each tourist spot they visited, Abby heard guides lecturing to groups in various languages. She recognized Spanish, Italian, English, German, and French. "I never realized that tourists came here from all over the world," she said when they returned to the bus.

Hannah smiled. "One of Jake's favorite verses from Isaiah says that in the last days all the nations will come to worship on the Lord's mountain. He pictures it like the Tower of Babel in reverse, with people of every language reunited here."

"You are wrong to think they will ever be united," Ari said, his voice sharp-edged. "It is true that people come here from all nations, but the walls dividing them are as thick and as high as the walls around the Old City. Even the name 'Jerusalem' is wrong. It is not a city of peace."

"But Isaiah is a *Jewish* prophet, Ari," Hannah said gently. "That verse is found in the Jewish scriptures. It *will* be fulfilled."

Ari gave the shrug of a skeptic, shaking his head. Nearly every day he seemed to find a reason to argue with Hannah. Since the arguments were usually in Hebrew, Abby didn't know what they were about most of the time, but she marveled at Hannah's patience with him.

The bus parked outside the Jaffa Gate, which led inside the walls of the Old City. While most of the college students hurried ahead, Ari and Abby stayed by Hannah's side as she maneuvered down the uneven, twisting lanes. Hannah seemed eager to continue the discussion they had begun on the bus.

"Do you call it a coincidence, Ari, that millions of followers of the three great world religions all come to worship God within these ancient walls?"

"I call it unfortunate," he said, frowning again.

"Three of the holiest sites in the world can all be found in this small walled-in area called the Old City," Hannah said, turning to Abby. "Muslims come to the Dome of the Rock, which is built over the place where Muhammad took his night journey into heaven. It's their second holiest shrine after Mecca. Muhammad said that one prayer in Jerusalem outweighs a thousand elsewhere. Christians worship at the Church of the Holy Sepulchre, built over the traditional site of Calvary and Christ's empty tomb. Jews pray at the Wailing Wall, which is all that remains of our Temple. Solomon built the Temple over the place where Abraham offered his son Isaac to God."

"Praying on the same scrap of land hardly unites the three," Ari said. "In fact, it has been the cause of many problems."

"They are also united by a common ancestor," Hannah said. "All three religions trace the roots of their faith to Abraham—the Jews and the Christians through his son Isaac, the Arabs through his son Ishmael."

"If we are one big happy family, why does the holiest Jewish site need to be fortified with guns and barricades?" Ari gestured to the army checkpoint they were approaching. Green-uniformed soldiers with guns slung over their shoulders searched backpacks and purses. Everyone was required to pass through a metal detector before entering the plaza facing the Wailing Wall.

"People who expect Jerusalem to have a holy atmosphere must be very disillusioned when they see these constant reminders of our hatred," Ari said.

"It was no different when the Jewish Temple stood here," Hannah said. "Worshipers who came to Jerusalem in Jesus' time saw Roman soldiers patrolling the streets and the Antonia Fortress dominating the plaza on the Temple's north side. Yes, this is 'holy ground' in a sense, but at the same time,

God expects us to live out our faith in a real world of pain and strife until His redemption is complete." Ari shrugged again but didn't reply.

Hannah gathered the group around her to explain that she would give them time to approach The Wall and pray if they wanted to—men on the left-hand side, women on the right. "Many people like to write out their prayers and place them in the cracks between the stones," she said as she passed around a small pad of paper. "But first, listen to the words of Solomon's prayer as he dedicated the Temple to God three thousand years ago." She opened a pocket-sized Bible and began to read. " 'As for the foreigner who does not belong to your people Israel but has come from a distant land because of your name . . . when he comes and prays toward this temple, then hear from heaven, your dwelling place, and do whatever the foreigner asks of you, so that all the peoples of the earth may know your name and fear you, as do your own people Israel . . .' You see, God's Temple was to be a place of refuge for all who sought Him. Jesus threw the money changers out of the court where the Gentiles were allowed to pray, reminding the Jews that God's house should be a place of prayer for all nations."

As Abby entered the enclosure and slowly approached The Wall, she wondered what she should pray for. She hadn't been able to forget Hannah's story of the Six-Day War and how the Israelis had miraculously won back the Old City and the freedom to worship at this site. But Jake's words still lingered in Abby's heart, pricking her conscience: *"Don't hate them . . . they win if you hate."*

Abby admitted that she hated Lindsey Cook for destroying her marriage. And she hated Mark for betraying her trust and forsaking his marriage vows. She knew it was wrong, but how did she get rid of all that enmity? What should she do with it? Forgetting what Mark had done was impossible. Her feelings couldn't be erased like a computer file with the simple push of the Delete button. Here in Israel she was able to put him out of her mind for several hours at a time, but eventually she would have to return home. She would have to face the empty closets, the lonely dinners, the vacant side of the bed. And her hatred would still be there like a carefully banked fire, waiting to re-ignite.

"Show me what to do, Lord," she prayed as tears welled in her eyes. "Show me what to do with all this pain. I'm so tired of carrying it around in my heart." As she swiped at her tears, the comment Jake had made after the war inexplicably came to Abby's mind: *"They intended to harm us, but God intended it for good."*

If He was a God of redemption, as Jake had said, could He possibly use even the wreck of her marriage to bring about something good? Abby wondered if she would have the opportunity to meet Jake before the summer ended. She would love to ask him.

At last she pulled a scrap of paper from her pocket and wrote simply, *Lord, please show me what to do.* Then, because the cracks were already stuffed with prayers, she stood on tiptoe to tuck it into the only empty space she could find between the massive stones. As she turned to leave she saw Ari standing where she had left him beside the low wall bordering the women's enclosure. He hadn't gone into the men's court to pray with the others. Instead, she had the unsettling feeling that he had been watching her.

"This house looks quite different from Leah's home in Degania, doesn't it?" Hannah asked the gathered students. They had all walked to the ruins of what had once been the wealthy Jewish Quarter during the time of Christ. It was now on display underground beneath a new building in the Old City.

"It looks like the villas I've seen in books on ancient Rome or Pompeii," one of the students replied. "Paved courtyards, mosaic floors, stuccoed walls . . . are you sure it was kosher for Jews to live like this?"

Hannah laughed. "You're exactly right about the Roman influence in architecture, but this is what gives it away as Jewish . . . these mikvehs, or ritual baths. Two thousand years ago, these homes sat on a hill across the Tyropoeon Valley from the Temple—with a breathtaking view of it, in fact. We believe that the occupants were temple priests—which leads to our discussion of the Sadducees.

"Most of the Sadducees were priests, and their response to the crisis of Roman occupation was cooperation. In return, the Romans allowed the Sadducees to control the temple rituals and sacrifices, turning the priesthood into a wealthy aristocracy. The Sadducees also controlled the Jewish ruling body, the Sanhedrin. Needless to say, the Sadducees were not too popular with the common people, who resented Roman rule and the crippling taxes they were forced to pay. The Pharisees had many more followers than they did, since the Pharisees opposed any foreign rule over God's people.

"The Sadducees accepted only the first five books of the Bible as God's revelation of Himself and didn't believe in a resurrection. They taught that righteousness could only be achieved by strict adherence to the temple rituals—which they controlled, of course."

"How convenient," Abby heard Ari mumble.

"The Pharisees, on the other hand," Hannah continued, "believed that God also revealed Himself through the prophets, the writings, and the teachings of the great rabbis and sages. They believed righteousness was achieved by carefully observing the strict day-to-day details of 'kosher' living—more than six hundred laws that had to be strictly followed."

Ari made a sound of scorn. "Leave it to religious leaders to change ten commandments into six hundred rules."

"Christians often forget that Yeshua—Jesus—was Jewish," Hannah continued. "He didn't come to start a radical new religion but to fulfill the revelation of redemption that the Jewish people had already been given. All His life, Jesus carefully followed Jewish Law. We know that He journeyed here to Jerusalem to attend all the feasts and sacrifices in keeping with the Sadducees, and He dutifully paid His temple tax. He must have angered the Sadducees when He quoted the authority of

the prophets and preached about a resurrection like the Pharisees, but what they probably resented the most was His claim
that 'One greater than the temple is here.' In other words, His
God-given authority superseded theirs."

Abby glanced at Ari as Hannah talked, curious about his
reaction to a discussion of Jesus. As she expected, his frown
was skeptical, disdainful. She wondered why he would even
come on this day tour to Jerusalem, knowing that the seminar
topic was "The Life and Times of Jesus." It couldn't be simply
to help Hannah get around; she seemed quite capable of
doing it on her own most of the time, and she wasn't afraid
to ask the students for help when she couldn't. Perhaps, Abby
thought cynically, it was because Ari couldn't last a day without an argument with her.

When Hannah finished her lecture and they all began
walking to the next site, Abby wasn't surprised when Ari questioned Hannah's conclusions.

"You said Yeshua challenged the priests' authority, claim-
ing His was greater. It sounds like a typical political power
struggle to me. Why spiritualize it? So they had different beliefs—so do all the other religions around here."

"Because the power struggle *was* spiritual—and God had
the final word. You know history, Ari. You know what happened to Jerusalem forty years after the priests succeeded in
having an innocent man crucified so they could stay in power.
The Romans destroyed it. They destroyed the Temple and the
priests' entire way of life. 'The stones will cry out,' Ari. The
Sadducees vanished from history, yet Yeshua is alive. His kingdom remains."

"Excuse me," Abby said, "but what you just said—'The
stones will cry out'—that sounds familiar, but I can't quite
place it."

"Jesus quoted those words on Palm Sunday," Hannah said.
"The Pharisees had demanded that He silence the people after
they proclaimed Him as the Messiah, but Jesus said that if
they kept quiet, the stones would cry out. Then He wept over
Jerusalem because He knew that it would be destroyed. Jesus

was quoting the Jewish prophet Habakkuk."

She stopped in the middle of the street and pulled her Bible from her pocket, paging through it until she found the passage. "Habakkuk wrote, 'Woe to him who builds his realm by unjust gain . . . The stones of the wall will cry out, and the beams of the woodwork will echo it . . . Has not the Lord Almighty determined that the people's labor is only fuel for the fire, that the nations exhaust themselves for nothing? For the earth will be filled with the knowledge of the glory of the Lord, as the waters cover the sea.' And that's exactly what happened, Ari. The corrupt house that the Jewish leaders built was destroyed, but the Kingdom of God, which Jesus proclaimed, has spread to every corner of the globe."

The group arrived at the southwestern corner of what had once been the Temple Mount. All that remained of it, Hannah explained, were portions of the huge retaining walls that King Herod built when he expanded the natural platform on which the Temple once stood. The Wailing Wall was only part of this retaining wall, not part of the Temple itself.

"Herod hoped that by rebuilding the Temple he would secure a lasting legacy for himself, but the construction work outlived him," Hannah explained. "Begun in 20 B.C., the Temple was still incomplete forty-six years later when Jesus was asked to comment on its beauty. The work was finally finished in A.D. 64, but the completed temple stood for only six years before the Romans demolished it in A.D. 70."

How tragic, Abby thought as she walked past the jumbled debris. She gazed at the huge stones that had been hurled from the top of the wall, and the fury of the Roman destruction amazed her. *The stones will cry out.*

"One of the ruined stones they found right here had an inscription," Ari said suddenly. It was the first time he had contributed to Hannah's lectures all day. "The stone was originally placed up there, on top of that wall, identifying it as the 'place of trumpeting.' It was where the priests stood to blow the *shofar*, signaling that the Sabbath or a holy day had begun."

Several of the college girls quickly gathered around him, hanging on his every word with adolescent infatuation. Abby saw why. Even she had to admit that Ari was quite good-look-ing—like her husband, Mark. She fought the urge to inform the girls that Ari was a married man.

"This street along the western wall was lined with shops in the first century," he continued. "They probably sold over-priced trinkets to all the tourists, just like the junk shops in the Arab market." He almost smiled.

"Jerusalem had tourists way back then, Dr. Bazak?" one of the girls asked.

"They were . . . eh, how do you say? *Pilgrims*, not tourists. The Torah required all Jewish men to travel to Jerusalem three times a year for the three religious festivals: *Pesach*, which you call Passover, *Shavuot*, and *Sukkot*. How do you call those last two in English, Hannah?"

"The Feast of Pentecost and the Feast of Tabernacles."

"Yes, thank you. Devout Jews traveled here from all over the Roman Empire three times a year. Hundreds of thousands of people. Over here," he said, pointing, "we found the re-mains of forty-eight mikvehs. The people were required to bathe to purify themselves before worshiping. These stairs, over here on the south side, date from that time period. They once led to doors, which you can see are now blocked. Inside are tunneled passageways leading up to the Temple Mount. I like to picture how it must have looked, with Herod's huge structure on the mountaintop and all the people streaming up to it with their offering baskets and sacrifices."

Abby could almost picture it, too, and she marveled at the depth of devotion that would inspire someone to travel so far in order to worship God. Back home, she could barely muster the energy to get out of bed once in a while on a Sunday morning and drive to church. She thought of Leah and the other villagers of Degania and the long, rugged journey they would have made to Jerusalem, probably on foot. She won-dered what they would have thought of the city and the Temple once they arrived . . . and if they had found the journey worthwhile.

I 've never seen so many people!" Leah said. She gripped her little brother Matthew's hand tightly so he wouldn't get lost and clung to the back of her brother Gideon's belt with her other hand as they threaded their way through the square below the Temple Mount.

"It's too crowded," Matthew whined. "I can't even see."

"It's a blessing," Abba said, turning to them. His weathered face was stern. "The Holy One promised to make Abraham's descendants as many as the stars in the heavens. We should not complain when the Holy One blesses us."

Leah didn't feel blessed. She felt damp and shivery from her required dip in the mikveh before climbing the Temple Mount. And as she gazed in awe at the dazzling array of goods for sale in the Street of the Vendors, she knew that her family was much too poor to afford even the cheapest trinket. Jerusalem was a city of great contrasts; rich men were transported by slaves in covered litters, while cripples in rags crawled to busy street corners to beg. But the majority of people were pilgrims like Leah's family, the men bearing lambs across their shoulders, the women baskets of tithes on their heads. Some of the pilgrims sang the Passover psalm as they climbed the stairs to the Temple: "The stone the builders rejected has become the capstone . . . blessed is he who comes in the name of the Lord." And like Leah, most of the pilgrims were gaping in wonder at the mammoth temple complex. The retaining walls alone seemed as tall as a mountain, the courtyard more vast than an entire village.

Abba stopped suddenly, herding the family to the side of the street as a squadron of Roman soldiers swept past. Their sandals and the stiff leather breastplates they wore over their tunics creaked like a new wagon harness when they walked.

Roman soldiers appeared everywhere in Jerusalem, policing the streets, standing guard to control the mob near the Temple Mount, parading in front of the royal palace and the Antonia Fortress, clutching their spears. Leah was more than a little afraid of them. The way they strutted around with their red capes swaying behind them, their swords swinging at their sides, their contempt for Jews barely disguised reminded her of Reb Nahum's cocky roosters strutting like bullies around the barnyard, pecking at the lowly hens. The soldiers were also an unwelcome reminder that she was a captive in an enslaved nation.

"If the Holy One set us free from slavery in Egypt," she wondered aloud as the soldiers passed, "why doesn't He set us free from the Romans?"

"Maybe He wants to," Gideon said angrily, "but our leaders won't act. The Torah says not to place a foreigner over you, one who is not a brother Israelite, but—"

"Doesn't the Torah also say to honor thy father and thy mother?" Abba's voice was sharp-edged, like flint striking flint, making sparks. His dark eyes flashed from Gideon to Leah and back again.

"Yes, Abba," Gideon said.

"Then you would both honor me by holding your thoughts and your tongues."

The crowd thinned slightly after Leah and her family began to climb the huge arched stairway to the top of the mount. As they paused to rest on the first landing, Leah gazed across the narrow valley to the Roman-style villas on the opposite hill, their red-tiled roofs supported by rows of white pillars. They were larger and more lavish than the villa back home in Degania where the district tax collector, Reuben ben Johanan, lived. Matthew noticed the mansions, too.

"There must be lots and lots of tax collectors in Jerusalem," he said.

"No, that's where the priests live," Gideon said, his contempt barely disguised. "And the members of the Sanhedrin."

Leah compared those mansions with the house where they

were staying while in Jerusalem. Abba's cousin Samuel was a stonemason who had moved away from Degania with his family to find work in the city. His home in the squalid laborers' district outside the city walls was dark and cramped. Samuel's wife had swept a storage room clean to provide a place for her guests to sleep.

Leah's legs ached by the time she reached the top of the stairs, but the view spread out before her was well worth it. The paved mountaintop was ten times larger than the entire village of Degania, the Temple itself so huge and majestic it made her feel insignificant. There was so much going on all around her in the outer courtyard that she was certain she could stay up here for a year and still not see it all. She followed Abba as if in a dream, past a covered portico where a rabbi taught his students, past more beggars and cripples in their pitiful rags, past a knot of Jewish men in foreign dress bickering at the table of the money changers. Gideon had explained how it was against Jewish law to pay the temple tax with foreign coins bearing pagan images.

The longest lines were composed of families like her own, who were waiting for a priest to inspect the lamb they had brought from home. Today, five days before the feast, was the day each family selected their lamb and had it declared acceptable for the Passover sacrifice. Families without lambs waited to purchase a "clean" one from the priests. Leah's father and brothers joined the inspection line, carrying the lamb from Abba's flock, the lamb Leah had secretly named Little One. As she joined them in line, she warned herself not to get sentimental. She knew from the time Saul first separated Little One from the flock and tethered him in the yard for Leah to feed that he would be their Passover sacrifice. She had tried not to become too attached to him, but she hadn't considered that the lamb would become so attached to her. He followed her around the tiny yard like her shadow, bleating piteously with his funny hoarse stutter whenever she disappeared from his sight, licking her with his scratchy pink tongue whenever she knelt to feed him.

When it was their turn for the priest's inspection, tears filled Leah's eyes as Saul brought Little One forward, cradling him proudly in his huge arms. Leah was proud of their lamb, too. He was perfect—clean, healthy, uninjured, spotless. She forced back her tears, not daring to cry. Abba would rebuke such foolishness.

As the priest set him on the table to inspect, he spread his broad hand awkwardly over Little One's head, clumsily poking his thumb into the lamb's eye. To Leah, the act seemed deliberate, and she nearly cried out along with the lamb. The priest frowned unpleasantly as he examined Little One, his expression that of a man who has just eaten sour grapes. He wore a white robe of very finely woven linen and a matching white turban on his bushy black hair. His fierce black eyebrows touched in the center when he frowned, and with his beaked nose, he reminded Leah of a raven. When he opened his mouth to speak, she almost expected him to crow.

"There is something wrong with this lamb," he said as he ran his swarthy hands over Little One's head. "Look . . . See here? His eye is running."

"That's because you poked it!" Leah cried out.

Abba whirled to face her, horrified that she had spoken. Mama grabbed Leah's arm and pulled her aside, shaking her. "Leah! You'll disgrace us!" she said in a harsh whisper. "It's shameful enough that you can't hold your tongue in Degania, but that man is God's holy priest!"

"But he poked our lamb's eye on purpose! I saw him—"

"Hush! Or you will never be allowed to come here again!"

Leah bit her lip as she turned back to watch the priest. His chin tilted arrogantly as he gestured to Little One.

"I cannot ignore this animal's rheumy eye. The lamb is defective."

Abba's shoulders slumped. He looked small and insubstantial beside the fleshy priest. "But . . . it's all we have, Your Honor," he said.

The priest's eyes were half closed as if the proceedings bored him. "The animal might bring a few shekels in the

Roman meat market, but it isn't suitable for Passover. I could spare you the trouble of selling it and exchange it for a clean lamb, but you will have to pay the difference in price."

"How much difference?" Abba said hoarsely.

"Your lamb and one shekel of silver in exchange for that animal over there." He gestured to one of the lambs tethered behind him. "It's the same size as yours."

Leah raged in silence at the injustice. The other lamb was much smaller than Little One, with scarcely any fat. The meager meat on its bones would barely feed her family and Cousin Samuel's, much less provide second helpings. She longed to protest, but Mama gripped her arm so tightly it hurt.

Abba removed his money pouch and slowly began piling silver pieces on the priest's scales. Gideon turned his back as if unwilling to be a witness. As he came to stand beside Leah, she could tell by his tight lips and clenched fists that he was as angry as she was.

"It's not fair," Leah whispered to him. "We're being cheated."

"I know," he said.

"Can't we do something? Isn't there a judge—"

"The priests *are* the judges."

The mound of silver Abba was forced to pile on the scale left his pouch nearly empty. The profits from the sale of his early grain crops were nearly gone, and he still had to pay the temple tax of a half-shekel apiece for Saul, Gideon, and himself. There would be nothing left to pay their Roman taxes by the time they got home.

"Abba ought to keep all the barley we brought," Leah whispered. "That crook doesn't deserve our tithe." It made her sick to think of the crow-faced priest sitting in his mansion on the hill, eating Abba's grain while they went hungry.

"Come," Abba said when the deal was finished. "We'll take this new lamb back to Samuel's house." Leah could tell he was disheartened.

"If it's all right with you," Gideon said, "I would like to stay and look around for a while. I know the way back."

"May I stay, too?" Leah asked. "Please?"

Abba nodded wearily. "Be sure to stay together, and don't wander too far."

Leah and Gideon explored the huge Court of the Gentiles first, acres and acres of stone pavement surrounded by pillared porches. "I want to get closer," Leah said, gazing at the gilded sanctuary near the center of the plaza. A thin plume of smoke rose heavenward from the holy altar.

"You can only go as far as the Court of Women," Gideon warned.

"I know. Will you take me there?"

"All right."

A thrill of excitement shivered through Leah as she approached God's dwelling place on earth. But once inside, the view from the women's court disappointed her. She had to peer over the other women's heads and look through a row of narrow openings just to see into the Court of the Israelites where Gideon had gone, and that view was obstructed by the backs of all the men who were inside. It was just like the Torah lessons in the synagogue back home—she was excluded because she was a woman. As the sweet perfume of incense drifted into her courtyard, she wondered what it would be like to be able to approach God's altar, to worship Him up close instead of from far away.

"There wasn't much to see," Gideon told her when he emerged through the Nicanor Gate a few minutes later. "We're much too late for the morning sacrifice and too early for the evening one."

As they skirted the edge of Solomon's porch, Leah's attention was drawn to a crowd that had gathered around a speaker. He wasn't a scribe, or a teacher of the law, or even one of the Pharisees' rabbis, but an ordinary working man like Abba with a lean, muscular body and sun-browned skin. With his smiling bearded face, pointed nose, and small round ears, he reminded Leah of the little brown-furred coneys that lived on the hillsides back home among the rocks. He spoke in the clear, plain dialect of her district of Galilee. But what drew

Leah to a halt was the fact that women as well as men sat listening at his feet.

"Gideon, wait." She pulled her brother to a stop beside her. "Can't we listen, too?" He shrugged, then leaned against one of the pillars with his arms folded to hear what the man had to say.

"The Prophet Jeremiah foresaw this day," the preacher said, gesturing broadly with his work-callused hands. "Jeremiah wrote, 'Woe to the shepherds who are destroying and scattering the sheep of my pasture!' The prophet was talking about the leaders and priests whose job it is to shepherd His people Israel. He said the wicked shepherds would be punished but that God Himself would gather the remnant of His flock. God spoke the same message through the Prophet Ezekiel, saying, 'I myself will tend my sheep and have them lie down . . . I will search for the lost and bring back the strays. I will bind up the injured and strengthen the weak, but the sleek and the strong I will destroy. I will shepherd the flock with justice.' "

Leah glanced at Gideon to see if he was also thinking of the corrupt priest who had just cheated their father. Her brother was standing up straight, listening with rapt attention.

"Isn't it enough," the preacher continued, "for these wicked shepherds to feed on the good pasture? Must they also trample the rest of the pasture with their feet? Isn't it enough for them to drink clear water? Must they also muddy the rest with their feet? Must God's flock feed on what they have trampled and drink what they have muddied? God says, 'I will save my flock, and they will no longer be plundered . . . I will place over them one shepherd, my servant David, and he will tend them and be their shepherd. I the Lord will be their God, and my servant David will be prince among them.' Yeshua the Messiah said, 'I am the good shepherd. The good shepherd lays down his life for the sheep.' And so Yeshua gave His life as our Passover sacrifice to remove the barriers that stand between us and God."

Who was this Yeshua? Leah wondered. She would gladly follow a leader who was as gentle and caring as her brother Saul was with Abba's sheep. Especially if that shepherd would break down all the walls that the priests and Pharisees had built and allow her to draw near to God.

She nervously glanced around, still unsure if she was even supposed to be listening, and saw that a woman had moved to stand close beside her. "I see that you're interested," the woman said softly. "Oh no, it's all right," she quickly added when she saw that Leah was about to flee. "You may stay. Yeshua the Messiah has many women disciples. God's Spirit was poured out on men and women alike, just as the prophet Joel said it would be. Divisions between rich and poor, slave and free, male and female don't exist in His kingdom."

Leah remembered the words of Matthew's Torah lesson that she had learned outside the synagogue window. " 'They will all know me, from the least . . . to the greatest,' " she recited aloud.

"Yes, that's right. Yeshua came—"

"It's time to go," Gideon said. He gripped Leah's arm and pulled her away.

"Gideon, wait! I want to hear—"

"Abba would forbid it." He propelled her across the courtyard toward the stairs.

"But they were talking about the Messiah."

"I know. Everyone wants the Messiah to come because our lives are so unbearable. People are willing to believe anything. But if he really came, then why are we still under Roman rule? Why are we still hungry? The real Messiah will fight the Roman armies. He'll feed us with manna when he comes, and we won't be hungry anymore."

Leah wondered what it would be like to have a full stomach all the time, like on a feast day or after a wedding celebration. At home, Abba and her brothers always ate first because they needed more food for their hard labor. Leah felt hungry most of the time, even after eating.

As they neared the stairs that led from the Temple Mount,

Leah suddenly heard a familiar sound. It was a lamb bleating with a distinctive hoarse stutter she recognized immediately. She turned and saw a well-dressed man walking toward her with Little One under his arm.

"Little One!" she cried. He bleated loudly in response to her voice and tried to wriggle free. "Gideon, that's Little One, that's our lamb!" Leah ran to him. Little One's stubby tail spun in happy circles when he saw her. The man had a difficult time restraining him.

"What are you doing?" he shouted angrily. "This is my lamb. I just purchased it for Passover."

"For Passover!" she cried. "Did the priests tell you this lamb was acceptable for the sacrifice?"

"Of course it's acceptable! Now get out of my way, girl."

"The priests cheated us!" Gideon shouted as he hurried to Leah's side. "We brought this lamb from our village in Galilee and the priests told us it was unclean."

"You must be mistaken." The man tried to edge around Gideon but he blocked his path.

"I'm not mistaken! My sister raised him, she knows him, and the lamb recognizes her!" Little One's cries grew louder as he struggled to free himself and go to Leah. "The priests stole our lamb," Gideon insisted, "and they stole Abba's money! You have to bring him back and tell the authorities what those lying, cheating priests did!" Gideon began wrestling with the man, trying to pull Little One from his arms.

"Hey, stop! Let go! This is my lamb! Thief!"

Suddenly two Roman soldiers appeared out of nowhere. Their beardless faces looked naked and ugly, their heads grotesquely small in their close-fitting helmets.

"Gideon, look out!" Leah cried. She backed away in terror.

"Get your filthy hands off me!" Gideon cried. "I'm telling you we were cheated! This lamb was stolen from us—!" All the air suddenly rushed out of him with a loud grunt as one of the soldiers punched him in the gut. Gideon doubled over, gasping in pain, but the second soldier cruelly yanked Gideon's arms behind his back, forcing him upright. The man holding

Little One thanked the soldiers and quickly disappeared down the stairs.

"No . . . stop! My brother isn't a thief!" Leah cried as the soldiers began dragging Gideon across the courtyard toward the Antonia Fortress. They ignored her, as if she wasn't even there.

Leah didn't know what to do. Too terrified to follow them, she stood alone, dazed. It had all happened so fast. *Please, God, let this just be a terrible dream!* But it wasn't a dream. They were arresting Gideon.

She was aware of people staring at her, skirting around her in a wide arc as she stood alone, weeping, but no one stopped to help. She was at the point of despair when she felt a comforting arm encircle her shoulder and heard a soft voice asking, "What's wrong, dear one? Can I help you somehow?"

Leah was surprised to see the woman who had spoken to her on Solomon's porch. Her face was so kind, so concerned, that Leah threw herself into the woman's arms.

"The Roman soldiers just took my brother away and it was all my fault! I don't know what to do!" The woman held Leah and allowed her to cry, gently rubbing her back.

When Leah's tears were spent, the stranger said, "What's your name, dear one?"

"I'm Leah, daughter of Jesse from Degania in Galilee."

"Is the rest of your family here in Jerusalem with you, Leah?"

"Yes, but Gideon knows the way back to where we're staying. I don't remember!"

"Tell me everything you do remember, and I'll try to help." Her voice calmed Leah, and she was able to explain to the woman about Cousin Samuel's house in the laborers' district outside the city walls. "I know where that is," the woman said. "It's a large neighborhood, but someone is bound to know Samuel the Galilean if we ask enough people."

She led Leah down the stairs and through the crowded streets to a gate that led out of the city. Leah recognized it as the one she had come through earlier with her family. At the thought of facing her father, she began to cry again. "It's my fault . . . it's all my fault!"

"Why is it your fault, Leah?" She told the woman what had happened, and when she finished, the woman said, "The Holy One will deal with the wicked priests in His time. But what happened to your brother wasn't your fault. The Scriptures say, 'Better a patient man than a warrior, a man who controls his temper than one who takes a city.' "

Leah knew it was true. "Gideon has always had a fiery temper," she said.

As soon as they entered Cousin Samuel's neighborhood, Leah saw her little brother playing in the lane with Samuel's sons. "Matthew!" she cried as she ran toward him. "Where's Abba? Tell him to come quickly!" In the panic and confusion that followed, Leah forgot all about the woman who had helped her. When she finally remembered and turned to thank her, the woman had vanished.

All the color drained from Abba's face as Leah explained through her tears how Gideon had been arrested. "Stay in the house," he ordered. "Saul and I will go back to the fortress and find him."

Leah tried to pray while she waited, but she didn't know what to say to God. Didn't she need to bring a sacrifice or an offering before she had the right to ask anything of Him? She heard her mother sobbing in the next room.

The sun was setting by the time Abba and Saul finally returned, supporting Gideon between them. "The Romans beat him with rods," Saul said, "his punishment for assault and attempted theft." Gideon moaned as they laid him on his stomach on the floor of Samuel's dingy storage room.

"Get some water and tend his wounds," Abba said gruffly.

"I'm sorry," Leah wept as she knelt beside him. "Oh, Gideon, I'm so sorry. . . ."

TEL DEGANIA EXCAVATION—1999

Abby pulled her Bible and book of devotions from her backpack and settled down in a patch of shade with them to take her morning break. It was secluded and peaceful on this side of the dig site, with birds singing in the grove of fruit trees below the tel and the glittering blue waters of the lake barely visible in the distance. She opened her Bible and read the day's passage from Psalm 66: *For you, O God, tested us; you refined us like silver . . . You let men ride over our heads; we went through fire and water, but you brought us to a place of abundance.*

The devotional explained how God sometimes uses difficult circumstances to accomplish His purposes and draw people closer to Him. It was the same thing Hannah's husband had said—that what others intended for harm, God could use for good. Abby still wondered what good could come from adultery and divorce. And she wondered, as she had every day, what she should do when she returned home.

Should she take the legalistic approach like the Pharisees, divorcing Mark for breaking his marriage vows, then withdrawing from her enemies and starting over someplace else? Someplace where she wouldn't have to hear the shocked whispers behind her back or endure the pitying looks?

Or, like the Sadducees, should she compromise with her enemies, amicably dividing up the household goods with Mark, and find another man to take Mark's place? Right now the thought of allowing herself to trust another man was too overwhelming for Abby to contemplate. She hadn't been one of the popular girls in high school, with dozens of boyfriends and dates. Studious and shy in college, she discovered she had much in common with quiet Mark MacLeod when they met while working at Turkey Run State Park one summer. Surrounded by the forest they both loved so much, falling in love had been as effortless as falling in step with each other on the wooded paths.

The Zealots had chosen to fight, and although Abby didn't want Mark back and wasn't interested in fighting with Lindsey Cook over him, she wondered if she should continue to fight *with* Mark, dragging out the divorce, suing him for the house and every cent he owned. But what good would money do her—or a house in which every floorboard creaked with memories?

Then there was Jesus' solution. Hannah still hadn't discussed what that was yet.

As Abby was about to close her Bible she noticed a strange series of markings on the page, as if certain letters and groups of letters had been underlined. She had noticed similar marks a few days ago in another place and had thought they were misprints. She tilted the page to the light to see if these were also typos, but the ink was dark blue, not black. When she flipped to the next page she could see the indentations a pen had made when it had been pressed down. How odd. This Bible was brand-new, a present from Emily. Had her daughter made the marks? If so, what did they mean? She hadn't underlined verses or even whole words—just random letters. Abby decided to ask Emily about them the next time she sent an email message.

Abby thought about Emily's last email letter as she walked back to the dig site to resume work. *Daddy came to church with me on Sunday,* Emily had written. *I introduced him to my pastor, and they're going to meet for coffee tomorrow night to talk. . . .*

Mark was going to sit down for coffee and talk? He never talked. He didn't have time. Throughout their last year of marriage, he'd simply swept into the house to change his clothes or to sleep or to check his mail. The rest of the time he was always busy working fifty or sixty hours a week—at least he'd said he was working. Abby felt her anger building again, churning her stomach like a stormy sea. How could God bring something good out of this?

Hannah was at Abby's work site when she got back, discussing something with Ari. The vans had left the hotel this morning without Dr. Voss and Hannah—which Abby had thought was strange. Now Hannah beckoned to Abby when she saw her.

"I was just telling Ari the bad news. Dr. Voss hasn't been feeling well these past few days, which is why he didn't come with us to Jerusalem. When he complained of chest pains yesterday, Ramona and I finally convinced him to go to the hospital for tests. The bottom line is, he needs bypass surgery. He and Ramona are flying home to Colorado today."

"Will he be all right?" Abby asked.

"With surgery, the doctors expect him to fully recover. But now I'm going to need someone to take over for him." She turned to Ari, but before she had a chance to ask, he held up his hands in protest.

"No, Hannah. Not me."

"But the work on the Roman villa has barely begun and—"

Ari answered her in a rapid burst of Hebrew, but it was clear to Abby from his expression and his tone of voice that he was refusing. It seemed odd that he wouldn't want to help out, especially since his specialty was the Roman era. Perhaps he was reluctant to elbow into Dr. Voss's territory.

"Please, Ari. As a favor to me," Hannah begged. "You know how important this dig is to me. I can't find anyone else at this late date . . . I'll lose my funding."

"I told you, I can't."

"But no one else is half as qualified as you are. Please."

Ari looked away, raking his fingers through his dusty hair as he stared off into the distance for a long moment. "Do you know what a difficult position you're placing me in?" he finally asked.

"Yes, I know. And you know that I wouldn't ask if I had any other choice. Listen, you won't have to write any reports. Give me your notes at the end of the season and I'll write them for you."

When Ari turned, he had a pained expression on his face. "Hannah . . ."

"*Please*, Ari." She reached up to touch his shoulder, and a silent acknowledgment of affection and respect passed between them.

"All right," he said quietly. He glanced at Abby. "But I would like my team from this area to move with me."

Abby wondered about Ari's request as she and the four college students gathered all their tools and equipment, then transported them by wheelbarrow across the mound to the far side of the village. There had been little rapport built between Ari and his team, let alone friendship. Why would he request that they all move along with him? But as Abby got caught up in the students' excitement, she finally decided that it didn't matter. They all knew that the chances of finding significant artifacts—even buried treasure—were much greater in the sprawling Roman-style villa than they had been in Leah's house. Everyone was eager to begin.

"I assume you know all your fellow volunteers by now," Hannah said when Abby and the others arrived at the new site, "but I want you to meet my good Palestinian friend, Marwan Ashrawi. I've hired him to help out with some of the heavy manual labor."

He gave a little wave, smiling slightly. He was a nice-looking man in his early thirties, with a square, clean-shaven face and a high, smooth forehead. Abby saw the biceps of a weight lifter beneath Marwan's sweat-stained T-shirt and wondered if it was from lifting rocks or weights.

"Marwan is a little shy," Hannah added, "but if you get to know him, you'll find that he likes to practice his English."

In the next few weeks, the volunteers began making spectacular finds under Ari's guidance—traces of decorated stucco walls; a hand mirror, comb, and other delicate toiletry articles; shards of ivory and Roman glass from furnishings and glassware. The difference between this elegant, spacious home and Leah's tiny hovel was dramatic. So was the change in Ari Bazak.

His enthusiasm became contagious as he climbed down into the pits to sweat and labor alongside his workers. He began to join in their conversation and laughter for the first time all summer and even took part in Hannah's daily lectures, adding extra tidbits of his own knowledge to hers. He became friendly and personable with everyone on the site— everyone, that is, except the Palestinian worker, Marwan. Whenever Ari and Marwan got within a few yards of each other, the tension between them made everyone uncomfortable.

"Who do you think might have owned this house, Ari?" Abby asked as they worked side by side one morning. He was teaching her how to recover and preserve the fine remnants of painted stucco that had once decorated the walls of the main reception hall.

"It could have been a wealthy landowner or a merchant," he said, swatting at a pesky swarm of gnats. "Or it could have been the local Roman tax collector's house. Degania was near a main caravan route, a convenient place for . . . eh, how do you say? . . . a customs booth."

"Why did everyone hate tax collectors back then?" Abby asked. "The New Testament talks about them as if they were the scum of the earth. I mean, I don't like to pay taxes either, but I don't take it out on the poor guy who works for the IRS."

"It was because most tax collectors cheated the people. It was an insult for Jews to pay taxes to their enemies in the first place, but the collectors took even more money than the Romans demanded, getting rich in the process. Do you remember when the Pharisees asked Jesus if it was all right to pay taxes to Caesar?"

"I think so. . . . Is that when Jesus asked whose picture was on the coin and said give to Caesar what is Caesar's and to God what is God's?"

"Yes. His enemies were trying to trap Him, and He knew it. If He said they should pay taxes to Rome, it would anger His followers, but if He said no, don't pay, his enemies could report him to the Romans for teaching the people to rebel. Jesus' answer was as wise as Solomon's was when he told the two women to divide the baby in half. His enemies were so amazed they walked away."

Abby had grown accustomed to hearing Hannah talk about Jesus, so it took her a moment to realize how extraordinary it was for Ari to mention Him. Before she could react, they were interrupted by a shout from one of the students digging in a nearby storage room.

"Dr. Bazak, come here! We found a bunch of painted pottery!"

"Let's go see." Ari offered Abby his hand to help her up. The smudges of dirt on his face made him look as endearing as a schoolboy.

The excited students showed them broken pieces of plates and bowls, all exquisitely painted. More remnants were still half-buried in a pile, as if the storeroom had once held a china cupboard. Ari handed Abby a potsherd. Unlike the chunky pieces they'd found in Leah's house, it was lightweight and delicate, with leaves and geometric designs painted in black on the brownish red clay.

"This is Nabatean pottery," Ari said as he carefully fitted two large sections together. "It's well known for its beauty and workmanship. We rarely find it unbroken because it is so fragile. Leave everything where it is and go get Dr. Rahov," he told the students. "Tell her to bring the camera."

"Oh my! It's beautiful, isn't it?" Hannah said when she arrived at the site. Her face seemed radiant. "God bless those clever Nabateans!"

Abby remembered that Hannah had met her husband while excavating Nabatean ruins. She kept forgetting to ask Hannah if she would have a chance to meet Jake this summer, but now wasn't the time. Hannah was busy snapping dozens of photographs, from every possible angle, to document their find.

Two days later, it was Abby's turn to make a discovery. While digging in the main reception hall, she found a slab of wood buried beneath the collapsed wall that Marwan was helping her remove. The board was about the size and shape of a book, with a narrow, raised border all around it like a frame. Remnants of a crumbly substance coated one side. She was carefully cleaning the frame with a toothbrush when she noticed something carved into the wood. Abby studied it closely, then stared in disbelief. It looked like the same three Hebrew letters she had found on the weaver's shuttle in the other house. She quickly called for Ari.

"Am I seeing things?" she asked. "Does that say what I think it does?"

Ari took his eyeglasses from his pocket to peer at it. "Yes . . ." he breathed. "It says *Leah* . . . Unbelievable!"

"What is this thing anyway?" she asked while they waited for Hannah to arrive. "What did I find?"

"It looks like a writing tablet. It would have been coated with wax—that's what this yellowish stuff is. When you wanted to write something, you carved into the wax, then you scraped it clean to erase it. Children used it like . . . how do you say . . . ?"

"A slate?"

"Yes, like a slate, to practice their letters."

"Do you think it could be the same Leah?" she asked Hannah after she'd arrived to examine it.

"Well, the name was common enough, but the ability to write it certainly wasn't."

"But why would she leave her personal things in two very different houses?"

"That's a good question," Hannah said. "Any ideas, Ari?"

He looked thoughtful as he combed his fingers through his woolly beard. "Well . . . if it is the same Leah, the only reason I can imagine is if the first house was her home but she worked here as a servant. Children were sometimes sold as servants if their fathers were unable to pay their debts."

"Sold!" Abby said. "That's terrible!"

"It was a fact of life back then," Ari said with a shrug. "We know from history that there was a famine here in the first century, around A.D. 46 or 47."

"Yes, good point," Hannah said. "Abby, you may recall the apostle Paul mentioning it in some of his letters. He collected funds among the Gentile Christians to help the Jewish brethren in Israel."

"The Jews were an enslaved people," Ari said. "Besides paying Roman taxes, every man also paid a yearly temple tax *and* a tithe of ten percent of all his crops to the priests. That left most farmers very poor."

"And a famine like the one in A.D. 47 would have ruined them," Hannah finished.

"How awful!" Abby said, shuddering. "To have to sell your own children!"

She thought about Leah that night as she lay in bed, wondering how she had coped after her life was thrown into turmoil. As turbulent as Abby's own life was at the moment, at least she wasn't facing overwhelming debt and servitude. Had Leah ever known happiness, or only poverty and disappointment?

THE VILLAGE OF DEGANIA—A.D. 48

You have no idea why Abba wants to see me?" Gideon asked as he and Leah hurried home through Degania's parched, dusty streets.

"No," she replied. "I already told you. Reb Nahum and Rabbi Eliezer came to the house with Reuben ben Johanan, that pig of a tax collector. Abba sent me inside while they talked, then Mama came inside and told me to run up to the fields and get you."

"Poor Abba," Gideon said, groaning. "If only it would rain. Nothing is growing in the fields. Saul's sheep can't find pasture . . . our grapes have all shriveled up. Reuben ben Johanan can't expect to collect taxes in the middle of a famine, can he?"

"I told you I don't know what he wants."

When they arrived home, Reuben and the other two men stood in the tiny courtyard with Abba, waiting. The tax collector wore a pale blue linen robe with a richly embroidered border of scarlet and gold threads. Leah knew she wasn't supposed to stare but she couldn't stop herself. It was the most beautiful garment she had ever seen. The coat that Jacob gave his favored son Joseph couldn't possibly have been more spectacular.

"This is my son Gideon . . . my daughter, Leah," Abba said.

His voice was so soft Leah wondered how Reb Reuben could even hear him. She felt the tax collector's gaze sweep over both of them. Then he gave Abba a curt nod and left with the other two men. The fragrant scent of perfumed oil trailed in his wake.

"Abba, what's going on?" Gideon asked. Their father didn't answer. Instead, he turned abruptly and ducked into the house. Gideon and Leah followed. "Why were they here, Abba? What did they want? And why did you send for me?" Fear made Gideon's voice shrill.

Abba paced in the cramped room, pulling at his beard as if he intended to pluck his face clean. "I can't . . . I . . . I need Saul. He can do a . . . a man's share of the work. Together we can grow enough to . . . and Matthew is too young . . . he . . ." Abba's voice sounded breathless, as if he had been the one to run all the way up to the pasture and back, not Leah.

"If this drought ever ends . . . if we can just grow enough

next year, I'll buy you back, Gideon, I'll redeem you—"

"You *sold* me?" Gideon cried. He shook his head in disbelief, as if trying to awaken from a dream. "Who . . . who did you sell me to?"

The lump on Abba's throat moved up and down as he swallowed. "Reuben ben Johanan. He agreed to take you . . . and Leah . . ."

"*Me?*" Leah cried. "You sold *me*, too?" She leaned against the stone wall, feeling dizzy. Her heart beat wildly, like the wings of a snared bird—for that was what she was. The district tax collector would be her master. If she burned the bread or spilled the soup, he wouldn't be patient and indulgent with her as Mama was. Leah would be beaten for her mistakes. What little freedom she had known was gone. Her life was over at age fourteen.

"You can't let him take us!" Gideon shouted. "It's bad enough that you sold me to that . . . that *sinner*, but not Leah! He probably uses his women as concubines!"

"That's enough!" Abba cried, halting his blind pacing.

Leah's terror rose up inside her like a flock of frightened sparrows at Gideon's words. She had dreaded the thought of marrying a village boy and sharing his bed, but to become the concubine of a man as hated and feared as Reuben ben Johanan was unimaginable!

"I had no choice," Abba said, his face stern. "I owed taxes to Rome. It was either this or . . . or my land . . . and how would we live if I sold my land?"

"How could you do this to us?" Gideon moaned. "Please, Abba . . . there must be some other way."

All of a sudden Abba's face seemed to crumble as the stern expression he always wore fell like a mask. He covered his face. "I'm sorry . . . I had no choice . . . Oh, God, forgive me!"

Abba had always held his children at a distance with his gruffness, but Leah suddenly saw what she had always suspected—that his outward manner really hid a deep, unfaltering love for his children. She wondered if God was the same—if the Pharisees' rigid code of laws and rules hid a loving Father from view? She went to Abba and tenderly rested her hand on his shoulder.

"I don't mind, Abba," she said softly. "I'm not afraid to work for him. The famine isn't your fault." For the first time Leah could ever remember, her father took her in his arms and held her tightly. But when she looked up, Gideon was gone.

Leah and Gideon left home at dawn the next day and slowly walked across town to the tax collector's villa. Leah carried her meager possessions bundled inside her shawl, but Gideon had taken nothing except the clothes on his back. Leah knew that word of their servitude had already spread throughout the village when their fellow townspeople quickly turned aside as they approached. No one would meet her eye. She now belonged to the most hated man in town.

"At least we'll eat," Leah said, trying to be courageous. "Even if the drought continues we won't starve to death. He has to feed us."

"You don't know that." Gideon kicked a stone in his path and sent it flying. "Reuben's servants never mix with the other villagers. We don't know what goes on in his house."

Leah had stayed awake all night, unable to sleep at the thought of what she faced. By dawn she was certain she had run out of tears, but they still rolled down her cheeks in spite of her efforts to stop them. "Do you think we'll ever go free again?" she asked, wiping her eyes. Gideon shrugged.

"The rabbi told me that according to the Torah, even if Abba can't redeem us, a manservant has to be set free after seven years."

"A man-servant . . . but what about a woman-servant?"

Leah could see from Gideon's face how upset he was, how reluctant he was to answer her. "He said that Reuben has a right to . . . to *take* you. But afterward, if he isn't pleased, he must let you be redeemed."

Leah drew a shuddering breath as she tried to compose herself. "Maybe Abba will redeem both of us before then. And who knows, I'm not much to look at, maybe Reb Reuben won't . . ." Fear choked off her words before she could finish them.

Gideon stopped walking. "See this?" He showed Leah a small knife in a leather pouch that he had hidden in the folds of his tunic. "I'll protect you, Leah. If that pig tries to come near you, I'll—"

"Don't, Gideon," she said, laying her hand on his arm. "It's wrong to kill. Besides, Abba would have married me off to someone in a year or two, anyway—probably someone as poor as we are. This way, at least I'll always be well-provided for."

Gideon exhaled as he hid the knife again. "The rabbi also said that when it comes time to set us free, Reuben can't send us away empty-handed."

"Do you really think Reuben ben Johanan will obey the Torah?" Leah asked. "Everyone knows what a notorious sinner he is. I've heard that he even eats with Gentiles."

"We could run away," Gideon said.

But Leah had considered that option during the night and decided it would be hopeless to run. "Where? Where could we go? He would probably send Roman soldiers after us. Either that or he would just take Matthew and Saul instead of us." She nudged Gideon to start him walking again.

A few minutes later the villa's red-tiled roof appeared in the distance above the trees. Leah's stomach lurched. It was a huge, rambling structure, nearly the size of the village synagogue, but very plain on the outside. They knew better than to go to the pillared main entrance, or the customs house door, which opened from the side of the villa onto one of Degania's commercial streets. Instead, they walked all the way around to the servants' entrance in back. A gate led into a walled-in courtyard with a huge outdoor oven and the villa's stables and sheds. The pungent aroma of livestock greeted them. An older woman who was shaking out a crumb-filled cloth for the chickens saw them enter the gate and beckoned to them.

"Ehud, they're here," she called into one of the sheds.

Leah dried all her tears and took a deep breath for courage. The woman smiled, though it must have been obvious to her that Leah had been crying. She appeared to be Mama's age or maybe a few years older, with gray-threaded brown hair that was neatly coiled into a knot on top of her head. Her full, round face was red-cheeked and pleasant, her body short and square.

"You must be Leah and Gideon," she said. "Welcome. Master Reuben told us you would be coming today. My name is Miriam, and this is my husband, Ehud." A brawny, barrel-chested man emerged from the shed and nodded to them in greeting. His sun-weathered face was rugged and forbidding.

"The first thing I should do," Miriam said, "is show you to your quarters—even though you won't be staying in them just yet, Gideon. You're needed right away to help tend the master's flocks. Ehud will take you there this morning. Have you eaten?"

Leah was about to answer that they had, meager though it had been, but Gideon spoke up first. "No, ma'am. There isn't much to eat at our house these days."

"Mmm," she purred. "Come inside, then, and eat something before you leave. It's a very long walk. Ehud says the shepherds must range farther and farther into the hills to find pasture because of the drought."

Leah worried that Gideon would go to Sheol for lying, but as Miriam led them into a small side room and began laying out bread, dried fruit, and even a precious lump of cheese for them to eat, Leah was very grateful that he had. She and Gideon dove into the food as if they hadn't eaten in a year. When they finished, Leah's stomach felt full for the first time since Passover.

"You were hungry, poor things," Miriam murmured. Leah felt her face flush. "I've cleared a place for you to sleep in here with the other serving girls, Leah. Gideon, you may put your things—"

"I don't have any things."

"I see. Well, you'll need to take a spare bedroll up into the hills, then. It gets cold at night."

As Miriam bustled around, putting together a warm cloak and other supplies for Gideon, Leah stole a peek at her new surroundings. The work areas were spacious and clean, and the two other servant girls, who were kneading dough and filling a tray with food, smiled pleasantly at her. When the girl with the tray slipped through the door with it, Leah caught a glimpse of a tiled courtyard in the center of the villa surrounded by rows of pillars before the door swung closed again.

"Is the boy ready?" Ehud stood in the outside doorway with a staff in his hand.

"Yes," Miriam answered. "Here, I packed you both some provisions for the journey."

Tears brimmed in Leah's eyes. Her brother couldn't be leaving her so soon. She wanted to beg Ehud and Miriam to let Gideon stay here with her, but she didn't dare. Their lives were no longer their own. "Shalom, Gideon," she whispered.

"Shalom." His voice was gruff with emotion. Leah wanted to run to him, cling to him one last time, but she couldn't move. A moment later, he was gone. For the first time in her life, Leah felt horribly alone.

Miriam and the other servants continued with their work while Leah stood in the middle of the room, struggling to come to grips with her sorrow. Her family and her home had been lost to her overnight . . . but she had never imagined that Gideon would be ripped away from her so suddenly, too.

"Leah, dear, would you please hand me that platter?" Miriam asked. She pointed to a low shelf where a pile of beautifully decorated bowls and plates were stacked.

Leah reached for the serving platter, her vision blurred by tears, and misjudged its weight. It was so light it flew right out of her hand and smashed into pieces on the cobblestone floor.

"Oh no! I'm sorry!" Leah sank to her knees, scooping up the broken pieces, desperately trying to fit the largest ones together with shaking hands. She cowered in fear of what her punishment would be. Miriam knelt beside her and gently caught Leah's wrists, stopping her.

"It's all right, honey. It's just an old plate. Master has plenty more." Leah began to sob.

"My goodness, you're shaking all over," Miriam said. "What are you so afraid of, Leah? You don't need to fear our master or anyone else in this house. If you do what you're told and don't steal from him or try to run away, no one is ever going to mistreat you. This was an accident. You have nothing to be afraid of, hmm?"

Leah knew she should hold her tongue. How many times had Mama scolded her for being too outspoken? But the words tumbled from her mouth before she could stop them. "The rabbi said the master could make me his concubine."

"No. Oh, honey, no. Not Master Reuben. He loves Mistress Ruth very, very much. He would never hurt her by taking a concubine."

Sorrow and relief and loss all flooded together in a surge of emotion. Leah covered her face and wept. Miriam gathered her into her ample arms and rocked her like Mama used to rock Matthew when he was a baby.

"Mm . . . mm . . . mm," she soothed. "You go ahead and cry if you need to, honey. I know just how you feel. I had to leave my home and go to work for Mistress Ruth's father when I was even younger than you are. I surely know how scared you are. But I promise you, no one here is ever going to lay a hand on you."

"Everyone in town says . . . what a terrible sinner Reb Reuben is . . . so I thought—"

"It's not true, honey. He's no more of a sinner than you and I. Just a kind, lonely young man who has been handed a dirty job to do. I've worked for Master Reuben for more than seven years—ever since he and my mistress were married. I could have gone free—Ehud and I both could have. But see here?" She fingered a loop of gold that pierced her earlobe, the emblem of a bond servant. "We've chosen to stay."

"I . . . I'm sorry about the plate."

"Never mind. I'm sure it wasn't easy to leave your family

or your brother like that. We've surely seen some hard times with this drought, yes? But we have to keep trusting in the Almighty One no matter what."

"How do we do that?"

"Why, once you know Him, it's easy—He's so very trustworthy. As the prophets said, 'Though the fig tree does not bud and there are no grapes on the vines, though the olive crop fails and the fields produce no food . . . yet I will rejoice in the Lord, I will be joyful in God my Savior.' Even in hard times we can find joy in the Lord."

For the next few days Leah was given only light chores to do—cleaning fish, sweeping the kitchen floor, keeping the kitchen fires going. "Until you get settled in," Miriam said, "and have time to adjust to your new home." She was very kind to Leah and much more patient with her than Mama had been. Leah saw nothing of the rest of the villa except for a few brief glimpses of the central courtyard through the swinging door.

As she sat outside in the servants' yard one morning, grinding grain with a hand mill, Leah realized that for the moment, she was alone—Miriam and all of the other servants were away on errands. She laid aside the grinding stone and smoothed a place in the dust to write. Matthew had taught her all the letters of the alphabet and the sounds they made, but she knew that if she didn't keep practicing them, she would soon lose her new skill. Humming the alphabet song she had learned from Matthew, she carefully scribed each letter in the dust with her finger until she reached *ayin*. She couldn't remember how to write the letter ayin.

Tears of frustration and homesickness filled her eyes. It was hopeless. Without Matthew or Gideon to help her, she would eventually forget all that she had learned. Leah lowered her head into her lap and wept as she struggled to remember. Suddenly she heard the outer gate open, then close. She didn't know which to wipe away first, the writing or her tears. She tried to do both, quickly swiping at her tears with dusty hands, smudging her face with dirt. When she looked up, she was horrified to see Reb Reuben in his beautiful blue robe standing over her. Why was he coming through the servants' gate? She was too stunned and confused to remember to bow to him.

"Your name is Leah, isn't it?" he asked. "The new girl?"

"Y . . . yes, my lord."

Leah took a good look at Reuben ben Johanan for the first time in her life and was surprised to see that he wasn't nearly as old as she had always thought. Because of his stature as the district tax collector, Leah had imagined that he must be as old as Abba, maybe even older. But up close, she saw that he was barely thirty. His dark brown hair looked shiny and luxuriant, like a lion's mane. His beard wasn't long, the way the village elders traditionally wore theirs, but neatly trimmed around the curve of his strong chin. His eyes were wide and deep set, a dark, plummy brown like sweet raisins. As they held hers in his powerful gaze, she was astounded to see that they were filled with compassion.

"You've been crying," he said. "Are you unhappy here?"

"No, my lord. It's nothing . . ." She wiped her eyes with her fists.

"Then why?" He was waiting for an answer.

"It's just . . . I couldn't remember something, and my brother isn't here to show me."

"You miss your brother?"

"Yes, my lord."

She bowed her head and stared down at her feet, then saw that she hadn't completely erased all of the letters.

Master Reuben must have seen them, too, for a moment later he said, "Did you write these letters, Leah?"

She nodded, too terrified to speak, afraid he would curse such foolishness as Abba would have done.

"Do you have an interest in learning?" he asked.

His deep voice was gentle, not critical. Miriam had said he was kind. Leah took a chance.

"Yes, my lord. My brother taught me the alphabet, but now I can't remember how to write ayin." She glanced up to see his reaction. One hand covered his chin as he thoughtfully stroked his beard. His hands were smooth, uncallused, his fingernails clean and oval shaped. He wore a beautiful ring on his fourth finger, with a deep blue stone the color of the sea.

"Come with me, Leah," he said suddenly.

Her knees trembled as she followed him into the kitchen and through the swinging door. She would finally see the beautifully tiled courtyard. But Master Reuben's stride was so smooth and swift she had little time to look around as she trotted behind him. He led her between two pillars, through another door, and into a side room. It was a workroom of some sort, with benches and tables that were littered with pots of ink, containers of reed pens, writing instruments, and piles and piles of scrolls—more scrolls than Leah had seen in her entire life. The musky smell of parchment filled the room. Two scribes worked side by side at the tables, beneath bronze lampstands. Leah was amazed to see that the oil lamps were lit in the daytime.

Before she could take it all in, Master Reuben picked up a wooden tablet coated with wax. She had seen the tablets Matthew and the other boys used in the synagogue to practice their writing, but those were crude blocks compared to this beautifully crafted one. Reuben sorted through a clutter of objects on one of the tables, found the writing tool he wanted, and carved something into the wax.

"Here," he said, holding the tablet out to her. "That's the letter ayin."

Leah was so stunned she could barely speak. "Yes. Thank you, my lord!" She bowed low again and began backing away.

"Leah . . ." She froze. "You may keep this."

She looked up, astonished as he held out the tablet and writing stick to her. "Yes, it's all right, you may have them," he said, "unless you like writing in the dust and getting dirt all over your face." His smile was so kind, so warm, she couldn't help but smile in return as she accepted his gift.

"Yes . . . I mean, no, my lord . . . I mean, thank you so much!"

"You're welcome."

He nodded in dismissal, and Leah fled to the servants' quarters on a cloud of happiness, clutching his gift. She carefully tucked it away beneath her sleeping mat before returning to her task of grinding grain. Then, as she rolled the stones together in rhythm, Leah's heart soared with the words that Miriam had taught her: *"Though the fig tree does not bud and there are no grapes on the vines . . . yet I will rejoice in the Lord. . . ."*

THE VILLAGE OF DEGANIA—A.D. 48

Gideon, come here. I want to show you something." Leah led him down the dark passageway to the tiny chamber where she and the other serving girls slept. He had just returned that day from tending the master's flocks after being gone all spring and summer. Leah barely recognized him at first. His skin was deeply tanned, his curly hair bleached golden by the sun. The oily smell of lanolin and sheep clung to his clothing. But it was Gideon's nature that seemed the most changed; he looked restless, angry, and deeply unhappy. She pulled her writing tablet from under her sleeping mat and proudly showed it to him, hoping it would cheer him to see that she had been treated kindly while he was away.

"Where did you get that? Did you steal it?"

"No, of course not! I would never do such a thing. Master Reuben gave it to me."

"You're lying!"

The accusation felt like a slap in the face. She stared at him. "What happened to you, Gideon?"

"The same thing that happened to you—we were sold. We're servants now, owned by the biggest sinner in Galilee."

"We have no reason to hate Master Reuben. He's kind to his servants, he feeds us better than we ever ate at home, he hasn't overworked us or abused us . . . and he did give me this writing tablet, whether you believe me or not!"

"He has grown rich by working for our enemies. That's more than enough reason to hate him."

"You're right, our master is very rich. But all the money in Galilee can't buy him happiness. This is a house of sadness, Gideon. Miriam told me so. She's worked for Mistress Ruth's family since she was my age, and she came here when Ruth married our master. He loves his wife very much, but her babies keep dying before they are born."

"That's God's judgment on him for his sin."

Leah was so angry she gave her brother a shove. "What's wrong with you? You sound just like the Pharisees! You're not the brother I knew!" She turned to storm out of the room, but he stopped her.

"Wait, Leah . . . I'm sorry." He ran his hand over his face as if to clear the anger from it, then sighed. "It's just . . . it's just so hard to take care of someone else's sheep all day, knowing that it will do me no good if they fatten and prosper— they'll never be mine. At least when I worked beside Abba and Saul, I knew that someday I would get a portion back from all my labor as an inheritance. But now everything is Reuben ben Johanan's—the wool is his, the profit is his. I can't even save for a wife or a future of my own. And nothing's going to change for the next seven years. I'll be an old man by then."

Leah rested her hand on his arm. "Miriam and Ehud are both servants and they got married. It was their own choice to stay and work here."

He smiled weakly. "Do you think any of the serving girls around here would want to marry me?"

"Well . . . not until you've had a bath."

Gideon laughed, and he was the brother Leah loved once again. He took the writing tablet from her and ran his fingers over its smooth frame. "This is nice. Did he really say you could keep it?"

"Yes." Leah told him the story of how the master had seen

her writing the alphabet and had shown her how to write ayin. "I want to learn to read, Gideon," she said excitedly. "Will you teach me how?"

"Why? What use is it for a girl to read, especially a servant girl?"

"I don't know. I just want to learn. Please? It will give us something to do together and help pass the time."

In the end, Gideon agreed. He sat down with her for a few minutes each evening after their work was finished and wrote new words on her writing board for her to practice. Leah carefully saved each sliver of wax whenever she scraped the board clean so that she could melt it down and coat the board with it over and over. By the time spring rolled around again and Gideon had to return to the master's fields, he had taught her to read all the words he could remember.

"Do you suppose I know enough to read an entire scroll?" she asked him just before he left.

"I don't see why not. Words are words, whether they're written on scrolls or tablets. But where do you think you're going to get a scroll, Leah? The master may have given you a writing board, but he's never going to let you near his scrolls."

Leah knew Gideon was right. She was a kitchen maid and wasn't even allowed inside the other rooms of the villa where the scrolls were kept. Except for the day the master had given her the tablet, she had never been beyond the central courtyard. Once in a while Miriam would ask her to sweep it, and Leah would try to peek inside the other rooms if the doors were open. The main reception room was her favorite, its stucco walls beautifully decorated with ornate friezes and imitation marble panels.

Leah was sweeping the tiled courtyard on a warm summer day when she noticed that the door to the room where Master Reuben had taken her stood open. She slowly worked her way around the square with her broom, then stole a peek inside as she swept. The room was dark, the lamps snuffed out, the scribes gone home for the day. Leah glanced all around the courtyard, and when she saw no other servants in sight, she peeked again. A scroll lay propped open on a table.

The temptation was too great to resist. Laying her broom beside the door, Leah looked around again, then slipped inside. Careful not to touch anything, she bent over the opened scroll and began to read. *And you present to the Lord offerings made by fire, from the herd or the flock, as . . .* She paused, not recognizing the next word, then continued. *. . . pleasing to the Lord—whether burnt offerings or sacrifices, for special vows or free-will offerings or . . .* Again she skipped an unfamiliar word. *. . . offerings—then the one who brings his offering shall present to the Lord a grain offering of a tenth of an ephah of fine flour mixed with a* something *of a hin of oil . . .*

She could read! Not every word, but enough of them to feel a surge of triumph that made her want to shout! She hugged herself in joy.

Suddenly the door from the street opened. Leah dropped to the floor like a stone dropping into water and hid beneath the table. She heard the door close, then footsteps crossing the room. She crouched into a tiny ball as Master Reuben glided past her. She saw his sandaled feet and recognized the fragrance of the scented lotion he always used. He was nearly through the door to the courtyard when he stopped.

Her broom! She had left it lying outside the door. He whirled around and saw her.

"Stand up!" he said angrily. She obeyed, trying to bow to him at the same time. "What are you doing in here?"

"Reading, my lord."

"What? Hold out your hands. What did you take?"

"N-nothing, my lord." She spread her hands, palms up, to show that they were empty.

"Untie your belt. Take off your robe."

Terrified, Leah did as she was told until she stood before him in only her undertunic. He gave her robe a shake so that anything she had hidden in it would fall to the floor. His face was very angry, not kind as it had been the last time.

"Tell me what you were doing in here," he said again.

"My brother has been teaching me to read words . . . on

the writing tablet you gave me. I wanted to see if I could read them if they were all written out on a scroll. I only looked at this one, my lord. I'm sorry." She trembled all over, certain that she had earned a beating.

"And could you?" he asked after a moment. She looked up at him, not understanding. "Could you read it?" he asked again, picking up the scroll, then tossing it down.

"Yes, my lord . . . most of the words."

"Show me." The scroll rattled as she held it in shaking hands. Leah began reading where she had started before and stopped when he said, "That's enough."

She quickly set the scroll down and stared at her feet, afraid to look at him. The silence between them stretched and lengthened like the spinning of a very long thread. And like that long thread, Leah's nerves stretched thinner and thinner until she was certain they would snap. Tears filled her eyes. The room was warm but she stood shivering in her under-tunic.

Suddenly Master Reuben crossed to the other side of the room. She heard him rummaging for something and wondered if he was looking for a stick to beat her. Then he came back to stand in front of her again. She saw only his feet, not daring to looking up.

"Leah."

"Yes, my lord?"

"Take this to your quarters and see if you can read it." She lifted her head and was astounded to see that he held out a scroll to her. She couldn't speak. "The physicians have confined my wife to her bed until our child is born. It would help her pass the time if you could read to her."

He thrust the scroll into her hands before she could reply, then strode from the room.

———

Leah was both excited and terrified as she followed Miriam into their mistress's bedchamber the following afternoon, clutching Master Reuben's scroll. She had practiced reading it the night before until it was too dark to see, guessing at the words she didn't know, recalling the plot from hearing it read in the synagogue. It was the beautiful story of Ruth, King David's ancestress.

Leah's mistress, also named Ruth, reclined on an ornate sleeping couch before an open window. Beyond it, water splashed in a small flower-filled courtyard. The scent of the mistress's perfume permeated the room until Leah could taste it on her tongue.

Confined to the kitchen, Leah had never seen Ruth up close before, and she was startled by how very beautiful she was. She wore cosmetics on her eyes, and her chestnut hair was piled on her head in the elaborate style of the Gentiles. But Mistress Ruth was painfully thin, even thinner than Leah, who had gone hungry most of her life. Her womb made a small bulge beneath her embroidered linen robe.

"Who are you?" she said when she saw Leah. "I didn't ask for another chambermaid."

"This is Leah, Mistress Ruth," Miriam replied. "Master Reuben sent her here to help you pass the time. She is going to read to you, my lady."

"Read! This slip of a girl can read? Why, who ever heard of such a thing!"

Her smile was radiant, briefly lighting her elegant face like a shooting star blazing across the darkened heavens. Leah couldn't help staring. No wonder Master Reuben didn't take a concubine. No other woman could compare with his wife. Leah was so mesmerized, it took her a moment to realize that her mistress had asked her a question.

"Um . . . where did I learn to read, my lady? My brother taught me, my lady. He learned at the synagogue school, my lady." She felt bumbling and crude beside her mistress, scarcely able to think or speak.

"Well, I can't wait to hear this for myself. Sit down, Leah. Tell me what you brought to read." Miriam shoved a small cushioned stool beneath Leah and she sank onto it gratefully.

"It's the story of a Moabite woman named Ruth. She was

the ancestress of King David. . . . It's a love story." Leah nervously opened the scroll, discovered she was holding it upside down, then blushed as she turned it over. She cleared her throat. " 'In the days when the judges ruled,' " she began, " 'there was a famine in the land, and a man from Bethlehem in Judah, together with his wife and two sons, went to live for a while in the country of Moab . . .' "

Leah put her whole heart into it, trying not to read in a boring monotone as Rabbi Eliezer always did, but adding life and drama to the words. When she glanced up from time to time, both Ruth and Miriam sat listening to her as if in a trance. The afternoon flew, until she found herself reading the final words:

" 'And the Lord enabled her to conceive, and she gave birth to a son. The women said to Naomi: "Praise be to the Lord, who this day has not left you without a kinsman-redeemer. May he become famous throughout Israel! He will renew your life and sustain you in your old age. For your daughter-in-law, who loves you and who is better to you than seven sons, has given him birth." ' "

Mistress Ruth had tears in her eyes when Leah finished. "What a beautiful story. I had forgotten. . . . It's been so long since I've heard it."

"Why don't you take a little nap now," Miriam said, tucking a shawl around her mistress. "I'm sure that Leah would be happy to return another day and read again, mmm?" Miriam's love for Ruth showed in the gentle touch of her hands as she smoothed the blanket.

"Does Mistress Ruth ever go out of the house?" Leah asked as she and Miriam returned to the kitchen. "I've never seen her in the village or in the synagogue."

"She goes to Caesarea or Sepphoris with Master Reuben sometimes, but she wouldn't be caught dead in Degania."

"Why not?"

"Because of the Pharisees. She's taken more than her share of abuse from them, so I don't blame her in the least. Imagine, men who claim to be godly, spitting on that poor woman!"

"But why?"

"Partly because she doesn't believe in following all their picky rules about baths and things . . . but mostly because she's the wife of the tax collector."

Leah was still thinking about the Pharisees' cruelty when she returned to Mistress Ruth's room a few days later to read the Book of Esther. As she closed the scroll, satisfied that Queen Esther's enemy had received the punishment he deserved, all of Leah's own frustrations with the Pharisees came bubbling to the surface like a pot of soup on a hot fire. Without thinking she said, "Have you ever noticed how all of the Pharisees in Degania resemble farm animals, Mistress Ruth?"

Ruth looked startled. "Farm animals?"

"Oh yes. The village is a regular barnyard! Take Rabbi Eliezer, for example—he's the very image of a billy goat with his long, thin face and that ratty gray beard of his. He's always butting into everybody's business, too, just like an old he-goat."

Ruth laughed out loud, and the sound reminded Leah of beautiful music, the notes ascending and descending in a rich, melodic sound.

"Reb Nahum is an old speckled hen with a fat breast," she continued. "He pecks all around the village with his sharp beak, examining every little particle of dirt or bug that he imagines he sees. He even has one of those chicken wattles beneath his chin that wiggles back and forth when he squawks."

"Leah, you're outrageous!" Ruth said, laughing helplessly. Her joy spurred Leah on. She stood to pantomime her victims as she described them.

"Reb Moshe is an ox—fat, slow, and dumb. He doesn't read the Scriptures. He plods over the words, trampling them beneath his heavy feet. I walked behind him in the street once, and his buttocks swayed back and forth exactly like an ox's hindquarters when he walked. Reb Joseph is a donkey—can't you tell by those huge ears? He uses them to listen to every word that's whispered in Degania. And have you ever heard him laugh? He sounds just like a donkey braying!" Ruth was laughing so hard she was in tears. "And Reb—"

Leah stopped when she looked up and saw Master Reuben. He was watching Ruth from the doorway. He saw no one else in the room but her, and when she stretched out her hand to him, he went straight to her side, kneeling beside her couch. Leah knew he had been drawn by the magical sound of her laughter. His eyes shone with love for her.

As Leah quietly slipped from the room, she heard Ruth say, "Thank you, darling, for sending Leah to me. She's so much fun!"

Leah read to Ruth nearly every day until her baby was born four months later. Ruth's labor was long and very difficult, and Leah was glad that Master Reuben had gone to Caesarea for a few days on business and didn't have to hear his wife's screams.

"Mistress Ruth had a little daughter," Miriam told Leah when it was finally over. "She named her Elizabeth. They're both resting now, but the mistress wants you to come and see her later on."

Leah fixed her mistress a supper tray that evening and took it to her. Ruth was holding Elizabeth, trying to soothe her, but the baby was fussing. "She just ate . . . I don't know what is bothering her," Ruth said. Miriam scooped the baby from her arms.

"I'll take her, Mistress Ruth," Miriam said. "You go ahead and eat some of that nice dinner Leah brought you." She bounced and jostled and cooed, but the baby only grew fussier.

"May I try?" Leah said at last. She took Elizabeth into her arms and began talking softly to her. Much to Leah's own surprise, the baby stopped crying and soon fell asleep.

"It's your voice, Leah," Ruth said. "She recognizes your voice from all the reading you did."

Leah was in Ruth's room, rocking Elizabeth, when Master Reuben arrived home. He went straight to his wife's side, still dressed in his traveling clothes.

"Ruth, thank God you're all right!"

Leah was surprised when Ruth suddenly burst into tears. "I'm sorry, Reuben. I'm so sorry . . . I didn't give you a son." He sat beside her on the bed and pulled her into his arms.

"Oh, Ruth . . . can't you see it doesn't matter? The child is healthy and strong, isn't she? Once you get well I'll be the happiest man alive."

Leah felt like an intruder. In her entire life, she had never heard a man speak to a woman as tenderly as the master spoke to his wife. Embarrassed to be eavesdropping, she tried to lay Elizabeth down as quickly as she could without waking her so she could slip from the room.

"No, bring her here, Leah," Master Reuben said. "I'd like to see my new daughter."

Leah carried Elizabeth to the bedside, folding back the blanket so he could see her tiny face. But it was Master Reuben's face that Leah watched. His eyes glowed with happiness as he studied his child, cupping the baby's cheek in his large hand.

"She's lovely, Ruth . . . nearly as lovely as you are."

Leah bent and laid the child in Mistress Ruth's arms, then tiptoed to the door. "When Elizabeth is older," she heard Ruth say, "maybe Leah can teach her to read, like a boy."

"Anything, Ruth. Anything you want. Just get well, my love."

While Miriam took care of Mistress Ruth, it became Leah's full-time job to take care of baby Elizabeth. With the help of a wet nurse, Elizabeth grew into a plump, happy baby with a sweet cherub face and her mother's chestnut hair. But Ruth was not getting well. Master Reuben hired legions of physicians who tried all manner of remedies and poultices in the months that followed. He even took Ruth to the Roman hot baths for a course of treatment. Nothing helped.

Leah now slept in the baby's room, next door to Ruth's, and she overheard Master Reuben shouting at the physicians one morning. "I don't care what it takes! I don't care what it costs! Make her well, do you hear me?"

Each day Elizabeth grew stronger and sturdier as Ruth grew thinner and paler. Elizabeth was walking by the time she was a year old, clinging to Leah's fingers, but Ruth had become too weak to rise from her bed. The slightest movement brought her pain, as if even her bones ached.

"She's dying, isn't she?" Leah whispered to Miriam as they left her room one day.

"Don't say such a thing!" Miriam cried. "Don't you even think such a thing!"

But Leah knew that it was true.

Swallowing his pride, Master Reuben went to the religious leaders at the synagogue. "Please . . . may I come to the Sabbath services? Would you help me, pray with me . . . for my wife?"

"We won't stop you from attending, but you cannot sit with the men of Israel. You and your household must sit with the Gentiles."

"Listen, I would like to donate some money to your synagogue or . . . or to the poor," Reuben said, pulling a leather pouch from inside his robe. "Whatever it would take to gain the Almighty One's blessing—"

The Pharisees spit on his money and threw it back at him.

Leah and Miriam also began going to the synagogue with him to pray for their beloved mistress. They were there one Sabbath when a visitor came. As custom prescribed, he was invited to read the Scripture. The prophetic passage was from the Book of Isaiah.

" 'But he was pierced for our transgressions, he was crushed for our iniquities; the punishment that brought us peace was upon him, and by his wounds we are healed. We all, like sheep, have gone astray, each of us has turned to his own way; and the Lord has laid on him the iniquity of us all.' "

The stranger looked familiar to Leah, but it wasn't until he mentioned sheep that she remembered why. He was the same man who had preached about the wicked shepherds in the Temple in Jerusalem a few years ago, the man who resembled a little brown-furred coney. She listened with rapt attention as he began to speak.

"Many of you remember Rabbi Yeshua, the Nazarene—how He walked among us, teaching us about the Kingdom of God and working wonders and miracles. Yeshua was the promised Messiah that the prophet Isaiah spoke about in the passage I just read. He brought God's promised redemption to all of us by becoming the Lamb of God, sacrificed to bear the iniquity of us all."

It was very clear that the man had only begun his discourse, but Leah watched in amazement as Reb Nahum rudely stood up and thanked the stranger as if he were finished. Then Nahum signaled to the rabbi to continue with the remainder of the service.

The preacher calmly held up his hand and said, "One more comment, if I may. The redemption Yeshua brought is not just for the Jews. It is for all people." His gaze swept the Gentile section where Master Reuben and his household were forced to sit. Then he said no more.

After the service, all of Degania lingered on the synagogue steps to hear more from the visitor. Leah and Miriam gathered with them, and even Master Reuben stayed instead of hurrying away as he usually did.

"I heard Yeshua the Nazarene preach once," Miriam whispered to Leah. "And I saw Him drive an unclean spirit from a boy. How I hoped that He was the promised Messiah, but when nothing changed . . . when we remained under Roman rule . . ." She sadly shook her head.

Leah inched closer, listening as the Pharisees argued with the stranger beneath the synagogue pillars.

"How could you call a man 'righteous' who died such a shameful death?" Reb Nahum shouted. "The Scriptures say, 'Cursed is anyone who is hung on a tree!' "

"You are exactly right, my friend. Yeshua became cursed by God for us. He bore the wrath of God that we deserve."

"The Scriptures say the Messiah will bring deliverance," Rabbi Eliezer added. "If Yeshua was the Messiah, why are we still burdened with Roman rule?" He gestured toward Master Reuben as if he were a hated Roman.

"Because the Messiah's kingdom isn't out *there*," the visitor said with a sweep of his arm. "His kingdom is within us. And it has come! When God brought redemption to our ancestors through Moses, they were set free from slavery, but they still had to cross the Red Sea themselves. They still had to walk through the desert and fight to conquer the land until God's kingdom of Israel was established. Yeshua *did* bring redemption. He canceled our sins so that we are no longer slaves to it, but we still must conquer the giants of sin and unforgiveness through His power in order to establish the kingdom that He died to bring."

As Leah looked around at the other villagers, she saw that they were listening just as attentively and as hopefully as she was. Rabbi Eliezer must have noticed, too.

"We're not interested in your heresy," he shouted. "Be on your way!" He nodded his narrow billy-goat head in the direction of the main road out of town as if he intended to butt the stranger off the steps. "Be gone! You're not welcome here!"

"You're welcome in my home."

Leah recognized Master Reuben's voice. He pushed his way between the gathered Pharisees until he stood before the stranger.

"I'm Reuben ben Johanan. Would you share the Sabbath meal with me? I would like to hear more."

"Yes, thank you," the man replied. "My name is Nathaniel ben Joseph." He followed Reuben down the steps as the crowd parted to let them through.

"You don't know the kind of sinner that man is!" Reb Nahum shouted behind them. "He collects taxes for Rome! He eats with Gentiles and sinners! Neither he nor his household keeps the Law!"

The stranger paused, turning back to Reb Nahum. "Yeshua the Messiah once said, 'I did not come to call the righteous into God's Kingdom, but sinners.' "

Back at the villa, Miriam supervised the kitchen servants as they hurried to spread the table for their guest. Leah ate in her room with Elizabeth as usual, but after the meal, Reuben assembled the entire household, including all of the servants, to listen to Nathaniel preach. Master Reuben himself lifted Ruth into his arms and carried her into the reception room. Leah sat on the floor beside Gideon, but she could tell by her brother's stiff posture and scowling features that he was skeptical.

"God extends His grace through His Son to everyone— even tax collectors," the preacher said, smiling. "In fact, one of Yeshua's chosen disciples was a tax collector."

"Was the man's name Matthew?" Master Reuben asked quietly.

"Yes, that's right. Did you know him?"

Reuben shook his head. "No, but my father did. Matthew invited Abba and a few other tax collectors to a feast with Yeshua the Nazarene. My father never forgot how . . . how compassionate the rabbi was. He said it was the first time in his life—the only time in his life—that a rabbi treated him like a man, with dignity. Later we heard that the religious leaders had the Nazarene executed."

"Yes, but Yeshua is alive! God raised Him to life on the third day as it was written: ' "You will not abandon me to the grave, nor will you let your Holy One see decay." ' I am a witness, as are countless others, that Yeshua rose from the grave."

For the rest of the afternoon, Nathaniel wove Scriptures together like a master weaver until he had produced a stunning tapestry of the Messiah—a portrait fulfilled in the person of Yeshua the Nazarene. He talked about the new covenant God promised His people through the prophet Jeremiah: " 'I will put my law in their minds and write it on their hearts. . . .' " Leah recited the beautiful words along with him: " 'I will be their God, and they will be my people. No longer will a man teach his neighbor, or a man his brother, saying, "Know the Lord," because they will all know me, from the least of them to the greatest. . . . For I will forgive their wickedness and will remember their sins no more.' "

"God sent His Son," Nathaniel said, "born of a woman, born under the Law, so that He could set all of us free from that Law. In Christ we have our rightful heritage as sons, the privilege of close conversation with God our Father, just as our own children call their fathers *Abba*. God's promised redemption is fulfilled, but it comes by faith, not by the Law, just as it did for our father Abraham."

Hours later, Nathaniel finished. The fire blazing inside him had finally spent its fuel. The silence he left was broken by a voice as fragile as butterfly wings. "I want to be baptized," Mistress Ruth said. "I need the forgiveness Yeshua offers. I've been bitter toward my enemies, and that bitterness has turned me away from God. I know that I'm dying—"

"Ruth . . . no!"

"It's all right, Reuben. I've accepted it. But I need to settle my accounts with God. I want to accept Yeshua's offer to be the sacrifice for my sins."

Master Reuben stood and lifted Ruth into his arms. Leah followed as he carried her to their private mikveh. She watched as her master descended into the water in his Sabbath robes, carrying his dying wife in his arms. His love for her and his helpless despair were written on his features as if carved in the wax on Leah's tablet.

The preacher crowded into the mikveh beside them, his hands raised to heaven. "My sister Ruth, I baptize you in the name of the Father . . . and of the Son . . . and of the Holy Spirit. Amen."

A week later, on a rainy Sabbath afternoon, Ruth died.

———

The sound of weeping awakened Leah in the night. She rose from her mat at the foot of Elizabeth's bed to comfort the child. Barely eighteen months old, Elizabeth was too young to comprehend what had happened to her mother, why the lovely woman in the room next door was suddenly gone, why the entire household had plunged into deep mourning. Nor had Leah herself finished grieving for Ruth. She had grown to love her mistress. The empty place Ruth left in Leah's heart seemed as dark and as vast as the cloudy sky above Galilee.

But when Leah knelt at Elizabeth's bedside, she saw that the child was still asleep. Listening in the darkness to the heartbreaking cries, she realized that they came from Mistress Ruth's room. She tiptoed to the adjoining door, thinking it might be Miriam. But the figure slumped in despair wasn't the gray-haired servant.

Master Reuben sat alone on his wife's sleeping couch, his elbows on his knees, his face buried in his hands. Leah knew she should turn away and allow the man to grieve in privacy, but the sound of his brokenness brought tears to her own eyes. He had no one in all the world to comfort him.

He didn't look up as Leah came into the room. Standing over him, she wrapped her slender arms around his shoulders and rested her head on his. "I loved her, too, Master Reuben," she said softly.

After a moment he reached for her, clung to her, and they wept together. When his tears were spent, he released her. Without a word, he stood and left the room.

Leah watched little Elizabeth devour a slice of melon, then stretch her chubby hand out for another piece. "More!" she said. It was her favorite word. They had just returned from their daily walk, and Elizabeth had been reluctant to come inside when she saw that the walk was finished, saying "More . . . more." Leah had lured her through the door with the promise of fresh melon, which Elizabeth was now stuffing into her mouth. She was a vibrant, curious child and the joy of Leah's life.

"I'm so worried about Master Reuben," Miriam told Leah as she cut more fruit into small pieces. "He hasn't left his room since Mistress Ruth's funeral, not even to go to work. We leave food for him, but he barely touches it—only the wine flask is emptied."

As Leah watched Master Reuben's daughter, she wondered

if it was possible for Elizabeth to fill her father's empty arms, for her simple, trusting love to take root and grow in his heart as it had in her own, filling the void that Mistress Ruth had left behind. She handed Elizabeth another piece of melon, then caressed her soft chestnut-colored hair.

"Miriam, I think that Elizabeth and I should take Master Reuben his dinner tray tonight."

Miriam's face registered surprise, then comprehension. "Mmm . . . it's worth a try, Leah. It's certainly worth a try. The child is the image of her mother at that age."

Leah didn't know what to expect as she knocked on the door of Master Reuben's private chamber that evening, the tray of food unsteady in her hand. "Your dinner, Master Reuben," she announced before opening the door. Miriam had warned her not to expect him to reply. Leah bent to whisper in Elizabeth's ear, coaching her, then gently pushed the child ahead of her into the room.

Master Reuben slouched on a chair in front of his shuttered window and didn't look up when they entered. He appeared disheveled, his gaze vacant, his beautiful robes torn in grief. None of the lamps were lit, and the room smelled strongly of wine. Leah set down the tray and gave Elizabeth another gentle push. The child stopped in front of her father's chair and looked up at him curiously.

"Abba?" Her tiny voice penetrated the gloomy silence of the room like birdsong. Reuben's gaze focused on her in surprise. "Abba . . . Abba . . ." she repeated. Leah handed her a piece of apricot, and Elizabeth held it out to him, as Leah had coached. Reuben didn't respond, sitting so still he might have been a piece of furniture. Finally Elizabeth grew tired of waiting and popped the apricot into her own mouth, then giggled at the trick she had played. "More!" she demanded.

Leah's heart was in her throat as she gave Elizabeth another piece. Once again, the child held it out to her father. This time Master Reuben slowly raised his arm from the chair as if it weighed more than he could lift and extended his hand to accept her gift. But instead of eating it himself, he bent

forward and fed it to her. Elizabeth gobbled it down, then
laughed again, obviously pleased with the way this game was
being played. After feeding her several more bites of fruit, Reuben lifted her to his knee, and she settled comfortably onto
his lap. As she offered him the next piece, Elizabeth saw the
tear coursing down her father's bearded cheek.

"Uh oh," she said and reached out to wipe it away. "Uh
oh, Abba."

Master Reuben caught her tiny hand in his and raised it to
his lips to kiss.

———

Every evening that he wasn't away on business, Reuben
called for Leah to bring his daughter to him.

"How is she? What did she do while I was away?" he
would ask, wanting to know every little thing Elizabeth had
said or done, every new tooth or word, every smile or tear. He
would surprise his daughter with trinkets and playthings he
had bought on his travels, then smile as he watched her play
with them. He laughed out loud as the child toddled curiously
around the huge reception hall with Leah chasing after her to
keep her from knocking over the lampstands.

When she grew tired of exploring, Elizabeth would crawl
onto Master Reuben's lap, and he would tell her stories of the
places he had been and the things he had seen. Leah loved
listening, too, as he described a pounding horse race in the
hippodrome, a colorful play he had watched in the amphitheater in Caesarea, or the bite of salt spray in his face as his
sailing ship plowed the waves of the Mediterranean Sea.
When Elizabeth grew sleepy he would kiss her tenderly, often
carrying her to bed himself in his strong arms.

Never in her life had Leah seen a father lavish his daughter
with so much love and affection. Just as she had forged a bond
of friendship and love with Mistress Ruth over the months
she'd spent with her, Leah now found herself drawn more and
more to Master Reuben. It was the highlight of her day, as well
as Elizabeth's, when he called for them in the evening. Leah

cherished the time she spent talking with him, watching him with his daughter. One evening Elizabeth tripped and fell as she bounded into the room to see her father, bumping her head on the leg of his chair. But it was Leah she ran to for comfort, not him. As she soothed the child's tears with her kisses, she was aware of Master Reuben watching them. He sat very still, his gaze intense.

"You are more than a servant to her, Leah," he finally said. "She loves you like a mother."

Leah knew he was right. She also knew that she had overstepped the boundaries of a servant's role by allowing it to happen. She gently pried Elizabeth's chubby arms from around her neck and turned her toward her father with a little push.

"Forgive me, my lord. We must do something to change that before it's too late. She needs to learn that I am only her servant . . . and yours."

Reuben appeared thoughtful as his daughter climbed onto his lap and nestled close. His blue ring sparkled in the lamplight as he stroked her curly hair. Leah held her breath, watching him. How would she ever bear being separated from Elizabeth—or Master Reuben? The evenings were lonely enough for her when he was away on business; what would they be like if she couldn't be with him at all? What if he gave her kitchen duties again and she could no longer kiss away Elizabeth's tears or listen to Master Reuben's stories and laughter?

As she watched him hug his daughter, Leah remembered how it felt when Master Reuben's arms had encircled her the night they had grieved together for Ruth. She remembered the scent of his silky hair, the dampness of his tears on her gown after he had gone. Her heart twisted inside her like a wrung cloth when she realized how much she longed to hold him again.

"No," he said after a long moment, "I don't want anything to change. I can see that she loves you, Leah . . . and that you love her. I can't deprive either one of you of that."

Leah bowed her head—as much to hide her tears of joy and relief as in humility. "Thank you, Master Reuben," she murmured.

That spring, the master was away for two long weeks, traveling to Jerusalem for the Feast of Passover. When he returned, he brought Nathaniel the preacher home with him, along with a small group of the preacher's followers. No longer welcome in Degania's synagogue, they held services every Sabbath in the villa's spacious reception hall. Nathaniel stayed until the Feast of Pentecost, teaching Leah and everyone in the household who wanted to learn about Yeshua the Messiah. What amazed Leah the most was the fact that the followers of Yeshua allowed women as well as men, servants as well as Master Reuben, to sit side by side at the teacher's feet and discuss the Scriptures. Several families from Degania and the surrounding villages began coming and were baptized in Master Reuben's mikveh. Many of the servants, including Miriam and Ehud, were baptized, too, but it grieved Leah that her brother Gideon wanted nothing to do with the meetings in the master's reception hall.

"Please come," she begged her brother. "Why won't you come? I know you would like what Nathaniel has to say if you would only listen."

"Reuben ben Johanan works for the Romans," Gideon said. His face was cold and hard, the way it had looked after the Roman soldiers had beaten him. "It's bad enough that he owns my body. I won't have him trying to own my thoughts, too."

Master Reuben listened thoughtfully to Nathaniel, but he always stopped short of declaring himself a Christian and being baptized. He had spent an enormous amount of money to purchase a set of Torah scrolls from the Essene community in Qumran, along with as many scrolls of the prophets as he could acquire. One day he showed Leah where he kept them. "I want you to read these to Elizabeth when she is old enough," he said. "I want her to know how the Messiah was promised to us in God's Word."

Not content to wait until Elizabeth was older, Leah began reading the scrolls to herself each night so that she could talk about what she read with Nathaniel and the others. God had satisfied the hunger of her heart, she realized one day. She could read and study Scriptures for herself, feasting on them as she had longed to do when she used to stand outside the synagogue windows. And in that Word, God had slowly revealed Himself to her, showing the fullness of His love. Leah marveled at how perfectly Yeshua had fulfilled all those prophecies.

"Five days before Passover," Nathaniel explained, "on the day the lambs are chosen, Yeshua made His triumphal entry into Jerusalem as our king, just as the prophet Zechariah had promised. 'Behold, your King comes to you, righteous and having salvation . . .' The people proclaimed Yeshua king that day, shouting 'Hosannah! Blessed is He who comes in the name of the Lord.' "

As Nathaniel explained the Scriptures, from the fall of Adam and Eve to Yeshua's death and resurrection, God's plan took form and shape before Leah's eyes, as if she had stepped back from her loom and suddenly discovered that the intricate pattern of stripes and colors were not individual threads, but a finished garment.

"I believe that Yeshua was the promised Messiah," she told Nathaniel one Sabbath afternoon.

"Would you like to be baptized?" he asked. Leah looked away. A cold chill washed over her, as if she had plunged into an icy bath.

"What's wrong, Leah?" Nathaniel asked when she didn't reply.

"I don't want anything to do with ritual baths. I have too many bad memories from when I used to go—" She stopped, embarrassed to mention the law that required bathing after a woman's uncleanness. She hadn't gone back to the public mikveh since becoming Reuben's servant.

"Yes, I know the Pharisees have misused it," Nathaniel said gently. "They demand meaningless cleansing from all our daily impurities, real or imagined. But their washing cleans only the outside. The Pharisees say nothing about cleansing the heart."

"Reb Nahum and Rabbi Eliezer keep watch like a couple of jackals waiting to pounce," Leah said. "They condemn everyone for transgressing the Law, yet they never keep it themselves. They make so many holes in the Law to slip their own sins through that it resembles a fishing net! And the priests in Jerusalem are just as bad. They demand a ritual cleansing before we enter their Temple, but they make themselves rich by cheating the poor people who only want to worship God!" She stopped, horrified to discover that she had spoken her thoughts so freely. It was one more reason the Pharisees had always condemned her, and now she had done it again—in front of Rabbi Nathaniel. She stared at her hands, folded in her lap, afraid to see his face.

"You're right. Baptism does symbolize our cleansing from sin," Nathaniel said. There was no shock or anger in his voice. "But Yeshua Himself was baptized, and we know that He was without sin. Baptism also symbolizes a new beginning as we leave the old ways behind and are born again into a new life in Christ. Our ancestors went through the waters of the Red Sea as they left slavery behind. Their children passed through the Jordan River as they began a new life in this land. We believe in one baptism, in Yeshua's name, for those who want to identify with His ministry, His sacrifice, His forgiveness."

Leah didn't reply. She knew that she wasn't ready.

Two days later, Nathaniel and the others returned to Jerusalem for the Feast of Pentecost. Master Reuben made the pilgrimage with them. Time passed too slowly for Leah after they were gone, like a very heavy cart moving uphill.

The evening Reuben returned, Elizabeth ran into her father's arms, crying, "Abba, Abba!" He lifted her high in the air, laughing with joy, then sat with her on his lap as he described Jerusalem and the celebration at the Temple. Even though she was too young to understand, Elizabeth loved listening to the sound of her father's voice. But Leah listened to his words, and she recalled her own disappointing visit to the Temple and the many barriers in the women's court that stood between her and God. She remembered the lamb she had helped raise, and how the priests had rejected him, just as they had rejected the perfect Lamb of God. Leah's lamb had known the sound of her voice and had responded to her; as Yeshua had said, "My sheep listen to my voice; I know them, and they follow me."

As she watched Master Reuben, a man of wealth and power, stooping low to allow his little daughter to rest in his arms, she saw a picture of her heavenly Father bending down to earth to draw her near to His heart. He was the God of David's psalms, the God who had created the beauty of a child's laughter, the tender shepherd who would lay down His life for His flock.

"Master Reuben," Leah said as he stood to carry his sleepy child to bed, "I would also like to be baptized."

CHAPTER 11

B lessed are those whose strength is in you, Abby read, who have set their hearts on pilgrimage. As they pass through the Valley of Weeping, they make it a place of springs. . . .

She stopped when she noticed more strange marks in her Bible. The p in pass was underlined, the w and the e in weeping, the g and s in springs. She scribbled the letters in the margin of her journal, spelling them forward and backward, then tried to unscramble them like a puzzle. They made no sense. She had forgotten to ask Emily about them. Abby had been too enraged to remember anything after reading Emily's last letter.

Please don't be mad, but Daddy is still living here at home, she had written. I overheard him talking to that woman on the phone and telling her that the affair was finished. He moved all of his stuff out of her apartment on Saturday, and so he has no place else to go. Mom, he has changed so much this summer. Wait until you see! My pastor invited Daddy and Greg to the Promise Keepers convention in Indianapolis next weekend, and Daddy agreed to go. . . .

It was a little late for Mark to think about keeping his promises. And it was much too late to suddenly decide he wanted to move back home. Not her home! How could Abby possibly trust him after what he had done?

Tell him he has *to move out by the time I get back!* she had written in reply. She would not share the house with him again for a single day.

Abby could tell from their letters that Emily and Greg had reconciled with their father while she was away. It would be childish and wrong of her to expect their children to take her side against him. They loved him, and Abby was certain that Mark still loved them. But every time one of them mentioned Mark, her temper flared. She had hoped her anger would ease and maybe even disappear while she was in Israel as she slowly began to write him out of her life, but now she realized that she would never be allowed to forget him. She and Mark were linked together by their children. Like it or not, she would be confronted with him for the rest of her life. Her anger was a fire that was never going to be allowed to die. Instead, it would be stoked and fueled each time she saw him— at Greg's and Emily's college graduations, at their weddings, with future grandchildren. Hannah's husband, Jake, had said "don't hate," but Abby needed to ask him how he managed to do that when he was forced to battle the same enemy again and again.

Abby closed her Bible and hurried to get dressed, styling her short brown hair with a curling iron and putting on lipstick and a dress. The Sabbath began at sundown, and that meant a celebration dinner with candlelight and special foods as the Israelis welcomed the Sabbath like an honored guest.

She happened to leave her bungalow the same moment Ari was leaving his, and they walked together to the dining room, talking about the day's discoveries at the site. The change in him continued to amaze her, as his frosty facade finally thawed. She no longer dreaded being stuck alone with him, finding instead that they could talk comfortably. As soon as they entered the dining hall, Hannah motioned them over to her table.

"We saved you both a place," she said. "Abby, Ari, I'd like you to meet Moshe Richman, his wife, Judith, and their three children, Dan, Gabriel, and Ivana. Moshe manages this hotel and Judith does all the bookkeeping."

They were a striking yet somewhat somber couple in their early thirties, with coffee-colored eyes and thick, wavy brown hair, which their two oldest children had inherited. The youngest, Ivana, a little girl of about six, had a radiant head of hair the color of an Irish setter's.

"Nice to meet you," Abby said. "Ivana and I have already met. She sometimes joins me for my walks around the hotel grounds in the evenings."

"I hope she has not been a bother to you," Judith said with a worried frown.

"Not at all. I enjoy her company. We don't speak the same language, but we've become friends, just the same."

Hannah said something to Ivana in Hebrew. She nodded and gave Abby a shy smile. The two boys, about eight and ten years old, were as solemn as their parents.

The Richmans accorded Hannah the honor of lighting the Sabbath candles. Abby listened appreciatively as the family recited the prayers and blessings in Hebrew. It surprised her that Ari prayed along with them after the skeptical comments he had made about religion when they'd visited Jerusalem. After a ritual hand washing, Judith uncovered two fragrant loaves of *challah*, and they began to eat. With Hannah translating, the children told Abby all about themselves and their activities at school. Judith explained how the adjoining kibbutz where they lived operated the resort hotel as a community venture.

"Moshe, why don't you tell Abby a little about yourself," Hannah suggested when Judith finished. "Tell her how your family came to Israel."

Moshe spoke without looking up from his plate, cutting his meat into small pieces with deliberate concentration, his face growing even more somber. "My grandfather was born in Berlin. He was not much older than my son Dan when Hitler came to power. His family tried to escape, moving from Germany to Amsterdam, but of course the Holocaust caught up with them in the end. The Nazis arrested them and transported them to concentration camps."

He stopped cutting, gripping the knife and fork like weapons, as if forgetting that he still held them. "My grandmother and grandfather were the only members of their families to survive the death camps. They met each other after the liberation and were smuggled ashore together, past the British, on a beach near Netanya."

Abby glanced at Ari, remembering his words to her the night they had stood on that beach. The hardships the Jewish people had endured awed Abby, making her own trials pale in comparison. That they could survive such horrors and still trust in God's unfailing love, as Jake would say, spoke volumes about their faith.

"When my grandfather was in the death camp, Psalm 102 became his testimony," Moshe continued. " 'My days vanish like smoke; my bones burn like glowing embers. . . . I am reduced to skin and bones. . . . All day long my enemies taunt me; those who rail against me use my name as a curse. For I eat ashes as my food and mingle my drink with tears because of your great wrath.' That was my grandfather's experience. But the second half of the psalm was his hope, a hope that has now been fulfilled: 'You will arise and have compassion on Zion. . . . For her stones are dear to your servants. . . . the Lord will rebuild Zion. . . . The children of your servants will live in your presence; their descendants will be established before you.' "

Moshe paused, and his gaze traveled briefly to each of his three children. Abby saw his love for them in its softness. Then a fierce flame kindled briefly in his eyes, a fire that told her he would do everything in his power to protect them.

"My father was born in Israel," he continued, "the same year that our nation was born. I was born here, on the Golan Heights, after Israel won all this land where we are sitting in the Six-Day War. Israel is built upon the blood and the ashes of our ancestors. That is why we must never sacrifice one inch of territory that others have bled and died to win."

"Not even for the sake of peace?" Hannah asked.

"There can be no peace until Israel fulfills her destiny to possess all of the territory that once belonged to King David and Solomon—from the Nile to the Euphrates."

Hannah broke her roll in half and began spreading it with margarine. "But what about all the Palestinians and Jordanians and Syrians who live in that territory?" she asked.

"Israeli rule will improve their standard of living," Moshe said, gesturing to the bountiful table spread before them.

"At what price?" Hannah asked softly. "Surely you must realize that such a conquest would cause insurmountable problems. We can't keep an entire population captive and expect them to be happy about it, no matter how many good things we provide for them. The Palestinians on the West Bank have taught us that lesson."

"If they don't like it, they can move elsewhere. Let their brethren in Iraq or Saudi Arabia take them, as we have absorbed our own Jewish people from all over the world. This land is *ours*, and we will own *all* of it one day."

Abby glimpsed the passion of Moshe's convictions in his reddening face, his tightly clenched hands.

The table fell silent for a moment, then Moshe turned to Ari, who sat between Hannah and Abby. "I know what Hannah believes, but what about you, Ari? You must have fought in the last war . . . are you willing to trade our hard-won land for peace?"

Ari stared at his empty plate for a moment, as if reluctant to speak his thoughts. He pushed it away from him before speaking. "Like you, I was also born in Israel—only I'm a third-generation Israeli. My ancestors were early Zionists who came here from Russia at the turn of the century. I have never known holocausts or pogroms. I have also never known peace. I grew up with the constant threat of Syrian shelling from the Golan Heights, and I slept in an underground bunker every night until I was twelve. When Israel won possession of the Heights, my village could sleep in safety for the first time. We must never give the Golan back, even for the sake of peace!"

His words had become more and more passionate, and he

paused for a moment to glance at Hannah, as if afraid he had offended her. Then he continued. "In 1973, three months after I graduated and began my military service, Israel was attacked again. It didn't matter that I was a new recruit; every man was needed to fight, so I fought. After that it was the war in Lebanon, then the Intifada, then the Gulf War—and all that time the terrorism against our people has never stopped. I am tired of fighting. It is tragic that every Jewish child in Israel must learn to use a gun; horrifying that every child must live with the constant threat of terror—"

He stopped abruptly. He had been looking at Ivana as he spoke the last sentence, but now he gazed down at his plate again, biting his bottom lip. When he finally looked up, his eyes met Moshe's. "I don't agree with you that we should go to war to win more land. I only want to live on the land my ancestors cleared and fought for and are buried on. It is the Palestinians who don't want peace, the enemies all around us who want to possess what we've worked so hard to build. All the years I was growing up, they wanted to push every last Jew into the sea, wipe out the nation of Israel. They rejected partition, refused to recognize our existence, attacked us all over the world—even at peaceful events like the Olympics. And now they say *peace*. The world can hardly blame us for being suspicious. I will never believe that our enemies want peace."

He folded his arms across his chest, and for the remainder of the meal, Ari was silent and withdrawn. The gradual thawing of his emotions that had begun after Dr. Voss's departure seemed to abruptly shift into reverse until Ari was frozen inside himself once again. Abby could understand his anger and bitterness—they were so much like her own. But what she couldn't understand as she walked home that night with him and Hannah was why Ari's heart had been hardened by his enemies, while Hannah's remained untouched by hatred.

TEL DEGANIA EXCAVATION—1999

Abby knelt in the dirt, carefully shoveling one tirea full of it at a time into plastic buckets for Marwan to haul away. The

Palestinian worker stood above her on the top of the balk, wiping the sweat from his dark face with his T-shirt.

"You're too efficient for me, Marwan," Abby said, smiling up at him. "You're hauling it faster than I can dig it."

"Perhaps that is because I am being paid and you are not," he said with a grin.

"Yes, or perhaps it's because you're ten years younger and in ten times better shape than I am!" she laughed. Abby had developed a warm friendship with Marwan Ashrawi as they had worked together for the past week, especially after discovering that he was also a high school teacher during the winter months. The stories he told about his students sounded remarkably similar to her own, regardless of the cultural differences. Marwan taught physical education, which explained his trim body and muscular build—not to mention his tireless endurance. His deep-set black eyes and thick black brows conveyed a wide range of expressions, from impish laughter as he joked with Abby about his students, to sullen withdrawal whenever Ari appeared.

"Pah! You American women worry too much about getting fat," Marwan said. "Palestinian men like their women to have a bit of meat on their bones."

"Yeah? Well, American men certainly don't." She couldn't help thinking of Lindsey Cook, a slender blonde. Mark's rejection had hurt Abby the most, as if he thought of her as a used car, easily traded in on a newer model. Abby hoped she had kept the bitterness out of her voice. "Hey, you can climb down here and help me dig, Marwan, if you're tired of waiting," she joked.

The smile instantly disappeared from Marwan's face. "Dr. Bazak would not like that. He would not trust me to do it correctly."

Abby wondered if the animosity between Ari and Marwan was personal or racial, but she was afraid to ask. She stood and passed the bucketful of dirt up to him, then watched him amble away with another wheelbarrow load. Abby was growing weary of dirt. She had it in every wrinkle and pore of her skin, in her hair, her eyes, her ears, and her throat. It mixed with her sweat and ran in muddy rivulets down her face as she labored without shade under the blazing Israeli sun. Hannah was right—archaeology certainly wasn't as glamorous as Hollywood portrayed it.

"Take a break, everyone," Ari suddenly called. "Dr. Rahov wants to show you what we found over here."

Abby took a long drink of tepid water from her canteen before joining Hannah and her co-workers in another part of the rambling villa. As soon as Abby saw the small outer chamber, the short set of stairs leading down to a deep plastered hole, she recognized the now familiar shape. "*Another* mikveh?" she said aloud. "Is this the culture that coined the phrase, 'Cleanliness is next to godliness'?"

Hannah laughed. "We've seen our share of ritual baths, it's true—but I'll bet you've never seen this before! I know I haven't!" She had somehow climbed all the way down into the chamber where people once immersed themselves. Now she stepped to one side, gesturing to a pile of rusty triangular-shaped metal wedges, about two or three inches long.

"Those look like arrowheads," one of the students said.

"Good guess. That's exactly what they are. Quite an arsenal of them, too, I would say. And do you see how there are several different sizes and shapes mixed together? That's because the Romans used troops from all over their empire as archers."

"Why would the Romans hide arrows in the bathtub?" another student asked. Hannah gestured to Ari, allowing him to explain.

"The Romans wouldn't," he said. "These weapons were probably stolen from the Romans and hidden here by Zealots."

"Were they like Palestinian terrorists, Dr. Bazak?" one of the students asked.

Ari seemed thrown off balance by the question. When he didn't reply, Hannah quickly said, "No, the Zealots were first-century Jews, freedom fighters who felt that only God should rule over the Jewish nation. Their 'zeal' was for the Lord. In fighting to overthrow the Romans, they saw their political resistance as a religious war, and they expected the promised Messiah to be a political leader. The movement started after the first Roman procurator in A.D. 6 held a census for taxation, inciting a rebellion. One of Jesus' disciples was a Zealot, but Jesus wasn't. He told Pilate, 'My kingdom is not of this world,' and He urged His followers to love their enemies."

At the breakfast break, Abby sought out Hannah and sat down beside her in the shade of the canvas canopy. She was surrounded by college students as usual, patiently answering their questions and listening as they told her about themselves. It was clear how very much Hannah enjoyed being with young people, and when Ari joined them, Abby recalled Hannah saying that he had been one of her first students.

"Seriously, Dr. Rahov, what is with all these baths we keep finding?" one of the girls asked.

Hannah smiled and set her paper plate on her lap. She always needed her hands free in order to talk. "According to the Law of Moses, ritual cleansing was necessary whenever something caused a person to become 'unclean'—contact with a dead body, certain illnesses, and so forth. Religious Jews today still have ritual baths. And bathing is also necessary before worship. Remember the baths we saw below the Temple Mount?"

Abby swallowed a bite of tomato and joined the discussion. "You know, there is an old custom in America of taking a Saturday night bath before Sunday morning church. I wonder if the mikveh is the origin of it?"

"Maybe so," Hannah laughed. She picked up her yogurt container and ate a couple of spoonfuls before saying, "Another law requires every woman to take a ritual bath a week after her monthly period ends. That's what Bathsheba was doing. Remember how some of the neighborhoods we saw in Jerusalem had houses that were built on the hillsides, looking down on top of each other? Evidently Bathsheba's mikveh was visible from King David's rooftop. Look up that Scripture passage sometime. It says that she had just purified herself from her uncleanness. In other words, the author wanted us to know that Bathsheba's monthly period was over, her husband was away at war, and so the baby had to be David's."

Abby was still thinking about King David's adultery when it was time to return to work. Against her will, she was also thinking about Mark. When she saw how all the young college girls flocked around Ari at the site every day, supposedly asking questions about archaeology, it made her furious. Ari was friendly but not flirtatious, and it angered her that the girls would flirt so shamelessly with a married man. He didn't wear a wedding ring, but then neither did Marwan or the hotel manager, Moshe Richman. Maybe wedding rings weren't customary for men in Israel. But Abby's husband, Mark, had always worn one, and it hadn't stopped Lindsey Cook from her pursuit.

Abby was chipping at the hard-packed dirt, trying to work out her anger, when Ari climbed down into the pit beside her. "You are within centimeters of first-century floor level," he said. "You must please dig very carefully."

"Do you think there might be a mosaic floor under all this dirt?"

Ari couldn't disguise his boyish excitement. "I am hoping there is. I will come back and join you myself as soon as I finish documenting the weapons we found in the mikveh."

A few minutes later, Abby's petesh struck something hard. She laid it aside and began carefully sweeping the dirt away with a small whisk broom. Her heart beat like a trotting horse. Even under a two-thousand-year-old layer of dust, the brilliance of the tiny colored stones shone through. She swept faster, quickly uncovering a foot-long section of border, fashioned like rolling ocean waves in shades of green and blue and white.

"Look at that!" Marwan said as he returned with his wheelbarrow. He jumped down into the pit to help her, carefully scooping the dirt she was loosening into the bucket with his hands.

When Abby saw that the border continued along the edge of the wall, she changed direction, sweeping toward the middle of the room. After cleaning another small section, she found herself staring at a fish—a cleverly fashioned gold and gray and green fish, with fins so graceful it seemed to swim. But it was what she found above the fish that took Abby's breath away—five Greek letters. She had seen them before, along with a fish, on the bumper sticker her daughter had pasted onto her car. They were Christian symbols.

"I think we'd better send for Hannah," she told Marwan. She was breathless, afraid to take her eyes off her discovery, afraid it would disappear if she did.

Ari and Hannah arrived at the same time. They looked down at the mosaic, then at each other, and something as powerful as a bolt of lightning seemed to pass between them. Abby didn't see who moved first—they might have moved simultaneously—but suddenly Ari and Hannah were in each other's arms. She couldn't see Hannah's face, but Ari's eyes were closed as he battled his emotions.

"You have to be the one to publish this, Ari!" Hannah said. "You have to be!" Then they parted, the moment passed, and Hannah celebrated by climbing down to hug Abby and Marwan and everyone else in sight, while Ari began snapping dozens of photos of the mosaic.

"This Greek word, *ichthys*, means fish," Hannah explained to the gathering students. Her voice was thick with emotion. "It was one of the symbols used by the early Christian church. It's an acronym for 'Jesus Christ, Son of God, Savior.' Do you have any idea what that means? We know Degania was a Jewish village. Yet some of the people who lived here were among the earliest Christians!"

Every available volunteer was put to work with Abby and Ari, uncovering the mosaic. Just before quitting time, a student working on another corner of the floor found Hebrew writing.

"It's a name," Ari said after examining it. "Reuben son of

Johanan. He was probably the person who commissioned the floor."

"Ari, does that name seem familiar to you?" Hannah asked.

He thought for a moment. "Sorry . . . but no."

"I'm positive that I've seen it somewhere before. Of course, I realize that Reuben and Johanan are fairly common names, but that combination . . . it seems so familiar . . ."

"Do you remember from where?" Ari asked. "A history book? Another dig?"

"I don't know."

As Abby rode back to the hotel in one of the vans, Hannah was deep in thought. Ari leaned forward from the seat behind them and tapped Hannah on the shoulder.

"Are you still thinking about the name on that inscription?" he asked with a wry grin.

"Yes. I *know* I've seen it somewhere before. It's going to drive me crazy until I figure out where!"

Ari nudged Abby, still grinning. "We'll have to fetch her for meals from now on, or she will forget to eat."

THE VILLAGE OF DEGANIA—A.D. 52

What's that strange sound?" Elizabeth asked.

Leah frowned as she tucked the bedcovers around the child, certain that the four-year-old's imagination was helping her find an excuse to avoid taking a nap. "I don't hear anything," she began, but then Leah did hear it—a sound like water rushing down a dry riverbed. Even as she listened, it grew louder, closer. "Lie down, Elizabeth," she said. "I'll go see."

She met Miriam and Ehud in the central courtyard, hurrying toward the main door of the villa along with several other servants. The concern on their faces made her afraid. "What's going on?" she asked.

"One of the Christian brethren just ran here to warn us—

there's a mob headed this way and it's out of control. We have to bar the door." But when they reached it, Leah's brother Gideon was swinging it wide open, instead.

"Gideon! What are you doing?"

"Giving us a chance for freedom!"

"No! Not this way!" She tried to wrestle with him but he was too strong. "Help me, Ehud!" she cried. The mob outside was just a few hundred yards away. Unable to pull Gideon back inside, the only solution was for her and Ehud to push him all the way through the doorway. Then the other servants quickly closed and barred it from the inside, leaving the three of them stranded outside on the steps.

"God help us," Ehud murmured as the crowd rushed toward them.

Many of the men brandished swords or clubs. Leah saw a few familiar faces among them, but most of the men were strangers to Degania. She was afraid they would trample over the three of them in their rush to break down the door, but Ehud held up his hands.

"Stop! Wait . . . please!" Their momentum miraculously halted. "What do you want here?" he asked.

Although Ehud was brawny from his years of heavy labor and his sun-weathered face was forbidding to strangers, Leah knew the servant had a gentle heart and an eagerness to serve his new master, Yeshua the Messiah. He would probably be no match for the mob's leader, a savage-looking man with wild, unkempt hair and a coarse woolen tunic.

"Hand over our enemy!" the stranger cried, brandishing a sword. "The Romans are God's enemies, and so is anyone who works for them!"

"No one in this household works for the Romans except Master Reuben," Ehud said quietly, "and he left for Jerusalem two weeks ago to celebrate the Feast of Tabernacles. You'll find only Jewish slaves and bond servants in this house."

"Is that true, Gideon?" the leader asked, turning to him.

Leah wondered how the stranger knew her brother's name.

Gideon nodded reluctantly. "Yes, it's true."

Ehud descended the stairs, stepping past the burly leader to bow to one of the village elders, a Pharisee. "Reb Nahum, I'm surprised to see you here. Would you tell me, please, what's going on?"

"The Samaritans attacked and killed a Jewish man," Nahum said, "a fellow Galilean who was passing through their district on his way to the feast."

"But what does that have to do with Reuben ben Johanan?"

"The Roman procurator will give us no justice," Nahum said. "These men think Reb Reuben would make a valuable bargaining chip."

"I'm surprised that a man of your integrity and devotion to the Law would permit such an evil as kidnapping to occur in our village," Ehud said. "After all, Master Reuben is also a fellow Jew—although not a Pharisee."

Reb Nahum looked uncomfortable. He scanned the crowd as if searching for another elder to back him up.

"Who are these men?" Ehud asked, gesturing to the leader, who seemed impatient with the delay.

"We are followers of the One True God," the leader shouted. He leaped up the steps to stand between Leah and Gideon.

He smelled like a wild animal's den, as if he hadn't bathed in a long time. But with the mob in front of her and the door barred behind her, Leah had no choice but to remain beside him. She shivered from cold and fear. The fall rains had begun, and she had come outside without a shawl.

"God alone should rule over the Jewish people," the man shouted. "The Torah says, 'Him only shall ye serve.' That means only cowards pay tribute to Rome. Only unbelievers tolerate mortal masters instead of recognizing God as their Lord. In the spirit of our ancestors, the Maccabees, I say, 'Let everyone who is zealous for the Law and who supports the covenant come out with me!' It's time for a holy war!"

A deafening shout went up from the mob as they waved their clubs and swords in the air. Leah unconsciously shrank back against the door. She had heard of this savage band of freedom fighters, the so-called Zealots. Their zeal for God had led them to foolishly take up arms against the Romans.

"This is the land God promised our ancestors," the Zealot leader shouted when the roar finally died away. "There is no room in it for anyone else. We must pay homage to no one but God. Why should our taxes support an emperor who considers himself a god? Why must we pay to erect statues to pagan gods and to build pagan temples? Why should we help the Gentiles live their immoral life-style, which contradicts the Laws of God? Remember the zeal of Aaron's grandson Phineas who put the idolaters to the sword. It's time to drive the pagans out of our land!"

Another huge cheer went up from the crowd. Leah was alarmed to hear her brother shouting, "Death is better than slavery!" as he waved his fist in the air.

Ehud turned and slowly ascended the stairs again, stopping one step below the leader and bowing slightly. Only Leah, Gideon, and the Zealot leader could hear Ehud's words above the din.

"Since Master Reuben isn't home, my lord, there is really no reason for you to terrorize your fellow Jews who are only his humble servants. The master keeps no silver or gold here, and while his household furnishings are valuable, they would be of no use to you, I'm afraid."

Ehud's humble words and gentle manner were meant to diffuse the Zealot leader's wrath, but Leah could see that he had worked himself and the crowd into a frenzy, and he needed an outlet for his energy. She feared for Elizabeth and prayed that no one would remind the leader that Reuben ben Johanan had a daughter.

"Very well," the Zealot said with a growl, "if we can't have the Roman collaborator, we will settle for the next best thing—the supplies in his storehouses!"

Ehud looked alarmed. "Should someone as zealous for the Law as you, my lord, resort to stealing, like a common thief or a tax collector?"

At these words, the Zealot lost his temper. He grabbed Ehud by the front of his tunic with one hand and raised his sword with the other. "It would not be stealing if a fellow patriot decided to contribute to our cause, would it?"

Ehud wisely backed down. "No, my lord."

The leader finally released Ehud and turned to Leah's brother, resting his hand on his shoulder in a gesture of camaraderie. "Gideon, you'll show us to your master's storehouses, won't you?"

"This way!" Gideon shouted.

Leah watched, appalled, as her brother gleefully led the mob around the building to the master's storehouses in the rear of the villa. "Oh, God, forgive him," she murmured as she huddled beside Ehud on the front steps.

She saw the damage the mob had made after they finally dispersed. The Zealots had broken through the gate into the servants' courtyard and had not only raided the storehouses, but had also taken several of the master's mules to help haul away his goods. Leah went to the servants' quarters in search of her brother and found Ehud already there with him. As steward over Master Reuben's household, Ehud would be held responsible for any losses during their master's absence. But in spite of the rage and the anguish she saw on Ehud's face, his voice was surprisingly gentle.

"*Why*, Gideon? Why would you betray our master like this? How has he ever harmed you or wronged you?"

"He made my father into his debtor! He forced Abba to sell my sister and me like . . . like animals!"

"Has it never occurred to you that Master Reuben could have sold you and Leah to another master, anywhere in the Roman Empire, to reclaim that debt? What did he need with two more servants, two more mouths to feed? Can't you see it was his kindness that allowed you to remain in Degania, to serve him here for seven years?" Leah herself had never thought of that fact, and it astounded her. Gideon seemed unmoved.

"Is this how you repay our master's kindness?" Ehud asked.

"God created us to be free," Gideon said. "If Reuben ben Johanan were a true Jew, he would gladly empty his storehouses to the men who are going to drive out the Romans and reclaim our freedom."

Ehud shook his head sadly. "It isn't an absence of shackles that makes men free—it is forgiveness. We are free to worship God only when we've found forgiveness for our sins. And we are free from the power of our enemies only when we forgive them."

"How can we forgive the Romans for desecrating our land?" Gideon shouted. "It's intolerable to have any ruler but God!"

"The Son of God said, 'Father, forgive them,' as the Romans crucified Him. He knew that violence and hatred weren't the way to bring the Kingdom of God into this world. It's our fallen nature that needs to be redeemed, not this land. What good will it do to deliver Israel from one tyrant when the next one will surely follow? The sons of King David and even the sons of the Maccabees eventually became tyrants, remember? Only God's grace and forgiveness can change man's nature. Only a changed nature will make us free."

"You're talking gibberish," Gideon mumbled.

"One of the Messiah's followers was a Zealot," Ehud continued. "Another was a tax collector. They should have been bitter enemies, but they became brothers. Yeshua said love your enemies. He said if the Roman soldiers force you to walk one mile, walk two. God's grace, not violence, changes people. The prophets said that all the nations of the world would one day come to seek Him in Jerusalem when His Kingdom is established. Do you think they will come to learn from us if we have no love? If all that we show the world is laws and rules and hatred?"

"I have no idea what you're talking about, old man," Gideon said.

Leah saw that his heart was as firmly closed and barred as

the front door of the villa had been. "Gideon, listen—" she began.

"No! I don't listen to traitors, even if one of them is my own sister!"

Gideon pushed past both of them and stormed from the room. He didn't return for dinner, nor was he found anywhere in the villa when it was time to bar the doors for the night. The band of Zealots had also disappeared from Degania, and Leah lay awake all night praying for her brother, terrified that he had run away with them. Under Roman law, a slave who stole from his master and ran away would be executed.

When Master Reuben returned from Jerusalem, Leah begged Ehud to allow her to help explain what had happened with the Zealots and with Gideon. She wanted to plead with the master for mercy. She followed the two men as they toured the ravaged storehouses and empty stalls, wondering how to interpret Master Reuben's cold silence as he surveyed his losses.

"My lord," Ehud finished, "I didn't have your authority to send word to the Roman garrison to pursue them. But I will leave immediately to summon them if that's what you wish."

Leah looked up at Ehud, confused by his offer to send for the Romans. Hadn't he begged Gideon to choose forgiveness, not revenge, just a short time ago? Why wasn't he urging the master to do the same?

Reuben stared into space with the same vacant look Leah remembered seeing on his face after Mistress Ruth died. Fearing for her brother's life, Leah dropped to her knees before him on the dusty floor of the storehouse.

"My lord, I beg you to have mercy on Gideon. I'll serve another seven years to pay his debt—or for the rest of my life if that's what you wish. But please don't send the soldiers after him. *Please!*"

Reuben looked down at Leah. She met his gaze, even though she knew that a servant shouldn't look at her master in such a direct way. Compassion flickered briefly in his eyes before he looked away.

"Let the boy go," he told Ehud.

Leah clutched her master's ankles to kiss his feet. "Oh, thank you—" But Master Reuben grabbed her by the arm, jerking her to her feet.

"Don't!" he said coldly. "Bow to no one but God." Then he turned and strode away.

THE VILLAGE OF DEGANIA—A.D. 53

See, Abba? Leah taught me the first two letters of my name."

Leah watched as Elizabeth proudly handed the writing board to her father, showing him what she had learned. From where she sat, Leah could see the master's face, see his love and delight in his daughter. Even though Elizabeth was no longer a baby, Leah still stayed in the reception hall each evening while the child spent time with her father. Master Reuben had never asked Leah to leave, so she quietly sat to one side, enjoying her time in his presence as much as Elizabeth did.

"And tomorrow night I'll show you another letter, Abba," Elizabeth said.

"Well, I'm afraid not. I have to leave tomorrow morning for Caesarea, remember? But you're such a clever little girl, I'll bet you'll be writing your whole name by the time I come home."

"May I go to Caesarea with you, Abba? Please?"

"I'm going there on business, Elizabeth. But I'll bring you a present, if you'd like. What will it be? What shall I bring you this time?"

Leah knew the effect Elizabeth's charm always had on her father. Master Reuben would bring her a camel caravan of jewels if she asked for it. Leah knew she should warn him that Elizabeth would soon be old enough to ask for it. But this time Elizabeth didn't request playthings and trinkets.

"Why can't I go with you, Abba?"

"Well, perhaps when you're older . . ."

Elizabeth planted her hands on her hips. "How old must I be? I'm already five!"

Reuben stared at her in surprise, a bemused look on his face. "Leah, do you think Elizabeth is old enough to travel?"

Leah was startled when the master suddenly addressed her by name. She seldom spoke now that Elizabeth was capable of conversing with her father herself. She often wondered if Master Reuben even remembered she was there.

"Old enough?" Leah hesitated, unsure from his expression what he wanted her to say. When she detected no warning in his eyes, she decided to tell the truth. "Yes, Master Reuben, I do. She is so active and curious that I think she must be quite bored with Degania. A new experience would be good for her. That is . . . if you think it would be safe, my lord."

"The Zealots have fled to the Negev for now," he said quietly.

"So may I go with you, Abba?"

He smiled. "All right. But you must come with us, too, Leah. Elizabeth will need you to care for her while I conduct my business."

Leah could scarcely believe it. He was offering her a chance to travel outside of Degania. To go to the nation's capital, Caesarea, and see the royal palace and the Great Sea. The only other trip Leah had made was when she went to Jerusalem for Passover, and that had ended in disappointment. Master Reuben must have noticed her surprise and excitement.

He winked at his daughter and said, "I think Leah is as thrilled as you are, Elizabeth."

Leah and Miriam worked by lamplight to pack all the things Elizabeth would need for the journey. Leah was so excited she barely slept that night and was up hours before dawn. But when she took Elizabeth to the master, dressed and

ready to go, it was Leah, not his daughter, whom he scrutinized from head to toe.

"Oh dear," he said, frowning. "Is that all you have to
wear?"

Leah's heart sank, certain he would decide to leave her behind. She was dressed in her usual servant's robes, the only
garments she had—the only garments that were necessary in
Degania.

"Miriam, isn't there something else Leah could wear?"
Reuben asked the older servant. "We can't have her running
around Caesarea looking like a kitchen maid."

"Well, my lord . . ." Miriam said hesitantly, "would one of
Mistress Ruth's old robes do?"

"Yes, that's fine. But be quick about it. It will take us more
than two days to get there as it is."

They arrived in Caesarea near sundown, so Leah didn't get
to see much of the city in the fading daylight. They stayed
near the royal palace in lodgings for employees of the Roman
government. Master Reuben allowed Leah to sleep in Elizabeth's room as she did at home instead of in the slaves' dormitories with his other servants. He sent for his daughter the
following afternoon when his business was completed.

"How about a tour of the city?" he asked Elizabeth as they
stood outside on the street. "Shall I rent a litter like that one
to transport us?" Four slaves trotted past, carrying the boxlike
conveyance on their shoulders by its poles.

"It's too small, Abba. We won't all fit."

"We . . . ?"

"Leah must come, too."

Leah knew by the look of surprise on Master Reuben's face
that he had pictured himself touring alone with his daughter.
But he quickly recovered and said, "Yes, of course she must.
Shall we walk instead?"

The pagan city fascinated Leah, yet it shocked her at every
turn. There were more Roman soldiers prowling the streets

here than in Jerusalem. But much worse, graven images sprouted everywhere among the fountains and fine homes, made in the likenesses of men and women and animals and birds. If she tried to avert her eyes each time she saw one, she would miss most of the city.

"Only the ones next to altars or inside the temples are worshiped as idols," Reuben explained. "The others are called statues. The Greeks believe that the human form is lovely to look at, like a sunset or a beautiful view. Some of these were made to honor men who did great deeds for Rome. And of course the eagle you see everywhere is a symbol of the empire—much like a menorah might symbolize the Temple in Jerusalem."

"This is so different from Jerusalem," Leah said as they walked down the wide colonnaded avenue toward the royal palace. "The streets were very narrow there, and they meandered like ants on a hot stone. But here they're so . . . so straight!"

"King Herod planned them that way. The streets are all the same distance apart as well. There was no natural seaport in his kingdom, you see, so he designed and built Caesarea and made it his capital. It took him twelve years to complete."

Dozens of questions poured from Leah, one right after the other, as they walked. She was only a servant, but she had grown so accustomed to talking freely with Nathaniel when he was in Degania and with her fellow Christians when they met to break bread every week that in her excitement she forgot herself. Master Reuben didn't seem to mind. He answered her queries as casually as he answered his daughter's.

Leah saw that he was fascinated with the Greek culture that had been imported here by Rome. He talked enthusiastically about the many plays he'd seen in the amphitheater facing the sea and the sporting events he'd attended in the hippodrome and the arena.

"Would you like to attend a play or a contest while we're here?" he asked.

Leah quickly shook her head. "No, thank you, my lord. I

could never feel comfortable at those places. I'm afraid that the forbidden things have been too deeply ingrained in me by the Pharisees." As soon as the words left her mouth, she worried that she had offended him. She glanced at him, but his expression was impassive.

"There is a Jewish quarter here in Caesarea," he said, "with about twenty thousand inhabitants. It would look more like home to you, I think. The Gentile population is much larger, of course. Unfortunately, there is also a great deal of tension between the two peoples."

"Why don't the Jewish people leave? This is obviously a pagan city."

"It isn't that simple," Reuben replied. "The Jews believe that since Caesarea was founded by King Herod, a Jewish king, the city is therefore Jewish. It's the capital of their homeland. They want to demolish the statues and pagan temples and make it like Jerusalem, where such things aren't allowed. The Gentile population says the city was designed as a Gentile city, that King Herod set up the statues and temples, and therefore he didn't design Caesarea for Jews. He even named it after the Roman emperor."

A sudden thought occurred to Leah. "You're caught in the middle, aren't you?" she said. "Between the two peoples."

Master Reuben looked at her in surprise. "Yes, I suppose I am."

Beyond Herod's royal palace where the Roman governor lived, the temple to Augustus stood near the water's edge. It was an impressive building with pillars on all four sides, dominating a plaza in the heart of the city. Leah wouldn't look at the colossal statue of Caesar inside it. She was much more interested in gazing out at the deep blue waters of the Mediterranean. Two massive man-made breakwaters stretched like arms to embrace the sea, encircling several acres of water to create the port.

"Oh, look! Could we walk out into the sea along those walls?" she asked.

"Yes, if you'd like to," Master Reuben said. As they strolled, he explained how Herod's engineers had sunk massive blocks of stone into the water to create an artificial buffer against the pounding waves. The walkway was two hundred feet wide, with towers evenly spaced all along it. The most beautiful one, Reuben said, was called the Drusium, after Caesar's stepson. White stone buildings with arched recesses for storage lined the inside of the breakwaters, their walls reflecting the afternoon sun.

When they had walked partway, they stopped to gaze out at the sea that stretched off into the distance until it met the blue sky on the horizon. "I've never seen a body of water that had no opposite shore," Leah murmured. She listened in awe to the cry of seabirds and the slap of the waves as they smashed against the wall below her. She followed the mast of a ship as it grew from a tiny white speck to a billowing sail, rising and falling on the waves as it slowly neared the port. She watched another ship maneuver through the narrow opening between the breakwaters.

Inside the harbor, dozens of masts bobbed on the waves as the ships lay at anchor, their sails furled like fat scrolls. Master Reuben let Elizabeth stop to watch a gang of stevedores, nearly naked except for their loincloths, load cargo that was destined for ports all over the empire—Nabatean incense, snowy bales of wool, and huge clay amphorae containing wine and fruit. The passengers waiting to embark spoke a babble of strange languages. Leah loved the combination of smells—the pungent aroma of fish and seaweed, the bite of salt in the air and water, the pine scent of pitch used to waterproof the boats.

"What is that thing, Abba?" Elizabeth asked. "It looks like a long, long bridge." She was pointing back toward the city where a row of perfectly symmetrical arches, joined at the top, marched along the beach north of the city until it disappeared from sight in the haze.

"It's not a bridge, it's an aqueduct," he explained. "It brings drinking water to the city from a spring on Mount Carmel, many miles away."

At last they turned back to the city, and Master Reuben led them through one of the more opulent sections of the marketplace. Seeing the master's fine robes, merchants scrambled to show him their wares as he passed, trying to outshout each other, each man insisting that only he could offer Master Reuben the best bargain in all of Caesarea. Not to be outdone, one young merchant stepped smoothly in the master's path, holding an exquisite golden chain set with semiprecious stones.

"Sir, why not buy this necklace for your wife?" he asked. "It would look beautiful on her lovely neck." He gestured to Leah.

Leah didn't understand why, but her heart suddenly began to race. She had once feared becoming Master Reuben's concubine, but now that she knew him the idea didn't frighten her at all. She remembered the night he had held her in his arms and found herself wishing that he would hold her again.

Master Reuben didn't correct the merchant. He didn't look at the man in outrage and disgust and say that Leah was his *servant*, not his *wife*. He simply shook his head, saying, "No, thank you," and walked on.

By the time they returned to their lodgings, Leah was nearly as exhausted as little Elizabeth was. "Let her sleep as long as she likes tomorrow," Master Reuben said. "My business affairs will take most of the morning, then we'll find something to do in the afternoon."

Leah had planned to sleep late as well, but someone shook her awake just as the sky was growing light the next morning. "Leah . . . Leah, wake up!"

She opened her eyes. Master Reuben stood over her, calling her name. He was breathless, his lungs heaving as if he had run a long distance. She saw the alarm on his face and sat up. "What's wrong?"

"You must . . . get Elizabeth . . . out of here," he said, panting. "Hurry!"

Leah heard it then—the same roar of rushing water she remembered from the day the Zealots had stormed their villa in Degania. But if that sound had been a river, this one was a tidal wave. She scrambled from her bed and grabbed Mistress Ruth's robe.

"No, don't wear that one, Leah. It isn't safe. Wear a . . . a servant's robe. You have to blend in with the others."

She stared at him, her fear multiplying with each passing second. "Why? What's going on?"

"A mob of Jews desecrated a pagan altar this morning. They're gathering in the plaza outside right now, preparing to storm the government buildings—like this one." Master Reuben was gathering his daughter's scattered belongings as he talked, stuffing them into her satchel. "You have to get Elizabeth out of here! Take her down the back way, through the servants' quarters. Gather the rest of my servants and leave—"

"What about you? Aren't you coming with us?"

"I can't. I'm a Roman publican. I would endanger all of you if someone recognized me." He found one of Elizabeth's sandals and crouched to look under the bed for the other one. When he stood again, his hair fell into his eyes. "The mob is Jewish, like you and the others, Leah. They won't harm you once they know you're on their side. Please . . . you must pretend that Elizabeth is your daughter—"

"But, Master Reuben, I can't leave you here!"

"You must! Aren't you listening to me? I'm . . . I'm *ordering* you to get dressed and get out of here! The mob will let you through, but once the Roman garrison arrives, you'll be slaughtered along with all the rest of the Jews!"

His shouts awakened Elizabeth. "Abba?" she said sleepily. "What . . . ?"

"It's time to go, Elizabeth. Come on, I'll help you get dressed." She was still limp from sleep.

Leah watched, unable to move as Reuben shoved Elizabeth's arms into the sleeves of her robe, then fastened her sandals on her feet. "You're caught in the middle," Leah said, remembering Master Reuben's words from yesterday. "The Jews will kill you because you work for the Romans, but to the Gentiles you're just another Jew to slaughter."

He whirled on her angrily, shouting, "Why aren't you

dressed? I told you to get dressed!" Elizabeth began to cry.

Suddenly Leah realized what she had to do. When Master Reuben's back was turned, she grabbed the ornate robe that had once been Mistress Ruth's and quickly put it on, then she coiled her hair on her head with shaking fingers. Master Reuben had Elizabeth on her feet and headed toward the door, trying to calm her tears.

"Master Reuben, wait!" Leah said, pulling him to a stop. She grabbed his sash and tore it off him. "Take off your robe! Put on this one!" She shoved her servant's tunic into his hands. The coarse clothing of the working class looked much the same for a man or a woman.

"Leah! What are you doing?" Master Reuben pushed her away as she tried to yank his outer robe off him. Desperate, Leah turned to Elizabeth.

"You want your abba to come with us, don't you?"

"Yes—"

"Then we need to play a little game. I'll pretend to be your mama, all right? That's what you must call me for a little while. But you mustn't call your father 'Abba,' do you understand? We will pretend that he's our servant. He's going to dress just like one of them and carry you to safety. Can you do that for me, Elizabeth?"

"No!" Reuben shouted. "I can't allow you to do this!"

"And I can't allow you to sacrifice yourself!" Leah shouted right back. "What would Elizabeth do if anything happened to you?" *And what would I do without you?* she silently wondered.

Reuben stared at Leah as if shocked that anyone would dare to speak to him like that, especially his servant. But Leah didn't care what happened to her once this was over. She had to save the life of the man she loved. She had been afraid to acknowledge it before, but at the thought of him being torn to pieces by the mob, she admitted to herself that it was true. She loved Reuben ben Johanan.

"My idea will work," she said in a softer voice. "Trust me." She tugged his robe off his shoulders while he was still frozen in shock, then helped him into her tunic. It was a tight fit, but it would do. "Take off your sandals," she ordered. "They're too nice. You'll have to go barefoot." While he bent to untie them, Leah dumped some oil from the lamp into the palm of her hand and mixed it with ashes from the charcoal brazier. Before he could protest, she rubbed the mixture into his silky hair. "It's much too clean and shiny," she said. "And give me your money pouch." She took it from him and fastened it to her own belt.

"Just hurry, Leah," he said, lifting Elizabeth into his arms. "We're running out of time." The noise outside in the street had become an angry roar.

Leah led the way through the maze of corridors to the slaves' dormitories and quickly rounded up the rest of Master Reuben's frightened servants. She was encouraged to see that they didn't recognize their master at first. She explained what she was doing and hurried them outside through the rear gate of the compound.

The streets behind the building were deserted. Anyone who hadn't joined the mob was barricaded inside his home. But as she neared the city gate, Leah saw a gang of armed freedom fighters standing in their path. She froze, hesitating as her courage suddenly deserted her. Then, realizing that it would look suspicious to fear her own countrymen, she quickly recovered and hurried toward them.

"Oh, thank God! You're on *our* side!" she cried. She rushed forward, as if to safety. "Please, can you help my daughter and me get out of the city? We're from Galilee and we're trying to get home."

"Galilee? What are you doing in Caesarea?" one of the men asked.

For a horribly long moment, Leah's mind went blank. It hadn't occurred to her that they would ask that question. Then a picture came to her of the stevedores loading cargo onto the boats in the harbor, the knot of passengers waiting beneath a canopy to embark.

"We came to see my husband off on a trading venture,"

she said. "He sailed for Crete yesterday, to the city of Lasea." She remembered the name of the port from one of Master Reuben's voyages. She tried to read the man's reaction to her lie and realized that he wasn't looking at her. He was studying the servants' faces behind her. She turned to follow his gaze and was horrified to see Master Reuben's blue ring glinting in plain sight as he held Elizabeth in his arms.

Leah hurried over to him, and reached to caress the child. With her own body blocking the strangers' view, she gripped Reuben's hand and tugged on his ring to draw his attention to it, then she lifted Elizabeth from his arms.

"Please, my daughter is very frightened," Leah said. As soon as Reuben's hands were empty, he quickly put them behind his back to slide the ring from his finger. "I would be happy to pay you for our safe conduct," Leah told the strangers. "My husband supports the cause of freedom. In fact, my brother Gideon joined a Zealot band a few years ago. Maybe you know him—Gideon ben Jesse, from Degania?"

The leader shook his head. "Is that where you're from? Degania?"

"I was born there, but I moved to my husband's village when I married." Leah knew she would start tripping over her lies if this ordeal didn't end soon. She shifted Elizabeth to her other hip and untied Reuben's money pouch. "How much—"

"Keep your money," the leader said with a growl. He gestured toward the gate. "Go. But I advise you to stay off the main roads."

Leah bowed to him in respect, fighting tears of relief. "Thank you, my lord. May God go with you."

———

When they arrived home two days later it was late in the evening. Leah had just finished putting Elizabeth to sleep and was preparing for bed herself when Miriam came to her room. "Master Reuben has asked to see you in the receiving room," she said.

"Now? But Elizabeth is already asleep and—"

"He said for just you to come . . . without Elizabeth."

Leah had already taken her hair down for the night, but she quickly coiled it on her head again and got dressed. What could he possibly want? He had never sent for her alone before. The thought of having his full attention, without Elizabeth, made her heart pound as if she were running a race. Then she remembered how disrespectfully she had talked to him in Caesarea, how she had ordered him around, shouted at him, and she was suddenly afraid. She started out the door, realized she was barefoot, and went back to tie on her sandals.

Master Reuben was seated in the chair where he always sat, with a small meal the servants had fixed for him on the ivory table beside him. It looked to Leah as though he hadn't touched the food. He was wearing one of his own robes again, and his hair was still damp from his bath. He glanced up when Leah entered, and his gaze followed her all the way into the room. She bowed to him, then stood waiting.

"Please sit down, Leah." He gestured to the leather stool where she usually sat when she came with Elizabeth. For a moment or two he didn't speak but sat with his hand over his mouth and chin, stroking his beard. He wore the blue ring on his finger again, and it glistened in the lamplight like dappled sunshine on a brook.

"I've been trying for two days," he said, "to find the words to thank you for what you did in Caesarea. I still haven't found them. I owe you my life." He lowered his hand from his face and absently twisted the ring with his other hand while he spoke.

Leah remembered the warmth of his smooth hand when she had grasped it, and she had to look away to keep from blushing.

"Since I can't tell you how grateful I am," he continued, "I will have to show you. I am setting you free, Leah."

Leah's head jerked up at his words. She stared at him in disbelief, her eyes meeting his plum-colored ones.

"I realize that your seven years are not quite finished," he said, "but in the morning we will go before two witnesses and officially end your servitude. You will be free to go." Leah was so stunned she barely heard the rest. "I have asked Ehud to prepare a gift of silver and two sets of clothing for you so you will not leave here empty-handed."

Leave? She couldn't leave Master Reuben! She was in love with him! How could she possibly go away and never see him again? She continued to stare at him, openmouthed, unable to speak.

"Leah? Is something wrong?" he asked.

Leah knew she was being very rude. He was offering her freedom and gifts besides, and she hadn't even thanked him for his generosity.

She slid off the stool onto her knees in front of him, trying to form the proper words of gratitude. But when she opened her mouth to speak them, what came out was, "I don't want to leave, Master Reuben. I want to have my ear pierced with an awl, like Miriam and Ehud did. I want to be your bond servant."

He shook his head as if it was out of the question. "No! You saved my life!" he said angrily. "How on earth can I make you my bond servant for the rest of your life? No! I am setting you free. That's the end of the matter. You're dismissed."

Her tears came once she was back in her room. Couldn't he see that he wasn't rewarding her, he was punishing her? What could she possibly do with her freedom? At twenty years of age she was too old to attract a husband, except an elderly widower, perhaps. Would any other man besides Master Reuben appreciate the fact that she could read and write— or even allow her to? And what about Elizabeth? Leah loved the child as her very own daughter. Why couldn't Master Reuben see that? Why couldn't he marry her and they could be a family, as they had been in Caesarea? But Leah knew it was hopeless to think that a man like Master Reuben would marry her, a mere servant. Even as a free woman she was far beneath him. Beautiful Mistress Ruth had come from a wealthy aristocratic family like his.

Leah loosened her hair again and lay down on her pallet as the horrible truth began to slowly sink in. Tomorrow she would have to leave the villa that had been her home for six years. Tonight was the last night she would spend as Master Reuben's servant. She thought of all the fears she'd had on the last night she had spent with Mama and Abba before coming here and how wrong she had been about what life in this house would be like. Her biggest fear had been that Master Reuben would make her his concubine, and now . . . now she remembered being mistaken for his wife in Caesarea and realized how much she wished for that very thing. Suddenly another thought occurred to her. As long as he still owned her, it was legal according to the Law of Moses for him to take her as his concubine. And if he did . . . if she became his mistress, then they could both have their wishes. He could set his concubine free, but Leah could stay with him always.

She lay awake for a while longer until she was certain that the household was asleep. Then, with the story of Ruth and Boaz on her mind, Leah crept from her room and across the darkened courtyard to Master Reuben's sleeping chamber. The lamps were out in all of the rooms, including his. She slipped inside and saw him asleep on his ivory bed beneath the window. Leah tiptoed across the floor and lay down on the bed at his feet as Ruth the Moabitess had done. He stirred in his sleep, then sat up a moment later, startled.

"Who . . . ? Leah . . . ? What are you doing here?"

She was trembling so hard she could barely speak. "I am still your servant, Master Reuben. According to the Law, you have the right to make me your concubine."

He stared, blinking in the darkened room as if wondering if he was dreaming. When he didn't say anything, she added, "I have come to offer myself, like the Moabitess Ruth offered herself to Boaz. You have the right to redeem me. I know I'm not beautiful like Mistress Ruth was—"

He reached to put his fingers over her lips, stopping her.

"You've grown to become a very lovely woman, Leah. . . . How old are you?"

"Twenty . . . nearly twenty-one."

"And I am almost twice that."

"Master Reuben, I love you." She wasn't able to stop the words. He stared at her in amazement.

"What?"

"Please don't send me away. I can't bear the thought of never seeing you again. That's why I saved your life, don't you see? I love you." His eyes filled with emotion.

"How could you love me? I took you from your father and your home, I'm hated by everyone in the district . . . perhaps in the country—Jews and Gentiles alike."

"But I know you, I know your heart. You're not the man people think you are. Please forgive my boldness in coming to you, but you're so sad, so lonely. I would do anything for you, Master Reuben."

"You will be set free tomorrow. Why—?"

"I don't want to be free. I want to become your concubine, as the Law says. I want to stay here . . . with you."

When he suddenly turned away and climbed from the bed, Leah felt shattered. She knew she should leave now that he had rejected her, but instead, she stood and went to him.

"Master Reuben . . . what's wrong?"

"I'm not the man *you* think I am. You know nothing of my business dealings, Leah. You don't know the people I've cheated . . . the money I've skimmed off the top like cream before sending what was required to Rome. I always figured those hypocrites deserved it. The Pharisees and everyone else in this miserable town deserved to pay for the way they treated Ruth. The more people hated me, the more I took from them, and I justified it in my own mind."

Leah touched his arm. "I don't care—"

"I care," he said, twisting away. "I deserved to die in Caesarea. But if I had . . ." He paused, pressing his fingers into his eyes. "I remember how Ruth asked for forgiveness and accepted Christ when she realized she was going to die . . . and I know I'm not right with God, either. I believe that Yeshua is the Messiah. I know in my mind that it's true. But there's no room for Him in my heart because of my hatred." He lowered his hand and looked at her. "You should hate me, too, Leah. I took you from your family when you were only fourteen. I stole six years of your life because of my own greed. Yet you risked your life for me. And now you're willing to throw away your future, too, by offering yourself to me?" He shook his head. "I can't allow it."

"I love you—" she began, but he gripped her shoulders almost painfully, cutting off her words.

"Would you love me if you knew that I only had to take your brother to repay your father's debt, not you? Would you love me even then?"

Leah closed her eyes as tears rolled down her face. It took a moment for her to comprehend his words. Master Reuben had cheated her father. He had cheated her. All these years she should have been free. She should have married, had a home and children of her own.

She opened her eyes again a moment later and looked up at him. "I forgive you," she whispered.

"How can you?" he cried, releasing her again.

"Because God meant it for good. If I hadn't left home, I probably never would have learned to read and write . . . I never would have loved Ruth or Elizabeth . . . I might never have had a chance to listen to Nathaniel and learn about Yeshua. I wouldn't have known that my sins were forgiven. . . . And I never would have known you, Master Reuben."

He sighed and ran his hand over his face. "I see the difference Yeshua makes in people's lives—yours, Ehud's . . . even Ruth's for the short time she had left. I wish I could believe that He forgives me, too, but there's just too much to forgive. I don't deserve it until I try to change—"

"It doesn't work that way. If we could change ourselves,

then Yeshua wouldn't have had to die. We could just win God's favor by sacrificing sheep and following all of the Pharisees' laws and taking their stupid baths over and over again."

Reuben groaned. "It's so difficult for me to accept something I didn't pay for, something that doesn't cost me anything."

"Do you make Elizabeth pay for the gifts you give her? Weren't you willing to sacrifice your life for her in Caesarea? That's what God the Father did for His children, because He loves us."

"And you risked your life for me," he murmured. He pulled her close and held her as he had three years ago. Leah clung to him, her heart pounding against his ribs. Then he suddenly released her.

"Not like this, Leah. I want to make you a free woman. . . ."

"But I don't—"

". . . and then I will make you my wife."

Leah wondered if she had misunderstood. When she realized that she hadn't, she said, "I'm not worthy to marry you, my lord."

He rested his hands on her shoulders, gently this time. "No, I must ask God to make me worthy of you. But before you agree to marry me, you'd better consider the burden you'll bear as my wife. You'll be ridiculed as a sinner's wife, hated, spat upon. You know how the people of Degania feel about me."

"I don't care. I love you, Master Reuben."

He reached to caress her hair, which she wore unloosed. "Don't call me master . . . just Reuben."

"I love you . . . Reuben." It was easier to say than she thought it would be.

"After Ruth died I never thought I would find another woman who could love me."

"I do," she whispered.

She thought Reuben would hold her again, but instead he said, "You need to go now, Leah. In the morning I will offer your father whatever dowry he asks."

She looked up at him, longing for him, but he turned her around and pushed her gently toward the door. "Go. While I still have the strength to resist."

The next day Reb Nahum and Rabbi Eliezer, the same men who had witnessed Leah's servitude to Master Reuben six years ago, followed him to Leah's house to act as witnesses again when he granted Leah her freedom. Then they watched in mute disbelief as he asked Leah's father to name his bride-price. Leah's parents were as dumbfounded as the Pharisees were. Reuben was a wealthy man. Why not make Leah his concubine? If he wanted her, why hadn't he taken her already, as he was legally entitled to do? No one could understand it.

Leah saw that her parents hated Reuben, as much as eve-ryone else in Degania did. When Reuben counted out twice the price of the dowry Abba had named, then poured the be-trothal wine he'd brought into a beautiful Nabatean cup, Abba was torn between accepting the money and refusing to allow his daughter to be joined to such a sinner. In a decision that astounded everyone, Abba said, "I will let you choose, Leah. The money is not important. I won't sell you to him a second time."

Reuben offered the cup to Leah. Her hand brushed his as she accepted it from him. She tipped it high as she drank so there could be no doubt that she was accepting his proposal. They were betrothed.

Very few villagers joined the merriment a week later as Leah and her wedding procession walked through the streets of Degania to Reuben's villa. The marriage feast, which she and Reuben would celebrate with their Christian friends, would be held in his home, along with his baptism into the Christian faith. The Pharisees and their followers stared at her in sullen silence as she and Reuben passed. She had married a man they all hated, a man condemned as a sinner for collab-orating with the Romans. A few even spit in her path. Leah remembered how the villagers had turned away from her six years ago as she had walked this route with her brother in shame. She had trembled at the thought of becoming Reuben's concubine. Now she walked beside him with pride, her head held high, not caring that she was reviled for loving him. She would be blessed to wake up beside Reuben ben Johanan for the rest of her life, until death parted them.

THE VILLAGE OF DEGANIA—A.D. 60

Reuben's workroom was nearly empty, his tax documents packed in bundles for shipping. Leah watched as a servant girl swept up the last of the dust. The room looked so different to Leah without the long tables and benches, the scribes bent over them beneath their lampstands, copying their endless rows of figures. She found it difficult to believe that fourteen years had passed since the day Reuben had led her into this room for the first time and given her the writing board. She had been a frightened servant girl, even younger than the one sweeping the floor.

"The room looks so empty," she sighed. "What shall we do with it?"

Reuben pulled her close. "I don't care. Lodge animals in it—board it up! I only wish I'd had the courage to give up tax collecting a long time ago."

But Leah knew it had taken time for him to complete his financial obligations to Rome and to pay back the money he had unjustly taken from his countrymen. He hadn't collected one shekel more than required from them in the years since his baptism and had given a great deal of money away to his fellow believers. Yet he still didn't feel as though he had done enough.

"Hush!" she said, brushing her lips against

his. "Our past is forgotten, remember? 'As far as the east is from the west . . .' "

Reuben looked down at her, and it was the same loving gaze he had once bestowed on Ruth. Leah could never quite get over her astonishment that Reuben ben Johanan loved her, too. They had been married nearly seven years—longer than the time she had spent as his servant—yet the years had flown so swiftly. They would celebrate their anniversary in two weeks, along with the anniversary of Reuben's baptism.

"The floor is clean enough," he told the servant. "Thank you, you may go." After the girl bowed and hurried away, Reuben reached to retrieve a cylindrical clay jar from the shelf, the only item that remained on it. He pulled off the lid. "I brought you here to show these documents to you, Leah. You may read them later, if you'd like. They are all my important legal papers and records, the deeds to the land I own, including this villa . . . and this one is my will. If anything happens to me . . ."

"Reuben, please don't say it—"

"If anything happens," he said firmly, "all of my property will go to you and Elizabeth. I want you to be familiar with my affairs so that no one will take advantage of you." He put the lid back on the jar and handed it to her. It was surprisingly heavy.

"I don't want to think about anything happening to you," she said.

"I know, Leah." He brushed a strand of hair from her face. "This is just a precaution. Hopefully this is the last trip I'll have to make to Caesarea. From now on we'll live here quietly, just the three of us."

Pain shot through Leah's heart like an arrow at his words. Reuben must have seen it in her eyes. "What's wrong?" he asked.

"I'm sorry that I haven't given you a son . . . to inherit all—"

"Haven't I told you, countless times, that it doesn't matter?"

"It matters to me. Why hasn't God answered my prayers, Reuben? Why have I never become pregnant?"

He lifted the jar from her hands and set it on the shelf behind him again so he could hold her close. "Listen to me," he said. "We live in violent times. The *sicarii* dagger-men have been terrorizing Judea, committing murders and assassinations, kidnapping high officials *and* their sons. I couldn't bear it if they kidnapped one of our children, and neither could you. The Holy One knows what's best. Let's trust Him, all right? He knows what our future holds—we don't."

Leah rested her head on the curve of his chest, drawing comfort from its solidity and from the familiar scent of him. "Nathaniel thinks we're living in the end times," she said.

"I think he's right. We should be prepared for it as Yeshua warned. He said when Jerusalem is surrounded by armies the Temple would be destroyed, and times would be difficult for pregnant women and nursing mothers, remember? Maybe that's why you . . ."

"You're right," she said, "I'm sorry." Then, remembering that tomorrow he would leave for Caesarea and be gone for two weeks, she held him even tighter. "I wish you would let me go with you."

"You know why that's impossible, Leah. Travel is becoming much too dangerous these days. Besides, wouldn't you prefer to watch the workers finish your floor?"

Reuben had commissioned a new mosaic floor for the reception room as an anniversary present after Leah had admired a similar one in Sepphoris. It fascinated her to watch the artisans turn piles of multicolored stones into a magnificent design. There were rolling waves along the edge in shades of green and blue that reminded her of the waves that washed against the great breakwaters in Caesarea. Above them, in testimony to their faith, she had asked the artist to add the believers' symbol of a fish and the Greek letters that stood for Yeshua the Messiah.

"Will you be back in time to break bread for the Sabbath?" she asked.

"Absolutely. You know I wouldn't miss it for anything."

But the sun was setting two weeks later, the Sabbath was beginning, and Reuben still hadn't returned from Caesarea. Wherever he was, Leah knew that he would now have to stay there an extra day, since travel wasn't allowed on the Sabbath. Their fellow believers had all arrived for the service, which was held in the villa each week, but Leah remained in the doorway, watching for her husband.

Miriam rested her hand on Leah's shoulder. "It's time to light the Sabbath candles."

"I'll be right there." She looked down the deserted street one last time, but Reuben's traveling party was nowhere in sight. That meant another day of waiting, another night spent alone. Leah hated the lonely nights when Reuben was away. Disappointed, she finally closed the door and went inside.

The others were already gathered around the table, seated on cushions on the newly completed floor. Everyone was admiring the mosaic, especially the fish symbols. Leah showed them where she had added Reuben's name in one corner for a surprise. She couldn't wait to show it to him.

When it was time to read the Word of God, someone asked to hear the copy of the letter the apostle Peter had written to encourage believers in these difficult times. Usually Reuben was the one who read from the scrolls, but tonight Ehud stood to read, instead. Suddenly Leah felt the Holy Spirit's nudge, making her sit up and take notice. *This is important,* He seemed to say. *This is for you.* The hair on her arms stood on end.

" 'As you come to him, the living Stone—rejected by men but chosen by God and precious to him—you also, like living stones, are being built into a spiritual house to be a holy priesthood, offering spiritual sacrifices . . . you are a chosen people, a royal priesthood, a holy nation, a people belonging to God, that you may declare the praises of him who called you out of darkness into his wonderful light.' "

The words seemed to be preparing Leah for something— she didn't know what. They seemed to be describing the new temple God would build after the old one was destroyed, a new priesthood that she was to be part of, declaring His praises.

Leah closed her eyes as the believers bowed for prayer. She tried to pray for Reuben, to pray that he was safe for the night somewhere, that he would return home safely tomorrow. But the peace she usually felt when she prayed never came. Instead, Leah felt a yawning emptiness and a fear that could not be measured.

THE GOLANI HOTEL, ISRAEL—1999

Abby was rinsing out her laundry in the bathroom sink one evening when the telephone rang. She picked up the receiver with dripping hands and recognized Hannah's excited voice on the other end.

"Abby, I found it! Remember I told you that name on the mosaic floor was familiar—Reuben ben Johanan? I figured out why! Come over if you're free, and I'll show you. It's unbelievable!"

Abby left the clothing to soak and hurried to Hannah's bungalow. She smiled when she saw the mess Hannah had made with storage boxes, papers, and bound field reports strewn all over the room. Hannah seemed oblivious to the clutter as she waved a sheaf of papers in triumph.

"I knew it had to be a first-century dig if it was the same Reuben, so I narrowed the search down to all the ones where we found first-century documents or inscriptions. That still left quite a few, but here it is! Gamla! We found a cache of documents belonging to Reuben ben Johanan during the excavation at Gamla in 1978! And wait until you hear this! One of the documents was a marriage contract between Reuben and a woman named Leah!"

"Wow!" Abby exclaimed. "Do you suppose it could be *our* Leah?"

"It's just too incredible to be a coincidence. The contract

says they were both from Degania."

Stunned, Abby searched in vain for a chair that wasn't piled with papers, then finally sat on Hannah's rumpled bed. "Where was this other dig? Is it near here?"

"Yes. Gamla is here on the Golan Heights, only twenty kilometers or so from Degania. It was a well-fortified Jewish stronghold during the Roman invasion of A.D. 67, so whoever carried Reuben ben Johanan's documents there probably fled to Gamla for refuge when the Romans attacked. Josephus describes Gamla in his book *The Jewish War*. I'll let you borrow my copy if I can find it." She rifled through the piles of books, searching as she talked. "Ah! Here it is." She brandished a well-worn volume.

"Josephus was a famous Jewish historian, wasn't he?" Abby said as she accepted the book.

"Or a famous Jewish traitor," Hannah said, laughing. "It depends on who you ask. He was born Joseph ben Mattathias, the son of a wealthy priest. When the war with the Romans broke out, he was given command of all the Jewish forces in Galilee. Of course, the Romans slaughtered his army, but Joseph somehow managed to safely surrender, then he wormed his way into the Roman general's favor. He was technically a prisoner when he began writing his eyewitness account of the war, including the battle at Gamla. He later changed his name to Josephus."

"When did you say you took part in that dig?"

"I was there for three summers, from 1976 until 1978." Hannah also searched for a place to sit, then finally scooped up the papers from one of the chairs and dumped them onto the floor. "I worked at Gamla at a very important time in my life," she said, her voice growing soft and wistful. "That dig will always be very special to me. I almost gave up archaeology—almost gave up on life, in fact—until Gamla. . . ."

JERUSALEM, ISRAEL—OCTOBER 6, 1973

Hannah sat in the synagogue pew with eight-year-old Rachel, trying to recite the prayers that were part of the ritual of

Yom Kippur. Her eyes kept straying from the prayer book to her husband, Jake, seated on the raised platform in front. He had been chosen as one of the six men called to read the Torah on this, the holiest day of the year. To Hannah, he seemed even more handsome at age thirty-six than he had been when they'd met twelve years ago. She couldn't keep her eyes off him. When Jake looked up and caught her gaze resting on him, Hannah winked. He tried to give her a stern look—she was outrageous to flirt with him during a holy ceremony—but she saw the corner of his mouth twitch as he looked away, suppressing a grin.

Yom Kippur had begun the evening before at sundown. As with the Sabbath and all the other holidays, Jake took the celebration very seriously. This was a day of repentance, a twenty-four-hour fast in which worshipers searched their hearts before approaching God to confess their sins. A deep stillness had blanketed the city as the three of them had walked together to the synagogue on this holy day, a peace that Hannah felt to the very marrow of her bones.

When the first interruption came—a messenger tiptoeing down the aisle to beckon to one of the men—Hannah thought little of it. But after four or five men had been interrupted while at prayer and handed notes, she began to wonder what on earth was going on. The atmosphere of solemnity cracked, then shattered as one by one, more and more men began to collect their families and leave. After one of the messages was brought to Daniel Ben-Ami, seated beside Jake on the platform, Jake also rose and strode down the aisle, motioning for Hannah and Rachel to follow him.

"What's going on?" Hannah asked as soon as they stepped outside onto the sidewalk.

"I don't know, but I think we'd better find out. I saw the papers they handed to Daniel. They were mobilization orders."

Hannah said no more, knowing that Jake would be reluctant to voice any fears or speculations in front of Rachel. As they hurried home, she tried to recall if anything had appeared in the news yesterday that might have prompted this. She could think of nothing except an incident involving Jews somewhere in Europe—certainly nothing that would require some of Israel's reserve troops to be mobilized.

"Abba, why are there so many cars on the street?" Rachel asked. "No one ever drives on Yom Kippur."

"I don't kn—" Jake's words were drowned out by the sudden screaming wail of an air raid siren. It was so close that Rachel shrieked and leaped into her father's arms in fright. Hannah felt her own heart leaping in her chest as they stood frozen in shock on the sidewalk.

"Do you suppose someone hit the wrong button by accident?" she shouted above the din. "They wouldn't hold an air raid drill on Yom Kippur, would they?"

Jake shook his head, bewildered. "It's not just one siren. Listen—they're going off all over the city!"

He grabbed Hannah's hand and they began to run, with Rachel still clinging to Jake for dear life. Hannah unlocked their apartment door with trembling fingers and raced inside to switch on the radio. Nothing. Stations didn't broadcast on Yom Kippur.

"We should go downstairs to the shelter," Jake said, "just in case it's a real air raid."

"Abba, I'm scared," Rachel whimpered.

"I know, love."

But by the time they reached the basement, the sirens stopped as abruptly as they had started. Hannah's knees felt rubbery as she climbed the stairs again. She left the radio turned on, the static hissing like steam while they waited.

"Are we going back to the synagogue?" Rachel asked.

"No, I think we'd better stay here until we find out what the sirens were for. If everything is all right, we'll go back this evening for *Neilah*, the closing." He settled on the sofa to wait, and Rachel snuggled beside him.

"I thought you were the best reader in the whole synagogue, Abba," she said. "Mr. Ben-Ami mumbles."

Jake smiled as he smoothed his daughter's dark hair, tangled from their wild run. "Why, that's very kind of you to say so—but you wouldn't be biased at all, would you?"

"What does that mean?"

"Playing favorites," Hannah said irritably. She didn't understand how Jake could sit there so serenely when it was obvious that something terrible was happening. She got up from her chair and started toward the kitchen, thinking she might keep busy by fixing something to eat, then she remembered that they were fasting. Jake gave her a pleading look when he caught her eye, shaking his head slightly, as if asking her to remain calm for Rachel's sake. Hannah sat down again.

"Did you understand what the passages meant that we were reading?" Jake asked Rachel a moment later.

"Some of them. Not the part about those goats, though."

"Let me see if I can explain it." Jake started to rake his fingers through his own hair, then stopped when he realized that he still wore his *yarmulke* on his head. "Every Yom Kippur we rehearse for the day when we will face God's judgment. We think about death by fasting and denying ourselves all of the usual pleasures of life for twenty-four hours. Then we confess our sins and repent—which means we turn away from them— and we promise to live better by God's strength.

"During the time when there was a Temple, the priests would lay their hands on the two goats' heads, symbolizing that the goats now carried all of the people's sin. One goat was sacrificed and its blood was brought before God's seat of mercy. The other one, the scapegoat, was set free in the Judean wilderness. By His grace, God allowed people to transfer their sins onto a sacrifice so they could be forgiven."

"Why don't we do the part with the goats anymore?"

"Because we no longer have a Temple."

"What happened to it?"

"The Romans destroyed it in A.D. 70," Hannah told her, "when they destroyed Jerusalem." She rose again, too restless to stay seated, and peered out of the window at the street. There shouldn't have been any traffic on Yom Kippur, but there was. More than when they had walked home from the synagogue.

"Can't we build another temple?" Rachel asked.

"Not on the original site, sweetie," Hannah said, sitting again. "The Muslims built the Dome of the Rock on our Temple Mount." She didn't realize how tense she was until the radio suddenly sprang to life, startling her.

"This is a special bulletin. The sirens are not a false alarm. If they sound again, everyone must go to their shelters immediately." The station began to play a recording of classical music—the slow, mournful strains of Beethoven.

"Why? Tell us what is going on!" Hannah shook the radio as if it were a stubborn person who refused to talk.

"Hannah . . ." Jake said gently.

She heard Rachel draw a deep breath, then slowly exhale. "Abba, is it okay to miss the rest of the Yom Kippur service?" she asked. Like her father, Rachel would try to keep her fear at bay by talking of other things. "Will we still be forgiven, even though we left early?"

"Yes, God knows if we're really sorry for our sins, and He forgives us. Would you like me to read the part of the service that we're missing? The *Haftara*, or prophetic portion for this afternoon, is the book of Jonah."

Hannah felt like screaming as she listened to Jake calmly read the story of the reluctant prophet who was swallowed by a great fish. But it had the desired effect of keeping Rachel soothed and occupied while they waited.

"I never did understand why they always read the book of Jonah on Yom Kippur," Hannah said irritably when he finished.

"Because repentance and forgiveness aren't just for the Jews, but for the Gentiles, as well," Jake explained. "God said that all nations would be blessed through Abraham. Do you realize that Jonah was sent to preach to Israel's bitterest enemy, Assyria? The story reminds us that God established His kingdom in His people so that we would bring His redemption to the whole earth—even to the people who hate us."

"Impossible," Hannah said. "Our enemies don't even want to admit we exist, much less listen to us."

At exactly 3:30, the music stopped and the radio crackled with another special bulletin. Hannah held her breath while she listened. *"Ladies and gentlemen, Israel has been attacked by both Egypt and Syria. Partial mobilization has been ordered—"*

It was all she heard as the air raid sirens suddenly began to wail again. Jake scrambled to his feet, pulling Rachel with him. "Down to the shelter!" he yelled above the sound of the siren, rising and falling like a woman's scream. Hannah grabbed the radio, yanking the plug from the wall. No one spoke as they huddled in the gloomy basement with their white-faced neighbors. Ten minutes later, the all-clear sounded.

"This is nerve-wracking!" the man who lived across the hall from them groaned as they trudged back upstairs to their apartments. "When do you suppose we'll find out what's happening?"

"You'd better keep your radio on," Jake told him. "I imagine our communications are in chaos because of the holiday."

Outside their living room window, Hannah saw three vehicles packed with soldiers racing down the street. A news bulletin asked that all nonessential traffic keep off the main roads. Another announcement stated that an emergency hospital had been opened for military casualties. Hannah and Jake looked at each other. If there were military casualties, the situation must be very serious. Coded mobilization orders were being broadcast off and on, in between musical selections. The three of them huddled around the kitchen table in numb silence, waiting for the next news report, listening for Jake's coded orders.

After what seemed an eternity, there was another bulletin at 4:20. *"Ladies and gentlemen, we are receiving reports of fierce fighting in the Sinai. The Egyptians have crossed the canal at several points and are on the East Bank. There is fighting on land and in the air."*

Jake stared at the radio in stunned disbelief. "If that's true, then our fortifications must have fallen. The only way the Egyptians could possibly be on the East Bank is if our line of defense collapsed."

"But how could it collapse? We have the best equipment and—"

"Hannah, it's a holiday. Nearly everyone was home on leave except for the newest recruits."

"Oh, dear God," she moaned. The unimaginable had happened. Egypt and Syria had declared war on the holiest day of the year.

Jake got up from the table and disappeared into the bedroom. When he didn't come back right away, Hannah followed him. He had already put on his uniform and was packing the rest of his gear into his kit bag. He looked up. She quickly turned away so he wouldn't see her tears.

At six o'clock that evening, Prime Minister Golda Meir came on the air to make a speech to her nation. The three of them gathered around the kitchen table again to listen.

"At two o'clock this afternoon," Mrs. Meir began, *"both Egypt and Syria crossed the cease-fire lines and opened hostilities on land and in the air—"* She was interrupted by a warning signal, followed by more coded mobilization orders. When Jake closed his eyes, Hannah knew that one of them had been his.

"Where, Jake?" she asked. He held up his hand, asking her to wait as the Prime Minister resumed her speech.

"I have no doubt that no one will give in to panic. We must be prepared for any burden and sacrifice demanded for the defense of our very existence, our freedom, and our independence."

Hannah remembered what Jake had told her after the Six-Day War—how he had been terrified during the battle, how he hoped and prayed that he would never have to fight again. But he would willingly shoulder the burden of combat, making that sacrifice for her and Rachel.

"How could we not have known?" Jake asked when the speech ended. "How could we have let ourselves be taken by surprise like this? Where was our intelligence?"

Hannah reached for his hand. "Jake? Where are they sending you?" His answer was barely audible.

"The Golan Heights."

She took a deep breath as she tried to control her tears and her trembling voice. "To fight against the Syrians with their Soviet-made equipment?" she asked bitterly.

"The Soviets are backing and supplying Egypt, too," he said. "They've had six years to analyze the last war and learn from it. And this time they were the ones who used the element of surprise." He bent to put on his boots, preparing to leave. They both knew that it was vitally important for every able-bodied man to join the fighting as soon as possible, but Hannah longed to cling to him, to beg him to delay his departure just a little longer.

"Do you think Jordan and Iraq will fight us, too?" she asked.

"It may not matter," he said, tugging his bootlaces. "Even if no other Arab country declares war, the Syrian and Egyptian troops outnumber us six-to-one. We're outnumbered in armor four-to-one."

Hannah and Jake looked at each other, then at Rachel, as if realizing at the same moment that she hadn't spoken for a long time, that they had been voicing their fears in front of her. Rachel's eyes swam with tears.

"I'll pray for you every day, Abba, and ask God to keep you safe." Jake pulled her into his arms and let her bury her head on his shoulder.

"If it's His will, Rachel . . . we must always yield to His will. Otherwise, we're putting ourselves in God's place, telling Him how to run the universe. No one must sit in God's place."

"But why would it be God's will for you . . . to die?" she asked as her tears were unleashed.

"Who can know the mind of the Almighty One? Many good men died in the last war, Rachel, and we don't know why. We can't see His design because we stand too close to it."

"What do you mean, Abba?"

"Here, come with me." He led her to the cluttered desk in the living room where Hannah's artifacts were piled in jumbled disarray. Hannah watched from the doorway as he sorted through potsherds and jar handles until he found what he wanted. He held up a small bean-sized square of green stone. "What is this?" he asked.

"A mosaic stone," Rachel answered.

"Yes, yes, but what is it? The eye of a fish? A piece of the border? Part of a flower?"

"I don't know."

"Neither of us do because we can't see the whole mosaic. We don't know what the artist's design was or where this piece fit into it. But you've seen mosaics, Rachel. You know how beautiful and intricate they can be, forming a picture that looks whole and complete from a distance, even though it's really made of tiny individual squares of stone."

He gently laid the stone in the palm of her hand and cupped his strong ones around hers. "We are those individual stones in God's design, Rachel. The Master Artist cuts us and shapes us so that we'll each fit into our place. The final picture is the redemption of the world. God is always working toward that redemption. I want to be part of it, and I know you do, too. We have to trust that no matter what happens to us, God is bringing redemption from it. We have to trust His unfailing love and take refuge in it."

Jake left a few minutes later. He said good-bye quickly, knowing it would be harder on all of them if he prolonged it. Hannah held her husband close, kissed him, and then he was gone.

Rather than face the emptiness he left behind, she decided to walk back to the synagogue with Rachel for the closing service of Yom Kippur. It began at twilight and lasted until the stars came out. She wasn't surprised to find the synagogue packed.

Hannah took Rachel's hand in hers as they stood for prayers and heard the reassuring words from Isaiah, "Those who trust in the Lord shall exchange strength for weariness." Together they recited the Sh'ma Yisrael, their creed of faith: "Hear, O Israel: The Lord our God, the Lord is one. Love the

Lord your God with all your heart and with all your soul and with all your strength." But Hannah shuddered, remembering Jake's words, as the rabbi gave the call for God's kingdom and His redemption to be made known in all the earth. She didn't want God's will if it meant taking Jake away from her forever. She wanted her will—that they would win the war quickly, that their lives would go on the way they always had, that Jake would come home to her again.

The service ended with the cry of faith, "God is Lord!" as the shofar sounded its final blast. But Hannah's heart wouldn't allow her to speak the words.

———

As the war dragged into its second week, a great cloud of gloom seemed to descend over the nation. There would be no easy victory as there had been during the last war. Each inch of land seemed hard-won as the Israelis slowly pushed the invaders back toward the cease-fire lines. Great Britain refused to resupply Israel, while the Soviet Union sent massive supplies of tanks, antitank missiles, and planes to Israel's enemies. Any Israeli successes were quickly canceled out as new equipment arrived in Egypt and Syria to replace what they had lost. The end was nowhere in sight.

Israeli citizens had been asked not to use the telephone except for emergencies, which is why Hannah was so surprised when hers suddenly rang. Devorah sounded breathless on the other end. "I think I'm going into labor," she said.

"Now? Isn't it too early?"

"Yes, two weeks early. Would you mind coming over to watch the kids? My mother can't get down here from Galilee."

Hannah's bags were already packed and sitting by the door in case she needed them for the air raid shelter. She and Rachel grabbed them and ran the few blocks to Ben and Devorah's apartment. Eleven-year-old Itzak let them in. His mother lay panting on the sofa.

"Sorry . . . I would have timed this baby better . . . if I'd known there was going to be another war."

"Listen, Devorah, didn't your last baby come very quickly? You'd better let me take you to the hospital. Itzak, Sam, and Rachel can watch the two little ones for an hour or so." She helped Devorah into Ben's car and raced through the streets, praying that there wouldn't be any air raid sirens to terrify the children while she was gone. Devorah's contractions were alarmingly close together, and Hannah added another quick prayer that she wouldn't have to pull the car over to the side of the street and deliver the baby herself. They were met outside the emergency room door by an orderly with a wheelchair.

"I'll come inside as soon as I park the car," Hannah promised.

"No . . . I'd rather you went home to be with the kids." Devorah smiled weakly and added, "I've done this before."

Hannah drove a bit more cautiously on the return trip to the apartment. Devorah and Ben had moved to a larger one four years ago after their fourth child, Miriam, was born. It didn't seem possible that little Rebeccah, whom Devorah had been expecting during the last war, was six years old already. Hannah envied Devorah's fertility. The large family she and Jake longed for had never arrived.

Devorah phoned while they were eating dinner to tell them that she'd had a baby boy. "He only weighs two and a half kilos, so they have him in an incubator. Otherwise, he checked out just fine."

"You sound tired, Dev."

"I am, but not from the delivery. Wait until you've fed, clothed, and chased my brood around that apartment for a day or two and you'll understand why I'm looking forward to a nice long rest in the hospital."

Hannah laughed. "Thanks a lot, sweetie."

"Oh, one more thing—Ben and I never settled on a name before he left. If you manage to get ahold of him, tell him to make up his mind. They need to know what to put on the birth certificate."

Getting through to Ben in a war zone proved nearly impossible. Hannah left phone messages at his command center, but since it wasn't an emergency, she was told not to expect a return call any time soon. In the meantime, she and the children nicknamed the baby *Katan* because he was so small.

The day before Devorah and the baby were due home from the hospital, a Sergeant Givati telephoned. Thinking it might be a message from Ben at last, Hannah shouted for the children to quiet down.

"Is this Mrs. Benjamin Rosen?" Sergeant Givati asked.

"No, I'm Ben's cousin, Hannah Rahov. Mrs. Rosen is in the hospital. I've been trying to reach Ben to tell him she just had a baby."

The long pause that followed terrified Hannah. "Hello? Are you still there?" she cried.

Sergeant Givati cleared his throat. "Could you please relay the message to her that Captain Rosen has also been hospitalized?"

"What happened? Is Ben all right?"

"This report says that his injuries aren't critical."

Hannah sank into the nearest chair in relief. "Where is he? May I see him?"

"He was transferred to the military hospital here in Jerusalem this morning, but you'll have to talk to his doctor before you can visit."

"Tell him I'll be there in half an hour."

Hannah convinced a neighbor to keep an eye on the children while she raced across town to visit Ben. She needed to see for herself how he was before breaking the news to Devorah and the children. It seemed to take forever for them to locate Ben's doctor, but when he finally arrived, Hannah was alarmed to discover that the man was a psychiatrist. He steered her into his office to talk.

"Captain Rosen's physical injuries aren't critical," he began. "They're not the reason he was hospitalized. I'm afraid he has suffered a very serious emotional breakdown . . . from battle stress."

"A breakdown?" Hannah didn't believe it. They had the

wrong person. "Ben has never been afraid of anything in his life!"

The doctor removed his glasses and laid them on his desk. "Captain Rosen's case is somewhat unusual. While the syndrome is most commonly triggered by fear, or perhaps horror at the carnage of war, your cousin's breakdown was triggered by extreme rage. He was not afraid to throw himself into battle—quite the opposite. He blazed into it as if he didn't care if he lived or died. I'm told that he fought very valiantly, too—if somewhat wildly. But he was endangering his men and himself by taking unreasonable risks and defying orders. They only got him to stop when he ran out of ammunition."

Once again, Hannah felt afraid. "How can I help?"

"Could you bring his wife here? We had him transferred to this hospital with the hope that if he saw his family he might remember all the reasons he has to live."

"She's in another hospital. She just had a baby. But Ben and I are very close, more like brother and sister than cousins. I'd like to see him."

"All right," the doctor said after a moment. He stood and they began walking down the corridor. "Captain Rosen still hasn't talked about what triggered his rage. He either can't or won't discuss it with me." They stopped again outside the door to Ben's ward. "Please don't be alarmed when you see him. He had to be sedated . . . and restrained."

Hannah watched Ben from the doorway for a moment before going inside. He wore a bandage above his right eye, and his face and hands appeared sunburned with first-degree burns. He was awake and restless in spite of the sedation, his hands trembling, his body twitching and jerking against the restraints. She drew a deep breath, forcing back her tears. Ben was alive. He would be all right.

"Shalom, Ben," she said as she bent to kiss his forehead. He stared at her for a long moment before recognition dawned.

"Hannah!" But instead of being pleased to see her, he looked wild-eyed, frightened.

"How are you, sweetie?" When he simply stared at her, she decided she would have to do all the talking. "Listen, I've come with some good news. You're a father again. Devorah had a baby boy. They're both fine, but she wants to know what to name him."

Ben went pale beneath his livid burns as if the news had unnerved him. His reaction was all wrong. He loved his children. He had looked forward to being a father again. "Ben? What's wrong?"

"How long ago?"

"Three days. But don't worry, the baby is fine except for a little jaundice. Dev is fine, too. They'll probably come home tomorrow. Rachel and I have been staying at your place, taking care of the other kids. Boy, I don't know how that woman does it full time. She deserves a medal. I'm afraid I've managed to trash your nice, neat apartment. . . ."

"You're at my apartment?"

His voice had the tone of slowly dawning horror, as if the conclusion he was drawing terrified him rather than cheered him. Hannah couldn't understand it. She decided to keep talking in the hope that her joyful news would finally register.

"Yes, it was easier for all of us. Your apartment is so much bigger than mine. I promised Devorah I'd stay another week and help her with the baby after she comes home tomorrow. Her mother can't get down here. But Dev wants to know what to name the baby. She said you never settled on a name, and the poor kid really needs one. I said she should call him Ben Junior since the little guy looks just like you. He even has your bald spot on top and—"

"You haven't been home—back to your own apartment—since Monday morning?" His words came out like a drowning man's, gasping for air. Hannah went cold with fear.

"No, there was no sense running back and forth. . . ."

"Then you don't know . . . you haven't been told!" Ben's voice caught as he choked back a sob.

Hannah lowered herself to the edge of his bed as she felt her knees go weak. She stared at her cousin and knew in an instant what had triggered his rage. *Oh, God. Don't say it, Ben. Please don't say it.*

Ben tried to cover his face so she wouldn't read the truth in his eyes, but his wrists were fastened to the bed rails. He closed his eyes and turned his head away. Hannah grabbed his shoulders, shaking him.

"I haven't been told *what*? Is it Jake? Tell me!"

"Please . . . don't make me . . ."

"Tell me, Ben, or I swear I'll beat it out of you! What happened!" Her own fear and rage had so overwhelmed her that she no longer cared about his.

Ben slowly stammered out the story, every word drawn out torturously.

"There was a skirmish. I took a hit with some shrapnel . . . above my eye. Jake thought . . . he said it needed stitches."

Hannah didn't want to hear it, but she knew that she had to—from Ben if he had witnessed it, not from some falsely compassionate government messenger sent to break the news to her.

"When the Syrian tanks withdrew and there was a lull in the fighting, Jake made me go to the first-aid station. I didn't want to go. I told him I was okay. I wanted to stay with our squad."

No . . . no . . . no . . . The words rang in Hannah's heart like a death knell.

"There were so many wounded at the station . . . all worse off than me. I couldn't help it that I was gone too long . . . that I got back too late . . ."

She touched the bandage above Ben's eye, as if her fingers could magically heal the wound and change the outcome of what Ben was trying to tell her.

"The order to advance came through while I was gone. . . . Six centurion tanks from our division were sent ahead to attack."

"Jake's?" she whispered.

Ben nodded. "I was too late . . . I had to stay behind in one of the tanks that was supposed to cover them . . . even though we were no good to them. We were no good to them at *all!*"

Ben was describing her premonition. Hannah watched it happen as vividly as if she stood beside him on the Golan Heights.

"As they neared the top of the hill, a hidden antitank battery opened fire. The Syrians had Russian-made Sagger antitank missiles powerful enough to break through armor plate. . . . There was nothing I could do. . . . They took a direct hit . . . all six of our tanks . . . exploded—"

"No!" Hannah screamed as she felt the impact, the heat, the searing shrapnel.

"I had to watch them all die . . . and there was nothing I could do!" Ben writhed in bed, fighting the restraints and the drugs that held him back as his rage rekindled. "But I blasted them to Sheol, Hannah! I got the monsters who did that to Jake! I would kill *all* of them if they would just let me out of this *bed*! Let me go back there!"

Ben's words faded in the background as the room pitched and reeled from the explosion. The last time Hannah had only imagined it. The last time it hadn't been real. Jake had come home to her, he had held her, loved her.

Please don't let this be real. Please let this be a dream, a mistake. Jake will be all right, he'll come home. . . .

But as she listened to Ben's cries of despair, Hannah knew that it was true.

"Oh, God, *no!* Jake!"

Hannah didn't realize she had screamed aloud until the nursing staff rushed into the room, prepared to give her a sedative. She fought them off.

"No, don't—I don't want anything, I have kids to take care of, I have to drive home," she insisted. "Don't give me anything. I'll . . . I'll be all right."

She couldn't fall apart yet. She had to be strong for Ben. For Rachel. For Devorah and the children. Who would take care of everyone if she fell apart?

Hannah unfastened one of Ben's wrists so he could cling to her. They wept for Jake in each other's arms.

Somehow, Hannah got home. She got through the day. And the next one, and the next. She thought only of the task at hand, not allowing the truth to find a resting place in her heart. *Take care of the baby. Take care of Devorah, the children.*

The war ended a week later on October twenty-fourth as both sides settled back on the cease-fire lines. The reserves returned home. Daily life slowly resumed.

At first Hannah couldn't comprehend that Jake was really gone, even when she moved back to her own apartment, even after the official death notice arrived. *When Jake comes home . . .* she would find herself thinking a dozen times a day. *Jake would like this* or *I must remember to tell Jake . . .* Mail still arrived with his name on it.

Then one day his kit bag was delivered to the house by a female soldier. Hannah carried it to their bedroom and opened it. She took out his Torah, his prayer shawl, a partially finished letter he had started writing to her. It was dated the day he died. The only words he had written in his strong bold print were, *Dear Hannah . . .*

"You didn't finish it, Jake!" she cried aloud. "You didn't finish our life together! We were just getting started! We were supposed to grow old, spoil our grandchildren. . . . Why didn't you finish it?"

The finality of her loss sank in. Jake was dead. Gone forever. Hannah wanted to wail and scream at God's injustice, but she heard a soft hurt sound, like an abandoned kitten, and looked up to see Rachel standing in the doorway. Her daughter was looking to her for strength.

"Come here, sweetie," she said, opening her arms.

"I miss Abba so much," she wept. "I want him to come home."

"I know, sweetie, I know. But if Abba could talk to you right now, what do you think he would tell you to do?"

"To . . . to trust in God's unfailing love."

"Then that's what we'll do, Rachel. That's what we have to do."

Even as she said the words aloud, Hannah knew they were lies. She didn't trust God anymore because He had betrayed her. How could a loving God take Jake away from them? How could a loving God allow a good man like Jake to die? A man who loved Him, trusted Him?

Hannah awoke that night and found herself listening for the sound of Jake's soft breathing beside her. The room was as silent as the grave. If she reached for him she wouldn't find the comforting warmth of his body, only the cold chill of empty sheets. Hell must be just as silent, just as cold.

Unable to endure it, Hannah climbed out of bed and wandered into Rachel's room. She brushed the hair from her daughter's face and found that it was still damp with tears. The blankets were rumpled from her restless sleep. As Hannah smoothed them and tucked them around her again, she noticed that Rachel's fist was clenched, as if clutching something. She gently uncurled her daughter's fingers and saw the tiny green mosaic stone.

Hannah knew she could never tell her daughter that Jake had lied to her, that the God he believed in did cruel things that made no sense. There was no design, no pattern. For Rachel's sake she would have to pretend it was all true, burying her doubt and her pain deep inside where no one could see them. It was much better for everyone if Hannah's life was a lie instead of Jake's.

JERUSALEM, ISRAEL—1973

Three months after the cease-fire, Ben arrived unannounced at Hannah's office at the Archaeological Institute. She had avoided him since his release from the hospital, knowing that his devastating guilt would heal faster if he wasn't forced to face her and be reminded of Jake. She also found it harder to hide her unending grief from Ben than from any other person. He knew her too well. He would see through her facade. She greeted his unexpected visit with strained laughter and a hug.

"You named that poor baby Mordecai? What on earth were you thinking, Ben!"

He didn't return her smile. "It was my father's name."

"Well, I know it was, but honestly, Benjamin! What a thing to do to a helpless child."

"You're too thin," he said.

"You should talk! How much weight have you lost—twenty, thirty pounds? As the proud papa of six kids, you could afford a little paunch, you know. You've earned it." He was much too serious. Hannah wondered if he was still on medication, if he had fully recovered from his shock.

"You'd better tell me why you're here," she said when she failed to lift his gloom. She closed her door and they both sat down,

Hannah's desk a messy buffer between them.

"Devorah insisted that I come and tell you in person," he said after a long moment. He was unnaturally still. "I have accepted a new position with the Israeli government. I've joined the Agency."

"The *agency*? Which agency?" She racked her brain, trying to think of any agricultural agencies he might have mentioned in the past or that she might have read about in the news. She drew a blank.

"I'm an undercover agent, Hannah."

She stared at him, fighting the urge to laugh out loud. She waited for his face to split into a grin, for him to tell her that it was all a joke. Ben, the father of six children—a spy? But his somber expression never changed.

"Are you out of your mind?" She said it without thinking, then wanted to bite her tongue off when she remembered his stay in the psychiatric ward. "Why, Ben?"

"To make sure we're never caught by surprise like that again."

"But . . . but you're a scientist, not a spy!"

"The Agency approached me several years ago. They said that my role as an agricultural expert would gain me access to all kinds of places worldwide. It would be an ideal cover for gathering information and making contacts. I finally agreed."

She stared at him, trying to comprehend. "Is the work dangerous?" When he didn't answer, she knew that it was. It was a long moment before she could speak. "Please don't do this, Ben. I don't want to lose you, too."

He gazed at the top of her desk, his eyes unfocused. "You should have already lost me. I should have died along with the others." When he finally looked up, his voice was as haunted and hollow as his eyes. "We had some of our newest recruits manning those fortifications along the Suez. They were children, fresh out of training. All the experienced troops had been allowed to go home on leave for the holidays. The Egyptians slaughtered them, Hannah. They rained down hundreds of rounds of ammunition in a matter of minutes! The kids in those trenches never stood a chance!" Ben paused when his voice broke. "Where was our intelligence? Why didn't we know? How could they have amassed so many troops on two of our borders and we never knew they were planning to attack?"

Hannah closed her eyes, remembering how Jake had asked the same question the night he left for the Golan Heights.

"My son Itzak will be old enough for the army in a few years," Ben said. "I need to make sure that something like this never happens again."

Hannah longed to plead with him, to convince him that it wasn't his responsibility, to beg him to think about his family. But she knew that Devorah had probably said all of those things. She gazed at her cousin's granite face and knew that she would be wasting her words. "Promise me you'll be careful," she said uselessly.

Ben never moved a muscle. "Of course, Hannah."

JERUSALEM, ISRAEL—1976

Hannah's grief seemed endlessly deep, silently eating away at her, leaving her hollow inside. When she first awoke in the morning, a brief moment might pass in which she forgot that Jake was dead, but then she would remember that he was never coming home, and the slow daylong spiral into despair would begin. But even as sorrow silently wailed in her heart, Hannah kept going, maintaining the facade of normal life for Rachel's sake. Like a wooden marionette with a painted smile, Hannah dutifully acted her part. *Get through today, get through the night, get through another day*.

Rachel wanted to continue attending the synagogue, so Hannah fulfilled all of the rituals with her, performing her lines by rote. When Yom Kippur rolled around each year and the rabbi promised that "Those who trust in the Lord shall exchange strength for weariness," she wanted to shout aloud that it was a lie, that God was a cruel tyrant. She and Rachel said prayers every morning, just as they had when Jake was alive: *"How priceless is your unfailing love! Both high and low among men find refuge in the shadow of your wings."* But they were words—empty, meaningless words.

Rachel clung to the tiny mosaic stone Jake had given her, trying to remember and believe that his death had meaning. Afraid Rachel would lose it, Hannah had it mounted in a jewelry setting and hung on a chain so she could wear it around her neck. For her daughter's sake, she mouthed Jake's words about God's design, but Hannah wanted nothing to do with God's purposes. Jake was dead. Even if He showed her how Jake's death fit into His grand design, she would never agree that it was worth such a terrible price.

As the third anniversary of Jake's death rolled around, and Hannah stood with Rachel at his grave, she longed to simply lie down beside him and wait to die. She was nothing but a hollow shell. She had reached the end of her strength. With the puppet strings stretched tight and ready to snap, she knew that she couldn't keep up the act much longer. But then Rachel looked up at her, her dark eyes trusting and hopeful.

"Abba isn't really in this grave, is he, Mama? He's in paradise, resting in Abraham's bosom."

"Yes, that's right, sweetie." Hannah knew she must keep dancing, keep performing for Rachel's sake.

———

Hannah sat alone in her office eating lunch one day in late winter, staring at the gunmetal gray sky outside her window. It was always so cold when it rained in Jerusalem and so depressingly dreary. She could have eaten lunch with her colleagues in the faculty lounge, but she was avoiding them, avoiding the endless discussions of their summer dig plans, the boastful stories of last summer's finds.

At work she staggered through her classes because she needed the income to live, but Hannah lacked the energy or the will to dig in the summer, afraid that it would be a painful reminder of the summer that she and Jake had met. He had played such an important part in her work after they married; she had dug for him, not for her career or for personal glory. Her discoveries always excited Jake as they proved again and again the truth of the Scriptures. He had been the one who had encouraged her when the work grew hot and difficult. But all the joy had gone out of archaeology without Jake.

She sighed and turned from the window to review her lecture notes. When someone knocked on the glass window of her office door, she looked up. Her department chairman, Jonas Zimmerman, opened the door a crack and stuck his head inside.

"May I come in?"

"Sure, Jonas. What's up?" Hannah's stiff puppet smile sprang into place as he leaned against her doorframe.

"I just got off the phone with an old friend of mine in America. His university has raised enough funds to start digging at Tel Batash next summer. He's looking for an Israeli colleague for a joint project. Are you interested?"

"Nope. Sorry." She quickly looked down at her notes again, as if too busy to entertain the idea. Her features carefully shifted into neutral.

"Just like that?" Jonas said. "You won't even take time to consider it?" She shook her head. He came inside her office, closed the door, and sank into the chair that faced her desk. "Hannah, don't you think it's time—"

"Please, Jonas, don't pressure me. I'm not ready to go back into the field yet."

"When will you be ready?"

"I don't know. Maybe when Rachel is older—she's only eleven."

"And next year she'll be 'only twelve,' then 'only thirteen' . . ."

Hannah heard the frustration in his voice and knew he would not remain patient with her much longer. She looked up, meeting his gaze, but said nothing.

"Will you at least think about it . . . and let me know if you change your mind?" he asked.

"Sure."

Jonas sighed and tossed a file folder onto Hannah's desk. "In the meantime, I'm assigning you a student. He just finished his three years in the army and wants to study archaeology."

Hannah held up her hands in protest. "Listen, I'm not sure I have anything to give—"

"No, Hannah, you listen." He leaned toward her, his words controlled and deliberate. "You have to start carrying your share of the work load. We've all tried to be sympathetic to your circumstances these past three years and not lay too much on your shoulders, but we're all overworked. You don't dig, you don't publish—the least you can do is advise a few students."

"I'm sorry." She was too close to tears to say anything more.

"I'm sorry, too, Hannah. Honestly I am. I thought the world of Jake." Jonas leaned back again, his expression softening. "I've met this new student. He's a bright kid. I told him he has an appointment with you today at two o'clock."

The frayed puppet strings strained as Hannah summoned the energy to perform another weary dance. "Of course, Jonas."

Shortly before her new student was due to arrive, Hannah set aside her lecture notes to read through his file. He was twenty-one, a *sabra*, or native-born Israeli from a town in northern Israel. He was quite intelligent, according to his transcript and all of his teachers, a thorough and diligent scholar. And he was also extremely popular with the opposite sex, according to a humorous postscript on one of his letters of reference.

"Shalom, Dr. Rahov." Hannah looked up from the file to find a very handsome young man standing in front of her with his hand extended. "Sorry I'm a little early. I'm Ari Bazak."

"Nice to meet you, Ari. I was just reading through your file. Please sit down."

Although he didn't resemble Jake at all, he reminded Hannah of him with his striking classic features in a perfectly proportioned face. Ari's hair and beard were darker than Jake's, his eyes a deep chocolate brown, instead of green, but his height and build were nearly the same, and he carried himself with the same confident self-assurance. She had misjudged Jake about being a woman chaser, but she didn't think she was misjudging Ari. It was easy to imagine swarms of girls fluttering around him.

His broad smile drew a genuine one from her, and they began to talk. Young Ari was very personable and articulate. Hannah sensed a sharp if somewhat unformed intellect, waiting to be shaped and molded. But he seemed so young to her—a few years younger than Jake had been when they first met.

Why was she comparing him to Jake? It unnerved her that she lacked the strength—or the will—to stop. As the interview lengthened, she found herself testing him, challenging Ari the way Jake's fellow scientists had challenged him that long-ago summer in the Negev. She wanted to see if Ari displayed the same strength of character and integrity under fire that Jake had. She silently cheered when, like Jake, he held his ground without rancor or retreat. Against her will, she felt a bond of simple friendship begin to form between herself and her new student.

"What made you decide to study archaeology?" she asked at last.

"A lot of factors, but visiting the dig at Masada clinched it for me. They took our commando unit there to be sworn in."

"Yes, Masada is a very impressive place."

He leaned toward her, his eyes intense. "But it wasn't just the historical importance of that place—the fact that it was the last Jewish stronghold before the exile, and all of that. I was intrigued with the overall design, the finely tuned details of the place."

"For example . . ." she prompted.

"The Roman mosaics," he said fervently. "Such artistry! All

those delicate shadings of color! I was amazed how each tiny, individual piece of the design had been carefully shaped and fitted together to form the bigger picture—" Ari halted when he saw Hannah's face. "Dr. Rahov? What is it, what's wrong?"

"Excuse me—"

Hannah barely made it to the ladies' room down the hall before the last of the puppet strings finally snapped. She collapsed onto the floor, weeping, knowing she had danced her final performance. The good-looking young man who reminded her so much of Jake, who spoke like Jake but who was not Jake, had severed the cords neatly with his devastating words. She lay on the imitation mosaic floor—small white hexagons that were cold and featureless, not part of any pattern—and finally cried out to God.

"How could you take him from me? How could you let Jake die? What kind of a God are you?"

Jake was dead. God had cruelly snatched him from her. She had covered the gaping wound he'd left behind as if placing a rug over a ruined floor, cleverly dancing around it, ignoring it for three years. God alone was strong enough to heal her wound, but she had turned from Him in anger, instead of turning to Him for refuge. Now the act was over, the festering wound exposed by a handsome young student named Ari Bazak and his ghostlike echo of Jake's last words.

"I can't go on, God," she cried, knowing she should have done so three years earlier. "Please . . . please . . . help me!"

———

Hannah phoned Devorah that night. "I know you've been begging me for ages to come up and visit," she said. "I was wondering if this weekend would be all right?"

"Yes, of course! Please come!" Devorah's voice revealed both surprise and pleasure. With Ben traveling so often in his work, Devorah and the children had moved back to the kibbutz in Galilee to be close to her family. "It just so happens that Ben will be home all weekend. He'll be thrilled. And Rachel can play with her cousins . . . it will be wonderful!"

From the first moment she arrived, Hannah was swallowed up in the warmth of family and memories, the relief of laughter and tears. She dropped her facade of unquestioning faith and strength and poured out her anger and hurt so that true healing could finally begin. Ben had no answers to her questions as they sat outside that evening beneath the sodden winter sky, but voicing them helped her. She slept better than she had for a long time.

"Come for a ride with me," Ben said after breakfast the next day. "There's someone I want you to meet."

He borrowed a pickup truck from the kibbutz and they drove around the lake, the pale winter sun trying to peek through clouds that were as soft as dove's wings. The wind had the breath of spring in it, the scent of new lambs and green grass. Galilee was beautiful this time of year, with the almond trees in full bloom and the hillsides speckled with scarlet anemones. Hannah was glad she had decided to leave the bleak, chilly city behind.

But when she suddenly realized where Ben was taking her, Hannah's heart went cold inside her. They had driven to the opposite shore of Galilee—to the Golan Heights.

"I can't do this, Ben," she said. "I'm not ready."

He looked at her, his eyes tender, then back at the road. "Trust me."

She fell silent as they climbed up into the hills. But instead of taking the main road, which led up through the heights to Mount Hermon, Ben turned south, then east again onto a narrow rutted road that wound into barren territory. After several bumpy minutes, she saw a jeep parked along the road up ahead, a man waiting beside it. Ben stopped the truck and got out to greet him.

"Hannah, I'd like you to meet Shmarya Gutmann . . . this is my cousin, Dr. Hannah Rahov."

"The archaeologist, yes," Gutmann said, shaking her hand. "I have read your work." He was a compact, muscular man in his midsixties with a cloudlike puff of white hair encircling his bald head. His knotted arm muscles and weathered face attested to years of physical labor, but his restless energy betrayed curiosity and a sharp mind. "I am what you might call a self-styled archaeologist," he said, "although in real life I am only a simple farmer from Kibbutz Na'an."

"A simple farmer?" Ben repeated, laughing. "Before statehood, Shmarya worked in military intelligence. He headed a top-secret unit of the Haganah."

Hannah knew that the Haganah was a forerunner of Ben's Agency. "Is that how you two met?" she asked.

The older man's eyes twinkled. "I met your cousin, the world-renowned agricultural consultant, when he came to my kibbutz to show us how to farm properly."

Ben laughed again. "Shmarya is the reason you and I are here instead of stuck in Iraq. He had a hand in the diplomatic negotiations that brought all of us Iraqi Jews to Israel twenty-five years ago. Although," he added to Gutmann, "Hannah certainly wouldn't have thanked you for it at the time!"

She smiled, remembering how she had wept with homesickness. "That's true, I wouldn't have. But I am grateful now. You said you were interested in archaeology, Mr. Gutmann? Have you been on any digs?"

"A few," he said, with a modest shrug. "I was very fortunate to have been part of Yigael Yadin's team at Masada. . . ."

"Yes! I knew your name was familiar," Hannah said. "You're the one who found the famous inscribed pottery shards—the ones that were thought to be the lots drawn for the suicide pact. You are hardly an amateur archaeologist, Mr. Gutmann! You've worked with more famous people than I have—Sukenik, Avigad, Mazar . . ."

"Tell her about your latest project," Ben said.

Hannah saw the excitement in Gutmann's eyes.

"After we won possession of the Golan Heights in 1967, I set out to find Gamla, the 'Masada of the North.' "

"Yes, of course, from Josephus' accounts. And have you?"

He grinned in triumph. "There!" he said, pointing to a place behind her. "Gamla—the camel!"

Hannah turned around to gaze at a narrow-humped ridge

of land that rose among the surrounding hills like the back of a resting camel.

"See? Inaccessible ravines on three sides, just as Josephus described it," Gutmann said proudly. "Take a walk down there and have a look for yourself. You'll be able to find Roman arrowheads and catapult stones without searching too hard."

"That's amazing! It certainly looks like the place Josephus described."

"I want to raise it from its ruins," he said. "It has taken six years to come up with the funding, but I finally have enough financial support to start excavating this summer. I would love it if you would join us, Dr. Rahov."

Hannah didn't reply. She continued to gaze in silence at the camel-backed hill and at the distant Sea of Galilee, barely visible beneath the lowering clouds.

"Can you take us down and show us around?" Ben asked.

"I'm sorry, I wish I could," Gutmann replied, checking his wristwatch, "but I don't have time today. Just follow that footpath. You can't get lost. This narrow neck of land is the only way to get there—as the Romans themselves soon learned."

They talked for a few more minutes before Gutmann apologized again for having to leave. "Hope to see you this summer," he said as he climbed into his jeep. Hannah felt the first few sprinkles of rain as he drove away. She turned toward Ben's truck.

"Wait," Ben said, stopping her. "Let's take a walk down there."

"But it's starting to rain."

"We'll get wet. So what? Please, Hannah."

She buttoned her raincoat and cinched the belt before following him down the narrow path. Gutmann was right—she could easily spot dozens of rounded catapult stones among the disordered ruins of tumbled foundations and fallen columns. Against her will, she felt a familiar prickle of excitement as she recalled Josephus' account of the battle that had raged here. The desolate scene started springing to life in her mind's eye. Ben led her all the way up the camel's spine until the trail ended at the edge of a steep ravine.

"Many of them fell to their deaths from here," Hannah said, recalling the story. "Just like Masada, they preferred death to being captured by the Romans." She shivered. The sprinkle had turned to a gentle rain, and drops of it sparkled in Ben's hair and beard. "You didn't make me walk all the way down here just to see the ruins, did you?" she said. He shook his head, then wrapped one arm tightly around her, pulling her close to his side.

"That's where Jake died," he said softly, pointing. "On that ridge of land right over there. You can't see the hollow where the ambush was waiting. And neither could he . . . until it was too late."

Tears welled in Hannah's eyes and washed down her face along with the rain as they stared in silence. She licked her lips and tasted salt.

"You know, Hannah, our government is being pressured by the international community to give the Golan Heights back to Syria." He scrubbed his own eyes with his fist. "Jake died to defend this land, and they want to take it away from us. This dig at Gamla could prove that the Golan is ours, that it always has been ours. Your other digs proved that Jews once owned Jerusalem and the Negev, now do the same for the Golan Heights."

He gripped her shoulders and turned her toward him, forcing her to face him. "Find the proof, Hannah. . . . For Jacob's sake."

Hannah signed on for the excavation at Gamla, which began on June 27, 1976. She returned for a second season in 1977, and a third in 1978. Her student assistant, Ari Bazak, joined her, attracting hordes of smitten female volunteers to the remote site.

"Hey, I want him for my assistant next year," one of Hannah's colleagues joked. "All you have to do is send Ari out to recruit volunteers and you're overstocked."

"Please, take him," Hannah said with a groan. "That boy is so busy chasing girls, I'm sure he'll be too exhausted to work. My daughter, Rachel, has a terrible crush on him, too."

"Oh, Mama, he's sooo gorgeous!" Rachel squealed after meeting Ari for the first time. "He's like a movie star! And did you see how he kissed my hand when you introduced us—like I was royalty or something? He's such a gentleman!"

"Yes, Mr. Bazak certainly does know how to be charming, but I should warn you—"

"He said I was beautiful!"

"I heard him. That's because you are." At thirteen, Rachel was emerging from childhood with willowy grace and poise, a carbon copy of her handsome father in female form. Yet she was gentle and sweet-tempered, as completely unaffected by her own natural beauty as Jake had been.

Rachel twirled in a happy circle before collapsing dramatically onto their sofa. "I'm in love, Mama!"

"Get in line, sweetie," Hannah mumbled.

"What did you say, Mama?"

"He's much too old for you. You're only thirteen, and Ari is a grown man."

"I'm not a little kid!" Rachel said indignantly. "And Abba was older than you were."

"Not ten years older. Only four."

Throughout the summer of 1978, Hannah watched helplessly as Rachel threw herself at Ari Bazak, following him around the excavation at Gamla like a love-sick puppy, turning up under his feet with every step he took. The boldness of Rachel's pursuit reminded Hannah of her own pursuit of Jake, but Ari was a very different person from her husband. While Jake had been naturally shy, Ari was the opposite—talkative, charming, and relentlessly flirtatious. He wasn't offended at all by Rachel's fan-club style of adoration but seemed mildly entertained by it—even though his many girlfriends weren't.

"He's very patient with her," one of Hannah's colleagues said after observing how Rachel shadowed him all day.

"Yes, he is," Hannah sighed. "I'm afraid it's only because

she's my daughter and Ari wants good grades. If he would just get annoyed and shoo her away once or twice, maybe we would all have a little peace and quiet." She told Ari as much the next day after she had to punish Rachel for practically sitting on his lap while he tried to eat. "You have my permission to do whatever it takes to get rid of her, Ari."

"Aw, she's just a little kid, Hannah. She really doesn't bother me. It must be pretty lonely for her being stuck way out here all summer with no other kids her age."

"Believe me, she doesn't think of herself as a child. In her mind she's the same age as all these college girls."

A few days later, instead of sitting around with Ari and the others after dark, Rachel made a big show of being sleepy and went to bed early. Hannah worked on reports in the field office for another hour or so before joining her in their tent. Rachel was tucked deep inside her sleeping bag and never stirred as Hannah came inside and yanked off her boots. She was about to set them by the tent door beside Rachel's boots, when she noticed that Rachel's boots were missing. She looked again at her daughter's sleeping form. There was something very odd about the way Rachel was hunched into a ball on her cot. Hannah peered inside Rachel's sleeping bag and found pillows.

Hannah shoved her feet back into her boots and grabbed her flashlight. The first place to look would be wherever Ari was. She hurried across the compound to where the college students sat around a folding table, playing a game of cards by lantern light.

"I'm looking for Ari. Have any of you seen him?"

"Ari? Gosh, he was here earlier, Dr. Rahov, but I guess he left."

"Do you know where he went?"

"I can take an educated guess where he might be," one of them answered mischievously. "Let's see . . . who else is missing?"

Everyone laughed but Hannah. She felt sick inside. Surely

Ari had more sense than to play his games with a thirteen-year-old!

"Hey, Deanna is gone," one of the girls said suddenly.

"Who?"

"The new girl. You know, 'Miss America' from New York University? Ari was flirting with her all day."

Hannah felt only mildly relieved. "Excuse an old woman's ignorance, but where might two people go on a 'date' around here?"

"Oh, Ari has several favorite spots," another girl said, slamming her handful of cards down on the folding table.

Hannah judged from her sarcastic tone that she had been jilted by him earlier in the summer.

"Try the synagogue ruins first," she added.

"You're kidding."

"Nope." She tossed her hair off her shoulders with a shake of her head.

"Ooo, sacrilege!" someone murmured.

"Is he in trouble, Dr. Rahov?"

"No, dear, I just need to ask him something."

"Do you want us to help you look for him?" the jilted one asked. Her voice was maliciously sweet.

"Yeah, we'll help you look, Dr. Rahov."

"Better make lots of noise so they'll know you're coming." Their comments were interspersed with giggles and laughter.

Hannah didn't relish a treacherous walk down the footpath to the ruined synagogue in the dark. She was trying to decide whether it was a good idea to let the students help her or not when she saw bobbing lights approaching up the hill and heard a loud voice—a distinctly American voice—telling someone off in a continuous tirade.

"For two cents I'd like to wring your miserable head right off your scrawny little neck! You've got a lot of nerve, you little sneak! I hope you get grounded for a week—for the summer . . . no, for the rest of your life!"

As the lights drew closer, Hannah was relieved to see the American girl dragging Rachel up the hill by the scruff of her neck. Ari trailed a few paces behind them.

"Just wait until I tell your mother what you did, you rotten little snoop!" she continued. "I hope she beats the tar out of you."

When she saw Hannah and the others, she pushed Rachel forward into the light. Hannah stared at her daughter and couldn't believe her eyes. Rachel was smirking!

"What's going on?" Hannah asked.

Ari couldn't answer. He was chewing his lips to pieces, trying not to laugh and make Miss America even more upset than she already was. But he didn't need to answer. Miss America answered for him.

"You'd better teach your snoopy little daughter a lesson or two about privacy, Dr. Rahov." She held up Rachel's pocket camera, waving it by the strap. "She must have eavesdropped on Ari and me this afternoon and decided to follow us! We thought we were all alone! We didn't know she was listening and watching our every move until she just popped up out of nowhere with her little flash camera, right when we were—" She stopped, shocked to discover that in her anger she was about to reveal far too much.

"Just when you were *what?*" Ari's former dream-girl asked sweetly.

When everyone hooted with laughter, Ari blushed clear to the roots of his beard. Horrified, Miss America thrust the camera into his hands and stormed into her tent.

"Well," Rachel said smartly, dusting off her hands, "that takes care of her."

Hannah's jaw dropped. "Rachel! Into our tent! Now!" She was astounded to see her daughter saunter away with a spring in her step. Hannah turned to Ari, who had stepped out of the circle of lantern light and was carefully backing away.

"Here." He handed the camera to Hannah like a hot potato.

"Ari, I am so sorry."

"No harm done."

"I'd like to promise you that it won't happen again, but—"

"It's okay, Hannah. I'll smooth things over with Deanna. Don't worry."

"Believe me, it's not you or Deanna that I'm worried about." She turned to go, then turned back. "Oh, and Ari?"

"Yeah?"

"In the future . . . please . . . not in the synagogue."

By the time Hannah returned to her tent, Rachel had tossed all the pillows onto the floor and had snuggled beneath the covers in their place. Hannah sighed. "I know you aren't asleep, Rachel. We need to talk about your behavior."

Rachel rolled over to face her. She looked up at her mother in a perfect imitation of an innocent little girl, her dark eyes shining in the moonlight. "Yes, Mama?"

Hannah prayed for patience. "I know Mr. Bazak laughed it off—"

"He lets me call him Ari."

"—but I'm not laughing, Rachel. Stay *away* from him. Leave him *alone*. Do you understand me? If you don't stop— if there are any more incidents like this one—I'll have to send you to Aunt Devorah's kibbutz to stay with your cousins for the rest of the summer."

"No, Mama! *Please* don't send me there!"

"Then will you promise me that you'll behave from now on? That you'll leave Ari and his girlfriends alone?"

"You don't understand, Mama!" Rachel sat up, gravely serious. With all the passion of a heartsick thirteen-year-old, she said, "I'm in love with Ari! I'm going to marry him someday!"

"Listen, Rachel—"

"But I *am*, Mama!"

"Sweetie . . ." Hannah stopped, recognizing her own youthful stubbornness in the set of Rachel's chin. There was nothing she could say to change her daughter's mind. Time and other-fish-in-the-sea were the only known cures for puppy love.

"Sweetie, go to sleep," she said wearily. But as Hannah crawled beneath the covers of her own cot, she wished—not for the first time or the last—that Jake was alive to help her cope with their daughter.

The following morning, Hannah decided to dig a few more test pits in the synagogue floor—not only to see what she could find, but to create enough of an obstacle course to discourage any future nighttime trysts among the volunteers. For some reason, the floor of the synagogue had never been paved two thousand years ago. She was wielding the pickax herself, hoping the vigorous labor would take her mind off her problems with Rachel, when she suddenly struck and shattered an earthenware jar, buried only a few centimeters beneath the surface. She sank to her knees for a closer look.

"Someone bring me a petesh, quick!"

Ari handed her one, and she swung the smaller pick carefully, clearing away the hard-packed soil. Her heart began to race with excitement when she peeled back the broken shards and saw that the jar held parchment documents, some with wax seals. Hannah knew even before she read them that they were the most important finds she had ever made.

Ari was on his knees beside her, carefully sweeping away the loose dirt with a whisk broom. He stopped when he saw what was inside the jar. "Wow!" he breathed.

Hannah looked up at him. His face seemed to shimmer through her tears. "Yeah. Wow."

15

THE VILLAGE OF DEGANIA—A.D. 66

D o you know what day this is, Miriam?"
Leah asked as she and the servant
poured wine and prepared the basket of unleavened bread for the communion service.

"Of course, my child. It's the anniversary
of your wedding to Master Reuben."

Leah paused to gaze at her beloved friend.
Miriam's hair was no longer gray but snowy
white, her fingers gnarled from age and years
of work.

"I was remembering that it was the anniversary of his baptism, too," Leah said.

Neither of them wanted to say that it was
also the night that sicarii assassins had murdered Reuben six years ago as he journeyed
home from Caesarea.

"How could the seven years that I was married to him fly by so fast," Leah asked, "when
these six years without him have plodded by
so slowly?"

Miriam didn't answer. She simply hobbled
over to Leah and wrapped her arms around
her—as she had done on the very first day
they'd met—and soothed her with her gentle
humming.

Leah's grief had dulled over time but had
never entirely disappeared, kept alive by the
haunting knowledge that Reuben's murderers
had never been caught. One of the villagers

CHAPTER

had found his body after the Sabbath ended. Reuben lay slaughtered in the middle of the road a half mile from Degania. He'd had no Roman bodyguard, since he no longer worked for Rome, and his loyal servants had been murdered along with him as they tried to defend him. Then the assassins had brutally cut off Reuben's finger to steal his ring. Leah had studied strangers' hands for six years, searching for that ring, wondering what she would do when she found the man who wore it, the man who had killed her husband.

She quickly dried her tears as the other believers began to arrive for the service. The little fellowship that met in the villa in Degania had grown to more than eighty people—so many that they could barely squeeze into the reception hall. But Leah knew it was probably the last time they would ever gather there for communion. Nathaniel had come to the village with disturbing news.

"We're meeting tonight to ask for the Lord's guidance for our future," he announced after everyone had arrived. "We have all watched the situation in our land grow steadily worse, especially since the new procurator, Gessius Florus, arrived from Rome."

Murmurs of outrage swept through the room at the mention of the hated procurator's name.

"A few weeks ago, Florus seized money from God's treasury in the Temple," Nathaniel continued. "Rioting broke out in Jerusalem with house-to-house fighting at times. It ended in countless crucifixions and the slaughter of more than 3,600 Jewish men, women, and children. The revolt that the Zealots have been clamoring for has finally begun."

Leah shuddered as a hushed silence fell over the room. She glanced at Elizabeth, seated beside her, and saw tears in her seventeen-year-old daughter's eyes. Leah took her hand. Elizabeth was betrothed to one of the believers in their fellowship, a young man named Judah, the son of a Pharisee. Judah's father had disinherited him for becoming a believer, forcing the young couple to wait to marry. Now the uncertain times threatened to postpone their marriage even longer.

"The apostles believe that the time has come for the remaining believers to get out of the country," Nathaniel said. "Listen to our Lord's warning to us: 'When you see Jerusalem being surrounded by armies, you will know that its desolation is near. Then let those who are in Judea flee to the mountains, let those in the city get out, and let those in the country not enter the city. For this is the time of punishment in fulfillment of all that has been written. How dreadful it will be in those days for pregnant women and nursing mothers! There will be great distress in the land and wrath against this people. They will fall by the sword and will be taken as prisoners to all the nations. Jerusalem will be trampled on by the Gentiles until the times of the Gentiles are fulfilled.' "

"What does that mean, Nathaniel?" Leah asked. " 'Until the times of the Gentiles are fulfilled'?"

Nathaniel smiled, erasing the sorrow from his gentle round face for a brief moment. "An amazing thing has been taking place in recent days," he said. "It began when the apostle Peter was sent by God to preach the Good News to a Gentile in Caesarea—a Roman centurion, of all people. The man, whose name is Cornelius, believed and was baptized.

"After the persecution of believers began and we were scattered, we had more and more opportunities to spread the news to the Gentiles. Some of our brethren—Saul, Barnabus, and Silas—have been preaching throughout the Asian provinces. Many Jews have believed, but many more Gentiles have become believers. They received the Holy Spirit, just as we did at Pentecost.

"You all know that two equal loaves of bread, the first fruits of our labors, are always presented to God at the Feast of Pentecost. I believe that it was God's design to show us that the first fruits of His Kingdom would be shared equally by Jews and Gentiles. Now we must leave Jerusalem, but we know that wherever God sends us we will be taking the Gospel with us—until the time of the Gentiles is fulfilled."

"Have the armies surrounded the city as Yeshua said they would?" Ehud asked.

"Not yet, but they're coming," Nathaniel replied. "Three Roman legions sent by Emperor Nero have landed at Acco. General Vespasian commands more than thirty thousand troops and support personnel. If he marches through Galilee, the village of Degania will be directly in his path. It's time for us to pray for our Lord's guidance."

The meeting went late into the night as the people prayed for one another and sought the Lord's leading for each family. Leah's entire household decided to flee the country with the main body of believers who would seek refuge in Antioch until it was safe to return. They would pack their belongings and leave together at dawn on the first day of the week. But in spite of Leah's fervent prayers, she found no peace in that decision.

When the prayer meeting ended, the fellowship in Degania broke bread together for the last time, remembering Yeshua's words: *"This is my body given for you; do this in remembrance of me."*

Leah was taking down her hair in preparation for bed when she heard someone pounding on the front door. Had one of the brethren forgotten something? She decided to let the servants answer it and had just climbed into bed when Miriam came to her room, lamp in hand.

"Who was at the door?" Leah asked.

Tears filled the servant's eyes. "Get dressed. You need to come. They're Zealots."

A lump of dread plummeted to the bottom of Leah's stomach as she quickly put her clothes back on and followed Miriam through the darkened house to the front door. She heard the clamor of men's voices, dozens of them, before she even reached the central courtyard and saw the flickering shadows of torches on the walls. At least fifty strangers were swarming into her house, peering into her reception hall and the other rooms, piling their bedrolls and weapons in her courtyard. She could tell by their filthy clothes and rugged appearance that they were one of the roving gangs of Zealots. They held old Ehud captive, roughly pinning his arms behind his back.

"What are you doing? Let him go!" she cried. At the sound of Leah's voice, one of the Zealots whirled to face her. "Gideon!" she breathed when she saw his face. He was barely recognizable beneath layers of dirt, a thatch of unkempt hair, and a scruffy beard.

"Leah?" he said in amazement. "Your servitude should have ended years ago! Why are you still here?" He roughly brushed her hair aside to see if she wore the earring of a bond servant in her ear. He seemed relieved to see that she didn't.

"Please, Gideon, tell them to let Ehud go," she begged. Gideon signaled with a wave of his hand, and the man holding Ehud released him. The latent power she glimpsed in that simple gesture unnerved her. "Are you in command of these men?" she asked.

"Yes."

Leah studied his face, searching for a sign of the brother she once knew, then shrank back from the glint of savagery she now saw in Gideon's eyes. "What are you doing here?" she asked.

"I happen to know that the tax collector is dead," he said. "Since he no longer needs this house, I've decided to appropriate it for my headquarters."

There was a note of triumph in his voice that sent ice down Leah's spine. She grabbed Gideon's hands and searched them for Reuben's ring. When she saw that they were bare, she dropped them again as if his touch would poison her.

"Did you kill him?"

He gave a lazy shrug. "What difference does it make to you who killed him? He was our enemy, Leah, a filthy Roman collaborator, and a—"

"He was my husband!"

Her words and the cold fury with which she spoke them silenced him. He stared at her for a long moment, then said, "That pig made you his concubine?"

"No, Gideon. He made me his wife."

"You're lying! Why would he marry you when he could have had you whenever he wanted?"

"Because he loved me . . . and I loved him."

Gideon shook his head. "I don't believe you."

"Ask Abba! Ask him about the dowry Reuben paid—twice the price Abba named! Abba told me it was my choice. He said he wouldn't sell me to Reuben ben Johanan a second time, and I chose to marry him! Do you want to see the legal certificate the scribes wrote?"

Leah could see that her words had shaken Gideon. But his stunned disbelief lasted only a moment before swiftly turning to rage. He drew back his hand and slapped Leah across the face.

"How could you! How could you prostitute yourself with that man? Wasn't it enough that he bought you the first time? Did you have to sell yourself to him a second time?"

"I loved him," she said as tears rolled down her stinging cheek. "Haven't you ever loved someone?"

He didn't answer.

The other Zealots had been searching the entire villa, rounding up all the servants. Now they herded them into the courtyard, most of them dressed in their nightclothes. One of the men had Nathaniel. Another held Elizabeth. Leah prayed that no one would tell Gideon that she was Reuben's daughter.

"The villa is mine," Leah said, drawing a deep breath for courage. "You and your men can have it, along with everything in it. I'll even give you the deed. But please, let the servants go."

"No," Gideon said coldly. "I'll need the women to run the household. The men will fight with us. Everyone stays."

He turned his back on her without another word and began issuing orders. He divided the servants into two groups—Leah and the women in one, the men in another—and assigned two of his men to guard them while they slept.

"We must pretend that Elizabeth and Nathaniel are servants," Leah whispered to the others in the darkened room. "They will do the same work as the others. We can't let Gideon know who you are, Elizabeth." Leah stayed awake for most of the night praying, trying to decide what to do. As the sun began to rise, she finally had a plan.

"We're going to prepare a huge feast for Gideon and his men," she told the servants the next day. "We will serve them Reuben's best wine, a year's supply if we have to. When the men are drunk, we'll quietly leave for Antioch with the other believers."

At first Gideon was reluctant to allow so much food to be wasted on a feast, but when he saw how the idea appealed to his men, he relented. He relaxed around the banquet table with the other Zealots, just as Leah hoped he would.

"Don't let the soldiers drain their wine goblets dry," Leah instructed her servants. "Refill them as soon as they're half empty." She made the rounds outside herself, making sure the sentries standing watch at the doors had plenty of wine, too. The guard at the back gate hesitated.

"I shouldn't drink, my lady. I'm on watch."

"What are you watching for in Degania?" she said, laughing. "Stray dogs? Why should the men inside have all the fun? Here." She gave him an entire wineskin filled with Reuben's aged wine. Close to midnight, the drunken sentry fell asleep, leaning against the gatepost. Most of the men in the banquet hall had passed out as well.

"It's time to go," Leah told Nathaniel and the servants. One by one they quietly filed past the sleeping guard with their belongings.

"Where are your things, Mama?" Elizabeth asked when she reached the gate with Miriam and Ehud.

"I need to distract Gideon a while longer so he doesn't notice that everyone is gone. I'll catch up with you later." But old Ehud saw through her words.

"You're not coming at all, are you," he said quietly.

Leah glanced at Elizabeth, dismayed to see that she'd heard, then shook her head. "I believe that the Lord wants me to stay here with Gideon."

"I can't leave you, Mama!" Elizabeth cried. "You have to come!"

"You belong with Judah now. The two of you must marry when you get to Antioch and begin a new life there together."

"Not without you!"

"Yes, with each other. You can read and write, Elizabeth, and you have your father's Torah scrolls. You and Judah and the others can help spread the Good News. We are to be Yeshua's witnesses to the ends of the earth, just as He said. People need to see God's Kingdom in us, the living stones of His temple. Your work is there, but mine is here. This is the spiritual sacrifice I need to make."

"These might be the men who killed Abba! How can you stay with them?"

"I don't know . . . but I do know that we're commanded to love our enemies. Gideon is my brother. It was my fault that he was once beaten by the Romans. And Reuben added to his bitterness by refusing to forgive my father's debt and making Gideon his servant. My brother has never seen what God is really like. The Pharisees showed him a God who is a nit-picker, waiting to reject him whenever he failed and broke His laws. The Sadducees showed him a God who favored the rich and despised the poor. The Zealots showed him a God who demands vengeance and wrath against unbelievers. How can I expect Gideon to see what God is really like, to see Christ's forgiveness and love, if I don't show him?"

"Oh, Mama!" Elizabeth cried, clinging to her. "How can I leave you?"

"You must. Take care of her for me, Ehud—for Reuben's sake. See that she marries Judah. Be happy, Elizabeth—"

"Where do you think you're going, Leah?"

The voice that suddenly came out of the darkness behind her was angry and harsh. She turned, startled, and saw Gideon standing just a few feet away from her, swaying slightly. His eyes were reddened with anger and wine, his voice slurred.

"I'm not going anywhere, Gideon. I'm staying here to see that the household is run for you . . . but please, let these others go."

"Why should I?" He pulled a knife from the sheath on his

belt and took a staggering step toward them.

"Because Reuben let you go free. I begged him to have mercy on you after you ran away, and he did. He could have sent the Roman troops after you."

Gideon gave a drunken laugh. "The joke was on him, then." He tipped his knife sheath upside down and caught something as it fell out of the bottom. He held it out to her.

Reuben's ring lay in the palm of Gideon's hand.

In that moment, Leah hated him more than she ever thought it was possible to hate someone. Rage and grief boiled up inside her until she was angry enough to kill him. He had brutally murdered the man she loved, had mutilated his body. She nearly rushed at Gideon, but the sound of Elizabeth's sobbing stopped her. It was more important that her daughter and the others go free.

"If you killed my husband, Gideon, then you owe me." She slowly dropped to her knees at his feet. "I once begged Reuben for mercy like this—for you—and he let you live. Now I'm begging you. Are you as much of a man as Reuben ben Johanan was?"

"Shut up!" The words exploded from him in a burst of rage.

Leah could see it churning inside him as Gideon's chest heaved, his face contorted. She feared she had gone too far. He grabbed her arm and jerked her to her feet, twisting it painfully.

"Go on! Get out of here, all of you!" he yelled, then turned to stagger back into the house.

Elizabeth reached for her hand. "Come on, Mama."

Leah longed to go with her, to turn her back on her brother and never see him again. She hated him for the murderer that he was. But the words of Christ pierced her heart, convicting her.

"I can't go, Elizabeth. I have to stay here."

"Mama, no!"

She took Elizabeth in her arms and held her daughter close for the last time. "Yeshua taught us to pray, 'Forgive our debts, as we have forgiven our debtors.' That's what I must do. God be with you, Elizabeth."

Then Leah released her and hurried into the house behind her brother.

THE VILLAGE OF DEGANIA—A.D. 66

Degania is impossible to defend," Gideon's dinner guest said flatly. "The village has no walls, no fortresses, and no buildings that are suitable to convert into a fortress in the short time that remains." Leah lifted the flask to pour him more wine, but he covered his goblet with his hand and shook his head. "You'll need to evacuate all of the townspeople."

"What about this villa?" Gideon said. "We could—"

"No. Impossible. This place is too . . ." He circled his hand in the air, searching for the right word. "Too rambling. There are too many approaches to defend."

Leah could see that her brother was unhappy with that decision, but his guest was Joseph ben Mattathias, the commander of the Jewish forces in Galilee. Gideon knew better than to argue with his commander in chief, even if the man was a few years younger than himself and inexperienced in combat.

"Very well," Gideon said stiffly. "Where would you like my men and me to serve?"

"I've decided to send you to Gamla," Joseph said, reclining against the cushions. He absently plucked a date off the platter Leah held out to him. "It's the main Zealot stronghold east of the Sea of Galilee."

"I know where Gamla is," Gideon said. He remained seated upright at the table, even though the meal was finished.

Leah thought that his dislike of the commander was ill-concealed. The only reason Joseph had been given the position, Gideon said, was because he was a relative of Jonathan, the Hasmonean high priest. Joseph had even argued against the Zealot rebellion initially, before finally joining it earlier this year.

"Then you know how important that fortress is to our cause," Joseph said. "The support we hope to receive from our Jewish brethren in Babylon will arrive by way of the main road that passes near Gamla."

"How many troops will be posted there besides mine?"

"Oh, not many at all," Joseph said, reaching for another date. "It isn't necessary. I supervised the reinforcement of its defenses myself. Gamla is quite impregnable."

Gideon raised his wineglass in salute. "Let's hope you're right," he said before draining it.

"I am right. In fact, my dear," he said, reaching for Leah's hand, "you would be wise to take refuge there as well."

His moves were as smooth as oil, too smooth for Leah's taste. He had shown a great deal of interest in her since learning that she was a wealthy widow and had tried to impress her during dinner by bragging about his travels to Rome. Gideon had warned her to bar her bedroom door tonight.

"That's kind of you to be concerned for me, Commander," Leah said. "But my refuge is in God, not in a fortress."

Commander Joseph ben Mattathias left early the next morning to continue the inspection tour of Galilee's defenses. Leah left Degania with her brother Gideon and most of the remaining villagers a week later for Gamla. The refugees and Zealots stripped Degania of every scrap of food before leaving, hauling a mountain of supplies with them to the fortress. While Rabbi Eliezer, Reb Nahum, and many of the others wept over the loss of their synagogue and their homes, tearing their robes and tossing the dust of Degania's streets onto their heads in mourning, Leah refused to look back. The only thing of value she took with her was the earthenware jar containing Reuben's documents.

"There it is. That's Gamla," Gideon said when they finally glimpsed the fortress from the top of an adjacent hill. "What do you think of it?"

"I can see how it got its name," Leah said.

The green hump of land on which Gamla was built resembled the back of a resting camel. The city itself seemed suspended in air, the houses clinging to the steep sides of the camel's back like saddlebags. Built like steps, the roof of one house served as the balcony of the next. Steep ravines guarded the fortress on three sides so that the only approach was by way of a narrow neck of land connecting the city to the neighboring hill. Workers had begun digging a trench across this land bridge so it could also be severed if necessary. Leah followed the others down the narrow path and through the city gate, built into a massive wall of black basalt boulders. A round lookout tower on the wall commanded the crest of the hill.

Inside, Gamla's streets were a maze of narrow alleyways, twisting along the steep ridge of land, opening suddenly onto small paved squares or turning sharply into steps. It would take Leah several weeks to finally learn her way around all of them. The highest point in the city was called the citadel, the southernmost peak at the very top of the camel's hump. Below it was the deepest ravine.

Gamla's synagogue perched along the edge of city, just inside the wall, and was built of the same black stones. It was larger than Degania's synagogue, with four rows of stone columns supporting its roof instead of three, and smooth tiers of black stone benches lining its walls. Like Degania's synagogue, its doors also faced Jerusalem. The villagers used it for Sabbath services or town meetings whenever necessary, even though it was still under construction, the stone floor paving still unfinished.

"Before the revolution started," Gideon told her, "Gamla was a prosperous city, a central processing center for the olive oil industry." As one of the Zealot leaders, Gideon appropriated a house for his family in the wealthiest quarter of the city, just below the citadel. Leah and her elderly parents, along with her brothers Saul and Matthew and their families, crowded into the house with Gideon and the former owners. By the time King Agrippa and his forces besieged Gamla a few months later, more than ten thousand people had packed into the fortress along with them.

All her life Leah had been criticized for being outspoken, but now her frankness became a gift that she used to persuade others that Yeshua was indeed the promised Messiah. It was as if all that had come before in her life—learning to read, studying Reuben's scrolls, listening to Nathaniel's preaching—had been in preparation for such a time as this. She worked tirelessly for the next several months, sharing her faith and caring for the elderly and the ill who were the first to die as the city slowly starved.

Leah's mother was the first of her family to believe, and she was also the first to die as disease ravaged the weakened community. They buried Matthew's two children a week later and one of Saul's daughters the following week. Abba also asked to be baptized, using just a few drops of Gamla's precious water supply. Then he quietly gave away his rations to his children and grandchildren until he also died. Leah herself had grown as thin as Mistress Ruth as the siege entered its seventh month. Yet she continued to pray, as she had taught the others to pray, "Thy will be done . . . give us what we need for this day . . ."

King Agrippa's men called out to them from the neighboring hill each day, trying to persuade Gamla to surrender. That's how they heard the news that city after city and village after village in Galilee had fallen to the Roman forces. But it was when they received word that the fortress of Jotapata had fallen and that Commander Joseph ben Mattathias had surrendered and been taken captive that morale in Gamla fell to its lowest point.

"I can't believe that coward surrendered!" Gideon raged. "He's a traitor to his people! All his men were willing to die fighting—why wasn't he?"

"Joseph was a failure as a military commander," the other Zealots agreed. "He wasted more time and energy trying to win support for himself than he did fighting the Romans."

"God is still on our side!" Gideon insisted. "We're not defeated yet! His Kingdom *will* be established!"

"I agree that His Kingdom will come," Leah said quietly. "But, Gideon, you're fighting for the wrong kingdom."

THE FORTRESS OF GAMLA—OCTOBER 12, A.D. 67

The Roman forces have arrived," Gideon announced. "Thousands of them."

Leah's empty stomach sank as if she'd swallowed a heavy stone. Gideon had hurried home from guard duty in the round tower after serving the first watch of the day. His voice betrayed fear for the first time since they'd come to Gamla.

"The Romans are building a fortified camp on the hill up there, overlooking the city," he said. "They've already put men to work filling in the divide we made so they can move their siege machines across the neck of land to Gamla. Come up to the citadel with me and see."

He was talking to Saul, but Leah grabbed her shawl and followed along behind them. From the top of the citadel, the Roman camp was an anthill of activity. Leah saw flashes of red from their capes, the glint of metal from their weapons. Whenever the Jews took aim to stop the workers on the land bridge, the Romans launched a hail of stones from their catapults, forcing the Jews to take cover.

"Look! They're down there, too!" Saul pointed to the base of the mountain where hundreds of soldiers tramped through the brush, peering up the slopes.

"If they try that approach they won't get

far," Gideon said. "We have boulders piled at the top of all the trails, ready to roll down on them."

But over the next few days it became apparent that the Romans weren't trying to scale the slopes. Instead, they had posted armed sentries around the base of the mountain to capture anyone who attempted to escape from the fortress. After seven months of siege, the Romans must have guessed that the defenders were low on supplies. The city leaders called for a meeting in the synagogue just after dawn a week later. Leah crowded in beside Gideon and Saul.

"King Agrippa has been asking for our terms of surrender for months," one of the elders began. "Perhaps we should consider negotiating with him, for the sake of the women and children."

"I'll never place my wife and children in Roman hands!" one of the Zealots cried. "I'd sooner place them in the grave."

There was a huge cheer of support, but when the noise died down, someone said, "That's where they'll be before long. We're nearly out of food."

"Listen," Gideon said, "Gamla is impregnable. The Romans will grow tired of besieging such a small prize and move on to more important cities, like Jerusalem. We know that Jerusalem is still in the hands of the Zealots and—"

An immense rumbling sound interrupted his words, a sound that could be felt in the trembling ground as well as heard.

"To arms!" Gideon shouted. He and his men quickly pushed their way through the crowd and ran from the building before most of the city elders had a chance to react.

"What is it, Saul?" Leah asked as she followed him and the slower moving mass of people toward the door. "What's that sound?"

"Roman siege machines. They must have finished the land bridge. Get home and take cover before—"

A thunderous explosion sounded above their heads as a hail of ballista stones the size of a man's head came hurtling through the roof of the synagogue, raining down on them.

Screams of panic mingled with the cries of the injured as the crowd stampeded from the building. Saul crouched down and shielded Leah with his body as the mob trampled past them, then he hustled her through the doorway when it was finally clear.

"No, don't look!" he warned as she tried to glimpse the carnage behind them. "Get up to the citadel—run!"

But Leah was too weak from hunger to run for very long, nor did she have the strength to climb to the top of the citadel. She went home instead and climbed to the rooftop with the other women and children where she had a view of the battle below.

Under a covering of ballista fire from the catapults, the Romans were transporting three monstrous battering rams on log rollers across the land bridge toward the city wall. Each time the defenders tried to fire on them, the Romans launched a shower of stones that drove them back. The wall was as much as twenty feet thick in places, but Leah and the others watched in horror as the machines took aim at three of the wall's weakest points.

"How could they know where to attack?" Matthew's wife, Rebeccah, cried.

Leah didn't answer, but she recalled how Joseph ben Mattathias had boasted about designing Gamla's defenses. Had he turned traitor?

The rhythmic boom of the rams echoed from the surrounding mountains as they pounded against the wall. From a distance, Leah could see the structure trembling and shaking beneath their force. When it became apparent that the first section of wall was about to crumble, the defenders backed away so the wall wouldn't tumble in on them and set up their line of defense in the street, ready to repel the invaders. But even with every man in Gamla standing ready, they seemed pitifully few against the horde of Roman soldiers that swarmed across the land bridge, preparing to storm the breach.

With a rumble like thunder, a section of wall finally collapsed as one of the rams broke through. For a long moment, the scene was blocked by an enormous cloud of dust, but Leah knew by the loud trumpet blasts, the sound of clashing swords, and the terrifying shrieks of the Roman battle cries that the enemy had broken through.

"We need to get to higher ground," Leah cried. "Up to the citadel!" Saul's wife seemed frozen in shock, unable to tear her eyes away from the battle. Leah and Rebeccah had to push her back from the parapet and force her down the stairs and out of the house. Herding the older children ahead of them and carrying the younger ones on their hips, the three women staggered up the rocky slope to the top of the citadel.

From there they saw through the thinning dust that the Zealots had stood their ground, battling in the narrow streets below. But as more and more Romans streamed through the breach like a tidal wave, Gideon's men were forced by over-powering numbers to retreat to the upper city, higher up on the camel's hump. Leah searched for her brothers in the swirl-ing mass of bodies and spotted Saul standing a head taller than the others, fighting beside his two young sons. Gideon fought near the front lines, bravely trying to halt the flood of Romans. There was no sign of Matthew.

As the defenders reached the higher ground of the upper city, they saw that the enemy attack had lost momentum. Roman soldiers wandered in confusion through the narrow, unfamiliar streets. Gideon quickly rallied his men for a counterattack, charging down the hill toward the startled Ro-mans with a barrage of slashing swords. The suddenness and ferocity of the attack drove the Romans who were on the front lines back on top of the others as they began a panicked re-treat. With no place to go and the streets too narrow for the trampling mob, the first soldiers to reach the cliffs on the edge of town began leaping onto the roofs of the houses below, stepping down from rooftop to rooftop as the hordes gradu-ally pushed them back.

Then, with a powerful rumble, the roofs suddenly began to collapse beneath the weight as too many soldiers crowded onto them. Houses toppled down upon each other, caving in, one after the next, as they avalanched down the steep slope. Hundreds of Roman soldiers fell buried beneath the ruins, and hundreds more suffocated in the billowing dust, unable to find their way out of the choking cloud. Leah stopped her ears against the screams and moans of those still alive who lay pinned in the rubble.

The Zealots gave a mighty cheer as if God Himself had intervened. They continued to press their attack against their retreating enemies, taking Roman weapons from among the dead as they battled forward. But Leah could see that too many Zealots were dying as well. When the main body of Romans finally managed to regroup and turned to link shields in order to halt the Zealot advance, they were too many for the remaining defenders. Gideon's men were forced back once again.

As the battle ended, the Romans completed their retreat through the breached wall. Gamla remained in the hands of the Zealots.

Gideon and Saul staggered up the hill with the others, trembling with exhaustion from the battle. While daylight remained, Leah combed the streets with the women and children, gathering weapons from those who had fallen, searching for the bodies of their loved ones. She found her brother Matthew lying dead near the breach in the wall, among those who were killed in the first assault. She helped his wife, Rebeccah, dig a shallow grave beside Matthew's two children, and they buried him beneath a pile of stones. They were both too weak to dig a deeper hole. Too numb for tears, Leah knelt to pray, reciting Ezekiel's prophecy over her brother's grave.

" 'This is what the Sovereign Lord says: O my people, I am going to open your graves and bring you up from them; I will bring you back to the land of Israel. Then you, my people, will know that I am the Lord, when I open your graves and bring you up from them.' "

Overcome with grief, Rebeccah lay down on the mound where her husband was buried and wept. Leah left her there to mourn and returned to the grisly task of picking among the rubble to strip the dead of their weapons. The mangled bodies that lay among the collapsed homes repulsed her, but she forced herself to search them, sometimes gleaning rations from their belts as well as knives and swords. Most of them looked so young to her—no older than her daughter, Elizabeth—and she had difficulty seeing them as her enemies. They had been mere boys, alive and vibrant just a short time ago.

The silence among the dead was so profound that Leah jumped back when a sudden sound startled her. The moan had come from a soldier lying at her feet. His bloodied head and torso protruded from the rubble of stones, his legs and lower body crushed and pinned beneath them. Leah knew he wouldn't live, and she also knew from his agonized moans that he was suffering. His right hand groped in the dirt, and she saw the deep grooves that his fingers had made as they sought his sword. It lay where he'd dropped it, just inches from his fingertips. He turned his head to look up at her as she crouched beside him. There was no anger or hatred in his eyes, only pain and silent pleading. Leah stood and pushed the sword toward his hand with her foot. Then she turned and quickly hurried away.

"God, you must be so sick of this," she wept as she staggered away from the ruins. "You must be so sick of the carnage our hatred reaps." She couldn't bear to think that God's Son had suffered the very worst of it, enduring the brutality of execution in a frail human body to redeem the people He loved. "I pray that it was worth it, Lord. I pray that those you've redeemed will spread your Kingdom to the ends of the earth."

She spent the rest of the day treating the injured, doing the best she could with limited water and scant medical supplies. As she wrapped a bandage around Gideon's wounded hand, he discussed the Zealots' next move with the remaining leaders.

"The Romans aren't used to defeat," he warned. "They lost

a lot of men today, and when they return it will be for revenge."

"Maybe we should send someone out to discuss terms of surrender."

Gideon shook his head. "They'll never accept surrender now. Not after suffering such a humiliating defeat."

"A siege will kill the last of us," one of the elders said. "We've already run out of food. The old and the weak are dying every day."

"They're the lucky ones," someone murmured.

"Isn't there a way we could escape? Down the cliffs, after dark?"

Gideon raked his uninjured hand through his hair. "I don't see how. The fact that Gamla is impregnable—the fact that the Romans couldn't get in—also means that we can't get out. They're standing guard at the base of the mountain, remember."

"Well, I would still like to try." One man stood to his feet and several others quickly joined him. "I'm taking my family down the ravine as soon as it's dark."

"Me too."

"You'll never make it," Gideon warned. "Those paths are treacherous . . . one false step and you'll fall to your death."

"I'll take my chances. Better that the mountain kills us than hunger or the Romans."

Gideon shrugged and gestured toward the door. "Go, then. Good luck to you."

Leah counted a dozen men who decided to risk escape.

"The rest of us have no choice but to man the breaches and wait for the next attack," Gideon said when they were gone. "We'll hold them off as long as we can—until every last one of us is dead."

But the attack they expected didn't come the next day or the next. The strain grew nearly unbearable as everyone waited to die. During the day, Leah and the strongest women and children collected ballista stones and formed a chain of volunteers to pass them up to the citadel so they could be hurled down upon their attackers. At night she listened to the sounds that carried on the wind from the Roman camp and tried to ignore the aroma of roasting meat and warm camp-fires that traveled on the wind along with them.

She slept restlessly, the constant gnawing of fear and hunger nudging her awake. When she saw a brilliant half-moon lighting the sky on the third night, Leah got up and went outside to gaze up at the stars. She thought of Elizabeth and Judah and prayed that they were safe in Antioch.

Would her land ever be at peace again? Would Elizabeth ever be able to return to the villa in Degania she had inherited from her father? Thinking about Reuben's will, Leah suddenly realized that his documents needed to be in a safer place—a place where they wouldn't burn if the Romans put Gamla to the torch. A place where they might one day be found.

She quietly slipped back into the house and retrieved the earthenware jar, then carefully made her way down the hill through Gamla's silent streets. The door to the synagogue stood open. Inside, the moon shone through the collapsed roof like a pale lantern. She found a broken chunk of beam from the roof and began scratching a hole in the unfinished dirt floor with it, stopping to rest often as her strength waned.

At last the hole was deep enough. Leah carefully lowered the jar into it, then stopped when she had a sudden thought. Wandering into the rear of the synagogue, she searched the adjoining storerooms until she found what she was looking for—a pen and ink. She also found a handful of parched grain someone had overlooked in a broken jar, and she tucked the precious kernels into a fold of her robe. Returning to her task, Leah's tears silently fell as she wrote God's promise to her people, from memory, on the back of Reuben's will. Then she scooped dirt over the jar and buried it in the earth.

When she emerged from the synagogue, a voice called out to her from the top of the guard tower. "Who goes there?" She recognized it as Saul's.

"It's me . . . Leah. May I come up?" She had to lean against the walls twice to rest, too weak to climb the stairs.

Saul and two other men were in the tower, but he was the only one who was awake. Leah gave him some of the grain she'd scavenged, and they talked quietly for a while. Saul reminisced about the flock of sheep he had once tended on the hills outside Degania. Leah talked about Yeshua, the Good Shepherd, who laid down His life for His sheep.

When the other men began to stir, Leah knew it was time for her to go. "Do you know where I can find Gideon?" she asked. "I want to give him the rest of this grain."

"Down there," Saul said, pointing to the breach the Romans had made in the wall. Leah prayed with her brother and held him tightly, feeling the strength that still remained in Saul's brawny arms. Then she left.

She found Gideon sitting alone, leaning against the crumbled wall, staring up at the moon. "What are you doing here, Leah?" he said as she knelt beside him. His voice was soft, as if he lacked the strength to speak louder.

"I couldn't sleep."

"No . . . I mean what are you doing here . . . in Gamla? Why didn't you leave Degania with your friends that night, when you had the chance?"

Leah didn't answer. Instead, she carefully unfolded her robe and brushed the scavenged grain into the palm of her hand, then held it out to him. "Here. This is for you."

Tears glistened in his eyes as he stared at the grain in wonder. Then he shook his head and folded her hand closed around her prize. "Why, Leah?" he whispered. "I killed your husband."

"I know." Leah swallowed, then whispered the hardest words she'd ever spoken in her life. "I forgive you."

Gideon slowly shook his head. "That's what I don't understand. How can you?" He closed his eyes, biting his lip as tears rolled down his cheek.

"I can forgive you because my own sins have been forgiven."

"But why did you stay with me? Now you're going to die in this terrible place."

"I stayed so you would see what God is like. He's a God who loves us and forgives us even though our sin killed His Son."

Gideon swiped his hand across his eyes, but his tears kept falling. "Here we are in the same place, facing the same end very soon, and I realize, too late, that you were right—I've been fighting for the wrong kingdom. I'm losing, Leah. Everything is crashing down around me, like the prophet said. 'You have shed man's blood. . . . shaming your own house and forfeiting your life. The stones of the wall will cry out.' This is the end of our nation. These fallen stones will bear testimony to God's judgment."

"But that's not the end of the prophecy," Leah told him. "A couple verses later it says, 'the earth will be filled with the knowledge of the glory of the Lord, as the waters cover the sea.' The kingdom Yeshua died to bring will fill the whole earth one day. And you and I can be part of that kingdom if we accept the Messiah's sacrifice."

"I don't deserve His forgiveness. I—"

Suddenly there was a sickening rumble, and the earth trembled beneath them. Above them on the crest of the hill, the guard tower where Saul stood watch teetered, then toppled to the ground like a child's toy, falling in a heap of rubble and dust.

"NO!" Leah screamed. "Saul!"

Gideon ran up the hill ahead of her, coughing in the choking dust as he pawed wildly through the debris, calling Saul's name. Archers on the wall fired in vain at the Roman sappers who had undermined the tower's foundation during the night. They ran unscathed into the darkness.

Leah helped Gideon dig, working frantically, the rough stones and splintered beams drawing blood as they gouged her skin. But there was no hope. When they found Saul and the other two men, their broken bodies were as limp as rag dolls.

Gideon cradled his dead brother in his arms.

"I'm sorry," he wept. "Oh, God, I'm so sorry. . . ."

The Romans waited until dawn to attack. There were no battle cries or trumpets this time, but Leah heard the tramp of thousands of feet as the soldiers marched across the neck of land to Gamla.

"To arms!" one of the Zealots manning the breaches shouted. They stood to fight their enemies, but the Roman forces mowed them down like ripe wheat. The cries and moans of the dying seemed to echo off the hills as Gamla's streets ran with blood once again and smoke curled from the burning synagogue. Leah fled to the citadel with the last of the refugees and helped them roll rocks and hurl stones down on their attackers. For a time, they seemed to be holding the Romans at bay. Then a fall storm blew in and the weather turned against them. The driving wind and rain blew in the defenders' faces and foiled their archers' aim, and it carried with it a hail of Roman arrows that they couldn't stand against.

Leah fled to the center of the mound as chaos surrounded her. She knew that this was the end. In front of her, Roman soldiers stormed the citadel, overrunning it. Some of the defenders fought to the very end, taking more Romans to the grave along with them. Others begged for mercy and died at the end of a merciless Roman sword. Behind Leah, people were trying to scramble down the side of the ravine in panic. Many lost their footing and tumbled to their death, others trampled each other in their rush to escape.

Leah slowly dropped to her knees. As she closed her eyes, waiting for the end she knew would come, she felt at peace.

"My Abba in heaven," she prayed. "May your name be hallowed in the earth through my life and even in my death. May your will be done here on earth, just as you have decreed it should be in heaven. Provide for our needs this day . . . and please forgive our sins, as we have forgiven those who have sinned against us. . . ."

THE GOLAN HEIGHTS, ISRAEL—1999

Abby clung to the grab bar in the backseat of Ari's car as it hurtled down the rutted road. Intrigued by Hannah's story and the documents with Leah and Reuben ben Johanan's names, she had stayed up late into the night, reading Josephus' account of the battle of Gamla. "Do you think we could tour Gamla on one of our days off?" she had asked Hannah.

"Sure. It isn't far. I'll ask Ari to drive us."

Now he stopped the car in a crude dirt parking lot at the end of the road. The sweeping view of the rugged hills and distant purple-rimmed lake took Abby's breath away. The camel-backed ridge was easy to spot, but the narrow trail leading down to it looked much too difficult for Hannah to traverse. Abby wondered if she had made a mistake in asking to come here, but Hannah was already climbing out of the car with her canes. Abby quickly scrambled out to help her.

"Aren't you coming with us?" Hannah asked Ari. He had remained behind the wheel of his car.

"No, thanks."

Ari had been coldly silent throughout their short drive, and now he stared out of his side window, not looking at either of them.

"Suit yourself," Hannah said, shrugging.

Hannah led the way down the trail, pointing out all the sights that Abby had just read about like a proud grandmother showing snapshots of her grandchildren. Abby saw the hole that the Roman battering rams had made in the city wall, the crumbled remains of the round tower. Catapult stones the size of bowling balls were heaped in piles everywhere.

"We found more than a thousand ballista stones," Hannah told her, "and 1,600 arrowheads. That should give you an idea of the ferocity of the battle. According to Josephus, Gamla fell to the Romans on November 10, A.D. 67."

Abby and Hannah sat down to rest on the synagogue's beautifully preserved benches. Hannah pointed to the spot where she had found the cache of documents that had once belonged to Reuben ben Johanan.

"We worked on preserving and translating them all that winter," she said. "One of them was Reuben's will, in which he left all his goods and property to his wife and daughter. It soon became clear after examining all the other papers that he had died beforehand, and that his widow had come to Gamla for refuge during the invasion. She must have buried the jar here for safekeeping."

Hannah gazed into the distance, silent for a moment as the gentle breeze blew her dark hair across her face. "Finding those papers changed everything for me. I'm not sure if I can explain how, but they helped me come to terms with my grief. The woman who had buried them and the woman who had discovered them were both widows with a young daughter to raise. Nearly two thousand years separated us, yet our paths crossed and we were both changed forever at the same place, here on the Golan Heights."

She swept her hair from her eyes with a graceful hand and turned to Abby again. "We found writing on the back of one of the documents, a verse from Isaiah 11, probably written from memory. Now that I know that Leah could write, I'm wondering if perhaps she wrote it herself. It said, 'In that day the Lord will reach out his hand a second time to reclaim the remnant that is left of his people. . . . He will raise a banner for the nations and gather the exiles of Israel; he will assemble the scattered people of Judah from the four quarters of the earth. . . . and the earth will be full of the knowledge of the Lord as the waters cover the sea.'

"Leah had claimed that verse in faith, even as the Romans were destroying her nation, killing or exiling all but a handful of her people. Two thousand years later, God fulfilled her hope through me when He brought my family here from Iraq. She and I were two pieces of God's mosaic. She played her part, believing that out of the ashes of her life, Israel would rise again. Now I would play my part, believing in faith that Jake's death was also part of His design, even if I couldn't see it. I would lay claim to Gamla, to Golan. I would trust in His un-failing love."

17

"May I join you, Abby?" Abby looked up from her outdoor breakfast on the dig site to find Marwan Ashrawi balancing his plate and a container of yogurt in one hand, a cup of coffee in the other.

"Sure, have a seat. This was the only patch of shade I could find besides the dining canopy. You're more than welcome to share it." Needing a break from the energetic college students, Abby had opened one of the vans' sliding doors and was sitting on the door sill. She moved aside so Marwan could climb past her and sit inside the van. "It's awfully hot in there," she warned.

"I'm used to it," Marwan said with a grin. "I'm not spoiled with air conditioning like you Americans are."

Abby laughed, enjoying his gentle teasing. "How long have you been doing this gut-wrenching labor during the summer months, Marwan?"

"Oh, a long time. That's how I earned money when I was in school. I met Dr. Rahov about three years ago, and she has given me work here during the summer ever since. She is a very nice woman."

"Yes, I've grown to love her dearly in a very short time. I'll miss her after—"

"Ah, there you are, Abby." Ari suddenly

rounded the corner of the van, interrupting them. "I was wondering . . ." He stopped when he saw Marwan, his expression changing from one of friendly ease to rigid discomfort, as if he had put on a mask. "Eh . . . excuse me. I didn't mean to intrude."

"That's okay." Abby didn't know what else to say. She knew that neither man would be comfortable if she invited Ari to join them. "Did you need me for something?" she finally asked.

"It can wait until later." He disappeared as quickly as he had appeared. Abby looked at Marwan and shrugged.

"He does not like me," Marwan said.

"So I noticed."

Marwan fidgeted on the seat, toying nervously with his bread, as if he had something he wanted to say. "I have been wanting to ask you, Abby, if you would be pleased to join my wife and me for dinner one night. I would like you to meet Zafina and our children. My home is not far from here."

"Yes, I would like that," Abby said. "How many children do you have?"

"Six."

She saw the pride in his eyes when he said it. "Six! Have mercy! I had my hands full with two!"

"Would you come tomorrow night? I could pick you up at the hotel. Let's say five o'clock?"

"That sounds great."

On the way back to the hotel, however, Abby decided to discuss it with Hannah, just to be sure she wasn't doing something wrong.

"You should go," Hannah said, "you'll enjoy yourself. Marwan is a good man. I've found him very trustworthy. I've met his wife and family, too."

"I've um . . . noticed that Ari and he don't get along," Abby said. "Is there a reason? Did something happen between them?"

Hannah shook her head. "As far as I know they never met until this summer. Sad to say, it's probably nothing more than the fact that Marwan is a Palestinian Muslim and Ari is an Israeli Jew."

THE WEST BANK, ISRAEL—1999

Marwan Ashrawi's house was a square flat-roofed building made from plastered cement blocks. It was clustered with a group of similar houses in a small Arab village not far from the dig site. Some of the rooms were hollow shells, without glass in the windows, as if the home was only partially built. Many of the other houses on his street looked incomplete as well.

"We finish one room at a time," Marwan told Abby, "as we have money and materials."

He parked his car in front and led Abby into a large all-purpose room with a polished stone floor covered with scatter rugs. It was bright and clean, the air fragrant with mysterious spices that made Abby's mouth water. His five youngest children, who had been watching television, ran to hug their father and be introduced to Abby.

"This is my son Jamil, my son Salah, my daughter Leyla, my daughter Najia, and my youngest son, Kamal. And this," he said as a handsome boy about fifteen years old came into the room, "is my oldest son, Basam."

"How do you do?" Basam said, shaking Abby's hand.

He was neatly dressed in a shirt and tie, and after greeting Abby, he headed toward the door, preparing to leave. Marwan frowned and began yelling at Basam in Arabic, but even though Abby didn't understand a word of it, she could tell by Marwan's tone and Basam's wry grin that it was all in jest.

"He must leave for work," Marwan explained. "He has a job clearing tables in a tourist restaurant." He punched his son's arm and tousled his hair before Basam left through the front door.

"He is a smart boy," Marwan said proudly, "and he loves

mathematics. I hope he will be much more than a waiter someday."

"Will it be possible for him to go to college?" Abby asked.

"I would like for all of my children to go to university. My people will need educated leaders to build a strong Palestinian homeland. But the Israelis think that all Palestinian boys are terrorists, and whenever they see two or three together, they assume they want to make trouble."

He motioned for Abby to take a seat on the sofa while he sat in a chair nearby. "Basam was arrested along with three of his Palestinian friends a few months ago," he continued. Pain filled his eyes and his voice. "They took him to the jail and searched him, interrogating all the boys and humiliating them, for no other reason than that they were Palestinian. Of course they found no reason to arrest them, but the police didn't care. They kept them locked up for five hours, frightened and shamed. I did not teach my son to hate. The Israelis are the ones who are teaching him. For this reason, many boys Basam's age don't want to wait so long and finish university. They want to fight for our freedom now."

Abby didn't know what to say. But Marwan's mood changed a moment later when a woman walked into the room with a tray of glasses.

He smiled broadly and said, "This is my number one wife, Zafina."

Abby's jaw dropped. "Do you have more than one?"

Marwan laughed. "Alas, no—if I did, it would be over Zafina's dead body!"

When Zafina smiled shyly, Abby could tell she didn't understand a word they were saying. She looked older than Marwan, although Abby knew that she probably wasn't—simply worn from a life of hard labor with six children and few modern conveniences. She was a bit plump, like many of the Muslim women Abby had seen, and wore a long skirt and a loose long-sleeved blouse, her head covered in a white scarf. Abby wondered why Marwan and the children could wear modern clothing, while the women were costumed like biblical characters.

"Thank you," Abby said as she accepted a glass. She took a sip of the sweet mint-flavored tea.

Marwan's youngest son, Kamal, plopped down on the sofa beside her. "Hello," he said with a grin like his father's. He was a beautiful child about four years old with large dark eyes like Marwan's and curly black hair.

"Well, hello. How are you?"

"Hello," he repeated.

"That is the only English word Kamal knows," Marwan said, laughing.

"You have a beautiful family," Abby told him.

"Thank you. Do you have any pictures of your family?" Abby pulled them out of her purse, proudly displaying prom photos and graduation pictures of Emily and Greg.

As Abby and Marwan talked about their children, his sons Jamil and Salah, who were about seven and eight years old, were engaged in a continual wrestling match—punching, hitting, pulling each other's hair. On a school playground, their behavior would have quickly earned them a detention, but Marwan and Zafina ignored them completely. It wasn't until Jamil formed his fingers into a gun and began making shooting sounds at the faces on the television news that Marwan hollered at him in Arabic and chased both him and Salah from the room.

Zafina sat on the floor before a low table, chopping vegetables for their dinner. She had a two-burner hot plate beside her and pans and dishes all around her, the rug beneath her protected by a plastic tablecloth. Leyla and Najia, who were about ten and twelve years old, helped her prepare dinner. As Abby watched them, she found it easy to imagine Leah preparing meals in much the same way in her first-century home.

When dinner was ready—spicy chicken and hot pita bread and several kinds of vegetable salads—Zafina and the children found seats wherever they could, and everyone ate with their plates on their laps. Then, just as Moshe Richman and Ari had shared the stories of their ancestors at the Sabbath dinner, Marwan shared his story.

"How would you feel if soldiers came to your home in America and told you that the land your fathers and grand-fathers have owned for centuries is no longer yours?" he asked. "That is what the United Nations did to the Palestinian people in 1948. They said that Palestine would be divided in half, that people who had lived in Europe and Russia and other countries would own half of it from now on, and the Palestinians who had lived and farmed there for centuries would have the other half. Of course we rejected this partition and went to war—wouldn't you?

"The Zionist soldiers ran my grandfather off his land when the war began in 1948. 'You must leave, it is not safe,' they told him. When he returned after the war, he found that his home and his village had been destroyed. The soldiers told him, 'You can't live here. You abandoned the land and fought for our enemies.' The world doesn't want to believe it, Abby, but the Zionists committed many atrocities against our people during that time.

"My father's family was homeless, forced to live in squalor in a refugee camp. My father knew that this was no place to raise a family, so he eventually left the camps and settled in Jordanian-held territory on the West Bank. Life was very diffi-cult. My father had no land of his own, so he was forced to work for other people. Then in 1967, Israel declared war by attacking Egypt's airfields. You know the outcome. When the war ended, the West Bank was no longer part of Jordan but of Israel. Once again, my family lived in occupied territory. And we were not alone. More than one million Palestinians in the West Bank and the Gaza Strip lived under Israeli military rule. I was only two years old in 1967, so I have never known free-dom. I have lived in captivity all of my life. All I want, Abby, is a homeland and freedom for myself and for my children. Is that asking so much?"

"No . . . of course not. It's what everyone wants." But she couldn't help thinking of Ari's story, how he slept underground because of the Syrian shelling, just a few miles from where Marwan lived. As she gazed at Marwan's family, she thought of Moshe Richman's children, Dan, Gabriel, and Ivana. Must they all grow up as enemies? Without the peaceful solution that Benjamin Rosen vainly sought, would they go to war once again? Would Salah and Jamil, Dan and Gabriel kill one another someday?

"The Jews have tried to cut off my people," Marwan said, "but we are like the olive trees—even if you cut them down, the roots continue to grow. The Jews would like to get rid of us, but we were also planted here by Allah. And our Father is also Abraham, through his firstborn son, Ishmael. Even the Jewish Scriptures say that this land was given to Abraham and his descendants. That means we also have a God-given right to it. I am sorry for what the Nazis did to the Jews. I know that they took away the Jews' homes and millions of their lives. But is that a reason to do the same thing to my people?"

"No, of course not." Abby's answer seemed inadequate. Again, she didn't know what else to say.

Leyla and Najia gathered the dishes when everyone finished eating and disappeared from the room with their mother. "Could I help them wash up?" Abby asked.

"No, please, you are our guest." He leaned back in his chair, thoughtful for a moment, then asked, "Why is it that Americans don't feel the same sorrow for the Palestinians that you feel for the Jews?"

Abby hesitated. "Well, I don't mean to offend you . . . but too many Palestinians have used terror to fight back. When Americans read about things like hijackings, suicide bombers, innocent people losing their lives—it gives all Palestinians a bad name. In the past, some of your leaders, including Yasser Arafat, have condoned violence and terrorism. There has even been terrorism in my country that was linked to the Palestinian cause. Most Americans don't realize that there are families like yours that simply want to live in their own homeland among their own people."

"I do not condone the use of violence, Abby. I never will.

But I know the frustration that many of my people feel. Not only was our land taken, but also our freedom. We now have self-government in some towns like Jericho and Bethlehem, but it is not enough. They offer us too little, too slowly. Didn't your ancestors in America also fight a war for their freedom? And because your enemy had superior weapons, didn't you also use . . . What do you call it? Guerilla warfare?"

"Yes, I suppose you're right." Abby had to admit that Marwan had broken all the stereotypes she once held of the Palestinian people. He wasn't a hate-filled, gun-wielding terrorist but a thoughtful, intelligent man who loved his home and his family. "I'm learning that the solution to a lasting peace in the Middle East is much more complicated than the nightly news portrays back home," she said.

"Many of my people are tired of waiting for that solution. Tell me, what would you do if someone took away your homeland and your way of life?"

"I don't know," she said quietly. "But I think I understand a small measure of your anger. I know what it is to have something you love stolen from you." She paused, still finding it difficult after all this time to talk about Mark. "A few months ago, another woman stole my husband. When she did, she also stole my home and my life. All the memories of what I had are changed, tainted. But unlike you, I don't think I want that life back."

"I am sorry," Marwan said. "Adultery is also a sin for Muslims and a very great tragedy when it destroys families."

By the time they finished their dessert of Arab pastries and strong coffee, it was late. "I should be getting back to the hotel," Abby said. "As you know, morning comes pretty early. Thank you so much for inviting me, Marwan." She started to rise, but Marwan waved her down.

"Wait. Before you leave I must tell you something. For an Arab to invite someone to eat with him is a pledge of friendship and trust, so I must be honest with you and keep that trust. I like you very much, Abby, and I am glad we are friends. But I had another motive for inviting you here tonight. I wanted you to see my Palestinian people for who we really are. It is my hope that you will return to America and tell your people that we are not all terrorists. We simply want a homeland."

"Thanks. I appreciate your honesty."

Abby waited. Marwan seemed to be considering whether or not to say something else. His youngest son had come to sit on his lap after they finished their dessert, and Marwan absently stroked the boy's hair.

"I wish I did not have to tell you this," he finally said, "but the Israelis have not been completely honest with you. They also have hidden motives."

"What do you mean?"

Marwan kissed his son's cheek and lifted him to the floor, telling him something in Arabic. Then Marwan stood. "Come with me, Abby. I will show you."

They went out through a back door, across a tiled courtyard, then up a darkened flight of stairs to the flat, open rooftop of Marwan's house. The night was clear and very warm, the air fragrant with the smell of frying garlic and onions. They stepped around plastic buckets and scattered children's toys in the darkness, then Marwan crouched behind the waist-high wall that formed a railing and pulled Abby down beside him. He pointed to the street below.

"See that car?" A dark sedan was parked on a narrow side lane down the street from the house. "It followed us here. Someone is waiting inside it, watching this house. When we leave, you will see that the car will follow us to the hotel."

A cold chill ran through Abby that had nothing to do with the night air. She never should have accepted Marwan's invitation. Agent Shur at the airport had implied that she was involved with Palestinian extremists—now perhaps she was.

"Why are they following you if you're not involved in terrorism?" she asked.

Marwan's large eyes looked luminous in the darkness. "Not me, Abby. They aren't following me. They are watching you. They have been ever since you arrived. It is because of the Israeli secret agent who died in the airport."

"But . . . but that's crazy! I didn't have anything to do with his death! Hannah believes me, and Benjamin Rosen was her cousin."

"I know. I believe you, too. But the Israelis obviously don't."

She shivered again. "I think I'd better go." Abby nearly ran down the stairs and back to the brightly lit living room. Marwan's children were sprawled on the rugs and the sofa, watching television.

"I am very sorry if I have upset you," Marwan said, kneading his hands together.

"No, that's all right. I'll be fine." But Abby felt frozen inside as she thanked Marwan's wife for the dinner. His youngest son, Kamal, gave her a kiss good-bye, and Abby thought again of her little Jewish friend, Ivana.

Abby's legs trembled as she walked to the car. She resisted the urge to look over her shoulder at the car parked down the lane. On the short drive back to the hotel, Marwan was silent until they reached the top of a hill. "Look in your side mirror, Abby. The car is following us with its headlights turned off."

Abby looked. She saw the car. She couldn't stop her tears.

"I am very sorry to have frightened you," he said. "I don't think you need to be afraid of them, since you have done nothing wrong."

"I'm more angry than scared, Marwan. And I'm glad you told me. I just hope that your family doesn't get into trouble because of me."

He gave a humorless laugh. "We live in occupied territory. We have no rights. My family will learn to be strong."

Abby remembered how frightened her daughter had been after their house was ransacked. If what Marwan said was true, if Abby was still a suspect in Ben Rosen's death, then the robbery was probably part of this nightmare. She had an overwhelming urge to run to her bungalow and call home, to hear her children's voices and assure herself that they were all right.

"There is something else I must tell you," Marwan said as he stopped the car in front of the hotel.

His dark face was so somber, Abby wasn't sure she wanted to hear it.

"They have deliberately deceived you. Dr. Bazak is not who he says he is. He is a government agent assigned to follow you."

"No! I don't believe you!" She saw immediately that her response had wounded Marwan, and she hurried to explain. "I mean, I don't *want* to believe it. Hannah is my friend. I . . . I can't believe that she would deliberately lie to me." But Abby remembered the way Ari followed her everywhere, staying in adjoining rooms, enduring Hannah's lectures about Jesus, assigning Abby to his work areas. Then she remembered his gun, hidden beneath his khaki work shirt. Her stomach rolled.

"Why don't you ask Hannah?" Marwan said. "She knows the truth. If she is really your friend, she will tell it to you."

Abby climbed out of the car on shaking legs, then stood on the front step as Marwan drove away. She watched for a long time, waiting for the mysterious sedan to pull up, waiting to see if Ari was behind the wheel. The car never came.

Maybe it wasn't the Israelis at all, she thought as she started down the path to her bungalow. Maybe it was one of Marwan's Palestinian friends trying to scare her. He had admitted that he wanted to win sympathy for his cause. But no, she would never believe that Marwan was a terrorist, he—

Abby stopped in her tracks. How had Marwan known about Benjamin Rosen? Even if the report of his murder had been in the newspaper, how had he known about Abby's part in it? Or that Ben had been a spy? Surely the press wouldn't have printed those details. And if it was true that Ari was also a spy, how did Marwan know?

She started to run as each bush and shrub suddenly seemed alive with danger. When she saw lights in Hannah's bungalow, she bounded up the steps and pounded on her door.

"Abby! What a nice sur—"

"I want to ask you a question," Abby said in a trembling voice. "Promise me you will tell me the truth."

"Of course, but . . . my goodness, you're shivering! Come inside!" Hannah pulled a sweater out of her closet and wrapped it around Abby's shoulders, then helped her into a chair. "What on earth is wrong?"

"Is it true that Ari is a spy like Ben was?"

Hannah was very still for a moment, then she slowly lowered herself to the bed. "Yes, Abby. It's true. Ari works for the same agency Ben did."

The truth jolted Abby like a slap in the face. The people she trusted as friends had been frauds—watching her, following her, betraying her trust. She could barely speak. "All this time . . . you've been lying to me?"

"No, Abby. I never lied—"

"Yes, you did! You said Ari was an archaeologist, one of your students! Are you a spy, too?"

"No. Never. And everything I told you about Ari is true. He has a doctorate in archaeology, and he was once my student. He resigned from the Institute five years ago and joined the Agency. This is the first dig he has worked on since then."

"But . . . you let him follow me? I feel so betrayed, Hannah. I thought you were my friend. I can't believe you would let him spy on me."

"I don't blame you for being angry, but it wasn't like that. I had no choice in the matter. I'm being used, too. The Israeli government would have assigned someone to follow you whether I approved of it or not. I know Ari, and I thought it was better that they sent him than some stranger. I have been defending your rights all along. That's what most of my arguments with Ari have been about. He has been pressuring me to get out of the way and let him invade your privacy even more, but I won't allow it."

"My email! He wasn't just being nice, was he?"

"I'm so sorry."

Abby thought about all that Ari had done for her, how close their rooms were, how he had even held her in his arms, and she felt so angry, so used, she couldn't speak. She shivered uncontrollably.

"Ari was very angry with me for becoming your friend," Hannah said. "He was supposed to get close to you himself, become your confidante, offer you solace . . . no matter what that might involve. But I wouldn't let him use you like that. I saw right away how fragile you were, how wounded you had been by your husband. You might have succumbed to his charms all too easily, and I couldn't allow him to manipulate your feelings that way. Our friendship is genuine, Abby. I liked you the very first night we met. And after losing Ben so suddenly, I needed a friend as much as you did."

As angry as Abby was, she knew in her heart that Hannah was telling the truth. She was a true friend. It frightened Abby to think that if it hadn't been for Hannah, she might have ended up in bed with Ari to get even with Mark. "Thank you," she whispered.

"I never believed you were involved in Ben's death. I don't know why the Agency sent Ari on this wild goose chase with you, but—" Hannah stopped. Her eyes suddenly filled with tears. "That's not true. I do know why they sent Ari. . . . It was an answer to my prayers."

She struggled up from the bed and retrieved a photograph in a silver frame from her dresser drawer. "There is something else I haven't told you, Abby. Something I haven't been allowed to tell you." She handed the photograph to Abby. It was of a much younger, much happier Ari Bazak with a strikingly beautiful woman.

"My daughter, Rachel, married Ari. I love him like my very own son."

18

CHAPTER

Hannah held the bronze coin beneath her desk lamp and peered at it through the magnifying glass. When the front-door security buzzer suddenly sounded, she nearly leaped out of her skin. It couldn't be seven o'clock already, could it? It was noon just a moment ago. She glanced out of her office window and saw that it was dark outside. She rose from her chair and hurried down the hall to open the door for Ari.

He had called that morning, inviting Hannah to dinner. "Sorry, I don't have time," she'd said. "I'm finishing my field report, and I have a publishing deadline to meet."

"You have to eat, Hannah," he'd said, then he'd laughed. "Oh, that's right! You usually forget to eat once you're buried in your work, don't you?"

"Is it something we can talk about over the phone?" She propped the receiver against her shoulder and continued scribbling notes to herself.

"No, I really need to see you in person."

They had agreed that he would stop by her office at seven o'clock that evening. This would be him at the door.

Ari had a huge grin on his face and an armload of soft drink bottles and paper carryout bags from King David Schwarma. "If you won't come to dinner, dinner will have to come to you," he said. He wasn't alone.

"Rachel! Sweetie, what a wonderful surprise!" Hannah said, hugging her daughter. "What are you doing here?"

"We've come to tell you our good news." Rachel slipped her arm comfortably through Ari's. "We're engaged!" She stood on tiptoe to kiss his bearded cheek. He grinned sheepishly behind the takeout bags.

"Very funny, you two," Hannah said as she led the way to her office. "Whose idea was this little joke?"

Ari set the bags on Hannah's desk, then draped his arm around Rachel's shoulder, pulling her close. "It's not a joke. I'm in love with your daughter. I've asked her to marry me." Hannah stared, incredulous. Rachel laughed and steered her mother to a chair.

"You'd better sit down, Mama, before you fall over. No doubt you forgot to eat again." She began opening bags and dishing food from the takeout containers onto paper plates.

"Y-you can't be serious," Hannah said when she finally found her voice.

"Why not, Mama?"

"Well . . . well, because you're a child and . . . and Ari is a grown man. How old are you, Ari?"

"Thirty-one."

"You see, Rachel? He's—"

"Ten years older than I am. I know. That's not so much. Here, eat your dinner, Mama, before it gets cold." She shoved a full paper plate into Hannah's hands, then licked her fingers. "It's not as though I'm marrying a stranger. Ari is already part of the family, isn't he? You always said how much you liked him, what an excellent scholar he was, how much you admired his teaching . . ."

It was true. Hannah had always enjoyed a close relationship with Ari Bazak. He had been invited to her home many times as Rachel was growing up. But she had never imagined that her daughter's adolescent crush would lead to this. She looked up at Ari, who was calmly chewing an olive.

"You can't be serious, Ari. Won't marriage interfere with your . . . life-style?"

He spit out the pit, then perched on the edge of her desk. "I am serious. I'm getting too old for that life-style. I've been wishing for a long time that I would find the right woman and settle down. And here she was all the time, right under my nose."

The food under Hannah's nose smelled too good to resist. She picked up her plastic fork and began to eat. "Would somebody please explain to me how this happened? The last I heard, Rachel was working on some sort of special project this summer and was too busy to come home."

Rachel sat cross-legged on the floor, unable to find any other spot in Hannah's office that wasn't overflowing with yellowing papers, dusty books, or priceless artifacts.

"Ari was my special project," she said. "I found out where *Doctor* Bazak was going to be digging this summer and signed up as a volunteer. I got up an hour early every day so I would be sure to look gorgeous; I shamelessly chased him from one end of the tel to the other all day; I plopped myself down at his dinner table every night to ask stimulating questions about the excavation; then I listened breathlessly to his fascinating answers."

"She's exaggerating," Ari said with a mouthful of food. "I wasn't suckered that easily."

"I told you eight years ago that I was in love with him, Mama. And that I was going to marry him someday."

"Forgive me for doubting, but you were thirteen."

"I know quality when I see it," she said, grinning. "You have to admit he's one-in-a-million."

"He certainly is. And you're not the only girl who ever thought so, sweetie. I wish I had a shekel for every heart he's broken. My dig would be funded for the next ten years."

"Pardon me for eavesdropping," Ari said, raising his hand like a schoolboy, "but may I say something in my own defense? I know I had a reputation . . ."

"As a notorious playboy."

"Well, yeah . . . but a leopard really can change his spots if he falls in love. Rachel isn't like—"

"All your other conquests?"

"You're being tough on me, Hannah . . . but I understand why. You have a beautiful, intelligent, incredible daughter, and I don't blame you in the least for being protective. But Rachel is no love-sick adolescent. She's mature beyond her years. And unlike my other so-called *conquests*, Rachel is refreshingly old-fashioned. She even has me attending synagogue regularly—something my family has been trying to accomplish for years. You raised her well, Hannah. You can be proud of her."

"I'm very proud of her. And her father would be, too." Rachel had always shared Jake's tenderhearted love for God, even though she had been only eight years old when he was killed. Hannah gazed at her beloved daughter and saw Jake's classic good looks on a slender female body—his thick, dark hair and beautifully arched brows; his wide, intelligent eyes and full lips. Her beauty was so extraordinary it took Hannah's breath away. She could easily imagine the effect Rachel would have on a man. Ari had been as helpless as a fly in a web.

"I fear my daughter has bewitched you, Ari. You, of all people, should have known better."

"Oh, please!" Rachel said, rolling her eyes. "You should talk, Mama. Weren't you the one who pursued Abba? Didn't you and Uncle Ben drive up to Tiberias after hatching your little plot to snatch Abba away from Aunt Devorah? And didn't you tell me that you kissed him first?"

"That was only because Jake was so shy. I had to do something—"

"Well, so did I!"

Hannah laughed. "No one would ever accuse Ari of being shy."

"And weren't you my age when you got married, Mama? And wasn't Abba older than you?"

"Not *ten years* older!"

"Hey, I'm hardly Methuselah!"

"Sorry, Ari." Hannah laughed.

He put down his empty paper plate and stood, pulling Rachel to her feet and into his arms. "So do we have your blessing or not, Hannah?"

She gazed at these two handsome young people—two people she loved dearly but had never imagined together—and her eyes filled with tears. She lifted one of the Coke bottles in celebration. "Of course, my dears. *Mazel tov!*"

JERUSALEM, ISRAEL—1990

Hannah knocked on the door of Ari and Rachel's apartment, breathless after climbing up four flights of stairs. "I'm recommending . . . that the Institute . . . give you a raise," she told Ari when he opened the door. "You two need an apartment . . . with an elevator."

Ari laughed. "That's why we chose this place—to convince you that I needed more money."

"I'm convinced!" The entire apartment had only a bath and three small rooms—their bedroom, a kitchen, and the living room, which had space for little else besides the back-to-back desks where Ari planned his lectures and Rachel studied to finish her college degree. Hannah found Rachel in her postage-stamp-sized kitchen and gave her a hug. "Want some help, sweetie?"

"No, thanks, I'm fine. Go ahead and sit down. Dinner's almost ready."

Hannah pulled out a kitchen chair, inhaling the fragrant aroma of garlic and roasting lamb. Ari finished setting the tiny table for their dinner, then sat down across from her. The table was barely big enough for their plates and glasses. They would have to serve themselves directly from the pots on the stove, buffet style.

Rachel was busy chopping, stirring, and cooking. But Hannah's eyes were on her son-in-law, not her daughter. She loved to watch Ari watching Rachel. Even after four years of marriage, he was still so deeply in love that he could scarcely bear to take his eyes off her.

"So what are we celebrating?" Hannah asked. "Is there an occasion for this dinner?"

"Not really," Rachel said. "It just seemed like a long time since we talked. Oh, and I did want to tell you about my senior thesis."

"Is this for your history major or your comparative religion major?" Hannah asked. Rachel was fascinated with so many subjects that she'd had a hard time deciding on just one major as she finished her degree.

"Both . . . but come on, grab your plates and dish up. I'll tell you about it while we eat."

"Mmm, this is delicious," Hannah said after she'd tasted her food. "Where did you learn to cook like this? It certainly wasn't from me."

"From her aunt Devorah," Ari said. Rachel frowned and punched his arm. "What? Did I say something wrong?" he asked.

Hannah laughed. "Don't worry, I know your aunt Dev is a better cook than I am. And I haven't been jealous of her since the day your father chose me instead of her. Now, let's hear about this thesis you're researching."

"I got the idea from Ari's lecture notes on the Roman era. You know how a lot of so-called messiahs appeared during that time? Well, I'm writing a paper on the Messiah, researching all the references to Him in the Torah and the Prophets, then comparing it with the historical records. Ari was a little upset when I brought home the Christian Bible, but Yeshua— Jesus—was the most famous of the messiah figures."

"You're reading the Christian Bible?" Hannah asked.

"Yep. I already read it twice." Rachel laid down her fork, too excited to eat. She played with her mosaic-stone necklace while she talked. "If someone invented the Christian religion, they went to an awful lot of trouble to do it. They knew our Jewish Scriptures and prophecies inside out."

"*If?* Rachel, you're not falling for this stuff, are you?"

"You know what surprises me the most, Mama? How *Jewish* this Yeshua was. The Christian Bible has him celebrating Passover and all the other feasts, quoting Jewish prophets, attending synagogue. Someone asks Him what the greatest commandment is, and He says the *Sh'ma Yisrael*: 'Love the Lord your God with all your heart.' He really wasn't starting a new religion at all. He was simply a Jewish rabbi with a breathtaking interpretation of Judaism. He was trying to move a very corrupt religious system back to what God originally intended. And the God He describes is the same one I believe in—a God of redemption."

Hannah was alarmed. "You've studied history, Rachel. You know all the atrocities that Christians have committed against our people in that name!"

"His followers did those things, Mama, not Him. Yeshua said to turn the other cheek when our enemies attack. He said the meek, not the powerful, would inherit the earth. Do you know that all of the earliest Christians were Jewish? The historical record also says that a large number of Temple priests became Christians, too."

"I'm surprised that such well-educated men didn't know better than to fall for it."

"That's the point. They fell for it because Yeshua fulfilled all of the prophecies about the Messiah. The book of Daniel, for instance, where it names all of the kingdoms that would follow the Babylonians in history. If you calculate those empires—the Medes and Persians were the chest and arms of silver, the Greeks were the belly and thighs of bronze—you'll see that Yeshua came during the Roman Empire—the legs of iron and feet of clay—just as Daniel predicted He would."

"You said yourself that there were a lot of other so-called messiahs during that time. What about Bar Kochba?"

"No one is following any of the other messiahs two thousand years later. No one rewrote the calendar to fit the date of Bar Kochba's birth. But the Kingdom Yeshua established has grown to fill the whole earth, just like Daniel's prophecy said it would."

LYNN AUSTIN

Hannah didn't know what to say. Her daughter's passion for the Christian's Jesus shocked her, but she didn't know how to refute it.

"Mama, think of all the prophecies that picture our Messiah as a shepherd, like King David. Do you know that Yeshua was born in a stable, that His birth was first announced to the shepherds who pastured the temple flocks? Isaiah prophesied that He would pour out His life as a guilt offering, and they crucified Yeshua on Passover."

"The Christians could have rewritten the account of his life and death, Rachel. They could have twisted it to make it fit whatever they wanted it to prove."

"Then why didn't the Jewish leaders come forward with proof to refute it? They never produced His body or contradicted the claim that He was killed on Passover. Do you know that all of Yeshua's disciples were martyred, yet not one of them ever called Him a fraud or denied that He was the Messiah? Would they have died as martyrs to a hoax? The most vicious persecutor of the early Christians, a Jewish Pharisee named Saul, later saw a vision of Yeshua and became a believer. He was tortured and eventually died for the faith he once persecuted. And if you read the Christian stories, you'll see that Yeshua's followers were very human. They doubted and denied and betrayed Him at first. In fact, it's written just like our Scriptures, with the same tradition of blunt honesty that gave us David and Bathsheba and Jonah running in the opposite direction from God. It's not a whitewashed account, but an absolutely amazing story!"

Hannah turned to Ari. He was sitting back in his chair sipping his coffee, listening to Rachel in relaxed contentment. "How can you put up with all this?" Hannah asked him. "Aren't you upset?"

"No, I'm intrigued," he said, smiling. "Rachel is a very smart woman. I trust her scholarship."

"Scholarship!" Hannah said in exasperation. "Honestly, Ari, you're so in love with that girl, you wouldn't care if she claimed to follow Muhammad!" Rachel laughed and leaned over to kiss Ari, then she got up to pour more coffee.

"So are you a Christian now?" Hannah asked her.

"No, I don't think so," she said, laughing again. "I haven't even spoken to any Christians, so they can't be brainwashing me. In fact, I've been asking several Torah experts to explain the Messiah to me and to explain why God hasn't fulfilled all those prophecies, like the ones in Daniel and Isaiah, when so many others have been fulfilled—like the nation of Israel being born in a day. And you know what? They can't tell me. None of their explanations hold up under close examination."

Hannah shook her head. "I sure wish Jake were here to talk to you."

"I do, too," Rachel said, fingering her necklace again. "He's the one who started me on this quest. He always said that the Holy One was a God of redemption. That's what Yeshua preaches, too. I'm starting to wonder if His redemption is the one we have all been waiting for."

JERUSALEM, ISRAEL—1991

The following spring, Rachel made a stunning announcement at the Passover seder. "I've become a believer in Yeshua the Messiah," she said. "I plan to be baptized."

Hannah was dismayed but not surprised by the news. The Messiah was all that Rachel had talked about for months as she finished researching and writing her thesis. "So . . ." Hannah said, exhaling, "I guess you must have finally met up with some Christians."

"No—at least not Gentile Christians. It was other Jewish believers in the Messiah, like myself, who finally convinced me."

"Is that why we're not celebrating Passover with Aunt Devorah and Uncle Ben this year, like we always do?"

"Sort of. I wanted to celebrate it with just you and Ari so I could explain what I believe and what this celebration now means to me. I wanted to take you through the process, step by step. I didn't think the others would understand."

"What makes you so sure I'll understand?" Hannah said. "Do you understand it, Ari?"

He looked from Hannah to Rachel and back again. "I'm . . . eh . . . trying to keep an open mind."

"Will you do the same, Mama?"

"Of course. But why are you even celebrating Passover if you're no longer a Jew?"

"But I am still a Jew! I haven't given up any part of our faith or our heritage. I don't have to. Yeshua the Messiah is the fulfillment of the Jewish faith."

Rachel had moved the table into the living room so they would have more room to relax while they ate. As they proceeded with the Passover seder, Ari, as head of the household, read the words of the liturgy. After he completed each portion, Rachel explained the familiar rituals in a new light.

When Ari held up the Unity cloth with the three pieces of unleavened bread, Rachel explained how the Godhead was a unity of three-in-one—Father, Son, and Holy Spirit—'unleavened,' without sin. When Ari removed the middle piece of bread, broke it, and hid it away in a shroud for a portion of the meal, Rachel explained how Yeshua left heaven and descended to earth, where His body was broken and hidden in the grave. They later sang the Passover hymn—*From the rising of the sun to the place where it sets, the name of the Lord is to be praised*—and Rachel told them, "Yeshua's redemption is for the whole earth, just as God promised Abraham that all nations would be blessed through him." And as they ate the meal itself, Rachel said, "When our ancestors ate this meal for the first time in Egypt, the blood of the lamb rescued them from death, just as Yeshua, our Passover lamb, rescues us from death."

Afterward, when the hidden piece of bread was found and "bought" with silver, Rachel told them that Yeshua's betrayal had also been bought with silver, as Zechariah had prophesied.

"When Yeshua got to this part of the seder," Rachel said, "on the night of His last Passover meal, He took the bread that had been hidden, gave thanks, and broke it just like we do, passing it to His disciples, saying, 'Take and eat; this is my body, broken for you.' It was like the fellowship offering of His day—the sacrifice that brought peace with God was also eaten by the worshipers." She held up a flat square of unleavened bread. "Look, Mama. It's striped and pierced, just as Isaiah said the Messiah would be pierced for us, and by His stripes we would be healed."

Throughout the meal, Ari poured each of them four cups of wine, each cup representing one of the promises God made to His people in Exodus. "This third cup is the cup of redemption," he said when he reached that part of the seder. "It represents God's promise that 'I will redeem you with an outstretched arm.' "

"Yeshua took this third cup," Rachel said, "and when He gave thanks He offered it to His disciples saying, 'Drink it. This is my blood of the covenant, which is poured out for the forgiveness of sin.' You know that God's covenants are always signed in blood. For the old covenant, that blood was sprinkled on the people, but this blood they drank, symbolizing that the new covenant is internal. His laws are written on our hearts, not tablets of stone. Passover was the commemorative meal of the old covenant, but it became the commemorative meal of His new covenant, the one promised in Jeremiah 31. It's the meal that Christians call Communion."

After Ari filled the fourth cup, the cup of praise, Rachel said, "Yeshua didn't drink this fourth cup. He said He wouldn't drink the fruit of the vine again until He drank it in God's Kingdom. That's because His Passover sacrifice hadn't been made yet. Our redemption hadn't been bought. He couldn't drink the cup of praise—where God promises to make us His people, His Kingdom—until after His resurrection."

Nearly four hours after the meal began, they sang the final

hymn—*The stone the builders rejected has become the capstone*—and Ari said the closing prayer.

"When Yeshua's Passover feast ended," Rachel told them, "He prayed, 'Father, the time has come. Glorify your son that your son may glorify you.' Then He went out to the Garden of Gethsemane where the priests arrested Him. Before that Passover Day ended at sundown, they had crucified Him."

Hannah had said very little throughout the meal, overwhelmed by Rachel's passion and by the enormous amount of research she had done. But now her daughter turned to her, waiting for her reaction.

"Well, you were right, sweetie," Hannah managed to say. "If someone did invent this religion, they worked awfully hard to make everything fit."

"But some of those things were beyond human planning, Mama. The Romans could have set Yeshua free. They didn't have to pass the death sentence. They could have crucified Him on any other day besides Passover. He died on that day by God's design. As the sun was setting, they laid His body in the tomb. You know as well as I do that the next feast, the Feast of Unleavened Bread, begins as the sun sets on Passover. Yeshua was buried on the day that we give thanks to God for the bread He provides from the earth. Yeshua said, 'I am the bread of life.' And He also said, 'Unless a kernel of wheat falls to the ground and dies, it remains only a single seed. But if it dies, it produces many seeds.' He died so that the Kingdom could grow through us.

"But that's not all, Mama. According to the historical record, Passover fell on a Friday that year, and so the Feast of Unleavened Bread was on a Saturday. The Feast of First Fruits is always celebrated on the first Sunday after Passover, so that year the three feasts fell on three consecutive days. You know that only occurs every so many years, because Passover can fall on any day of the week. Yeshua rose from the dead on the Feast of First Fruits. He told the people that a sign would be given, the sign of Jonah, who was in the belly of the fish for three days. Isaiah wrote, 'After the suffering of his soul, he will see the light of life and be satisfied.' Yeshua was the first fruits of God's new Kingdom. We will all share His resurrection life."

"All right," Hannah conceded, "I can see that it would have been pretty difficult to orchestrate all those things."

"There's more if you want to hear it. Fifty days after Yeshua rose from the dead, on the Feast of Pentecost, God's Spirit was poured out on a group of early believers. It was the fulfillment of Joel's prophecy where God said He would pour out His Spirit on *all* people. Remember how Moses said he wished the Lord would put His Spirit on all the people after the seventy chosen elders prophesied? God's new covenant was for all people, not just the leaders—from the least to the greatest. The Feast of Pentecost celebrates the day the Law was given, and Exodus says that three thousand people died on that day. But on the day God's Holy Spirit was poured out, three thousand people who witnessed it became believers and His Law was written on their hearts."

Ari leaned forward and took his wife's hand. "You should have been an attorney. You present a pretty impressive case for this Yeshua fulfilling all the Messianic prophecies."

"Not all the prophecies," she said. "There are three Old Testament feasts that still haven't been fulfilled. But the prophets say that the Lord is coming again in judgment when the trumpet sounds. And what are the next two feasts of the Jewish calendar? The Feast of Trumpets and Yom Kippur. That fits what Yeshua said, too. When the harvest is over, when all nations have heard the Gospel, He will come again for the final judgment. Then, when the earth is redeemed from the corruption of sin, we'll celebrate God's rest—the last feast, the Feast of Tabernacles. Zechariah prophesied that in the last days the whole earth will celebrate that feast. Remember how Abba read the book of Jonah to me on Yom Kippur? He said that God establishes His Kingdom in His people in order to bring His redemption to the whole earth."

When she finished, Hannah and Ari looked at each other. "I have to admit," Ari said, "it does all seem to fit together in one pretty impressive design."

"Just like a mosaic," Hannah murmured. She sat back in her chair as memories of Jake drifted into her thoughts. She wondered what he would think of all this. Would Jake also have become a believer in Yeshua? While she was still deep in thought, Rachel went into the kitchen and returned with dessert—a layered chocolate torte made from matzah.

"No more lectures tonight," Rachel said. "I promise."

Hannah wiped imaginary sweat from her brow. "Phew! That's good news. I can barely absorb what you've already said."

Rachel cut them each a piece of dessert. "We have another announcement to make, Mama. One I think you'll like a lot more than the first one."

Hannah looked at her daughter and smiled, already guessing what she was about to say.

"Ari and I have decided to start a family. We're trying to make a baby."

Hannah beamed as she lifted her cup of wine. "Mazel tov, sweeties! I'm so happy for both of you! But please, tell me you didn't invite me here to share that process with you, step by step! I forgot my camera."

Ari was still laughing five minutes later.

19

TEL AVIV, ISRAEL—1994

O h, sweetie . . . look!" Hannah's voice was hushed with emotion as she watched the shadowy form on the ultrasound monitor. She gripped Rachel's hand in her own. "Your baby!"

Starting a family hadn't been as easy as Rachel and Ari had hoped. But after three years and many specialists, Rachel was pregnant at last, just starting her fourth month. Hannah stood beside her in a clinic in Tel Aviv and watched her unborn grandchild on the screen, heard the reassuring sound of its heartbeat.

"I wish Ari could see this," Rachel said tearfully.

"Don't make him feel any worse than he already does for missing out. He accepted the offer to speak at that conference before you were even pregnant. Besides, his loss is my gain. I'm so glad I had the chance to see this . . . this miracle!"

The technician smeared more gel on Rachel's stomach and studied the monitor as she slid the instrument around. "There," she said suddenly, "that's an excellent view of her."

"Did you say . . . *her*?" Hannah asked.

The technician's face reddened. "Oops!"

"It's all right," Rachel said. "I want to know, and so does Ari."

"Yes, it's a girl," the technician said, smiling.

The baby's face and tiny nose were in profile. Hannah watched her granddaughter lift spidery fingers and begin sucking her thumb.

"Oh, Mama, I can't wait!" Rachel cried. There were tears of joy in both of their eyes. When they finally emerged from the clinic, Hannah pulled Rachel toward a department store down the street. "I feel like going on a shopping binge," she said. "Let's buy a ton of pink ruffles! What do you say?" They emerged two hours later looking like pack mules, burdened with bags of baby clothes. But when Hannah tried unsuccessfully to hail a taxi or even a seven-passenger *sherut*, she knew they had shopped too long. It was now the height of rush hour.

"Never mind, let's just grab a bus," Rachel said, flagging one down as it approached. They climbed aboard, and an Orthodox gentleman graciously gave them his seat.

"Whew, I'm exhausted," Hannah said. "Are you all right?"

"I'm excited! I can't wait to show Ari these ultrasound pictures when he comes home!"

The short ride seemed to take forever as the bus stopped at nearly every corner to let people on and off. Hannah grew impatient. She should have tried harder to find a taxi. But Rachel didn't seem to mind the delay as she pulled tiny pink shirts and sleepers and ruffled hats from her bag of baby things, examining them one by one.

"Look," she said, showing Hannah a pair of white satin booties with delicate pink embroidery. "I can hardly imagine a pair of feet this tiny, can you? Her toes would be the size of pearls!"

"Your feet were once this small," Hannah said, taking the booties from her. "I can still remember how Jake would hold one of your little hands or feet in his own and just silently marvel at the wonder of it."

"You know what absolutely amazes me when I see how small and vulnerable a baby is?" Rachel asked. "The fact that the Almighty One would become a baby with hands and feet that were tiny enough to fit into those booties. Yeshua was the very fullness of God, yet He squeezed himself into a defenseless human body with tiny hands and feet. The psalmist said we are engraved on the palms of those hands. Isaiah said that they were pierced for us."

Hannah heard the awe in Rachel's voice and saw the passion of her beliefs shining in her eyes. After listening to her daughter talk about Yeshua for four years, Hannah found that she was almost convinced, in spite of her arguments to the contrary. She lifted the delicate booties to her cheek and brushed the soft satin against her skin as the bus stopped, once again, to take on passengers.

"Mama, do you know what Yeshua said as they drove those nails into His hands and feet?" Rachel asked.

"No, sweetie. Tell me." Hannah glanced up as a young Palestinian boarded the bus. Their eyes met. The naked hatred she saw in them made Hannah draw a breath as she instantly perceived his intent. She never had the chance to scream.

"*Allah Akbar!*" he shouted, and the world erupted in a deafening blast of fire and heat. Hannah's entire body absorbed the impact of the explosion. The force of it lifted her, flung her tumbling through the air, then slammed her down again with heedless fury. She lay stunned, half conscious, numb and racked with pain at the same time.

She opened her eyes. Instead of the bus there was sky above her. High, thin clouds blew past like wisps of tissue paper. The smell of hot metal and burning rubber and flesh filled her nostrils. She heard the roar of the ocean in her ears, the clamor of a thousand bells.

Suddenly a dark figure blocked her vision, a man Hannah didn't know. He crouched beside her, his expression dumb with disbelief. Dark blood oozed from a gash on his forehead near his hairline, his face bloody, his shirt torn. He seemed unable to speak, but he removed his belt as if in slow motion, and Hannah felt him slide it under her thigh and pull it tight. She wanted to ask him what he was doing and why, but before she could make herself form the words, the man was gone.

For a long moment Hannah simply lay there, trying to understand what had happened and where she was, trying to remember where she was supposed to be. *On a bus . . . going home . . . with Rachel . . .*

But Rachel was no longer beside her.

She struggled to her elbows and looked around. The montage of images that met her gaze was from Sheol itself—smoke and fire and terror and death. The street resembled the black-and-white photographs she'd seen of Europe in the aftermath of bombing raids, only this scene was in brutal color—the twisted wreckage of seared metal; a dangling tire, vainly spinning on its axle; a blasted storefront, gaping with glass and debris; shattered bodies littering the road like pieces of a broken jigsaw puzzle.

"Rachel!" Hannah yelled her name, but it was as if she called from the bottom of the ocean. Her voice was lost in the shrill of screams and sirens.

Then a small movement caught her eye, fluttering on the ground behind her. Something yellow, like the blouse Rachel had been wearing. Hannah twisted around, ignoring the pain, and saw Rachel's head and one outflung arm. Her dark hair was glossy with blood. The rest of her lay buried beneath twisted pieces of the bus. Shards of glass all around her twinkled like diamonds in the sun. Hannah tried to crawl to her and nearly blacked out from the pain. Her own leg was pinned beneath the seat they had been sitting on. She stretched out her arm and touched Rachel's face, caressed her cheek.

"Rachel . . . sweetie . . . ."

Rachel turned her head and met Hannah's gaze. Her eyes were dazed with pain, but there was no fear in them. "Abba . . ." she whispered.

"No, Rachel, it's Mama . . . I'm here. Hang on, sweetie. Help is coming." The wail of sirens grew louder.

"Abba . . ." Rachel whispered again. "Abba, forgive them . . ." Her eyes closed.

"No!" Hannah cried. "Rachel . . . no!" She struggled to roll onto her side, desperate to crawl to Rachel, to hold her. But

when she moved, the pain in her leg was so overwhelming, so unbearable, that the world instantly went black.

———————

Hannah opened her eyes to bright lights. Chaos. Shouts. Screams. A man in green hospital scrubs was looking down at her, talking to her. The white ceiling above her was moving . . . or was she moving?

"Can you hear me, ma'am?" the man asked. "We're taking you into surgery."

Hannah closed her eyes to signal that she had heard, that she understood, and awoke in a white-draped bed in a dark, shadowy room. Everything was quiet. Too quiet. As her vision cleared, she saw Ben and Devorah standing over her. For a moment she didn't know what had happened or where she was. Then she remembered the young Palestinian, the look of hatred on his face, his strangled shout cut short by the deafening blast. A shudder of horror rocked through her.

"*Oh, God . . . No!*" She tried to move, to flee, but her body was heavy and limp, unresponsive to her commands.

"It's all right," Ben soothed. "Shh . . . hush, now . . ."

He stroked her cheek, crooning as if she were a baby. Hannah remembered Rachel's baby, the comforting sound of her steadily throbbing heartbeat, the softness of her tiny satin booties. Hannah had held those booties in her hands only a moment ago. She looked at her hands, but they were empty. An IV tube snaked from one of them. Her heart pounded with fear. She heard the echo of it beeping rapidly on the machine beside her bed.

"Rachel! Where's Rachel?" Ben took her hands in both of his and gripped them tightly.

"She's gone, Hannah." His eyes filled with tears. "Rachel's gone."

"No . . . Oh, God, please . . . no . . ."

Ben lowered his head and sobbed as he had when Jake died, and she knew it was true. Rachel and her baby were dead.

"Then let me die, too," she wept. "Please, Ben . . . I don't want to live."

———————

Hannah had no way of knowing how much time had passed as she wavered in and out of consciousness. The array of machinery surrounding her bed told her that she was critically ill, but she wouldn't join the battle to keep herself alive. With Jake dead, and now Rachel and the baby, there was no reason for her to live. She was aware that the doctors were fighting hard to save her, but she floated away from them, away from the pain, toward death.

"Come on, Hannah! *Fight!*" Ben shouted at her. "You've been stubborn all your life, for crying out loud. Don't quit now!"

She could tell he wanted to shake her, as he had when they were children. "Let me go, Ben," she whispered.

He pounded his fist against the bed rail in frustration. "No! You can't let them win! You have to live!"

"I'm not afraid to die." She closed her eyes, allowing sleep to swallow her again, hoping she would awaken in paradise with her loved ones. Instead she awoke to a face in a surgical mask, telling her she needed more surgery.

"We tried to save your foot, Mrs. Rahov, but it was badly mangled. There isn't enough circulation, and the infection isn't responding to antibiotics."

Hannah didn't care. "Let me die," she whispered. But she awoke in her bed again, floating in and out of sleep, still disappointingly alive.

The door opened and a tall stranger entered her room, a honey-skinned Arab sheik with a handsome chiseled face. He sat in the chair beside her bed. Hannah knew she must be dreaming because she'd never seen the man before, but when he spoke her name it was so vivid, so real, she decided that he was the angel of death, waiting to take her.

"I'm ready," she said aloud.

"Good," he replied with a smile.

She expected him to rise and take her by the hand, but instead he opened a book and began to read: " 'In the beginning was the Word, and the Word was with God, and the Word was God. . . . Through him all things were made; without him nothing was made that has been made.' " His voice was resonant and deep, and he read the Hebrew words with an Arabic accent. " 'In him was life, and that life was the light of men. The light shines in the darkness, but the darkness has not understood it.' "

Hannah didn't understand what he was reading, but she allowed his voice to soothe her to sleep. The next time she awoke, the man stood over her. She could tell by the pale sunlight that washed past the shuttered window that it was very early in the morning. The room seemed to glow and shimmer, as if the earth trembled before the dawning sun. Again she thought he must be an angel summoning her to paradise, and she welcomed death.

"Here," he said. "I brought her for you to hold." Hannah could barely take her eyes off his face, the face of an Arab prince, but when she followed his gaze, she saw that he held a newborn baby. He bent and laid the child in Hannah's arms.

Hannah inhaled her clean sweet smell and stroked her soft curly hair. She allowed the baby's tiny delicate fingers to curl around her own. The baby was awake, and her dark eyes searched Hannah's with a gaze that was so intense it was as if they knew each other. Hannah stared until the dainty face blurred behind her tears.

She understood. The stranger was an angel sent from God. He had brought her granddaughter for her to hold so that she would know she was safe and whole. " 'I am the resurrection and the life,' " the man said softly. " 'He who believes in me will live, even though he dies; and whoever lives and believes in me will never die.' " Hannah held the child until they both fell asleep.

When she awoke again, the baby was gone. Devorah sat in the chair in the stranger's place. "You're off the critical list," she said.

Relief and love brimmed in Devorah's eyes, but Hannah felt no joy at the news that she would live. "Where's Ben?" she asked. A curtain seemed to close over Devorah's face as she looked away.

"He was called in."

Hannah knew what that meant. The Agency needed him. Devorah was never told where Ben would be sent or what he did or how long he would be gone. But Hannah hoped it meant retaliation for what the terrorist had done. The Israelis would strike back at the enemy ten times as hard for every blow they received. An eye for an eye. She remembered the young Palestinian's face, his shout of "Allah Akbar," the deafening, heat-filled roar, and for the first time in her life she was grateful for Ben's work. She wanted every Palestinian in Israel to die. Devorah must have recognized her hatred.

"Oh, Hannah, don't . . . don't . . ." Devorah covered her mouth and wept.

———

"I want to see my leg," Hannah told the doctor a few days later.

"When you are stronger."

"No, right now. If I have to live . . . and if I have to live this way, then I may as well get used to it."

The nurse cranked the bed and helped Hannah sit up, then carefully pulled the covers away. Hannah's leg ended below the knee in a stump that was swathed in bandages. When Hannah nearly vomited, the nurse quickly replaced the cover.

"Please leave me now," Hannah said as the nurse swaddled her in blankets to control her shivering. She needed to grieve alone. The doctor administered a sedative before he left, so Hannah was only half-conscious when the dark-skinned stranger entered her room.

"Are you real?" she asked.

"Yes, Hannah. I'm real." She felt the warmth of his hand as he laid it against her cheek to brush away her tears. She wanted to touch him, but the drugs had turned her body to lead. As she sank into sleep, the last thing she heard was his soothing voice.

"Lord, you have touched blind eyes and caused them to see . . . you have healed the lame and raised the dead. Lord, I pray that you would open Hannah's eyes, fill her with your life, raise her up to walk before you . . ."

Against Hannah's will, she got better. As the nurse was changing her dressing one morning, Hannah asked, "Who is the tall Arab man who sometimes comes into my room?"

"Isn't he your pastor?"

"My *what*? I'm Jewish. I don't have a pastor. And he certainly isn't my rabbi."

The nurse shrugged. "That's what he told the head nurse. He showed us his chaplain's credentials. He must have come into your room by mistake."

But after the nurse left, Hannah remembered that he had called her by name.

Not long after the doctor transferred Hannah to a rehabilitation hospital, Ben returned. He seemed unusually subdued as he bent beside her wheelchair to give her an awkward hug. Hannah waited, certain that he brought news, knowing he would tell her what it was when he was ready. He finally sat on the edge of the bed, facing her.

"I thought you would want to know that we traced the bomb materials. We found the group responsible for the attack. We raided their headquarters a few days ago and made several arrests. I know that won't bring Rachel back—or the twenty other people who died—but there will be justice, Hannah."

She turned her wheelchair toward the window, gazing out at the broken, wounded souls like herself who hobbled around the exercise yard.

"Why did I live, Ben? Why couldn't Rachel have lived? Why not my granddaughter?"

"Why did I live instead of Jake and the others?" he said in a hoarse voice. "God alone knows the answer."

Hannah remembered the blurred outline of her granddaughter on the ultrasound monitor, the steady thumping of her tiny heart. Rachel's child. Rachel's and Ari's.

"Ari!" She said the name aloud, struck by a sudden thought. "Ben, where's Ari? I just realized that I don't remember seeing him. Did he come to visit me in the hospital? My memories of those first weeks are so foggy." When Ben didn't answer, Hannah wheeled her chair around to face him.

"Ben, where is Ari?"

He hesitated for what seemed a very long time. When he finally reached out and gripped her hand, she felt a tremor of fear. "Tell me!"

"Ari fell to pieces, Hannah. You can't imagine—"

"But I can imagine, all too easily! I know how deeply that boy loved Rachel! Please tell me that Ari is all right!"

"Yes, he's all right . . . but for a long time he wasn't." Ben released her hand and stood, crossing to the window to stare out as she had. "He blamed himself for what happened. He said he should have driven Rachel to the clinic himself. He insisted that she would still be alive if he hadn't let his work come first. No one could reason with him. His grief and despair just . . . overwhelmed him, consumed him. We were afraid he would harm himself—or worse, get a gun and slaughter some innocent Palestinians like Baruch Goldstein did at the Tomb of the Patriarchs. Ari had that look about him, like he needed to kill someone in revenge, and he didn't care if he died in the process. He had nothing more to lose. When he disappeared for two days we were all worried sick. I had him tracked down. Then I convinced him to come to work for the Agency."

"Ben, no! Please . . . you can't let him do that! Not Ari!" She wanted to climb out of her wheelchair and stop him, but of course she couldn't.

"You have no idea how distraught he was before he disappeared or how cold and empty he was when I found him. He's not the same man you knew, Hannah. He's no longer a scholarly archaeologist, content to dig up the past. He's a man who was pushed over the edge, and it changed him into someone else. He thinks he failed to protect the people he loved. He failed to keep his wife and child safe."

"But working for you isn't the answer. Can't you see that it's a death wish? He's still trying to kill himself, only he's doing it through the Agency."

Ben turned from the window to look at her. "You're wrong. In Ari's case, it is the answer. I know, because I felt the same way after I watched Jake's tank burn. I had the fleeting thought, 'Thank God it wasn't me,' and I'll have to live with the guilt of that thought for the rest of my life—along with the guilt of being alive when I should have died with everyone else. You know exactly how that feels, Hannah."

His stare was hard, cruel. She did know.

"After Jake died," Ben continued, "I went a little crazy, too, like Ari. You and I both did, remember? I joined the Agency. It was my way of doing something to fight back. It helped me. Healed me. This will help Ari, too."

"*Help* him? By teaching him to kill? He's an archaeologist, a teacher!"

Ben sat down on the edge of the bed again. "I swear I've never killed anyone, Hannah, except during wartime. My work with the Agency has prevented deaths."

"Please . . . you can't let Ari do this! It's not fair to exploit a man's grief and rage for your purposes."

"You don't understand, Hannah. In work like this, it's dangerous to use a man who might falter at a critical moment and begin to question his motives. But a man who isn't afraid to die will be much safer—whether you and I agree with his motives or not."

"So you'll harness Ari's hatred, like a horse to a plow?"

Ben's eyes bored into hers. "Do you mean to tell me you don't hate them, Hannah?"

She didn't reply. What she felt was much deeper than hatred.

"I thought so." Ben rose and moved toward the door. "It's done, Hannah. It's already done. Ari began training three weeks ago. He was in a commando unit in the army, so he was

halfway there. And he has a gift for languages, as you well
know. He speaks flawless Arabic."

"I'm afraid for him, Ben."

"If he doesn't do this—if he has no opportunity to fight
back—then *I'm* afraid for him."

THE GOLANI HOTEL, ISRAEL—1999

By the time Hannah reached the end of her story, Abby was
numb. All the anger she had felt when she stormed into the
bungalow had drained away as she slowly comprehended the
enormity of Hannah's losses. And Ari's. She remembered the
night they ate dinner with the Richmans, and the way Ari had
looked at little Ivana as he talked about Palestinian terrorism.
Ivana was about the same age his own daughter would have
been. Abby couldn't speak.

"So you see, I lost Ari, too," Hannah said. "I love him like
my own son, but he became a stranger five years ago, someone
I barely know. This assignment, following you, is the first time
he has returned to archaeology since Rachel died. When I
asked him to lecture for me that first day in Caesarea, I wasn't
even sure he would do it."

Abby suddenly recalled the look of surprise on Hannah's
face that morning when Abby stepped off the bus wearing the
shorts and blouse Ari had loaned her. "I wore Rachel's clothes!
That must have been so hard for you, Hannah. I'm so sorry.
He never told me . . . I didn't realize."

"Don't be sorry. I'm glad he loaned them to you. All these
years he would never let me or anyone else touch her things,
so it was a good sign. You are almost the same size as her, with
the same dark hair . . . only she wore her hair long."

Abby looked down at the picture again and blinked away
tears. "She's so beautiful. They look so happy."

"For Ari to come on this dig was an answer to prayer. He
was returning to the work he once loved and finding healing
in that work—like I did at Gamla. I've watched his excitement

grow each day as he dug a little deeper."

"I have, too," Abby admitted. "Especially since he started excavating the Roman villa . . . and when we found the mosaic."

"Yes, the mosaic! All my life I've dug through ruins to prove that this land belonged to our Jewish ancestors. Now these Christian symbols on the floor of a Jewish home prove that some of those ancestors believed in Yeshua the Messiah! Ari has seen it. God used the part of his work he was most passionate about—mosaic floors—to prove to him that Rachel was right, that Yeshua was Jewish. And, that He was the Jewish Messiah our ancestors had been waiting for.

"But that isn't all," Hannah continued. "Ari had to stick close to you, Abby, and that meant listening to the message of Christ. He knows it's what Rachel believed. He didn't declare himself a believer or ask to be baptized before she died, but he went to church with her." She paused. "Oh, Abby, please forgive me for not telling you. Please believe that it was for Ari's sake. And please pray for him."

Abby stood and accepted Hannah's embrace. "Of course I forgive you, Hannah. Of course I do."

"Then if you're free tomorrow night, would you join a friend and me for dinner? There is someone else I would like you to meet."

Abby couldn't stop thinking about Hannah and her daughter after she returned to her room. If anything ever happened to one of her own children, Abby knew that her grief would be unbearable. Unable to sleep, she calculated the time in Indiana, then picked up the telephone and called home.

"Hello."

It was her husband, Mark.

Abby's heart pounded in her throat. Her mouth opened, but nothing came out.

"Hello?" he repeated.

"Um . . . is Emily there?" she finally managed to ask. Her

voice sounded so hoarse she doubted if he would even recognize it.

"She just ran out to pick up a pizza. Can she call you back?"

At the sound of Mark's voice, Abby battled to push away a horde of memories, as if fending off a swarm of bees. Some of them stung her painfully. She and Mark had attended colleges that were miles apart, and much of their courtship had taken place over the telephone. She had once loved the sound of his rich baritone voice and its power to warm and enliven her— like smooth, strong coffee on a wintry evening. She remembered sitting on her bed in the dormitory, wrapped in a blanket as she talked to him, watching the snow falling outside her window, waiting for spring when they would be married.

"Hello . . . ?" Mark said again. "Hello, are you there?"

She realized she had kept him waiting a long time. "This is Abby," she finally said. "Emily doesn't need to call me back. I just wanted to remind her that I love her . . . in case she forgets."

She gently laid the receiver back in its cradle as the tears came. That was how Mark used to begin his phone calls. *I just wanted to remind you that I love you . . . in case you forget. . . .*

20

CHAPTER

EAST JERUSALEM, ISRAEL—1999

Abby, I'd like you to meet my good friend Ahmed Saraj . . . Ahmed, this is Abby MacLeod, from America."

"Hello, so nice to meet you," Abby said, shaking his hand. The moment Ahmed opened the door to greet them and Abby saw his handsome chiseled face and honey-toned skin, she guessed that he was the Arab stranger who had visited Hannah in the hospital. He was about the same age as Hannah, and he greeted her with a warm embrace. Even dressed in Western-style clothing he resembled an Arab sheik.

"Ahmed is the pastor of the fellowship of believers I attend," Hannah explained. "He also taught me to walk . . . in more ways than one."

Ahmed invited them into his house, which was very similar to Marwan's, except that more of the clustered rooms had been completed. He shared his home with his youngest son, Ibrahim, his daughter-in-law, Safia, and his beautiful five-year-old granddaughter, Nada. The child climbed onto Hannah's lap as soon as she sat down and barely left Hannah's arms the entire evening. When Safia announced that dinner was ready, Nada and Hannah seemed reluctant to part. Abby suddenly realized that Nada must be the baby that

Ahmed had brought to Hannah in the hospital.

Safia had spread the meal on a cloth on the floor, and everyone sat on rugs and cushions scattered around it to eat. Abby took helpings of couscous and lamb and fresh pita bread, along with a variety of the delicious Middle-Eastern salads that she had grown so fond of while in Israel. When Ahmed said grace, it was a Christian prayer, in Jesus' name.

"I'm probably showing my ignorance," Abby said as they began to eat, "but I always thought that all Palestinians were Muslims."

"Most are," Ahmed said, "but there is also a small population of Palestinian Christians in Israel. Their faith in Christ dates back many centuries. Sadly, my family was not part of them. I was brought up in the Islamic faith."

"Tell Abby how you became a Christian," Hannah urged.

Ahmed laughed. "It was through the back door, you might say. My father was a gardener for a Christian church on the Mount of Olives here in Jerusalem. My grandfather had been the groundskeeper before him, and so on, all the way back to the time when the church was first founded. It was a great honor to hold this job, an honor that I, as the eldest son, would one day inherit. But I was much more interested in listening to what went on inside the mysterious sanctuary than I was in trimming shrubs and pulling weeds. And so whenever I had a chance, I cracked the door open and listened.

"What I heard for the first time in my life was the message of God's love. I saw His love portrayed on the crucifix in front of the church. I learned that through Christ, I could become a child of God—a new idea for me. I had been taught that to earn Allah's favor I must follow the five pillars of Islam: believe in one God; pray five times a day; fast during the month of Ramadan; give alms to the poor; and fulfill the *Haj* or pilgrimage to Mecca during my lifetime. I was taught that prayer would carry me halfway to God, fasting would bring me to the door of His palace, and giving alms would gain me admission. But that was wrong. The Christian God had already thrown open the door of His palace through His Son, Jesus Christ, removing all the sin that stood in my path. To walk through, all I had to do was repent and believe."

Ahmed was a fascinating man to watch. He had a natural dignity and gracefulness in the way he walked and sat, and his gestures conveyed a sense of royalty. Abby had never been in the presence of princes or kings, but she could imagine none more regal than Ahmed. She saw that it had nothing to do with human pride and everything to do with the Spirit of God within him. She would have loved to hear him preach the Gospel.

"Eventually, a very kind priest wedged the sanctuary door open for me from the other side," Ahmed continued. "He offered to educate me for free at the school, which his religious order sponsored. This was a very difficult decision for my father to make. He knew the advantages that a Western-style education would bring me, an education that he could not afford. But he also feared that it would draw me away from the faith of my ancestors. He didn't know, of course, that I had already been drawn to Christ by His message of grace."

Abby was so intrigued by Ahmed's story that she had forgotten to eat. She took a few mouthfuls of food and let Ahmed eat some more before asking, "Was your family upset when you finally became a Christian?"

"I am no longer their son. They mourned for me as if I had died. They no longer speak of me."

"That's a very great price to pay for your faith," Abby said.

"Yes. But God has given me new brothers and sisters in Christ," he said, smiling at Hannah. "I had the privilege of meeting Hannah's daughter, Rachel, first. It was only through the great tragedy of her death that I met Hannah. . . ."

TEL AVIV, ISRAEL—1994

Hannah was no longer on mind-numbing medication when the handsome Arab stranger walked into her room in the rehabilitation hospital one afternoon. She knew he wasn't an angel, but a flesh-and-blood man. A Palestinian man. Her enemy.

"Who are you?" she demanded. "I don't know you. Why do you keep coming here?"

"I am Ahmed Saraj. I was a friend of your daughter. I baptized Rachel into the Christian faith."

"You did *what?*"

"I am the pastor of the church she belonged to."

"Get out! Get out and don't come back!" When he didn't move, Hannah looked around for something to throw at him. There was nothing within reach.

"I understand how you feel—"

"How dare you tell me you know how I feel!" Hannah shouted. "You *don't* know! It was one of your people who killed my daughter!"

"Yes, Hannah, I do know," Ahmed said gently. "It was one of your people who killed my wife."

His voice held none of the terrible rage and bitterness that Hannah knew hers did. She saw sorrow and kindness in his ebony eyes, but she walled off her heart to them. Ahmed took another step into the room.

"When my wife's father was dying, she went to his home in Hebron to care for him. Israeli commandos raided the wrong house, searching for terrorists. They didn't look. They just opened fire on the occupants with their guns blazing. Nada and her father were both killed instantly."

His words, and the gentle, dignified way he said them, left Hannah shaken. She still wanted nothing to do with him, but when she spoke to him again it was less vehemently than before.

"Get out, or I'll ring for someone to come and throw you out." She tried to wheel her chair toward the telephone, but the brake had been left on. She was too rattled to remember how to release it.

"You wanted to know why I've been coming to see you," he said.

"I don't care why you've been coming. I want you to leave!"

"I would like to do that, but I can't . . . I came because God told me to come."

"What a ridiculous thing to say!"

Ahmed slowly walked across the room and sat in the visitor's seat facing Hannah's wheelchair. He leaned forward with his elbows on his knees so that their eyes were level. The intensity of his gaze and the compassion in his eyes left Hannah defenseless.

"Whenever I pray for you, Hannah, God speaks the same verse of Scripture from the Psalms to me, over and over again. 'How priceless is your unfailing love! Both high and low among men find refuge in the shadow of your wings.' "

Tears filled her eyes as the stranger recited Jake's words. She hadn't heard them spoken aloud since Rachel died. How could this man possibly have known? She covered her face and wept.

"I knew that message was for you. . . . We can trust God's unfailing love, Hannah."

He left her alone to grieve, but he returned the following morning. "I have come to help you with your physical therapy," he announced. "I understand that your cousin has work he must do, and that his wife lives in Galilee. I told them I would be happy to come each day and work with you. I have had experience with such therapy before."

Hannah turned away from him. "I don't want your help."

"I know," he said softly, "but I will work with you just the same." He gripped the handles of her wheelchair and released the brake.

"We're enemies—Jew and Arab," Hannah said.

Ahmed sighed. "This strategy of an eye for an eye has blinded all of us. What both of our people long for and cannot find is grace."

It was the first of many days that Ahmed spent with her. Once Hannah had been fitted for a prosthesis, she needed to strengthen her atrophied muscles, adjust to her new limb, practice walking.

"This is impossible," she wept one day after tripping for what seemed like the hundredth time. "I'll never get the hang of this. It's too hard."

Once again, Ahmed helped her up. "Rest a bit, Hannah, then we will try again."

"No. I quit. Why should I walk?"

"For Rachel's sake. Rachel loved you. She would want you to be whole."

"Rachel is gone, and I don't care if I walk or not. I can lecture to my classes in a wheelchair. I won't be excavating anymore, so why bother?"

"You must also walk for your son-in-law's sake."

"What does Ari have to do with it? He resigned from the Institute. He hasn't even come to see me."

"As long as you're in this wheelchair, you are a reminder to him of what happened. You must walk so that Ari will be able to look at you without feeling guilty, so that he can forgive himself. You must go on with your life and return to archaeology so that he won't blame himself for destroying your career. If you won't do it for yourself, then do it for him. Rachel loved him. He is a shattered man just now, and Rachel would want him to be whole, too."

Hannah's muscles slowly grew stronger. She gradually adjusted to the artificial limb. She learned to walk. Hannah also reached an uneasy truce with Ahmed. As she learned to lean on him, she also learned to trust him. He was strong when she felt weak, compassionate when grief overwhelmed her, a companion when she felt all alone. No matter how angry or depressed she became, Ahmed always returned her harsh words with gentle ones. And she also grew accustomed to his prodding lectures. He talked about the Holy One the way Jake used to do. And he talked about Yeshua the Messiah the way Rachel had.

"Why do you still come around to annoy me now that I

can walk?" Hannah asked when he showed up at her apartment one afternoon.

"Because my job is not finished. There is something even more important than walking that you must learn."

"What?" she said irritably.

"Come for a walk with me and I will tell you."

Hannah had papers to grade, an exam to write, lecture notes to review. She didn't have time for games. But Ahmed had removed her jacket from the coatrack. He held it out for her to put on.

"All right, but just to the corner deli and back," she said, picking up her canes. "I need to buy coffee anyway. I'm all out."

They rode the elevator to the lobby and walked outside to a cool spring day. With its soft gray clouds and brisk damp breeze, it reminded Hannah of the day she first walked down to see the ruins of Gamla with Ben. Ahmed's unusual solemnity made this walk seem just as momentous.

"All right, what is it that I must learn?" she asked as she limped along.

"You must learn to forgive." His words hit a wounded place in Hannah's soul like an arrow striking its mark. "You could grow a new leg," Ahmed said, "but you still won't be whole until you forgive. Bitterness will eat away at you until you stop living, until it destroys you. It is like pouring bitter salt water on a plant. You will slowly shrivel up and die."

"Did you forgive the soldiers who killed your wife?" she asked bluntly.

"Yes. I had to, for all the same reasons. God sent someone into my life with the same message that I'm telling you."

"I don't think murderers deserve to be forgiven."

"Murder, hatred, and vengeance are part of man's fallen nature. In the first generation after the fall, brother killed brother. God is as sick of murder and hatred as we are, but what is He to do? Destroy us all? It's His purpose to redeem the world."

Hannah looked at Ahmed in surprise. "That's what Jake always believed."

They reached the tiny corner store, and Hannah pulled a pound of coffee from the shelf. After she paid for it, they headed back to her apartment.

"I've lived through the same wars and conflicts that you have, Hannah, only on the other side. My people lost their freedom. My family disowned me. My wife was brutally murdered. The burden of unforgiveness that I hauled around with me was just as great as the one you carry. I was enslaved to it, crippled by it. I finally grew weary of it. Aren't you tired of it, too?"

Hannah didn't answer. They reached her apartment building, and Ahmed held the door open for her. They rode the elevator in silence. When they entered her living room, he was still waiting patiently for her reply.

"Yes," she whispered as her tears began to fall. "Yes, I am sick of feeling this way. Tell me what to do."

"Add it all up, Hannah. All that they have done to you. Make an accounting of what it is that your enemies owe you. Tally the debt." Ahmed sat with her, crying with her as she poured out all of her hatred and anger.

"They killed Jake! They killed Rachel and my grandchild! They destroyed Ari. They stole my family, my life, my future!"

"Now, forgiveness is this," he said gently. "Not that you forget, not that you say what they did was all right—it wasn't! Forgiveness is canceling that debt, tearing it up, clearing the account. Only you have the right to do it. The debt is owed to you. You might think that means they're going free, that they're getting away with it, and you're right. Your enemies *don't* deserve it. But when you forgive, you'll discover that your enemies aren't the ones who go free—you are."

"I can't do it. It's impossible. I'm not strong enough or good enough to forgive them."

"The only way you can find the strength to do it is by remembering that God did the same thing for you. Add up all your crimes, tally the debt you owe Him. It's what you do every year on Yom Kippur. You come before the judgment seat of God and discover that you also deserve to die.

"When Jesus stood in the judgment seat before the Jewish Sanhedrin, He was innocent. Yet they saw guilt and condemned Him to die. Why? How could that have happened? It was because the guilt they saw was yours. It was as if they pointed the finger of God's justice at you, but Christ stood up in your place to die for your crimes. He became the scapegoat for you. And so God tore up the accounting of your sin. Yes, the Scriptures say, 'He does not treat us as our sins deserve.' That was only because of the sacrifices at the Temple. Yom Kippur balanced the accounts each year. But the blood of lambs and goats couldn't permanently take away our sin. That's why animals had to be sacrificed over and over again. God's justice demands a man's life for a man's life. Christ was that man. Read Isaiah's prophecy. It says, 'He was pierced for our transgressions, he was crushed for our iniquities; the punishment that brought us peace was upon him, and by his wounds we are healed.' "

"I know I don't deserve forgiveness," Hannah said.

"And your enemies don't deserve it, either. It's unjust. It's unfair. But that's the definition of grace—forgiveness that is undeserved. It always costs the giver everything and the receiver nothing. It cost God His Son. As they crucified Him, Jesus said, 'Abba, forgive them.' "

Hannah lowered her hands from her face and looked at Ahmed in stunned surprise. "Those were Rachel's dying words. . . . We were talking just before the bomb exploded, and she asked me if I knew what Yeshua said as they crucified Him. She was trying to tell me the answer afterward. She said, 'Abba, forgive them. . . .' "

Ahmed drew her into his arms and held her tightly. "It's very appropriate, isn't it? Rachel wanted more than anything else to be like Jesus, to show His grace. I think she meant those words for the Palestinian bomber, too. Jesus' disciples are to be dispensers of His grace. That's how we bring Christ's redemption to completion. The world will never believe in God's grace until they see it demonstrated in our lives."

WEST BANK, ISRAEL—1999

When Ahmed finished, Abby knew that his words were also meant for her. She would never be free of her anger and bitterness unless she forgave Mark.

"Where . . . how do I start?" she asked.

"You start by asking Christ to forgive you," Ahmed said. "Once His Spirit lives inside you, He'll give you the strength to forgive others."

"I'm not even sure I can face Mark yet."

"Do you want to be free from the pain and the anger?" Hannah asked.

Abby nodded. "Yes. I'm so tired of feeling this way. I want . . . I want to feel joy again."

"Then forgive him, Abby. Even if absolutely nothing changes with your husband—and it probably won't—the person who will be set free by forgiveness will be you."

When it was time to leave, Ahmed embraced Hannah and kissed her good-bye. Abby saw the tender love they shared. They were followers of Christ; His cross had bridged the gap between Jew and Palestinian, making them one. Canceling the debt, not settling the score, was the only solution to lasting peace with her enemies. It was Jesus' solution.

"God's grace is the most powerful force in the universe, Abby," Ahmed said. "Once it is spread abroad through us, Christ's followers, it can defeat hatred and prejudice and sin. It can even redeem mankind."

21

THE GOLANI HOTEL, ISRAEL—1999

W hy not start by trying to forgive Ari?"
Hannah asked Abby when they returned to the hotel.

"Should I tell him I know he's a spy?"

"Yes, I think so. Tell him how you found
out."

The light was on in Ari's bungalow. Abby
could see him through the window, seated at
his desk in jeans and a T-shirt, typing on his
computer. She knocked on his door.

"May I come in for a minute?"

"Sure." His expression was neither friendly
nor wary.

"I . . . um . . . I need to tell you something," she said after he'd closed the door.

"Oh? What's that?"

"I know you're a government agent. I
know that you were assigned to follow me . . .
that you work for the same people that Ben
did." There was a long silence as Ari stared at
her, his features unreadable.

"Where did this idea come from?" he finally said.

"Marwan showed me the car that was following me home from his house the other
night. I didn't believe him at first when he
told me you were a spy. So I asked Hannah to
tell me the truth . . . and she did."

Ari still didn't reply. He became the cold,

unfeeling secret agent she had met at the beginning of the dig, not the fervent archaeologist that had gradually emerged as they uncovered the Roman villa. She understood what Hannah had meant when she said that Ari was lost to her. Abby didn't like this man that Ari had become, either. She wondered if her own bitterness toward Mark had changed her the same way.

"I know it's true because I know that Hannah wouldn't lie to me," Abby said. "She also told me that you're her son-in-law."

He motioned for her to sit, then sat down in the desk chair across from her. He still said nothing.

"I want you to tell me the truth," Abby said. "Was the break-in back home part of this?"

"I was never given that information," he said stiffly. "I can only guess that if it was, they were searching for evidence of your involvement . . . or else they wanted to apply pressure to see if you contacted someone."

"Have you been reading my email?" When he didn't answer, Abby's temper flared. "If you've done anything to put my children in danger, I'll—!"

She would . . . what? Retaliate? That's what Ari was doing. That's why he had become an agent. If Abby felt this much hatred toward the people who merely threatened her family, what must Ari feel to lose his wife and unborn child? She could understand why he would want revenge. But then Hannah had lost everyone she loved, too, and Hannah had found a force stronger than hatred and vengeance. She had found the strength to forgive.

"It was my job," Ari said quietly. "I was simply doing my job."

Abby drew a deep breath to calm herself. "I know you don't believe me, but I had nothing to do with Ben's death."

He shrugged slightly. His arm was draped on his desk as he sat back in his chair, and he toyed with the keys on his laptop computer as he talked. "It doesn't matter if I believe you or not. I was assigned to follow you, so I did."

"I'm trying to find the strength to forgive you for invading my privacy . . . for using me that day you held me when I cried—"

"You're wrong," he said sharply. He sat up straight and his eyes met hers, refusing to release them. "If I used you that day, it was not in the way you think. I was sent as a professional—to do a job. I was supposed to crack down on you, pressure you, scare you if I had to. I wasn't supposed to let personal feelings get in the way. But for the first time in my career, I slipped. Ben's death hit me hard. I needed comfort just as badly as you did that day." His gaze finally broke its hold on her, and he looked away. "Ben was my mentor and a good friend—as well as Rachel's uncle. I can't imagine why Shur even assigned me to the case, under the circumstances. I guess he needed a convincing archaeologist."

"Wait a minute . . . You work for Agent Shur? You mean that whole little scene where he was questioning me and you arrived in time to rescue me from him . . . was an act?"

"Dov Shur is my boss. He was also Ben's boss."

"Do you know why Ben was killed?"

"I can guess." Ari paused, playing with the computer keys again. "Ben was one of the middlemen in the peace process. From what I gather, he secretly shuttled back and forth between the Israelis and the Palestinians, relaying the terms each side was willing to offer for peace and what concessions each was willing to make. Lately, there have been a lot of setbacks—inside information was being leaked to some of the militant groups opposed to peace. There was even some sabotage. Ben was trying to find the source of those leaks. He must have gotten too close."

"Listen, Ari, I would like to find Ben's killer, too. But it's a stupid waste of your time to follow me. Why don't you look for the real killer? Ben said he'd found the traitor, remember? Why aren't you looking for him?"

Ari grew very still. "What do you mean?"

"Those were Ben's last words before he died. He said he was sure there was a traitor."

"I was told that he hadn't said anything before he died."

"But he did! I told your boss and that other agent who questioned me at the airport what Ben said."

"Told them what?"

"Ben's last words. He mumbled something that sounded like tore or torn . . . and he said there was a traitor. He was sure there was a traitor."

"Any information Ben carried was never found. We assume his killer took it. But I know Ben. If he had evidence of a traitor—and especially after the bomb threat in Amsterdam—he would have made a backup copy of that information and hidden it somewhere. One of the reasons I was following you was on the odd chance that if you had that information, you would try to pass it to someone."

"But Ben didn't give me anything."

"You could have it and not know it," he said quietly. "But I assume they thoroughly searched your things, right? I know they searched the airplane."

"You mean he might have planted it on me?" The thought terrified Abby. "What would this information look like? Microfilm? A computer disk?"

"Nothing technological. Ben didn't have time. If he gave you something, it would have been while you were on the airplane."

"He was right beside me all that time except for when he—" Abby stopped, too shocked and frightened to finish her sentence. She *was* involved in this. She had been all along.

Ari grabbed her shoulders, his grip almost painful. "Except for what? Tell me!"

"My Bible . . . I've been finding strange markings in it . . . and Ben borrowed my Bible when we were on the airplane."

"Show me!" Ari hauled her to her feet by one arm and they hurried next door to her room. Her hands were shaking as she pulled her Bible from her knapsack.

"The Torah," Ari breathed. "You said he mumbled tore or torn . . . could he have been saying Torah?"

Abby realized that what she had mistaken for a sigh or a

moan at the end of the word was actually the second syllable. "Yes. That's exactly what he said."

"Show me these markings."

Abby had found most of them scattered throughout the Psalms. She opened to that book and paged through it, tilting the Bible to the light until she found some of the underlined letters.

"Here . . ." she said, handing the Bible to Ari. He put on his eyeglasses to examine it closely.

"This looks like a very old-fashioned code I've heard about that uses the chapters and verses of Scripture," he said.

"Can you decode it?"

"Not unless I know Ben's starting verse. Otherwise, they are just random markings, some of them decoys to make computerized unscrambling long and difficult. The chapter and verse of the key Scripture tell how to decode it."

"I'm not sure I understand. How do we find out the key verse?"

"Ben probably told it to you in the course of your conversation. Do you recall him reciting any verses to you?"

Abby struggled to remember, but anxiety wiped her mind blank. "He was reciting psalms when we took off because I was so scared and—"

"No." Ari shook his head, impatient with her. "Later in the flight. After he talked to you. After he was sure you weren't involved in the bomb threat. After he decided to put the code in your Bible. When did he borrow it?"

"He took it to the rear of the plane when he went back there to pray with the other men."

"Did he quote any verses after that?"

Abby closed her eyes, trying to put herself back in the airplane, trying to imagine Benjamin Rosen seated beside her, trying desperately to recall his words. Nearly a month had passed. She had read many verses of Scripture since then. "I'm sorry . . . I can't remember."

His anger and frustration showed on his scowling face. "I will take this, please," he said, holding up her Bible. "Shur will want to try unscrambling it on the computer. This is my pager number. Call and leave me a message if you remember anything else."

It was only after Ari gave Abby his card and left that she began to wonder if she had done the right thing. Whoever had killed Ben had wanted to sabotage the peace process. Ari hated the Palestinians for killing his wife and child. He'd said he would never believe they wanted peace.

Why hadn't Ari's boss told him about Ben's last words? Was it because he also suspected that Ari Bazak was the traitor?

TEL DEGANIA EXCAVATION—1999

Abby was very surprised when Ari arrived with everyone else at the dig site the next morning. He proceeded to direct the work at the villa as if he was nothing more than an archaeologist. These would be their last few days of work. Abby was sorry to see them end. Hannah gathered the group together at the close of the morning to give one of her final lectures.

"We've seen how Israel was a land in crisis in Jesus' day," she began. "The people who lived here suffered under their enemies. We've talked about the Pharisees, the Sadducees, and the Zealots, and their responses to this crisis—withdrawal, compromise, fighting back. When the promised Messiah arrived, all three groups missed His coming because they had false expectations.

"You see, all of them expected to be set free from their enemies, the Romans," she continued. "But Jesus knew that the real enemy who keeps us in bondage is not 'out there'—it's within us, our own sinful nature. Jesus extended God's grace to mankind. It was the key to freeing us from that bondage, the key to His Kingdom."

From where Abby stood, she could see both Ari and Marwan standing on opposite sides of the gathered volunteers. Marwan had his hands in his pockets, Ari stood with his arms folded across his chest—but they wore nearly identical expressions on their faces. Neither was willing to forgive. Both wanted to strike back at their enemies to avenge their loved ones. For them, the score would never be settled. She recalled Ahmed's words—the strategy of an eye for an eye blinded everyone.

"Peace with our fellow man isn't won by military victories," Hannah told them. "It's won when we extend God's grace to each other. Peace with God doesn't come through our good works or by following a set of rules and rituals—nor is there any need for sacrifices. The sacrifice that brings peace has already been made through Jesus Christ; the price of our redemption has been paid. Jesus' followers have received grace—undeserved, freely given. We in turn are to be dispensers of that grace, demonstrating His redemption to the world.

"We've uncovered two very different houses here; one very lavish, the other very poor. Most rulers, like the Romans, build their kingdoms on the backs of the people. But Jesus' Kingdom is upside down from all earthly kingdoms. His rulers don't lord over their subjects but are their servants. They don't grow rich and powerful at other people's expense, but like a shepherd, they willingly lay down their own lives for their sheep. His Kingdom comes, His peace comes as we forgive each other's debts, even as our own debts have been forgiven. We've been taught to pray, 'Thy kingdom come, Thy will be done on earth.' That means according to God's design and pattern.

"I want to end by reading you this verse from Psalms," Hannah said. "May it be a reminder to you that we can all become one in Christ: 'How good and pleasant it is when brothers live together in unity . . .' "

The Scripture verse jolted Abby as if someone had grabbed her by the shoulders and shaken her. That was it! As soon as the words were out of Hannah's mouth, Abby recognized them as Benjamin Rosen's key verse. He had read it to her before returning her Bible. She must tell Ari right away.

But when she glanced at him again, a prickle of suspicion

crawled up her spine. The verse wouldn't help solve Ben's murder if Ari was the murderer.

Abby didn't know what to do.

She pondered her dilemma as she rode back to the hotel, as she showered, as she listened to the other volunteers talking to each other at lunch. When she passed Hannah's bungalow on her way back to her own, she realized that more than anyone else, Hannah would want to capture Ben's killer. She knocked on Hannah's door.

"Please forgive me for asking such an insensitive question," Abby said as Hannah invited her inside, "but I need to hear the answer from you. I think I might have the key to solving Ben's murder—I've had it all along and didn't know it. But now I don't know who to trust with it. The last thing Ben said was that there was a traitor." Abby took a deep breath, then exhaled. "With Ari feeling the way he does about making peace with the Palestinians, is it possible . . . could he have had anything to do with Ben's death?"

Hannah didn't react with anger or shock. She sat on the arm of the chair as she stared at the carpet, deep in thought. It took her a long time to answer, but when she did, her words were spoken with quiet certainty. "No. It isn't possible. Ari's love for Ben was stronger than his hatred for his enemies."

"Thank you," Abby breathed as she hugged Hannah in relief. "Then Ari is going to find the person who killed Ben."

Abby hurried back to her own bungalow and pounded on Ari's door. There was no answer, so she tried the knob and found it locked. His curtains were closed. She decided to write him a note, asking him to come and see her as soon as he got back, and wedged it into his doorjamb. Then she returned to her own room to wait.

She tried reading her devotional but didn't get very far before remembering that she no longer had a Bible. She stood, nervously pacing the narrow room, peering through the window each time she passed it, watching for Ari. Suddenly she remembered the card he had given her with his pager number. Abby dug in the pocket of the pants she had worn last night, then quickly dialed the number. The recording told her to leave a message after the beep.

"Ari, this is Abby. I remembered Ben's verse! Call me as soon as you can!"

Shortly before suppertime, someone knocked on her door. She opened it, expecting to see Ari, and faced Dov Shur, the agent from the airport with the curly white hair and milk-commercial mustache. He was dressed in casual clothes— slacks and a sport coat without a tie—and wore his identification badge clipped to his pocket. He was smiling and waving the note she had written to Ari, acting much friendlier than he had the last time she'd met him.

"Hi, I'm Dov Shur, Ari's boss. He won't be back, I'm afraid. There's really no point in having him follow you any longer, since you know who he is. May I come in?"

Abby moved aside to allow him to enter. He closed the door behind him, stuffed the note into his pocket, then pulled out the desk chair and sat down. "Whatever you needed to tell Ari, you can tell me. I know all about the code Ben wrote in your Bible."

Abby couldn't speak. She didn't know this man, and his sudden appearance made her uneasy. She had been suspicious of Ari being a traitor just a few hours ago . . . how much more so this stranger. Until she knew for certain, she decided to trust no one. The information had cost Ben Rosen his life.

"It . . . it was . . . nothing important," she stammered as she sat on the bed. "Just a question about the mosaic floor we found."

He leaned forward in his chair, his expression sincere, remorseful. "I came to apologize on behalf of our government for keeping you under surveillance. You had a right to privacy, and we violated that."

Abby exhaled. "I was angriest about the break-in of my home in Indiana."

"But we had nothing to do with that."

He looked her directly in the eye when he said it. Abby was so relieved that she could only nod.

"It's my sincere hope, Mrs. MacLeod, that Agent Bazak explained everything to you, that you now understand why we had to follow you, and that you will forgive us."

Abby swallowed. "Of course. I already told Ari that I forgive him."

"Thank you." He leaned back in his chair and seemed to relax slightly. "Benjamin Rosen was one of my best men . . . and a good friend. I would do anything to find his killer. Am I correct in assuming that you would be willing to help find his killer, too?"

"Yes, of course."

"Good. Then I would like to ask you to do something for us. I would like you to call your Palestinian friend, Marwan Ashrawi, and invite him to come here."

"But why?"

"So I can talk to him. He knew, somehow, that Ari was an agent. I need to know where he got that information."

Abby hesitated, unwilling to come between the Palestinians and the Israelis. Marwan trusted her. He said it was a sign of that trust that they had eaten together.

"I don't think I can do that," she said.

Shur sighed. "Don't get me wrong—we could come down hard on Ashrawi without your help if that's what we intended. We could have already picked him up for questioning. He was at the work site today, wasn't he? I'm afraid that if we did corner him, he would deny that he ever told you such a thing. But if you were present as a witness . . . well, he could hardly deny it, could he?"

Abby felt confused. She couldn't think. Something about this didn't feel right.

"Please, Abby," Agent Shur begged. "I want to talk to him in a nonthreatening environment. I would rather not have to drag him into a police station."

Abby recalled Marwan's story about his son being detained and questioned for no reason. She didn't want Marwan to be put through a humiliating scene like that, but she was still reluctant to agree.

"I don't know his phone number," she said.

Agent Shur reached into the pocket of his sport coat and produced a piece of paper with a number written on it. Then he slid Abby's telephone over to the edge of the desk where she could reach it.

"If he wants to know why you're calling, you may tell him it concerns Ari Bazak, which is the truth. You don't need to mention my presence."

Abby didn't feel right about what he was asking her to do, but she also felt as though she had no choice. She would feel worse if they arrested Marwan and forcibly interrogated him. Drawing a deep breath, she dialed his number.

"Marwan, this is Abby," she said when he answered the telephone. "Could you please come over to the hotel right away? I need to ask you something."

"What's wrong?"

"I'd rather not say over the phone. It's about what we discussed the other night. I'm in bungalow twelve." Marwan took a long time to reply. Abby almost hoped he would refuse.

"All right," he said at last. "Give me twenty minutes."

"You don't feel right about this, do you?" Shur said after she hung up. His tone was sympathetic. "I understand. But I assure you, if Ashrawi has a logical explanation for his inside knowledge, then everything will be all right."

"Marwan told me that he has been working on digs every summer for several years. Maybe he heard about Ari quitting. I know there were rumors about it, because Dr. Voss heard them, too."

"You see?" Shur said. "I'm sure there will be a reasonable explanation, and then Mr. Ashrawi will be free to go."

But as Abby waited, trying to make small talk with Agent Shur, she realized that she couldn't explain how Marwan knew about Benjamin Rosen. She was having serious regrets about getting involved in this and possibly betraying Marwan when someone knocked on her door. Agent Shur motioned for her to answer it.

"Thanks for coming, Marwan," she said when she saw him. "Come in."

She stood aside to let him pass, then closed the door. When she turned to Agent Shur, he had a gun pointed at them.

"Don't scream," he said as she gasped. "Just sit down on the bed, please, and don't say a word."

But Abby had already collapsed onto it involuntarily as her knees gave way. A wave of shock coursed through her like a jolt of electricity. Shur pressed the gun to the back of Marwan's head and quickly searched him for weapons, then pushed him down onto the bed beside Abby. All the color had bleached from Marwan's face. She prayed that Shur would question him about Ari quickly and get it over with instead of prolonging his terror. Shur consulted his watch. When he finally asked the first question, it had nothing at all to do with Ari.

"Did you drive your own car here?" he asked in a low voice. Marwan nodded. "Is it parked outside?"

"Yes."

Several long minutes passed as Shur sat down in the desk chair again, waiting. He said nothing, but the gun pointed at the two of them was steady in his hand. Abby trembled from head to toe. She could sense Marwan's rising fear as he waited beside her. His breathing grew ragged and shallow.

"Why—" Marwan finally started to ask, but Shur silenced him by cocking the gun with a loud snap and pointing it at Marwan's face. As he did, Abby noticed for the first time that Shur was wearing a pair of very thin gloves.

Suddenly she knew with terrible certainty that Shur was the traitor who had killed Benjamin Rosen. That's what Ben had been trying to tell her—not that he was *sure* there was a traitor, but that *Shur* was the traitor.

"Oh, God!" she whispered. Cold nausea slithered through her. "I'm sorry, Marwan, I didn't know."

"But you would have figured it out," Shur said in a cold, quiet voice. "You would have eventually remembered the verse for Ben's code and figured it out." He sighed and shook his head as if he were truly sorry. "You should have gone home after we ransacked your house, Mrs. MacLeod. It would have been the wisest thing to do."

Abby fought the urge to be sick as she stared at the gaping gun barrel. Shur planned to kill her. The thought of dying wasn't as terrifying as waiting for it to happen, wondering how it would feel. Her throat ached as she labored to breathe. A few more agonizing minutes passed before Shur checked his watch again, then spoke.

"All right, Abby. I would like you to take off your shoes, pull back the covers, and lie down on the bed, please."

"No—" Before the word was barely out of her mouth, Shur was on his feet with the muzzle of the gun pressed to Marwan's head.

"Do it." He didn't raise his voice. He didn't need to. She fumbled to unfasten her sandals with shaking hands, then pulled back the bedspread and lay down on the sheets.

"I'm sorry. . . ." she whispered to Marwan again.

"You're next," Shur told Marwan. "Remove your shoes and lie down beside her."

"I refuse," Marwan said. "You may as well kill me and get it over with." He didn't flinch, even with the gun barrel pressed to his head.

"Oh, you *are* going to die," Shur said coldly, "but I will give you this choice—you either make it appear that you were her lover, or I will make you into her rapist. How will your wife and children like that?"

Marwan closed his eyes. He did what Shur asked, lying down on his back beside Abby.

Shur returned to his chair and began groping through his jacket pockets with his free hand, searching for something. As Abby watched, she wondered if either she or Marwan, or maybe both of them together, dared to make a move. Shur couldn't possibly keep one gun trained on two people at the same time, could he? Marwan was in much better physical shape than the paunchy, round-shouldered agent. They had nothing to lose by trying, since they were both going to die anyway.

But before she could nudge Marwan, Shur removed a pair of handcuffs from his jacket.

"Raise your arms above your head," he commanded. "Both of you."

He locked one end to Marwan's wrist, then slipped the cuffs around one of the brass headboard rails and locked the other end to Abby's wrist. Neither one of them could get up.

Shur laid his gun on the desk and dug into his pocket again, removing a plastic bag containing a smaller gun. As he carefully unwrapped it, Abby guessed that it was the weapon that had killed Benjamin Rosen. Shur pressed it into Marwan's free hand.

"Don't be afraid," he taunted. "It isn't loaded—yet." He forced Marwan to grip it and squeeze the trigger so it would have his fingerprints on it, then took it away from him again. When Shur removed a clip of bullets from his pocket and began to load it, Abby started to sob. She knew that she would die first. Shur would make it appear that they had been lovers, that Marwan had killed her, and then was stopped by Shur as he tried to flee. Abby closed her eyes and began to pray. Not for deliverance—it was too late for that—but for forgiveness. She knew she didn't deserve it unless she forgave Mark, but she also knew that God was merciful.

Oh, God, please forgive me, she silently prayed. *I'm so sorry for—*

Suddenly the bungalow door slammed open as it was kicked from the outside.

"Drop it, Shur!" someone shouted.

A deafening explosion of gunfire filled the room. Abby screamed and huddled against Marwan for protection. She heard the crash of breaking glass, the splintering of wood. If she was hit, she didn't feel any pain.

When the gunfire stopped, her eyes flew open and she saw Agent Shur falling to the ground as if in slow motion. The gun he had been loading slipped from his hand and dropped to the floor seconds before he did. Shards of the bungalow's shattered window littered the carpet.

Ari Bazak stood in the doorway, holding a gun.

"Are you all right?" he asked them.

"Yes . . . I think so," Marwan said shakily.

Abby was sobbing too hard to reply. Ari sat down on the bed beside her and drew her into his arms. His body trembled as much as hers did.

"It's all right," he soothed as she clung to him with her one free arm. "Everything is going to be all right."

22

CHAPTER

THE GOLANI HOTEL, ISRAEL—1999

Abby stuffed the last of her belongings into her suitcase and flipped the top closed. "I guess that's everything," she said, glancing around the hotel room one last time.

"Here, let me help you with that." Hannah leaned on the lid to hold it down while Abby zipped it shut. When they finished, the two friends gazed at each other.

"There's so much I want to say," Abby began, taking Hannah's hands. "Thank you hardly seems adequate. I don't think I could have recovered from that . . . ordeal . . . without your help."

In the aftermath of the shooting, more agents had swarmed into Abby's room behind Ari. They'd called an ambulance for Shur, then combed the room for evidence, taking statements from her and Marwan, piecing together the chain of events. Later, Abby had taken refuge in Hannah's bungalow, moving her things into the empty room beside Hannah's for the last four days of the dig. Now, much too soon, it was time to say good-bye.

"I'm glad I could help," Hannah said, hugging her. "I'm sorry you had to witness the violent side of my country—not once, but twice. Let's hope that your next visit to Israel will be an uneventful one. Until then, will you pray for the peace of Jerusalem, as King David asked us to do in his psalm?"

"Yes, I promise I will."

Hannah released her, and Abby hefted her suitcase from the bed to the floor.

"I'll be praying for Ari, too," she said. "I'm sorry I didn't get a chance to say good-bye to him."

"I went to see him yesterday," Hannah said.

"How is he?"

"Still trying to recover from the shooting. It was a terrible shock to learn that his own supervisor was a traitor and a murderer. Harder still to aim a gun at his friend and fire. He'll be all right, though."

"I never thanked Ari for what he did. Things were pretty crazy afterward . . . and I was a wreck."

"Who wouldn't be," Hannah said, "after such a close brush with death."

Abby set her carry-on bag on the floor beside her suitcase and sighed. "They say your life is supposed to flash before you at times like that, but mine didn't—even though I thought I was going to die. If anything has given me a new outlook on life, it has been this dig. It was like glimpsing time and history from God's perspective, and it made me realize just how short life really is . . . how important it is. It could come to an end so suddenly. Mine nearly did."

"Jake used to say that life was God's gift to us. We should enjoy it and not waste a moment of it by wallowing in bitterness. He used to love the wonderful view of the bigger picture that my archaeological discoveries provided."

"Me too. I keep thinking about all those layers of civilization, all those people like Leah and Reuben who have lived and died, leaving behind the record of their lives. They each played their part in God's plan . . . and now it's my turn. What I leave behind is up to me, isn't it?"

Hannah nodded. "Have you decided what you'll do when you get home?"

"No . . . not exactly. I know that I want to play my part in

God's design . . . and in His Kingdom. I'm just not sure what that is yet."

"He'll show you. In the meantime, be careful you don't get bogged down trying to see the purpose in everything that happens to you. You may never see where your husband's affair fits into God's plan, for instance—just as I may never fully know why I had to lose Jake and Rachel. We're still much too close to see the bigger picture."

"I think I understand what you're saying," Abby said slowly. "When Leah died at Gamla, she probably didn't comprehend why her nation was being destroyed and her people scattered, either."

"Probably not. It's only when we stand at a distance of two thousand years that we can begin to see how it was part of God's plan to spread His Kingdom to the whole world. I can't fathom a design on that grand of a scale, can you, Abby?"

"No," she murmured. "It's beyond my comprehension."

"But you know what amazes me even more?" Hannah's voice grew hushed. "God also cares deeply about each individual person. Two thousand years ago, He had that mosaic floor created for His purposes. Then He kept it buried all that time, waiting for Ari to discover it *this* summer. That's how much God loves us. Now Ari knows it, too. He knows that finding that floor was much more than a coincidence. It was God's gift to him, showing him that Rachel's life, Rachel's faith, was part of the bigger picture."

There was a knock on Abby's door. The porter had arrived to carry her bags to the waiting taxi. Tears filled Abby's eyes at the thought of leaving her friend.

"Oh, Hannah . . . it's so hard to say good-bye."

"Then let's not say it. Let's say *Shalom*, instead." She drew Abby into her arms for the last time. "Shalom, my dear friend. May God's peace be with you. And may His face always shine upon you."

LOD AIRPORT, ISRAEL—1999

Abby's plane was scheduled to leave Israel shortly after midnight. She had still been crying as the taxi pulled out of the

hotel parking lot for the airport, with Hannah waving to her
from the front step. Now it was nearly eleven o'clock, and
Abby was exhausted. She thought she might even be able to
sleep on the plane for once.

Inside the terminal she joined a long line of passengers
waiting to have their luggage inspected. She listened idly as
the agents interrogated them. "Are you carrying any packages
for another person? Did you pack your own bags? Have they
left your sight since you packed them?"

She thought of Hannah and Ari and Marwan—how they
had to live with this constant suspicion and fear. Abby would
pray for the peace of Jerusalem.

At last it was her turn to have her suitcase inspected. The
young agent motioned for her to come forward. But before
Abby had a chance to lift her bag onto the table, she heard
Ari's voice behind her. "It's okay. You can pass her through.
She's with me." His hand rested briefly on her shoulder.

Ari showed the agent his identification badge, and the
man put Abby's suitcase on the cart with the others. Ari carried her tote bag as they walked in silence to the boarding
gate. He stopped to show his badge once again as they passed
through airport security. Ari then found two seats for them in
a deserted corner of the departure lounge.

"How are you?" he asked at last. "Have you recovered?"

"Yes, I think so. Hannah was a big help. How about you?"

He shrugged and made a so-so gesture. "Dov Shur died on
the way to the hospital," he said quietly.

Abby laid her hand on top of his. "I never thanked you for
saving my life."

His eyes met hers for the first time. "You're welcome. I'm
glad I got there in time."

"Are you allowed to tell me what made you come back . . .
just in time?" she asked.

He drew a deep breath, then exhaled. "I went to the
Agency's archives, looking for the tape recording they made
when they questioned you after Ben's death. I thought you
might have quoted the Scripture verse during the interview

while it was still fresh in your mind. The tape was missing. So was the written transcript of it. There was no explanation—they had just . . . vanished! I learned that Kol, one of the agents who questioned you, had been assigned to undercover duty and couldn't be contacted. The other agent was Dov Shur. You had misunderstood Ben when he said 'Torah,' so I wondered if you could have also misunderstood the rest. Could Ben have said *Shur* was the traitor, not that he was *sure* there was a traitor? I had just decided to go back and ask you when you paged me. I tried to locate Shur, but no one knew where he was, so I requested back-up assistance. . . . Then I prayed that we would make it in time."

"Thank you, Ari."

He simply nodded.

As Abby studied him, knowing she would probably never see him again, she sensed the struggle between the two very different men who both claimed Ari Bazak. She wondered which man would win—the archaeologist or the secret agent. Then she noticed that he was wearing a yarmulke on his head. She reached out to touch it.

He smiled sheepishly and yanked it off, stuffing it into his pocket. "I guess I forgot about it. I went to church tonight, the one that Rachel and I used to attend. I talked to an old friend of hers, Ahmed Saraj."

"I'm glad."

"Yes. I am, too."

"So what are you going to do next, Ari?" she asked quietly.

"Well, I'm officially on leave from the Agency until the investigation is complete." He smiled slightly. "Hannah says that will give me just enough time to help her publish our findings at Degania."

"The mosaic floor?"

"Yes." The smile spread across his face. "It's a very unusual discovery, you know—Christian symbols in a first-century Jewish home. It will be a very important find."

The loudspeaker crackled suddenly, announcing Abby's flight. They both stood.

"Before you go," Ari said, "I have something for you." He held out a small box, wrapped in plain paper. "It's a present from Hannah and me. Don't open it now. Wait until you're on the plane. Oh, and I need to return your Bible to you." He pulled it from his jacket pocket.

"Were you able to decode Ben's message?"

"Very easily, once we knew his verse. Here, we're finished with it."

"I want you to keep it," she said, pushing it back into his hands.

"Your Bible? Abby, I know how important it is to you. . . ."

"Please, I want you to have it. To remember me."

Ari accepted it, then drew her into his arms for a brief embrace. "I could never forget you. . . . Shalom, Abby."

"Shalom," she whispered.

Abby was at peace as she boarded the airplane and buckled herself into her seat. She felt strangely calm as they prepared for takeoff, then roared down the runway and lifted off. When the plane was finally airborne, she opened the gift from Ari and Hannah, removing the wrapping carefully as if she planned to use it again.

Inside the jeweler's box was a small green mosaic stone, hanging from a golden chain. She lifted it out and slipped it around her neck. Tucked beside it was a note in Hannah's writing: *One small piece of God's design to remind you that His redemption is displayed to the world through us—one small act of grace at a time.*

The final leg of Abby's flight, from takeoff in New York until landing in Indianapolis, seemed longer to her than the flight from Israel to New York. She was eager to see her children again and glad that Emily and Greg were both coming to pick her up at the airport. As she stepped off the de-boarding ramp, she searched the crowd for their faces. But when she finally spotted a familiar face, it wasn't Emily's or Greg's.

It was her husband, Mark.

Abby stopped walking, frozen in place. Mark saw her, too, but he also remained where he was. His face was somber, his eyes questioning, sorrowful.

Daddy has changed, Emily had insisted, and he did look different somehow—less certain of himself, more vulnerable. He reminded her of the serious mathematics major she had fallen in love with twenty-three years ago, not the smooth computer executive he had become.

Abby slowly walked toward him, stopping a few feet away. Tears brimmed in Mark's eyes, then trailed down his cheeks. He didn't wipe them.

"Hello, Abby."

She fingered Rachel's necklace, remembering God's unfathomable design.

"Hi," she managed. Then her own tears began to fall.